How can I give him an answer?

Someday, she thought, I'm going to have to decide whether I want to sacrifice everything to a career, or to experience the guilt of being part mother and part tycoon. Damn it. Men don't have to make these kinds of choices.

She knew what she wanted to say: I know I'd love this business. I could hold my own with any hot-shot you've got around here after I learn the ropes. But that's not what he's asking me. He isn't questioning my ability. He's worried about the conflicts I face because I'm a woman...

PLAYERS

LAURA BRADFORD

A JOVE BOOK

PLAYERS

A Jove Book / published by arrangement with
the author

PRINTING HISTORY
Jove edition / May 1985

ISBN: 0-515-08183-3

Jove books are published by The Berkley Publishing Group,
200 Madison Avenue, New York, N.Y. 10016.
The words "A JOVE BOOK" and the "J" with sunburst
are trademarks belonging to Jove Publications, Inc.

PRINTED IN THE UNITED STATES OF AMERICA

*To Paul Paalborg,
without whom this book
could not have been written*

In a pride of lions it is the female that does the hunting . . .

L.B.

Chapter 1

SHE STOOD IN the center of the small converted attic room, pacing nervously back and forth, absentmindedly passing the long Victorian window with its half-raised Japanese shade. A shaft of light from the April sun threw speckled shadows on the off-white wall, casting a path of splintered tiny refractions that drew her gaze to the small garden whose brick wall looked defenseless against the looming maples that shadowed St. Vincent's Avenue with the new green of spring.

She sat down on the bed and held the letter, and looked over to the writing desk, which was a long wooden tabletop set on painted white columns of cinder block. A gooseneck drafting lamp, a portable electric typewriter, and a pile of thick textbooks cluttered the desk. There was a picture of her mother and father taken in the yard of their house in Falmouth, Maine. Her father had his arm around her mother, tenuously, hesitantly, as if he were an embarrassed guest who had been asked to stand and be photographed. Her mother's expression was condemning in its resigned, intent compliance.

The other picture was of Peter. He was tall and slender with broad shoulders that tapered to a narrow waist. He stood with his hands in his pockets; his expression was one of humorous irony. He seemed an observer at life's party, whose guests he found amusing, but in whose company he felt uncomfortable. An outsider.

She saw the other letters, unfolded, spaced across her desk. She got up from the bed and went to look at them again. She picked each one up. The first was from Citibank; the second was from the Chase Manhattan Bank. One was from Morgan Stanley, the prestigious New York investment banking firm. Another was from First Boston, another investment firm located not in Boston, but in New York. She knew the letters by heart. They were offering her a job upon graduation in May from the Harvard Business School.

But now her dilemma lay in the choice she had decided to make. She knew herself well enough to realize that she had really made up her mind in September, when representatives from many of the firms who were seeking out the top graduates in her class had come to Cambridge to interview her along with other students who had achieved outstanding records in the Business School. She stood third in her class, and she had been chosen as a Baker Scholar, one of the most coveted awards given by the Harvard Business School. She read the letter she held in her hand for the twentieth time.

Baldwin Cooper, Inc.
1221 Avenue of the Americas
New York, N.Y. 10019

George R. Hall
Managing Director

Miss Elizabeth Reed Clark
15 St. Vincent's Avenue
Cambridge, Massachusetts

Dear Miss Clark:

We would be pleased to invite you to our New York office on April 20 to meet the principals of our firm, Mr. Lawrence Baldwin and Mr. Robert Cooper.

If it is convenient, I would like to meet with you first in my office at 11:00. Plan to have lunch with us at 12:15. After lunch I would like to introduce you to other members of our staff.

If you are able to accept our invitation, please call me and I will send your airline tickets and make a reservation for you at the St. Regis Hotel. I will also enclose a check for your expenses while visiting us in New York.

I look forward to seeing you again on the twentieth.

Cordially,

George Hall

She kept tapping the letter against the palm of her hand. She knew she was going to accept George's offer if the other officers of the firm decided they wanted her. They seemed to. She was trying to analyze why she wanted to work for Baldwin Cooper, a small venture capital firm, rather than the more prestigious and larger financial institutions that were also interested in hiring her.

She knew that very few women had made careers as venture capitalists. It was an arcane specialty where the firm invested seed money in young companies with great growth potential. Most of these investments were lucky to break even or even luckier not to lose money. The payoffs when they came could be enormous, but so were the risks. What was there about her, she wondered, that attracted her to such a perilous career, a career in which there were so few women?

She had gone over the reasons in her mind until her head ached. Had George Hall sold her a bill of goods? She had thought about that. God knows, Hall was a salesman.

Her mind went back to that September day, when she had stood in the lobby of the Ritz-Carlton and watched him walk off the elevator. She didn't know how, but she knew it was him, and he knew it was her. He walked toward her smiling.

"Miss Clark." He extended his hand. His eyes looked at her approvingly.

"Most people call me Liz, Mr. Hall."

He laughed. "You've got a deal, but only if you call me George."

"Deal," she said, smiling at him.

Their eyes met, his a dark brown, hers a cobalt blue with tiny flecks of hazel in the irises. She felt an almost instantaneous intimation that they understood each other. He must be at least forty, she thought.

He was forty-three.

He's going to suggest Lock-Ober's. Where else would a hot-shot businessman eat?

"Do you like Italian food?" he asked.

She tried not to show her surprise. "Yes, I do. Very much."

"I know a little place on the North Side. It's small and charming, and the food is quite good. Would you like to try it?"

She looked at him with those cool, analytical eyes that he would learn to know so well. "That sounds like fun, Mr. Hall."

He stopped. "Hey. Wait a minute. You're going back on our deal. It's George, remember?"

"Okay, George."

They sat facing each other in the small grotto of the restaurant near an incongruous fountain of cherubic cupids bathed in blue light.

"May I ask you a question that's been bothering me, George?"

"That's what I'm here for."

"Why did you select me as one of your candidates?"

He smiled amiably. "This really is delicious fettuccine."

He put his fork down on his plate. "Liz, we don't recruit anyone lightly. We want people of the highest intelligence. We need people who can not only work well with their peers but who will also impress our clients and our institutional partners. We need people who are creative and who have initiative, but who can work within a disciplined environment."

"What do you mean, 'disciplined'?"

"I'm talking about teamwork. We have our own way of doing things, and it has proved pretty successful. We can't have people running off in different directions doing their own thing."

She toyed with her veal. She was waiting for him to answer her question. So far he hadn't.

"Ours is one of the most exciting and at the same time one of the most demanding businesses I know of. We take our own capital and combine it with far larger portions of capital from insurance companies and banks who know us, who respect our record for making money for our investors. We select a com-

pany—maybe one company after looking at two hundred—
and then we bet our chips on that company. We nail down
everything we can with the entrepreneur. We make sure he is
invested to the level of his resources." He began to laugh. "To
paraphrase General Rommel, we believe that 'mortal danger
is a sufficent antidote to stimulate performance.'

"A small company in a high-growth environment is one of
the most unpredictable investments you can make. We often
choose an inventive genius who is a nightmare as a manager.
We have to see that his talent and ego remain stimulated, but
we also have to find someone who can mind the store.

"When these babies have a problem, it can appear suddenly,
escalate fast, and quickly become terminal. We have to monitor
our geniuses closely enough to catch any snag before it becomes
too serious.

"If we've done our job right, if our judgment has been right,
the company we've invested in grows. Maybe we go public
with the stock. We sell some and keep some. Maybe we sell
the whole company if the price is right. Maybe we use it as a
vehicle to acquire other companies . . ."

He was watching her closely as he spoke. He saw the slight
compression of her lips, the muscles along her jawline tighten.

"I know I haven't answered your question yet. I'm coming
to that."

"It's not that . . ."

"What is it?"

She hesitated. "It's—it's just that it sounds a little cold-
blooded to me."

He watched her closely. She had averted her eyes.

"Why?"

"These investments. They involve people's lives, don't they?
It's not like selling a stock or a bond."

He waited before answering. He poured her some more
Verdicchio and refilled his own glass. "That's true. They do.
But in the meantime, Liz, we've given a talented human being
a chance to build something he otherwise would be unable to
build. We create jobs for hundreds, sometimes thousands of
people. Sometimes it gets rough. If we have to clean house in
a company to save it, we do it. In the end, it's a combination
of insight, guts, determination, drive, initiative, and experience
that pays off. And, I might add, luck. If you don't have luck,

you might as well throw the rest of it in the wastebasket." He smiled at her and touched her hand. "Liz, remember this regardless of whether you choose to come with us," he paused, "or if we choose to have you..."

He said this looking at her carefully, searching her eyes. She felt a small chill of anxiety. Did they want her or didn't they? His last remark sounded as if they were still undecided. Maybe her own confidence had been premature. She'd had a strong feeling that she was in if she wanted to be. Now it seemed that she was still being tested. She felt her confidence begin to slip away, but as young and inexperienced as she was, she realized she couldn't let this show. She tensed slightly, sat a bit straighter in her chair. She looked at him directly. There was a shadow of challenge in her eyes. She sensed that he felt it.

"If you have to decide between luck or brains," he said, "always choose luck. I know a lot of guys who are smart as hell but they're sick, broke, or unhappy. You've got to be lucky, Liz, regardless of how much talent and drive you have."

She sipped her wine. "But why me?" she asked quietly. This time she had to make an effort to control her voice, to seem outwardly calm. She knew instinctively that the question itself presumed a confidence she didn't feel.

He took out his cigarette case and offered her one. She shook her head. She noticed that his lighter was a gold Dunhill.

"First of all, Liz, we look for brains. Your record at Radcliffe and Harvard tells us all we need to know about that." He paused, then started to smile. "I keep in touch with some of my old professors here. They know the kind of talent I'm looking for. Alex Rostov thinks very highly of you. He sent me a copy of your résumé. It was very impressive."

Liz had wondered why her quantitative analysis professor had asked for a copy of her résumé. Now she knew. She felt flattered but annoyed. Alex could at least have mentioned this to her.

"We never would have interviewed you if you had ranked lower than tenth in your class. But what intrigued me about your résumé was that you made it through undergraduate and graduate school on your own. On scholarships and odd jobs. No one handed you a damn thing. That's what impressed me most."

A young waiter with a carefully trimmed dark beard and wearing a gold necklace stood tactfully to one side. "Is everything all right?" the waiter asked.

"Would you like some dessert, Liz?"

"What do you have?"

The waiter purred. "If you like cheesecake, ours is absolutely spectacular."

"I'm a sucker for cheesecake, Liz."

"I'm afraid I am, too."

"Make it two cheesecakes."

"Want an after-dinner brandy?"

"I'd like that."

"Two Courvoisiers and coffee."

Liz was still surprised that George had selected a restaurant like this. She laughed inwardly at how out of place they both looked in this small dimly lit restaurant where the other men wore open-neck shirts and slacks; the women sported a clutch of eclectic styles, like different species of brightly colored birds.

She had dressed conservatively, as she was sure George Hall would take her to Locke-Ober's or Joseph's or the Algonquin Club, three bastions of Boston's business elite. But instead, he had chosen a charming, intimate little restaurant on Boston's North Side where the streets were narrow and the houses and apartment buildings were of old brick squeezed one on top of the other. It was a neighborhood of closely knit Italian families where the streetlights were old gas lamps that had been adapted to electricity. A small triangular park faced an old Catholic neighborhood church.

George was immaculately tailored in a blue pinstripe suit. Liz had to force herself not to laugh as she noticed he was the only man in the room wearing a jacket and a tie. She also noticed that being different didn't seem to bother him. He was obviously a far more complex person than she had expected, and she found herself attracted to the surprise.

George sipped at his brandy. "You asked why we picked you." He hesitated. "I wanted to see for myself a young woman who had accomplished so much all by herself. Now that I have, I can tell you that I'm impressed." She was looking at him carefully, probing the depth of his sincerity. As a woman she sensed more than just the carefully reasoned explanations of his interest in her background and academic skills. She knew he was attracted to her physically. She could feel it. She wondered if he was aware that his objectivity might be less clouded if a man were sitting opposite him rather than the attractive young woman she knew herself to be.

She watched the dark brown eyes meet hers, and then she realized that his thoughts had turned inward. For some reason his face seemed to tighten, and his lips compressed. He fingered his wineglass absentmindedly.

I wonder what it would be like to start all over again with someone like her, he thought. His mind picked up the scene in his former wife's apartment, just before coming to Boston to interview Liz.

Claudia had telephoned him from her office and had asked him to come to her apartment at Seventieth Street and Fifth Avenue. He hadn't been to her apartment since he had moved out after their divorce.

Twelve years, he thought, as the cab let him out in front of the building. We were married for twelve years. It was good in the beginning.

"Ms. White is expecting you," the doorman had said. How he hated that goddamn Ms. And for some reason it irked him that she had returned to using her maiden name.

She opened the door to the apartment when he rang, holding it ajar for a moment, looking at him appraisingly. She looked pale and thin to him, but then she always had looked that way. She wore a black dress that accentuated her slenderness. She was carefully groomed as always. She must be going out for dinner, he thought.

He entered the living room, which overlooked Central Park. It was nearly dusk. The lights in the room were muted, but the apartment was pure Claudia. Modern with severe Scandinavian furniture, light wood. Splashes of color from original paintings that were carefully hung. Abstract sculptures lit from recessed spots in the ceiling. There was an almost regal simplicity in the way she lived. He saw the light reflected from the silver tray on a glass coffee table. On the tray stood a shaker of liquid and two glasses.

"You look fit as always," she said.

"And you still look like a white iris."

She stopped when he said it and turned to face him. "That's very poetic. I can't tell if it's a compliment or not, coming from you."

He swallowed hard. He felt the first cuts of annoyance. "It was supposed to be a compliment," he said evenly. "A white iris is a beautiful flower."

She laughed softly. There was an edge to it.

"I'm flattered," she said. "I'm not used to compliments. Especially not from you."

"Claudia, did you ask me over here to fight with you? If you did, I'm not in the mood."

She ignored his remark. "Is it still martinis?"

"They'll do."

She shook the shaker vigorously. "You always told me that you should shake until your hand feels pain from the cold." She paused. "A rather prophetic statement about us, don't you think?" She poured a drink and handed it to him. Her fingers felt like porcelain. She motioned to the long beige sofa. He sat at one end and she at the other.

"What did you want to see me about, Claudia?"

She was looking at him analytically, seeing what the years had done to him. They had been kind. Kinder than they had been to her. She resented that, and her bitterness showed.

"I hope we can be civilized about this, George."

He didn't reply. She could see the muscles contract along his jawline.

"I want to talk to you about the money you owe me."

He sighed heavily. "Christ. Not that again."

"As I don't have to remind you, George, I'm a lawyer, and a very good one. I have a special sensitivity toward contracts, especially when I'm a party to one." She paused, sipping her martini. "You owe me a good deal of money, George."

"Oh, Jesus." He was trying hard to keep from exploding. "Claudia, I'm aware of the money I owe you, but what I can't understand, contract or no contract, is your lack of pride. What the hell do you need my money for? You make more money than I do. And I've told you fifty times, I'm in an unusual business. I need what capital I can get my hands on for the business. And then it's locked up long term. My assets aren't liquid. I don't have a thousand shares of Exxon that I can put on the market. We invest in medium-sized privately held companies that we have to nurture along. You know that."

"I do know that, George. I also know that every now and then you and Larry Baldwin and Bob Cooper sell off some of those lockups at handsome profits."

He shook his head in weary resignation. "We do, Claudia, we do. But we haven't had a real winner in a hell of a long time."

She smiled at him, with less than repressed sarcasm. "You *are* in a difficult business, George."

"You're goddamn right I am." He stopped for a moment and looked at her with equal bitterness. "One of these days we'll hit one, and then I'll make some kind of settlement with you. I don't want to spend the rest of my life with your claws in me."

They were at it again. They couldn't be in the same room for fifteen minutes without ripping open old wounds.

"Would you be willing to discuss a deal when that time comes?" he asked, his voice laced with anger.

"Something's better than nothing, George," she said quietly.

"Well, something is what you're going to get. I'm sick to death of being bled by you."

"You haven't bled much recently, George."

He knew that if he stayed a minute longer he would lose control. He got up, put his drink on the table, picked up his coat, and without a word left her sitting there sipping her martini like a pale ghost.

"George." Liz's voice brought him back.

She had watched his face mirror his thoughts, and she could see that he had been ruminating in troubled waters.

"I'm sorry, Liz." He looked at the vital, attractive young woman sitting opposite him and the thought returned to him: I wonder what it would be like to start all over with someone like her. He dismissed the idea as preposterous and forced his mind to return to the business at hand. He was supposed to be interviewing Elizabeth Clark for a job in his firm. He had better get on with that.

She could see the change in his mood. The small knot of anxiety she had started to feel began to disappear.

• • •

As she sat on the bed, the letter from Baldwin Cooper in her hand, she could visualize George's face as it had been that night she sat opposite him in the restaurant. She remembered the intensity that seemed to sweep across him like a brushfire when he began to discuss the business. She felt the excitement in him. It was palpable. She knew that was one of the things he was searching for that night in her. Did she have it? Did she have the guts and determination that he had told her were necessary?

She got up and walked to the worn, cheap maple dresser and looked at herself in the mirror that hung above it. It was as if she were looking at someone else. She never thought of herself as attractive, although she knew that men did. She touched her cheek. She saw the quiet, serious reflection stare back at her. Could she cut it if they gave her a chance? She had up until now. She had worked like hell to accomplish what she had. She'd been building credentials so that companies like Citibank, Chase, and Baldwin Cooper would make her an offer; now they had. She looked at the person staring back at her from the mirror. She remembered what George had said: "You've got to be lucky, Liz. If you don't have luck you can throw the rest of it in the wastebasket."

"Are you lucky?" she asked the mirror. The face that looked back at her held no answers.

The phone rang. She was so wrapped in her own thoughts that she let it ring four times before she picked it up.

"Liz, were you asleep?" Peter asked her.

"No. I was—" She hesitated. "I was just caught up in a few things."

"You're not grinding away on a beautiful day like this, are you?"

"No."

"How about going for a walk? We can get something to eat. What do you say?"

She saw the wind stir the maples on St. Vincent's Avenue. The sky was azure. She shrugged off the girl in the mirror.

"Okay, Peter."

"Pick you up in twenty minutes?"

"I'll be ready."

• • •

They walked along the banks of the Charles River, the red brick Georgian buildings of Harvard behind them. They held hands and watched the puffy breeze strain the skill of the sailors in the small sloops. The white sails of the heeling boats looked like the wings of diving gulls. The towers of the new Boston across the river rose toward the April sun.

"You're pretty quiet, Liz."

"I'm sorry."

"Want to talk about it?" He had come to know her well. He knew the reasons for her withdrawal. In many instances he felt that he knew her better than she knew herself. Loving her had not cost him his objectivity.

"For a gal who's about to conquer the big city with a fat job offer, you look mighty glum."

She turned toward him, the light catching her face. He felt the pressure of her hand.

Liz looked up at him and she knew; they both knew.

Peter Wells was the only man she had allowed to approach that special place, that private preserve that she guarded so carefully. She was a lot like her mother that way. They were both reserved. Maybe it was their stoic Yankee heritage; those Calvinist genes that were molded by the granite coast, the rock-strewn fields, the long, cold, implacable winters.

She continued to look at him, her lips trembling. She drew his head toward her and kissed him with great tenderness. They sat down on the grass oblivious to the joggers, the strollers, the running, yapping dogs, the kites.

They had started dating seriously when Liz was a senior at Radcliffe. Peter was working on a doctorate in modern Western European history at Harvard. She used to kid him about that. "What is a limey doing coming over here to read Western European history?" she'd asked. "Wouldn't they let you into Oxford or Cambridge?"

He had applied for a scholarship to study in the United States. He wanted to get away from the insularity of Britain and learn about life in the States.

"You've taken over from us," he had jokingly told Liz, "and you're welcome to it. England is going to become the repository of Western culture. An island museum, a library. When you Americans and Japanese and Germans exhaust yourselves chasing your materialism, you can always stop off and rest in our little island. We'll be poor, but you know how charming we are. You can visit our ruins, rest up in our hotels, seek your roots in our antiquity. Just put your feet up by our cultural fire and warm yourselves. We shall become the roadside shrine, the place to pause for all you strivers."

He brushed her hair back from her face. He rested on his elbows looking at her eyes that were the same color as the sky.

How do you die just a little on a beautiful April day? she thought. They had said very little. What was there to say? He is so dear, she thought. "Sweet" was the word she used to describe him. He was manly but sweet. He was not impatient with her moods, which she knew could be irritating. He would wait until she came back to him, and when everything was right—it had to be absolutely right for her—they would make love. It wasn't just sex with either of them; it was truly making love. But the place so deep inside her, that private sanctuary where even Peter had not been allowed to fully enter, tormented her with its insatiable logic. Sometimes she wanted to scream and smash her head against a wall. What the hell are you doing? she thought. She would tear at herself in the depths of her mind. He's the best person you'll ever meet. You love him, you know you do. He loves you. Goddamn it, Liz, what's wrong with you! She lay on her back looking up at him. How do you die a little on an April day as beautiful as this? she wondered. The thought possessed her.

He gently kissed her. Then he looked at her with pain in his eyes. "Why are we acting out this Greek drama, Liz? Why do we allow ourselves to be bound so by the fates? We don't have to. Why are we doing it?"

She couldn't answer him, because she couldn't talk. Her throat felt as if she were choking.

"Don't cry, darling," he said softly. He kissed the tears that glistened on her cheeks, and felt like crying himself. He knew everything about her, and yet he knew nothing. "Liz," he said quietly. He was fighting to retain some semblance of control. "I know you love me, darling," he paused. "Liz, you know I adore you. We could have such a marvelous life together. You could even wrap yourself up in your bloody business and become the richest and most famous woman in America."

She watched his eyes fill with tears.

"I would stay over here, Liz, not go back to England. When

I've got my doctorate I'll find something in New York. We could work it out." He lowered his head and placed it on her breast. He could hear the rapid beating of her heart. "We've got so much, darling, so very much. How can we just let this go?"

Why had she known almost from the first that it just would not work? She kept resisting in every way, but in time, less and less. She rationalized that somehow they could find a way to make it work, but some inner voice kept telling her that she would ruin it for him. He would try to fit an academic life around her career, but in the end she would make him unhappy. She knew she would need an almost selfish mobility and freedom to compete in an overwhelmingly male world. That kind of commitment required a dedication and sacrifice she could only make at this point in her life, *now*. It would be too late if she waited, married, and had a child. She had made up her mind that she didn't want to break herself into pieces being a part-time wife and career woman. She had worked too hard to get this chance, and now that she had her chance, she wanted to take it, but she hadn't known it would be so hard. She had underestimated the cost.

Her chest began to heave with silent, wracking sobs. They lay there in the dappled light, the river flowing its serpentine course between the cities that had brought them together; in which they had learned of love. Now, she would be leaving these cities, Cambridge and Boston, that had been so much a part of her life for six years. She was leaving Peter. She knew that, he knew it, and they both found the pain unbearable.

How do you learn to die a little on a day in April on the banks of the Charles River? The only answer her mind was able to grasp as she ran her fingers through his hair was the ineluctable awareness that she was voluntarily letting go of a precious piece of her life that she could never regain. This awareness frightened her, this realization that she knew what she was doing. Her reasons for doing it frightened her even more.

As she lay there under the azure sky with his head on her breast, she let her mind drift back to that winter night almost three years ago when they had first made love. They had drunk a lot of cheap Italian red wine. As they left the small restaurant, the shattering cold and damp winter air bit at their faces. They were laughing, she remembered that. The snow on the streets of Cambridge was freezing as the temperature dropped. She kept slipping and had to hold on to him to keep from falling.

"My God, it's cold," she said.

"Trouble with you Americans. Take you away from your central heating and your whole world falls apart. My room at Oxford was about this temperature most of the term. You would have loved it. Very bracing."

She slipped and nearly fell. "Damn these heels," she said. He almost fell himself trying to hold her up. She was a tall girl, and he was having no easy job of it.

"Do you think you can manage another few blocks? There isn't a cab in sight. My flat isn't far from here," he said tentatively.

She stopped for a minute, holding tightly to his arm. She looked at him. She was smiling, but her eyes had a look of measured analytical appraisal. "Are you trying to seduce me?" she asked laughingly.

"I'm trying." He laughed. "I hoped you would prefer it to freezing to death on the streets of Cambridge or breaking a leg."

He could feel her eyes measuring him. They had been dating since September.

"You sound like W. C. Fields," she said. "'I'd rather be in Philadelphia.'"

He looked at her quizzically. He didn't get it.

She put her arm around him. "Fields was a great American comedian."

"Yes, I know," he said languidly.

"Someone asked him how he wanted his obituary to read and he said, 'On the whole, I'd rather be in Philadelphia.'" She slipped again, and he caught her.

"Have I missed something?" he asked. "Is there some sort of symbolic connection between Fields and my asking you up to my flat?"

She laughed. "Well, the alternatives you present—freezing to death or breaking a leg—seem to point in the direction of your apartment—I'm sorry, flat." She laughed again as they walked gingerly on the packed freezing snow that glistened in the sporadic light of a pale moon swept by January night clouds.

She had been in his apartment before, but only briefly. Just a glass of sherry. She had been attracted to the orderly male simplicity of how he lived. Maybe it was because he was British that the small rooms seemed to have a different quality about them, a solidity, a simple dignity, a feeling of warmth, comfort, and repose; the place was almost a retreat. His flat reflected him. There was an inviting security about the way he lived. The smell of pipe tobacco; old tweeds neatly hung. Books and papers in orderly piles. She had felt safe here before, sheltered. Now she felt the added sensation of anticipation. He would make love to her, she thought, and through the haze of the wine she had drunk she felt the stirrings of excitement. Somehow she knew it was going to be right with him.

"Why don't you take your coat off? I'll get you a brandy."

She put her coat over a chair and sat down on the worn sofa. She watched him go over to the bar, which was a partition that separated the kitchen from the living room. He poured two snifters of brandy and turned toward her. Her eyes met his as he handed her a glass.

"This should warm you up."

She held the glass and looked at him. He was quite tall with broad shoulders. He was lean and angular. He seemed to fill the small living room.

She could feel him looking at her with a gaze that was tender, almost melancholy. There was that about their relationship, she thought. There was something sad about it, even now, when they both knew that they were going to make love.

She felt the brandy burn inside her. Her eyes never left his as he sat down beside her.

What would it be like to spend my life with him? she wondered. She imagined some snug faculty house or apartment with a fire in the grate. She imagined the isolated, protected academic life, a life spent with liberal intellectuals. The picture in her mind frightened her. She could never live that kind of a life, she thought. It was claustrophobic. It gave no rein to her own ambitions. She was headed in an entirely different direction. She was going to go to the Harvard Business School, if she could get in. That was one of the most competitive academic environments she could have chosen.

He kissed her with great tenderness. She put down her glass and drew her arms around him and responded more avidly, more hungrily than she had thought she would. He let his hands move gently to her breasts. She began to undo his tie and unbutton his shirt. She felt his hands and arms under her. He was lifting her from the couch.

He carried her effortlessly to the small bedroom. Her mind was a maelstrom of pure passion and work-ridden guilt. She had so much to do. Her desk was piled with work. This was supposed to have been an early evening. She would be exhausted in the morning, and it would show. On her it always did. That pale, almost translucent freckled skin worked rapidly into dark rings under her eyes when she was tired, and she had an eight o'clock economics class. She didn't give a damn. She wanted him, not just sexually; she wanted to take a part of him and keep it with her. She realized as the thought formed that she wanted to *take* from him. What did she want to give? Could she give him love? She could. She was in love with him. Could she continue to give to him? She reached for him hungrily, and they made love. He was far more experienced than she. His hands were gentle and knowledgeable. He made her wait, made her reach the extremes of her passion until her ecstasy was almost pain.

"Now, for chrissake, Peter. *Now!*" She understood in the starburst of her release that few men would ever make love to her as he had. Her heart beat so heavily she felt it must be audible. She wanted more. She had so rarely given herself to a man that she had stored a reservoir of passion inside her that was consuming her.

He cared enough to understand her need and fulfill it. He gave to her when there was nothing left to give but his skill. But he gave. He had long ago fallen in love with her. As they lay looking up at the ceiling in the darkness listening to the muted sounds of Cambridge traffic and the raw night wind, their thoughts had combined.

And now it was three years later. They had come to the fork in the river, yet they couldn't bring themselves to part. There had to be a way to stay together; there had to be.

How do you die on the banks of the Charles on a beautiful April day? she asked herself. Her silent tears mixed with his own were the only answer.

Chapter 2

SHE STOOD IN the softly lit foyer of Baldwin Cooper. The ambience of the reception area came as a surprise. She had expected it to be chrome and glass tables, with leather designer chairs. Maybe her preconceived notion of what Baldwin Cooper's offices would be like was a result of her impression of George. Why, she asked herself, had she thought of George Hall in a metaphor of chrome and glass?

She looked about the reception area at the tall polished-bonnet-topped secretary that stood next to the far wall. Its patina could only have been acquired with age. She knew it was a genuine and very expensive antique. The wallpaper behind it echoed the image of a Japanese screen, the subtle forms of travelers climbing the winding paths of a snow-covered mountain.

She seated herself in a wing chair and looked at the receptionist, who smiled at her.

"Mr. Hall knows you're here. He'll be tied up for a few more minutes. Would you like to look at the *Wall Street Journal* while you're waiting?"

"No, thank you. I read it on the plane coming down."

She knew that she was as tense as a tightly wound spring. It was like the Harvard Business School, she thought, and that thought gave her a grim confidence. She had conquered the West Point of business schools, and if she could do that, she could handle an interview with the principals of this or any other firm.

Isn't that what they taught you? she thought. Wasn't the inhuman work load designed to weed out the mentally and emotionally weak? The whole confrontational structure of the curriculum. If she could handle that and the quantum of case studies that had kept her up until three o'clock in the morning when her classes began at eight-thirty, if she could cope with subjects like managerial economics, quantitative analysis, and financial accounting, why was she so uptight about this interview?

She forced herself to relax. She crossed her legs and sat with her hands resting casually on the arms of the chair, looking down at her new suit.

She had chosen her suit carefully.

My God, she thought, I spent $175 dollars on this outfit. She had shopped for it for weeks. It had to be just right. Not too insouciant, but not too severe either. She had never spent that much on an item of clothing in her life. Her shoes and bag had cost almost as much, making a deep hole in her meager savings. She knew that her mother had never spent that amount on clothes. The thought of her mother increased her determination to make this interview a success.

She was so accustomed to the analytical case study system at Harvard that she sat there unconsciously applying it to herself. Let's look at the package from a marketing point of view, she thought. She knew she was attractive. She was conscious of her shapely legs as she waited. Her figure was good, and her face and hair should benefit from the modulated lighting, so the package should be reasonably presentable. The ability of the product to perform had already been demonstrated, at least academically; they knew her record. But what about the intangibles? she asked herself. How will a team of high-powered males react to a lone female who wants to join the club? She was intuitive enough to understand that some men felt intimidated by a woman with her intellectual credentials, especially given the additional asset of her sexuality.

Liz was under no delusions. She knew that being a woman in an all-male environment had its drawbacks, but it also had its advantages. She could sense that with George. She knew instinctively that George was physically attracted to her. But if that became evident to her younger peers it would make them hostile toward her. If Baldwin Cooper chose to hire her, she would have a difficult line to walk. Her male peers could concentrate their energies on doing their jobs, but she would always have to be aware of that invisible aura of sex that men reacted to either positively or negatively in a competitive business environment. It would not be easy.

She saw George Hall come toward her, his hand extended, a broad smile on his face. He had acquired a tan, and looked quite handsome with his full dark hair. She wondered if he had his clothes made in London. Liz never missed much, and the impression she had of George was an extension of what she originally felt when she had first met him in Cambridge.

George was not old money; she knew that. He was too careful with the details of how he looked, the impression he was making on others, to be old money. Nonetheless, George's look suited him, and he wasn't pretentious about it.

"How nice to see you, Liz. I'm so glad you could make it. I know how difficult it is to leave the Point."

So he was a Harvard Business School grad, she thought. "The Point" was an inside joke. They referred to the rigorous B School as West Point. It figured, she thought.

Liz stood up. She could feel him looking at her; she wondered what kind of vibes he was picking up. As a woman, she knew that physically he liked what he saw.

"Let's go to my office. We can chat for a few minutes and then we'll meet Baldwin and Cooper for lunch."

He touched her arm and led her down a hall of waxed parquet floors covered with scattered Oriental rugs. The hall held framed old maps and etchings of New York when the Dutch were still its principal source of financial power.

"Here we are." He held the door for Liz, who entered his office trying to hide her surprise. There was no attempt to conform to the impression of subdued elegance that was evident in the reception area. George's office was a Scandinavian extract from the *Journal of Modern Design*. The wall opposite his desk burst into color with deftly textured mauves, blues, sweeping strokes of red and green. It looked like an original Hans Hofmann. It was.

"Do you like it?" He was smiling as he saw her surprise.

"Why—yes, I do."

"Please sit down."

He pointed to a chrome-framed leather chair that looked challenging. She found it surprisingly comfortable.

He understood her response and was amused by it. Almost everyone reacted the same way. His office was a complete switch from the ambience the firm offered to its visitors in the reception area. It annoyed the hell out of Baldwin and Cooper, but it said a lot about George.

Liz felt more comfortable now. She could feel George watching her as she looked around his office and beyond the open gauze drapes to a view of mid-Manhattan.

She knew he was waiting for her to remark on his office. She had a stubborn inclination not to say anything, but her intuition told her he expected her to. She played to her intuition. "I must say, George, your office is a lot more lively than that reception area."

"Don't tell that to Baldwin. He hates this office. Thinks it ruins the whole atmosphere of refinement and success." He laughed. "Larry isn't a stuffed shirt. He's just hooked on antiques. Bob Cooper goes along with him because he knows that the clocks, maps, chairs, rugs, and paintings are a hell of a lot better investment than some of the deals we've made."

She instinctively knew that she had to play it carefully with George. She would be working for him if the firm decided to hire her, and she sensed that his light manner was probably misleading. Her intuition told her that George had to have another side, one that was tough and sharp and capable of cutting deeply. He would not be managing director of such a compact meritocracy as this one unless there was far more to him than surface geniality.

"You look very attractive, Liz. I like that suit."

"Thank you."

He leaned back in his chair. "How's everything back at the crunch factory?"

"Under control." She paused. "I'll be glad to get out. It seems as if I've been going to school forever."

George lit a cigarette, and she watched the blue-gray smoke hang in the air.

"One of the things about your background that most impressed me was that they accepted you at the B School right out of Radcliffe. They don't make a habit of doing that. Tell me, why did you make the decision to go for your M.B.A. before you had any work experience? Do you think in retrospect that was a mistake? Don't you feel that business school would have been more meaningful if you had approached it from the background of a real work environment?"

She wondered if he always asked three questions at once. "I didn't want to get just any job after Radcliffe," she answered. "I had majored in political economics. With just a B.A. I couldn't expect much. If I had gone after a Ph.D., I probably would have wound up teaching or working with some think tank. I didn't want either of those jobs; I wanted the challenge of making some money and having fun doing it. I thought if I could get into the B School and do relatively well my chances of getting the kind of job I wanted would be a lot better."

He watched her while she spoke. She was quiet and somewhat reserved, the way he had remembered her. The light from his window picked up the copper highlights of her hair. He saw the sheen of her crossed legs. He knew he was looking at a young woman with a penetrating intelligence. What he didn't know until he saw her under fire was how gutsy and determined she was; how badly she wanted the golden apple.

They had never hired a woman before, and Baldwin and Cooper were not at all sure that they should.

Why *did* he want to hire her? he asked himself. He knew all of the reasons he had articulated to Baldwin and to himself, but after he had met her that first evening in Cambridge, did some switch flip on?

She had all the credentials that could be expected at her age, and she had done it on her own. She had cracked one of the world's toughest academic environments. She had done better than he had. Her class rank was higher than his—but what the hell did that have to do with anything? If it had been some young stud sitting in front of him, not dry behind the ears, it would have been easy, but as she sat before him, flexing her leg like the twitching tail of a big relaxed cat, he knew that he would have a difficult time being as objective with her. Why? Because she was a woman? Was there something special about Liz that he responded to? Could he be objective with her without being affected by the sexual mist that was always present between a man and a woman? Would it unconsciously influence his judgment?

He smoked quietly, listening to her, watching her, seeing the cloud shadows soften the light as it played about her face. Hiring her, he thought, will be my decision. Baldwin will leave it to me. He wondered as he put out his cigarette if he had already made that decision. And if he had, had he been honest with himself about his reasons for doing so?

"Let's get some lunch," he said. He came around his desk to her chair. She stood up, and he could smell the faint trace of her perfume. He touched her arm—a habitual gesture of his with women—and followed her out of the room.

They sat in the firm's dining room whose ambience was much the same as that of the reception area. There was a large English sideboard on which were displayed two exquisite Chinese export porcelain jars. A broad, carefully polished mahogany dining table reflected the light of a brass chandelier. The table was set with cut crystal and heavy shell-patterned silverware on four off-white linen placemats. In the far corner of the room stood a tall clock, beautifully inlaid, showing not only the correct time but the different phases of the moon relative to the day and month of the year.

On the wall over the sideboard was what appeared to be a Charles Willson Peale portrait of Alexander Hamilton in a heavy wooden frame.

She remembered the contrast of George's office, and she had to hide a smile.

"Since you are the guest of honor, Miss Clark, how about sitting here?" Larry Baldwin held a chair for her at the center of the table facing George. Larry and Bob Cooper took seats at opposite ends of the table.

Liz was struck by how young they seemed. She'd expected two men in their fifties or sixties, but Larry and Bob looked about the same age as George, whom she had judged to be in his early forties.

"Miss Clark, how about a drink? We're not as stuffy as our banking friends. Can we tempt you?" Larry Baldwin was short and slight with quick blue eyes. He smiled easily and seemed to have a pleasant, relaxed manner, until you noticed the slim fingers in almost constant motion as if he were playing an invisible piano. Liz noticed the thinning hair, which she assumed had been blond when he was younger.

The waiter, Carlos, stood quietly near the swinging door that led to the kitchen.

"I'd like a dry sherry."

Liz noticed that Carlos never moved.

"My usual, Carlos," said Bob Cooper. He was a tall, broad-shouldered man with hair that was beginning to gray. There was a sense of physical strength about him. He had a strong masculine air that was almost palpable. Liz was struck by the contrast between the two principals of the firm.

Bob turned to Liz, his bass laugh booming throughout the room. "Wait till you see what our managing director likes to drink. We call it sex in a glass." He tilted back his chair, his jacket open, and pointed a thick finger at George.

George laughed. "Don't let Coop give you a playback of his libido. It's three raw clams in clam juice and tomato juice."

Carlos placed an enormous martini in front of Bob Cooper, who pointed to George's glass shaking his head. His expression was one of feigned disgust.

Liz felt as if she were intruding into the male essence of the room. Here was the cave of the leaders. Every instinct told her that few if any women ever saw its interior.

"Check off on the menu what you want, Liz," George said. She started to look over the menu. The phone on a small stand near Larry Baldwin's chair rang.

They all automatically looked toward the short, slim man whose eyes and fingers never stopped moving.

"Nice to hear from you, Bill," Larry said, his face tightening. Liz felt the tension come into the room like a chill blast of wind. "You what?" Larry asked. "Say that again." Larry held his hand over the mouthpiece and whispered to Bob and George. "He's telling me he can't meet this month's payroll."

"Jesus Christ!" Bob's face was livid. He brought a meaty fist crashing down on the table so that the china and silver rattled.

"Bill. Calm down," Larry continued. "Did you talk to the bank?"

A pause.

"They won't go along? Bill, hold it. We're having lunch here. I have Bob and George with me. I want to put you on the speaker phone. We also have a young lady as a guest, so clean up your language a little, okay? I'm going to switch you on to the speaker now so that we can all hear you."

He flipped the switch on the speaker phone and hung up. "Can you hear me now, Bill?"

"Loud and clear."

"You're coming through fine."

Liz started to get up. "I'll wait for you outside."

Larry shook his head and motioned for her to sit down.

"Why should you have trouble with the bank, Bill? They've seen the contracts."

"Sure they've seen the goddamn contracts," Bill answered. "But some son of a bitch has them convinced we can't lick our production problems and that we'll either be way over budget or late on the delivery schedules." Bill paused. "You know our tit's in a wringer, Larry, if we can't make those delivery dates."

"This is George, Bill. Give it to us straight with a little less color. Can you make those deliveries on time?"

"I can't make them, George, if I can't pay my people."

"Never mind that for a minute. Are you now, at this moment, able to deliver those laser micrometers on schedule at contracted prices?" They all waited. The silence on the speaker phone drew them like a magnet.

"You can't paint me into a corner, George."

"The hell we can't," Bob Cooper's voice boomed through the room.

Larry motioned to him to take it easy.

"Screw that!" Bob shouted.

"What did you say, Bob?" Bill asked on the other end.

"I wasn't talking to you, but I am now. You've been waffling with us on these goddamn chronometers for months, Bill."

Larry kept shaking his head, signaling Bob that this wasn't going to get them anywhere.

"I'm going to tell him once and for all, Larry—"

"Bob, who the hell are you talking to?" Bill asked, angry now.

"I'm trying to talk to you, but one of my partners is waving at me like a signal officer on a carrier deck."

They all heard the laugh come through the speaker phone.

Liz watched their faces. This was supposed to be a lunch interview. Not only had there been no interview, but as yet there had been no lunch. She felt the pressure building in the room until it seemed palpable.

"Goddamn it, Bill. George was down there not less than six weeks ago, and the deal he glued together with the bank was based on those contracts. You told him then." Bob turned to George. "If my memory is correct, didn't you come back and tell us that Bill had stated unequivocably that he would be able to meet both the specs and the delivery dates?"

"That's exactly what Bill told me and I told you and Larry," George said.

"Jesus Christ, Bill," Bob roared, "what the hell do you expect the banks to do? They've bent over backwards to accommodate you because of us and our insurance company partners—"

"Hold it, Bob." The voice was as level and as cold as steel. It came from the small man at the foot of the table. Liz watched him with a fascination bordering on awe. Somehow Larry had stopped everything, held control of everyone, and he had accomplished this through some indefinable quality of intellectual toughness that was known to these men and to which they responded with respect.

"We can't solve this over the phone, Bill. George will fly down there tonight. If he can't make it, we'll send Howard. George can be on deck by phone. There's no question about meeting the payroll. That simply has to be done, regardless of how we do it. We'll find some way to satisfy the banks. I'm also going to call some people we know, consultants, at Arthur D. Little, and have them fly down so that we can get an unbiased opinion as to just where you are. That will appeal to the banks as well as to us, Bill. And one more thing. We'll bill your company for the expenses of the consultants."

"Like hell you will! I know what consultants are. They're a bunch of make-believe hot-shots who, if they had any brains or balls, would be running their own businesses."

"Bill," said the voice whose intonation brooked no argument, "that's the way it's going to be. Now, I'll have George call you after lunch." Larry Baldwin flipped the switch on the speaker phone, and the conversation was over.

Bob Cooper was seething. "That little son of a bitch calls us on the twentieth day of April and gives us less than ten days to work out his goddamn payroll."

Larry's face was the color of chalk. The muscles in his jaw worked like a cat under a blanket. "Carlos, would you see what Miss Clark will have?"

Carlos stood beside Elizabeth's chair. Her hands were moist with perspiration. Her stomach felt as it had during her first

year at the Business School when she was called on to answer
a question by a particularly demanding and abrasive professor.

"The veal is excellent. The red snapper is very good, miss."

She hesitated. "I'd like the veal, please."

"A shrimp cocktail or perhaps some vichyssoise to start?"

"Shrimp, please."

The energy in the room seemed to disappear slowly like the
setting sun. They ate silently. The early, easy humor seemed
difficult to recapture.

"I'm sorry about the interruption, Liz," George said. "But
that's our business. That phone call could just as easily have
come to any one of us at two in the morning or on a Sunday
afternoon. Even when we're lying on a beach someplace, if
they've got a phone, and it works..."

Bob and Larry ate silently.

Liz understood the problem—it was childishly simple—
the problem, not necessarily the solution. Evidently this Bill
had used some contracts as a means of inducing a bank to
advance him working capital, money he needed to run his
business. Somehow the bank had gotten wind of the fact that
he might not be able to meet the conditions of those contracts,
and the bank was refusing to lend him any more money. He
didn't have enough money to meet his payroll. She didn't have
anything but these skeletal facts, but they fascinated her. Here
was a chance to do what she had been learning in theory, to
apply her skills and training to a real business problem. The
excitement of confronting this challenge and doing something
about it stimulated her so that she knew her face was flushed.
She could feel it, and with her pale, almost translucent skin,
she knew they could see it.

The lunch continued, and the men made several awkward
attempts to return to the interview, but they were less than
successful.

They were eating dessert. Bob Cooper was quietly blowing
rich blue-gray smoke from a Havana cigar. Larry pushed back
his chair.

"George, would you give Bill a call and set things up? I
want to talk to Miss Clark for a minute." Larry looked at Bob.
"You want to stay and chat with us?"

"I'd love to, but I have some people coming to see me at
two." He looked at his watch. "If they're on time I've already

kept them waiting for ten minutes." He stood up. "Miss Clark, it was a pleasure meeting you. I hope we'll be seeing a lot more of you around here."

Liz smiled. "I enjoyed it, Mr. Cooper."

He laughed. "You did? Well, then, you must be as nuts as the rest of us." Liz watched him as he left the room.

George got up. "When you're through with Larry, come back to my office, Liz. I've got a tight schedule this afternoon, but we'll see if we can't work around it."

She was left sitting in the center of the long dining table, looking at Larry Baldwin over rumpled napkins and the debris of lunch. He stared at her, his eyes reflecting his simultaneous preoccupation with the problems in which he was absorbed while at the same time taking the measure of the young woman sitting at his table.

"Not quite the way things happen at Morgan."

She smiled. "I don't know, Mr. Baldwin. I've never been to Morgan."

"Didn't you apply to any of the major banks?"

"I got offers from Chase and Citibank."

He laughed. "Well, this is not quite how things are at the Chase, Miss Clark. I can assure you." He sighed in response to some inner thought. "How did you come to apply to an outfit like ours?"

She hesitated. "I didn't."

"You didn't?"

"No. I received a letter from Mr. Hall, who arranged to meet me in Cambridge. He told me that he kept in close touch with the Business School and that one of my professors with whom he was friendly suggested he contact me. He described what you do here, and I thought it might prove challenging and exciting."

"Like this lunch."

She laughed again. "Is it always like this?"

"Not always. Sometimes it gets a good deal more intense." He paused. "That may be the understatement of the age, Miss Clark."

She knew without being told that Larry Baldwin was an extraordinarily capable man. She sensed that he *was* the firm, although she was sure that no one in this meritocracy did much sleepwalking.

"Miss Clark, we're in one of the most exciting businesses I can think of. We are really professional gamblers, only in our game the odds aren't with the house. As a matter of fact, they're stacked quite heavily against us. Our job is to make sure that the gap between risk and reward is as narrow as we can make it, and that's a very difficult thing to do. It takes a special person to have the intelligence, the drive, the guts, and the staying power to hang in there and retain perspective when everything is falling apart. And, conversely, not to go on any ego trips when things are going your way." He looked at her coolly. "Do you think you're that kind of person?"

Her mind was on the telephone call that had come during lunch. It had ignited her. She couldn't repress the flood of desire to be a part of what was going on here. She was thinking about Bill, whoever Bill was, and his payroll, his people. But she knew she was not a missionary, and she felt guilty that her thoughts were not focused solely on the plight of Bill's workers. Her excitement came from the problem itself and how to solve it, and she wondered whether there was some deficiency in her character that made her feel this way.

"What are you thinking about right now?" Baldwin asked her.

She looked at him, her face flushed with excitement; her eyes were bright with an intensity and preoccupation that almost matched his. When she answered him, it was as if she were talking to herself.

"I'm thinking about this client of yours and the problem he has with his payroll."

"What about it?"

"I think it would be absolutely fascinating to be involved in straightening something like that out."

"Why?"

"Because it's a crunch situation."

"And you like crunch situations?"

"Not if they can be avoided. But if the crunch comes, I find it exciting to meet it."

"And handle it?"

"And handle it."

"Wouldn't you say you're a little short on experience?"

Her face flushed.

"Let me tell you how it works around here, Miss Clark. We

know you're bright, and have the discipline and determination that got you through the Business School with your record. First-class, absolutely. What we don't know is how well you will adapt to the exigencies of this business. It's highly specialized, Miss Clark, and you can't learn it in business school." He shifted in his chair and noticed Carlos waiting to clear the table.

"We'll be through here in a few minutes, Carlos. Just leave everything until we're finished." He turned back to Liz. "What I'm going to say to you, Miss Clark, will be very frank. We don't have the time around here to be oblique—nor, might I add. do we have the inclination.

"If we decide to make you an offer, and if you decide to accept, we will begin the process of training you under fire. You'll start off crunching numbers with two young associates who have been with us for about two years. They've built up enough experience to have some account responsibility, although they're not yet responsible for any single client. They are highly competitive young men. Very aggressive, or we wouldn't have kept them on. Their *raison d'être* is this business. It comes first with them, as it does with all of us. If there are fires to put, opportunities to explore, those become our priorities. Many times, those priorities interfere with our personal lives, with our families. But that can't be helped. It's the price this business demands." He watched her closely. "Are you ready to pay that kind of price? Before you answer, think about it from my point of view. You're a very attractive young woman. I'm not sure that you won't prove a distraction around here." He smiled. "It's been known to happen. But what concerns me more is the possibility that after the time we put in training you, when you finally become really useful to us, you may decide to quit and play wife and mother."

She stared at him, not sure how to respond to his quick personal comment.

"Forgive me. I can't think of a job more important than that. Only it doesn't fit in with this business. You can't be worried about picking up the children at school while you're on a plane to the West Coast. Miss Clark, I assure you it's a lot better to make the decision now, for both your sake and the firm's. We don't want to find out several years from now that we've sharpened a talent we're going to lose."

He had gone to the heart of the matter swiftly, she thought, cleanly, like a surgeon laying open an incision. It was something she had kept forcing to the back of her mind on those exhausted nights in her cell-like room at Harvard. She had always been too busy to confront the problem as directly as Baldwin Cooper was presenting it. She had kept it hidden in the recesses of her mind, afraid to bring it out into the open to analyze it. Peter had forced her to look at it, and it had ruined their relationship. She wasn't sure she could go through that again. She knew that Larry Baldwin sensed her confusion. She didn't know how to respond to him.

"There are many other careers in finance, Miss Clark, that are less demanding than our business. Financial analyst with a good-sized brokerage firm. Loan officer with a bank. With your record, you could do lots of things that won't require the kind of commitment we will." He watched her as she withdrew into herself in reflection.

How can I possibly give him a truthful answer? she thought. I've already torn myself in half over this with Peter. He's right. Someday I'm going to have to decide whether I want to sacrifice everything to a career, or to experience the guilt of being part mother and part tycoon. Damn it. Men don't have to make these kinds of choices.

She knew what she wanted to say: I know I'd love this business. I could hold my own with any hot-shot you've got around here after I learn the ropes. But that's not what he's asking me. He isn't questioning my ability. He's worried about the conflicts I face because I'm a woman.

It just slipped out. She couldn't have prevented saying it if she wanted to. "Mr. Baldwin, your business offers the excitement and challenge that I would enjoy and the rewards that go along with that. But you're asking me if I'm willing to give up a part of my life as a woman." She shook her head. "I'm not sure I can commit myself to this firm for the rest of my life. It would be dishonest of me to make a promise like that."

She was looking at him directly. Her eyes met his. She could see no reaction on his part.

He looked at his watch and stood up. "I have to be going." He hesitated. "Did you and George ever discuss money?"

She was standing now, and she realized she was taller than he. She saw the quizzical expression. "No. Mr. Hall and I never talked about money."

They were facing each other, standing beside the dining table.

"What do you think you're worth?"

She had rehearsed this carefully with herself. It was a topic of continual discussion at the B School. Her fellow M.B.A.'s had developed a network of information concerning the differing starting salaries of the companies in which they were interested. She looked at him evenly, her voice well modulated but firm. "I think I'm worth forty-five thousand to start, Mr. Baldwin, with suitable bonuses for exceptional performance."

It was a high salary for someone straight out of graduate school. But companies were willing to pay that much for someone with her class rank, graduating with a master's degree in business administration from the Harvard Business School. She was one of an elite group of young men and women.

"If you'll follow me, Miss Clark, I'll show you to George's office."

She sat in the small reception area outside of George's office, reading *Forbes,* occasionally looking up at his secretary, who had been eyeing her furtively, with quick, furtive little smiles.

I haven't the faintest idea of what his reaction was, she thought. I blew it. I know it. He was waiting for me to give him the old do-or-die for Baldwin Cooper, and I couldn't. She felt the tearing unfairness of her sex. It really is a man's world, she thought bitterly, especially in a place like this. She felt the maleness all around her. It was reinforced by George's secretary who probably knew why she was here. This sort of thing goes out on the office grapevine, she thought, and she knew that she must have been the topic of a good many conversations. She could feel her face flush. She was mad as hell at the silent confrontation that she felt. Maybe it's a good thing I blew it, she thought. This is no job for me. It won't be enough for me to be as good as the young studs they have around here; I'm going to have to be better.

The door opened and George stood there, his face grim. He motioned for her to come in.

"Sit down, Liz."

George offered her a cigarette. She shook her head. He sat down wearily and buzzed his secretary. "Is Howard in?" he asked her.

"I saw him this morning."

"Tell him I'd like to see him right away." He looked at Liz.

"We have a novel way of recruiting."

She laughed. "It isn't dull."

"That's one thing it never is around here, Liz, dull. How did you get along with Baldwin?"

"I don't know. I couldn't read him. I don't have the faintest idea what he thought."

"What did you talk about?"

Her lips compressed. She looked directly at George. "He wanted to know if I was willing to put my career first, over the considerations of a family." She sighed audibly. "I told him I didn't know. It was the only honest answer I could give him. I don't know how I'll feel about a career five or ten years from now. It will be a tremendously important part of my life, but will it be my whole life? I can't answer that question at this stage of my life."

He was looking at her carefully. She could feel his appraisal, but she sensed a certain disappointment. The protégée had let her mentor down. She was frustrated with the whole afternoon. All she wanted to do was to get on the first plane back to Boston.

A tall young man stood in the doorway.

"Come in, Howard. This is Elizabeth Clark. Howard Grayson."

Howard Grayson smiled thinly. "Miss Clark."

Liz looked at the thin young man with the full head of wavy chestnut hair. The swift impression Liz received of Howard was one of a discerning blandness. She was sure there had to be some hot coals banked inside that cool exterior, but they didn't show.

"Howard, can you get down to Atlanta tonight?"

"I suppose so. But it will mean a lot of shuffling around. I've got to be in Houston on Thursday, and I have a heavy schedule tomorrow."

"Anything you can't postpone?"

"I guess not. What's up?"

George looked at Liz and then at Howard before he spoke. "I'll fill you in later. Make arrangements to be in Atlanta early this evening. Set up a dinner appointment with Bill Folsome and plan to spend all day tomorrow with him. Try your best to get things squared away down there before you come back to New York. I'll be on deck if you need me."

Liz caught the guarded glances that ricocheted between them. She realized that George didn't want to go into details in front of her.

"I'll catch up with you a little later, Howard. Ask Martha to get started on reservations for Atlanta."

Howard's face betrayed little emotion. If he was annoyed at having his plans turned upside down at the last moment, it didn't show. He smiled thinly again at Liz. "Pleasure, Miss Clark."

Liz watched him leave the room. There was an impersonal quality about Howard that made him seem remote. She looked at George. "You have a busy afternoon ahead, George, and I'm getting in the way." She started to rise.

"No. Please sit down. I want to talk to you—"

His secretary stood hesitantly in the doorway.

"What is it?"

"I have a note from Mr. Baldwin."

He took the envelope and removed the note, and the secretary vanished.

Liz watched his smile broaden as he read it. He handed it to her.

"You want me to read this?"

"I think you're entitled to."

She took the note. It was handwritten in bold strokes of black ink:

George—

If she'll have us, hire her.
She's the only Harvard M.B.A. I've met fresh out of the tank who knows when to keep her mouth shut. I think she also may have the intemperate liability of being honest.

Larry

Liz was dumbstruck. She had been sure she had blown it. She tried to cover her surprise. "I don't know what to say."

George laughed. "That's our beloved leader. It looks as if you've got a job if you want one."

The realization that she had somehow conquered this day was slow to sink in. What surprised her even more was her own doubt as to whether she now wanted what they were offering her. Larry Baldwin's questions had struck deep.

"Well? What do you say? Are you going to join us at this Mad Hatter's tea party?"

She had to be very careful how she answered George. There was a limit to any further demonstration of a lack of decisiveness. "George, I've got some other offers I haven't had time to evaluate," she lied.

"How long will that take?"

"I should be able to let you know within a week. Will that be soon enough?"

George looked at her appraisingly. "I guess it will have to be."

She thought she saw a flicker of doubt in George's eyes. She didn't care. She needed more time to make the commitment she knew they would demand of her. She needed to know if she wanted to spend a part of her life in this venture capital company. Maybe Larry Baldwin was right; there were other jobs that demanded less. But then, Larry Baldwin had just hired her.

Chapter 3

PETER WELLS LOOKED quietly out of the window at the walk-ways crowded with happy graduates and their families. Behind him he could hear Liz packing as he watched the kaleidoscope of people spill over the lawns that fronted the brick Georgian buildings of Harvard College.

Liz's mother sat in the single straight chair, which she had turned to face the bed so she could watch her daughter pack. "You're sure there isn't anything I can help you with?"

"No, thanks, Mom. I'm almost through."

The three of them felt each other's presence and seemed uncomfortable in the strange quiet of the cell-like room as the sounds of laughter and the general exuberance of post-graduation excitement carried to them on the soft, warm May air.

"I've got to take my gown back," she said as she bent over her suitcase. "I bought the hood." She straightened up and turned toward them. "Peter, would you take my gown back to the gym? I want to talk to Mother. We can get started when you get back." She looked at him as he seemed to fill the room. She started to laugh. "It's a good thing you didn't have to spend two years in this cell."

"I don't see how anyone could spend two years in it," her mother said.

Peter took the gown. "I'll be back in twenty minutes."

She touched his hand as he started to leave the room. He stopped and looked at her, his eyes filled with resignation. He looked at her mother. "I'll see you soon, Mrs. Clark." They waited until they heard his footsteps on the stairs.

Liz sat down on the bed and looked at her mother. She tried to smile. "I only attended these ceremonies for you, Mom. Almost nobody from the B School bothers about graduation."

"You certainly don't act like someone who has just picked up all the marbles." Betty Clark watched her daughter as she listened to the continuous cacophony of the crowds outside.

"I don't feel like it."

Her mother shook her head. "You've worked so hard and done so well, and now you have this job, forty-five thousand to start! A young girl fresh out of college. My God, Liz, it's almost scandalous."

Liz looked at her mother sitting there in the new spring dress she had bought for Liz's graduation, looked at the pale blue eyes that had seen little joy. It was hard enough to articulate the problem to herself, let alone try to explain it to her mother.

"Mother, I don't know what's wrong with me. I've worked like a dog to get a chance like this and now . . ."

"And now what? You don't know whether you want it or not, is that it? You don't know whether you want Peter, either."

Liz started to speak. Her mother held up her hand. "Liz. I want to get this off my chest before he comes back. We may not have much time alone together when we get home. I've got to get back to the hospital. Do you remember that day you came down for breakfast and picked up the morning paper—"

"Please, Mother. Don't bring that up. For God's sake."

"Do you remember what I told you when you read about your father's death?"

"Mother, please."

"It was hard enough to learn that your father had been killed in that accident, but the woman he was with—"

"Mother, for God's sake. Why must you bring this up now?"

The spare figure seemed charged with a strange ferocity. "Because I don't want you to be like me. I don't want you to know a life of empty rooms and lonely meals. It didn't have to be that way for me. I made that hell myself. I let pride and shame isolate me from people and from life. All I had was my work, and I'm not even good at that."

Elizabeth reached out and clasped her mother's hands. "That's not true. You know that's not true. You're the best nurse they've got in that hospital."

Her mother's voice was low; her thoughts far back in the past. "No, I'm not, Elizabeth. A good nurse is interested in people. I—I lost that a long time ago." Her eyes focused back on Liz, bringing a force to bear that Liz had never known her mother possessed. "I don't want you to make my mistakes. I want you to meet life head on. Reach out and grab it. Suppose you make some mistakes. So what?"

"But, Mother, you don't even know what the problem is."

"I know this much. You made up your mind when you were at Radcliffe that you wanted a career in business. You worked like a slave, like someone demented. They searched you out before you even graduated."

"They do that with all the top students here."

"And you were one of the brightest. They sought you out first—"

"Mother—"

"Don't 'Mother' me! Is it the challenge you're afraid of?" Liz shook her head.

"Then what is it?"

Liz hesitated. "It's hard to explain."

"Well, explain it to me before Peter gets back."

Liz sighed. "Mother, the firm wants one hundred percent from me. They want the job to be my whole life." She hesitated. "But I may want to get married someday, have children."

"Plenty of women have a career and a family."

"Not this kind of a career, and not this kind of a firm. Mother. If I don't give them everything I've got, I won't last a year there."

Betty Clark looked at her daughter carefully, a gaze that carried the accumulated wisdom of lost opportunities. "If you're sitting between the horns of a dilemma, Liz, there's only one way to get off. You've got to grab hold of one horn or another and swing yourself down. You just can't sit there. If you do—" She paused. "If you do, Liz, you'll end up like me."

They sat there, the laconic woman whose life had been changed by a newspaper headline, and her daughter, a tigress about to try her new claws and teeth. They held each other's hands in that small womb of a room, oblivious to the noise outside.

Liz's eyes never left her mother's face. She watched her mother

momentarily reach back into her own past to a time over thirty
years ago when she was a pretty young woman with dreams, and
a life of hope and expectation stretched out before her. Betty was
buying a pair of shoes in Benoit's on Congress Street in Portland,
Maine. The clerk, a round-faced, ebullient young man with dark
chestnut-highlighted hair, was being overly attentive. His manner was quietly engaging. There was a joy about him that she
found almost infectious. She was quiet and reserved with a serious look. Her friends in school called her Hoot because one of
them had said, "Betty, you look as solemn as an owl. I'm surprised you don't hoot." The boys in her high school class had
picked up the nickname, and it stuck. That's how they had au-
tographed her high school yearbook: "To Hoot, the best friend I
ever had."

She remembered all those scrawled signatures. She also remembered the round-faced clerk who kept offering pair after pair
of shoes, suggesting first this one, then that one until she was so
confused she didn't know which pair to choose.

"My name's Randy Clark," he said in a continuing mono-
logue. "Not going to be working at this store all my life, I can
tell you that."

"What are you going to do?" she asked quietly, hesitantly.

"Goin' to work for the Brockton Shoe Company as soon as
there's an opening. They've promised me Northern New England. From Bangor to Kittery. That's the life for me. Movin'
around. Meetin' people. Good money in it, too." He looked up
at her with those laughing, ingratiating dark eyes. "What you
goin' to do?"

"I'm going to be a nurse."

"That's a good career," he said admiringly. And that's how
they had met.

As the years passed and she had time to think, Betty decided
that what had attracted her to Randolph Clark was his personality his joy of life. He was certainly different from her parents,
who were careful and respectable. Her father was a vice-
president of the Casco Bay National Bank. Her mother had always referred to the importance of her father's job. Her mother
thought her husband's position gave status to the family, and she
was always admonishing Betty not to do this or that. "What would
people think?" was her mother's constant concern. Betty's life

was constricted by her mother's stern attitudes and her mother's home had become like her own house was now, stiff and dark and without compassion.

Her mother was beside herself when Betty started keeping company with Randy Clark. "He's a shoe salesman," her mother kept reminding her with haughty disdain. "I don't understand you, Betty. There are so many eligible young men at the bank." But Betty had selected the one joyous person who seemed to care about her. And he did. The years exposed his lack of practicality, but nothing had diminished his ebulliency. They had been happy in the beginning, but Randy began to understand why his wife's high school yearbook had autographs scrawled all over it that read, "To Hoot . . ."

Then Liz was born. Randy adored his daughter, but he traveled so much. He was away from home so often. And the years passed, with the gulf widening between Betty and Randy.

He seemed to make excuses not to come home, and when he did, he spent all his time with Liz. Betty had become like her mother, a reproving presence. She felt guilty about this, and jealous of the adoration Randy lavished on their daughter. "You come home like some migrating bird and spoil that child rotten, and then I have to deal with it," she would say. After the accident, after the scandal that had brought her and her parents irredeemable shame, she began to wonder what part she had played in the estrangement of her husband, and in the scandal, but those thoughts were quickly killed by a protective self-righteousness. The years had eroded that shell, however, and she had grudgingly admitted her own responsibility for what had happened. She had been consumed by the sin of pride, and she had never learned to give, really give of herself out of love. Even with Liz she had always held back a part of herself.

Her eyes came back from her past, and she looked at her daughter and felt she was really seeing her again. She embraced Liz almost desperately.

"Liz, I pray every day that you won't be like me. I pray that you will meet life with joy and not bitterness. Not hide from its challenges. Not be afraid to take chances." For the first time Liz could remember, she felt the anguish of her mother's tears.

Peter stood in the doorway. They hadn't heard him come back. Liz saw him first, and it broke their mood. She rose, kissed her mother's dry, cool cheek, and stood up.

"Do you think that old Chevrolet of yours will make it to Falmouth?" Liz asked him.

He laughed. "It's never let me down."

She looked at her mother. "Come on, Mom. Let's get back to real Yankee country."

The fog hung thick and fat, glistening droplets in the late morning sun. The upper layers of wind-torn mist were beginning to burn off, exposing patches of blue sky. They had parked on the deserted asphalt road and walked down to the cove watching the receding tide leave a lace of white foam over the dark rocks. Seaweed and devil's tails of kelp floated on the shallow breaking waves.

The morning was still cool, and they were dressed warmly in heavy woolen sweaters and pants and rubber boots. They held hands as they walked in silence at the water's edge of the crescent-shaped cove. They could hear the squawking of gulls in their relentless search for food.

"Have you made up your mind what you're going to do?" Peter asked.

She hesitated. "I'm not sure. I think so."

"Isn't your uncertainty an indication that maybe you aren't cut out for this sort of thing? How many of your classmates would hesitate if they had the opportunity you've had?"

"Most of my classmates are men. The only decision they have to make is what job to take." Her voice was tinged with irony. "Despite the women's movement and ERA, this is still a male-dominated society."

She kicked a small stone and sent it clattering into the water. "If I had majored in art or design or something that I could fit in with a role as a wife and mother, or if I had wanted to teach, it would have been a lot easier. You can still have kids and work them in around those kinds of careers. But I was never interested in that. For some reason, it was business that turned me on, and when I got into Harvard, I understood why. Those cases we studied. I *knew* what to do with them. It was almost instinctive, the way other people paint. Working out those problems was exciting." She paused. "That's the reason I didn't take the offers from Chase or Citibank. I want to be a part of the action. A part of something smaller, less institutionalized where what I do per-

sonally will have an impact on the company. I could have interviewed at a place like Morgan Stanley or First Boston, but they
act as agents in most of the deals they're in. I want to be part of
something where the company is a principal, where the firm's
own money is on the line. And some day, when I become a partner, it will be my money that's at risk. It's what Larry said—"

"Who's Larry?"

"Larry Baldwin. He's one of the principals of the firm. He
said that their business was like professional gambling, only the
odds were stacked against the house, and it was their job to narrow those odds, to make them as small as possible, and then make
the decision to go or not to go. And they work like hell to make
it all pay off."

Peter watched her face, damp from the mist, the droplets of
moisture beginning to glisten from the sun that was burning off
the fog. He saw her excitement; he could hear it in her voice. She
was a Diana. The hunt, the quest, the excitement it generated in
her was a force he could feel.

"When I was having lunch with them, a client with a serious
problem called while we were about to start ordering. From the
conversation I could tell what the problem was." She paused and
turned to look at him, his hair wet from the fog. "Oh, Peter, I
wanted so much to be a part of that. To go down there and help
straighten out the mess. I knew I could do it." She started to laugh.
"When I told that to Larry, he asked me if I wasn't a little short
on experience. I know I am, but I also know in my bones that the
business they're in is for me. Larry said it was the most exciting
business in the world, and I think he's right. To take a chance on
a small company you believe in after you've weeded out those
you think are going to be the losers, then to be a part of making
it grow, building it, and helping it become successful—I can't
think of anything I want to do more."

He held her arm and turned her toward him. He looked at her,
her face aglow with the excitement of what she had been de-
scribing to him.

"Then what's the problem, Liz? If something means this much
to you, you have to do it."

She put her arms around him and looked up at him. "But look
what this is doing to us. With a career like that, I could never be
the wife you want. I can't even see myself having children under
those circumstances." She paused. "What's tearing me apart, Pe-

ter, is that I'm not sure it's worth it. What I have to give up seems too much to ask."

He put his arms around her and drew her close to him. "Everyone isn't cut out to be a wife and mother, Liz. That's a full-time job, and so many people do it badly. You have special talents," he paused, "and I believe you have a need to use those talents. Liz, you can never have it all. No one can. You've got to take your shot and see what happens."

As he held her, she had the strange sensation that she was looking back on her life. This was the kind of conversation people who loved each other had after they found out it wouldn't work. She was having her divorce before her marriage.

"Let's go back to the house," he said.

They got in the car and drove back to Falmouth and parked in front of the small wooden frame house on Beach Road. The large maple on the front lawn gave protective shade.

They entered through the screened porch on the side of the house.

The house was silent, almost forbidding in its frozen solitude. The waxed furniture glistened in the unused rooms. The thin gauze drapes framed the living room windows with their half-drawn shades. The dining room table with its bowl of wax fruit, carefully dusted, underscored the lifelessness of the house. It was as if the house were waiting in morbid somnolence. It depressed him.

She took his hand. Her voice was determined. "I want you to come upstairs with me."

He looked at her closely.

"I want you to make love to me."

He felt uneasy in her mother's house. It was as if she had read his thoughts.

"Mother's working from eleven to seven." She smiled. "It's very convenient." She guided him up the stairs to her bedroom.

They entered her room with her Harvard and Radcliffe pennants on the wall, her dolls and stuffed animals from childhood on the window seat. A shaft of dust-held sunlight came through the window striking the hooked rug on the polished wooden floor. Her narrow four-poster bed, with the handmade quilt, seemed to chastise him.

"Liz—"

She walked over and drew the shade. The sunlight was still

censorious. "Don't say anything. Just hold me."

He could never deny her anything. Not from the first day. As he felt her warmth, her softness, his reluctance yielded as he knew it would. The house was so still that he could hear the ticking of the tall clock downstairs in the living room.

She pulled back the quilt and drew him to her. They didn't say a word. What was there to say? They both felt caught in the swift diverse currents of life that were pulling them apart. But she didn't want to think of that now. She wanted to think only of him, of having him. She wanted his skill to manipulate her body so that her mind would be consumed by passion, blowing away the torments that had clawed at her soul since the day she realized she had fallen in love with him. Even though the respite would be brief, even though the pain of their relationship would return when the ecstasy of their lovemaking was over, she wanted that reprieve. And she wanted to give to him. She wanted her body to transmit to him the depth of her love.

They lay in each other's arms as the cloud shadows mottled the light against the closed white bedroom door.

"Will you go to England this summer?" she asked.

"I think so. I want to spend some time with Mother and Dad."

"I wish I could get to see you."

"I wish you could, too." He paused for what seemed a long time before continuing. "That means you've made up your mind."

"I—I guess I have."

"When will you tell them?" he asked quietly.

She hesitated. "I'll call them Monday. I think they would like me to get started as soon as possible."

"You won't get much of a summer vacation."

"I don't think I'll get any." She looked at him. "Will you be working on your dissertation this summer?"

"I'll have to if I'm going to get that bloody degree by next June."

"And then what?"

"I really don't know. I think I can get a teaching job at Oxford if I want to go back. It all depends on whether or not I want to remain in the States."

"There's always Columbia or NYU."

He chuckled. "What's so special about them?"

She jabbed him gently with her elbow. "Stop kidding."

"I'm not kidding."

She rolled over, looking at him, propping herself up on her elbows, her chin resting in the palms of her hands. "Are you serious?"

"Of course I'm serious."

"You limey bastard—"

He started to laugh. Then he looked at her face and saw the fear in her eyes. He stopped teasing her. "You want a poor English scholar of Western European history to come home to between business trips?"

"Peter—"

He pulled her close to him, his lips brushing her cheek. "The only reason I wouldn't go straight back to Oxford is you, you silly goose. But Liz, who are we kidding? When you get wrapped up in that crazy business world of yours, I'll be lucky to see you once a month." He paused. "I had a hard enough time seeing you in Cambridge. You were always working. Let's just play this by ear until we see what your life is going to be like. If there's any room in it for me."

They had been through this so often that the wound was rubbed raw. It hurt too much to touch it. "I suspect your mother will be happy to hear you've made up your mind." He waited for her to reply. It was slow in coming. He saw her glance stray to the small photograph of her father that stood on the bureau. He was holding Liz on his lap. She must have been about six years old, he thought. There was a joyous quality about her father. The round face and large eyes smiled happily back at him. They were both looking at that moment of life, frozen in time. He had the strange sensation that if he could push a button at the back of the photograph Randolph Clark would burst into laughter as would the child he held with a relaxed adoration.

Liz rarely spoke of her father. Peter knew the subject was painful, but he didn't know why. He felt her come back to him. She had forced herself to break with something in her past.

"I've got an idea. Let's liven this place up a little," she said. "You're going back to Cambridge. I'll be going to New York. Let's have an old-fashioned New England party."

He looked up at her, her eyes now bright with what she was

thinking. "What's a New England party?"

She kissed his nose. "It's fish chowder, steamed clams, and lobster. And, of course, blueberry pie. Why don't we surprise Mom when she comes home? We can even have a bottle of champagne. California, of course. We'll make it a blast."

She sat up in bed pulling the sheet over her breasts. The unconscious attempt at modesty under the circumstances made him laugh.

"What's so funny?"

"You."

She smiled, smoothing his hair with her hand. "Will you help?"

"You'll have to show me what to do."

The sunlight in the room made him uncomfortable.

"I'll shower," she said, "and see if I can find some blueberries for a pie." Her face was aglow. "We'll decorate the dining room. Come on, it'll be fun." She was sitting up looking at him, clutching the sheet to her, her mood shifting as quickly as her thoughts. "Oh, darling, it's going to be so quiet here without you, and so lonely in New York." She hesitated. "When I find an apartment, will you help me move?"

"What do you think?"

She kissed him and got out of bed, taking her clothes from the chair, hurrying out of the room.

He lay there staring at the ceiling. She was moving on, he thought. And he would do what? Hold his life in abeyance waiting to see whether anything could be salvaged from the career she was beginning? He was too realistic for that. He sensed somehow that this small surprise party for her mother was in part to hide the anguish they both felt, an anguish he knew would deepen in the small hours of the morning when they were apart. He felt the loneliness begin to seep into his mind like the chill from damp stone walls. How could he possibly let her go? How could he possibly interfere with her going? It was the first time he had really loved a woman, and it was the most painful experience he had ever known.

Chapter 4

SHE FOUND NEW YORK staggering. She had never experienced anything like its pace, its variety, its anonymity, its congestion both vertical and horizontal, its aggressiveness. It was one thing to fly in for a day and go back to the relative scholastic charm of Boston. But to live in this city whose pulse was quickly becoming her own was an awesome adjustment.

George had asked her if she could start by June 15, and she had said yes. She smiled as she thought of their conversation.

"We're looking forward to having you with us, Liz."

"So am I."

"You'll have to find a place to live."

"I know. I've been worried about that."

"I think you should come down right away and start looking." He hesitated. "It isn't going to be easy finding something you like and will be able to afford."

"That's what I've been told."

"We can probably find you a furnished studio apartment. We'll pay one month's rent and a month's security. We'll pay up to eight hundred dollars a month. Anything above that is on you. Two months is all we give to any employee moving here from out of town. Oh, of course we'll pay for your move."

She had spent two solid weeks vainly looking for an apartment. She was to report to Baldwin Cooper on Monday. That left just three unhampered days to find a place to live. Once she started working, she would have only the weekends to look, and that would cut down drastically her opportunity to find something.

By now she had become used to the twisting black asphalt streets of the Village, its eclectic racial mix, the occasional derelict poking through the dented trash cans, the pushcart fruit stands and the tired-looking antique shops with their unwashed windows.

The Village was colorful, but at times it made her feel depressed, like a character in a Hopper painting, with its stark gray and brown buildings and its black skeletal fire escapes.

It was the old story. The streets and the apartments she liked, she couldn't afford. What she could afford, she didn't like.

She got used to taking the hot, dirty, graffiti-splashed subways uptown to the elegance of the East Side. She had to admit that even the sterility of her efficiency seemed preferable to the apartments she had seen downtown.

She had spent her time alone in this enormous uncaring city, and felt the chill of its anonymity. She had not heard from George, which surprised her. She knew no one else. She ate alone, spent her days and her nights alone. She had gone to the top of the World Trade Center and was held breathless by the sweeping panorama of the granite reef that is Manhattan. She felt that she was part of the sky, some kind of stationary bird standing on this incredible building, seeing the vertical towers, the placid rivers and bay, the steel gray spiderwork of connecting bridges.

She had taken a bus tour of the island, but the sights of New York blurred in her loneliness. Her only refuge was the relief she felt when she spoke to Peter. She thought of their last phone call.

"How's the big city?"

"Big."

"You sound depressed."

"I guess maybe I am." She paused. "I've got too much time on my hands. About the only people I speak to are superintendents, landlords, and the girls at the checkout counters."

He laughed. "It will fall into place once you start working."

She waited a long time before replying. "I miss you so much, Peter. I hate eating alone, always being alone. I hate waking up in this damn plastic apartment the firm rented for me, and seeing myself in the mirror, and knowing another day is beginning without a soul to share it with, without another human being to talk to. Peter, the anonymity of this city is incredible. You have to be here by yourself, not knowing anyone, to appreciate it. Millions of people come and go every day, but it's like watching a crowd scene in a movie where someone has turned off the sound. You're both a spectator and one of the mob at the same time. You want to reach out and touch someone and say, 'Hey, stop. Look at me. I want to talk to you.' But it's like grasping at fog. The blurred faces just keep rushing by."

He sighed. "You've got a bad case of the resettlement blues. You'll feel a big change when you start working on Monday. You'll feel an even bigger change when you find a place of your own. You still looking in the Village?"

She sighed. "Yeah. I think I could write a real estate guide called 'How I spent My Life Looking for an Apartment in Greenwich Village.'"

"Sounds dull."

"It is." She paused. "Peter, I miss you so very much."

"I miss you, too."

"I wish you were here."

There was a long silence. "Liz, I've wanted to come down a hundred times."

His voice was disappearing in her mind. She had to fight back the tears. Each time she hung up after talking to him, she felt as if a small piece of her had been torn away. Once she started to work, she knew her loneliness would abate a little. She would meet people, make friends, but this introductory period was hard, and for the first time in a very long while she felt isolated and vulnerable.

She stood looking up at the street. The notion of living below street level struck her as ridiculous and she started to laugh. She watched the strange ballet of shoes and legs move past the living room window. The building superintendent, whose accent she couldn't place, watched her with a faintly derisive smile.

"What's so funny, lady?"

She turned to him. "I guess it's looking up at the people.

I've never been in an apartment below street level."

"You like? Good price." He laughed and pushed back his stained woolen cap. "You want see the rest of it, lady?"

Liz laughed. "There doesn't seem to be much more to see." She stood in the living room, which opened off to the left to a small bedroom. The dining room was an extension of the living room with a window overlooking a bleak courtyard. Faint gray light was barely able to find its way between the buildings and showed the begrimed bricks of the opposite wall. The only other window was in the bedroom looking up at the street.

"Eet needs to be painted, and the floors scraped and varnished."

Liz looked at the small kitchen with its grease-stained cabinets. The gas stove was so old that she couldn't remember ever seeing one like it. She turned on a burner and heard the hiss of gas, but saw no flame. The janitor came over with a lighted match. "No pilot, lady. You need match."

Liz ran the water in the sink. There was a distant throbbing of pipes. She held her finger under the hot water tap. "Well, at least the place has hot water."

She bent down and opened the small cabinet under the sink. A large roach fled from the unaccustomed light.

"Bugs!"

"All old buildings got bugs, lady. I spray for you, but they come back."

Liz admired his honesty. She walked into the bedroom. The light from the street was unkind to the chipped dark walls and peeling ceiling. The bathroom was ancient with white square wall tiles. The raised tub stood on cast-iron feet. She ran the tap in the sink and flushed the toilet. Strange gurglings. She started to laugh.

"You mean you really expect to rent this place?"

"I only work here, lady. I don't care if she rent it or not."

"She?"

"Yah. Lady owns dis building."

Liz walked into the living room of the unfurnished apartment. She turned and saw the legs and shoes walking by on street level. The place was a mess, but to her it was unique, fun. Something intrigued her about being in a place where you looked up at people.

"How's the heat?"

"Steam. We got plenty heat. Plenty hot water. Mrs. Colchek put in new boiler last year."

"How many tenants does she have?"

"She got three and then this apartment."

"The ad said six-fifty a month with utilities."

"Dat's right."

"How long a lease?"

"She like a year."

"How about two?"

"You gotta talk to her."

Liz stood there biting gently on her thumbnail. "If she paints this place in the colors I want, and does the floors. And if you can get rid of the bugs, I'll take it."

"You gotta talk to her, lady."

"Have you got her number?"

He took out a battered card from his shirt pocket and handed it to her.

"I'll call her."

Liz walked up the short flight of steps to the wooden door that opened on the street. She walked to the opposite sidewalk and looked at the small building whose dark brick facade blended with the other vertical rectangles. She looked up and down the block. On the south side of the street about three houses down she saw a small tree in a square of earth on the sidewalk. She walked over to it and saw that it looked like a sycamore. Its leaves were sparse and its branches pathetic, but it was a tree. In this compression of stone and brick, this was a living tree. She was thrilled at the sight of it.

She could hear the noise of the traffic on Sixth Avenue and started walking in that direction. She saw an eclectic collection of small restaurants, a delicatessen, a grocery store, a drugstore, a newsstand, a Chinese laundry. Within less than two blocks she had what she had been looking for—a real neighborhood and her very own tree! This might not be George Hall's idea of a neighborhood, but it was hers. It was livable and affordable, and if Mrs. Colchek would fix the place up for her, this was where she was going to start out living in New York: 115 Weymouth Place was going to be home.

Chapter 5

HER FIRST DAY at Baldwin Cooper was a day of introductions and quick hesitant smiles; she felt like the new girl at school, only this was an all-male milieu, and her reception was cool. She had still not seen George, and she found herself annoyed at that. When she looked at it rationally, she knew there was no reason for him to show her any special attention. Now that she was on board, the big brass would be farther removed from her than during the easy get-acquainted meeting when they were trying to interest her in the firm.

"Here's your office." Howard Grayson pointed to a small room with two desks whose single long window faced the north side of Forty-eighth Street. She could see the flow of traffic on Sixth Avenue and a line of office towers as dull as boxes set on end.

"It looks as if I have a roommate."

"You do. Curt Von Loutich. He's very bright. A real charmer. You'll have to be careful not to fall under his spell." Howard laughed. "You wouldn't be the first, and I'm sure you won't be the last."

Liz let it pass. She would judge the charmer for herself. She was quite sure she would find him resistible.

"I share my digs with Arthur Dunham. Until you came along, we were the 'three must-get-theres.'" He laughed. "Now, we'll have to initiate you into the club."

Howard leaned against Curt's desk, which was piled with folders and reports. It also held a marble desk set with twin pens and a small silver plaque that she couldn't read from where she was standing. Her desk was noticeably barren. She walked to the window and looked out at the splash of spring colors and the traffic on Sixth Avenue. She could feel the pulse of the city reach up to her from forty-eight floors below.

"George told me to give you his apologies for not having been in touch since you came to New York, but he's had a hellish schedule. He's been out of the office for the better part of three weeks. 'Fires and opportunity,' he calls them. Oh, well. You'll soon get to know what it's like. They don't waste much time around here." He paused. "Speaking of that, I've been elected to get you started. As I said, we don't give you an awful lot of time to settle in. No great training programs like the Chase. We sort of throw you into things and let you start digging your way out."

She had been watching Howard, who had been quietly appraising her. Howard was lean with a somewhat languid manner. He looked like some of the Englishmen she'd met at Harvard. She knew it would take a while to learn to read Howard. He let very little show. His brown-flecked hazel eyes seemed to be constantly measuring, weighing, trying to gauge the strengths and weaknesses of the competition.

"I have a meeting at two with a company that wants us to raise some money for them," Howard said. "I've spent a fair amount of time looking into it, and I've prepared a preliminary memorandum that I'll give you to read. It should give you most of the pertinent details. We're nearing the stage where I'll have to make a decision on whether or not this is worth having George, Larry, and Bob take a look.

"We have a rather informal system. If a proposal comes in that looks as if it has any promise at all, Curt, Arthur, and I discuss it. If two of the three of us think it's hopeless, we simply turn it down. If we decide to go ahead, we get permission from George to do the necessary arithmetic, meet the people, and check out their backgrounds and financial connections. When that's all done, one of us writes up the kind of a memorandum I'm going to give you. We distribute that among the three of us"—he smiled thinly at her—"now the four of us, and we meet again to decide if it's still worth bringing to the brass."

Liz sat on the window seat and felt the air conditioning blow against her dress. She got up, feeling timid about sitting down at her desk, but she did it anyway. She leaned back and looked at Howard who was watching her flick her right leg, which was crossed over the left. Howard's gaze lingered with an unaccustomed fixation.

"What you're telling me, Howard, is that in the initial selective process you, Arthur, and Curt are the ones who decide what deals this firm is going to consider."

He nodded. "We're offered so many deals that if there weren't some screening process, Larry and Bob and George would be overwhelmed. We must see two or three hundred proposals a year. Most of them we dismiss very quickly. One of the tough ones is coming in this afternoon. These people may have something, and we have to give them a fair hearing." He paused. "I'm having lunch with them. I'd invite you to join us, but I think your time would be better spent boning up on my memorandum on this company. It's complete, with all the financials I could lay my hands on. The earnings projections are my own. I discounted the company's own projections rather heavily. Also, the estimates for capital requirements over the next five years are mine. The owners of the company, like most of them, badly underestimated the amount of money it will take to get them off the ground. I'll have Mary Rawlings bring it in to you. She's our secretary and girl Friday. She's overworked as hell, with the three of us. Now that you're here, maybe you can persuade George to get her some help. Once you really get going, there's absolutely no way she'll be able to handle the four of us."

"You're damn right there isn't."

Howard turned to face the squat, sturdy woman standing in the doorway with her hands on her hips and a broad grin on her square pug-nosed face.

Liz looked at the girl. She appeared to be in her late twenties or early thirties, and she wore her dark blond hair short, with bangs.

"So this is the new gal who's going to make you guys get up and move." Mary walked into the office, her hand extended. "Mary Rawlings."

Liz stood up and shook Mary's hand. "Elizabeth Clark, Mary. I'm looking forward to working with you."

Mary looked at her appraisingly. "High time they hired a

woman around this place. I was going to start picketing the
building if they waited much longer."

Liz was aware of the distinctions between herself and Mary.
She tried to ignore them but Mary was too smart and too
experienced to pretend they were equals.

She pointed to Howard. "What this hot-shot says is right
down the middle, Miss Clark. I've got too damn much work
to do already, handling the three of them. My first suggestion
to you, if I may, is to talk to Mr. Hall and get him to hire
another secretary. If he doesn't, I'm going to quit." She looked
at Howard. "I'm not fooling, Howard. Enough is enough."

Howard's tone was soothing. "I'll talk to George."

Mary laughed. "You'd better let her talk to George. I have
a sneaking suspicion she'll get a lot more out of George than
you will."

Liz saw Howard's face flush. Tact was not one of Mary
Rawlings's long suits. She was a female sergeant major and
would never change.

Howard turned to Liz. "My office is just the other side of
this wall. Come with me and I'll give you the memo myself."

Mary started to walk out of the room. "Nice to have you
aboard, Miss Clark. Let me know if there's anything I can do."

"Thank you." Liz made a mental note to handle Mary Rawlings carefully. She also was determined to see to it that George
hired another secretary.

One of the first things Liz found out was that you ordered
lunch at your desk by phoning the receptionist, who ordered
what you wanted from the Midtown Deli. She was sitting with
her shoes off, leaning back in her chair, eating a ham and
cheese on rye and occasionally sipping milk through a straw
from a cardboard container.

She was reading Howard's memo, and she was impressed.
Howard's style was concise. He avoided any effort to persuade.
His purpose was to give the partners as concise and accurate
a picture of Computer Caterers as possible. If Howard, Curt,
Arthur, and she agreed that the firm should consider backing
Computer Caterers, they would recommend it.

As she read the memorandum, she found that the concept
behind Computer Caterers appealed to her. The company was
small, only about $5 million in sales, and its earnings before
taxes weren't bad—$250,000. The owners had only been in
business for three years, and yet they had landed a substantial

contract to cater for Mid Continental Airlines, based in Chicago. From what she read, their food and service was good, and the airline was satisfied that their prices were competitive.

They had started their business by serving the cafeterias of some of Chicago's larger banks and insurance companies, but they saw their future potential in an entirely different direction. They were proposing that BC raise $5 million dollars for them to build new facilities to prepare food for the patients and staffs of several big hospitals in Chicago from one central plant, obviating the need for duplicate kitchen facilities at each hospital.

With the aid of computer terminals installed in the offices of the head dietitians in all the hospitals, they could provide individual patient meals and deliver better food at lower cost than the hospitals were now serving. The real savings for the hospitals would come from closing their kitchens.

The savings Computer Caterers had projected were enormous. For the city of Chicago, it would mean lower hospital costs. Howard's memorandum stated that the city was seriously considering a test program at St. Luke's. The most ingenious part of Computer Caterers' program was their intention to be paid a percentage of the money they saved each institution.

Liz had read through the memorandum once, and then went back to make some notes.

Her telephone rang. She was startled by her first phone call.

"Liz, Howard Grayson. I have some people here I'd like you to meet. We're in the main dining room. Can you come down?"

"I'll be right there."

She opened her purse and took out the small mirror. God, I look awful, she thought.

She reached for the yellow pad on which she had made some notes of Howard's memorandum. She saw Mary Rawlings sitting at her desk in front of Howard's office.

"Where's the powder room, Mary?"

Mary laughed. "The john's the first door around the elevators to your left. You'll need the combination."

"The what?"

"The combination. A girl was nearly raped here six months ago by some goddamn delivery boy. Since then, all the johns have combo locks."

"What's the magic number?"

"Today it's one-five-three."

"How often does it change?"

"Every day. Just ask me."

Liz looked at Mary and started to laugh. "I certainly hope you're not out when I really need you."

Mary chuckled. "You can always ask the receptionist if I'm not around."

Liz walked toward the bathroom, again wondering about Mary Rawlings. Her instincts were flashing her all the red warning lights. "I'm probably all wrong," she thought as she pushed the numbers and opened the door.

She looked in the mirror at her slightly long, angular face. She combed her hair quickly, put blush on her cheeks, and spread it deftly with her fingers. She quickly added some lipstick and a few touches of mascara, and then surveyed the results. It's all I've got, she said to herself, envying the sultry sex appeal of the receptionist with her full breasts and long chestnut hair.

Liz walked down the curved stairway to the forty-seventh floor and entered the main dining room.

"Ah, there you are. Gentlemen, I'd like you to meet my colleague, Elizabeth Clark."

They all stood up.

"This is Miles Bateman, president of Computer Caterers; Harry Roche, vice-president of finance; Leo Montelli, the company's counsel." Howard pointed to a chair next to Mr. Bateman. They all sat down.

"Miss Clark has just read the memorandum I prepared on your company. I haven't had time to find out her reactions. If you have no objections, I'd like to ask her if she has any questions for you."

Liz was on the carpet, and she had only just sat down. She didn't know if this was Howard's idea of a joke, but if it was, it certainly didn't seem funny to her. She had hardly had time to think about Computer Caterers, let alone formulate any intelligent questions.

She looked at Howard, her expression cool. "I just finished reading Howard's memo, and I have one or two thoughts in mind," she said, still looking at Howard.

Miles Bateman was looking at Liz as if he were buying meat, wholesale. The small dark eyes in the round fleshy face had undressed her in fifteen seconds. Liz felt naked in front of the porcine little man. She turned in her chair to face him, forcing herself to smile benignly.

"Mr. Bateman, your concept seems logical and intriguing." She paused. "If you can do what you propose—"

"We can, Miss Clark. I assure you. When we have the test results from St. Luke's there won't be any more doubts."

"And when will you have those?"

The dark eyes looked at her wryly. "When you get us the money to build our new facility."

Liz wanted to ask him if that wasn't putting the cart before the horse, but she smiled pleasantly. She also noticed the long, inquiring look of Leo Montelli. She had the palpable sensation that he was asking himself what she was doing here.

"Miss Clark." Harry Roche leaned his forearms on the table, looking at her intently. He was a thin young man with wide designer glasses and carefully styled hair. "We have the best cost figures in the industry. I think that reflects our management. The numbers we've worked up for the city of Chicago alone will help get the mayor reelected. The potential savings are enormous. So are the profits for us."

"Do you expect any labor problems?" she asked quietly.

Leo Martinelli's jowly face and heavy eyebrows could not disguise his penetrating brown eyes. "Our contacts with organized labor are pretty good, Miss Clark. We haven't had any trouble yet that we couldn't handle."

Liz nodded. There was something about this group of men that she didn't like and didn't trust. It was ridiculous to give credence to such superficial first impressions. She knew that, yet she knew, too, that they wouldn't go away.

"Whom did you displace when you got the Mid Continental Airlines contract?"

Miles Bateman had turned his chair around so he could look at her directly. "Why?" he asked quietly.

"Just curious."

"We took the business from Serv-Air."

"In Chicago?"

"That's right."

Howard could sense the shift of rapport.

Miles turned to Howard. "Howie, Harry and I have spent a lot of time giving you all the information you've asked for.

If we can't give St. Luke's a fairly firm date as to when we can start this test program, we might lose it. We can't afford that." He paused. "We need a decision from your firm, Howie, one way or the other, and we need it soon."

"How soon?"

Bateman looked at Roche and Montelli. "We have to know within ten days." Montelli nodded. Bateman stood up. "I've got to be downtown by two-thirty. I'll never make it in fifteen minutes. Come on. We gotta go." Montelli and Roche stood up. "Nice to have met you, Miss Clark."

"My pleasure."

"I'll walk you to the elevators," Howard said. "See you upstairs, Liz."

They walked to the elevators, leaving Liz behind, out of earshot.

The elevator doors opened. Bateman held the door firm. "Ten days, Howie. Remember. Then we gotta go someplace else."

Howard watched the doors close. As he walked slowly back to the curved staircase, he felt the pressure of his dilemma. The deal had sounded good, but now they were pushing him. He recalled what George had told him: "Never get yourself so mentally committed to a deal that you can't walk away." It was good advice. Howard's problem was that he was having a hard time following it. He called Mary Rawlings and asked her to set up a meeting with Curt and Arthur as soon as they returned.

Curt Von Loutich was a charmer, there was no doubt about that. He was a tall, handsome young man with light blue eyes that seemed to find life ironically amusing. He wore his clothes, which were European in cut, with ease and style. Curt came from an old Munich family who had recaptured some of their wealth after the war. He had spent most of his youth as an educational expatriate in schools in England and Switzerland. He had the easy, fluid manner of someone who would be at home in any society. Elizabeth was impressed, but her cautious nature flew storm-warning flags where Von Loutich was concerned.

Arthur Dunham was known as the Marine. He was of medium height, compact in build, and there was a controlled competitiveness about him that was apparent, but not offensive. He had spent three years in the Marine Corps after he graduated from Dartmouth, but he decided that the military life lacked financial as well as most other rewards. He went back to Dartmouth and received his M.B.A. at the Tuck School of Business.

As Liz looked at the three of them—Howard, Curt, and Arthur—she realized that BC had done a good job of recruiting. These young men had very impressive backgrounds. They looked outstanding, and they probably were. This was going to be a tough crowd in which to compete. She made the mental note that she would have to have sharp teeth and claws to win a place among these Young Turks.

"I don't care how much you guys have to do," Howard told them. "We've got to come to a decision on Computer Caterers. Do we show it to the brass or don't we?" Liz was standing near the window with the morning sun backlighting her. Curt was looking at her with a calm analytical assurance. Howard and Arthur were seated at their desks with their chairs swiveled around so they could face Liz.

"I've read your memorandum, Howard," Arthur said. "The company seems to have a good concept. They have a short but good track record. What's the problem?"

Curt was standing by the door, looking at Howard. "I, too, have read your stilted prose, Howard. I agree with Arthur. What's your problem? Don't you have confidence in these people?"

"I do. But—"

"But what? Either you think they have a sound proposition or you don't."

"It isn't that, Curt. These guys are in a tough business. They have to deal with the Teamsters, who move all their trucks around, and the Food and Caterers Union isn't exactly a Sunday school choir."

"Have they had any serious labor problems?"

"No."

"Then what are you worried about?"

Liz watched Howard. He hadn't even glanced at her, hadn't asked her opinion. She was too new to the firm to have their confidence, but it would have been simple courtesy to include her in the discussion. She watched Howard's intense preoccupation.

"Howard," Arthur cut in. "Curt and I have to be in Minneapolis by six. I've got a mess of phone calls to clean up. I vote that we submit this to the brass."

"I agree with my impatient associate," Curt said. "I'll go along with Arthur."

Howard nodded as if talking to himself. "Okay. That's it. We'll show it to George and BC." He still didn't acknowledge that Liz might make a contribution, even though she, too, had read Howard's memorandum. She boiled with controlled anger.

"Shall we leave these two alone and adjourn to our private lair, Elizabeth?" Curt was watching her carefully. Liz looked at Howard and Arthur. She managed a strained smile and walked back to her office followed by Curt.

She sat down silently, her thoughts a mixture of anger and frustration at having been so blatantly ignored. She remembered the similar reactions earlier this afternoon from the officers of Computer Caterers. They had treated her like an intruder, an unwelcome guest with a bad cold.

"When I get back from Minneapolis," Curt said quietly, "I think you and I should have a little get-acquainted dinner, don't you? After all, we are sharing the same office."

She looked at him. He was still regarding her with a worldly sophistication that she found irritating.

"Let's wait until you get back from Minneapolis." Her voice had an edge to it.

He laughed and picked up his telephone.

Liz sat back in her chair trying to ignore his telephone conversation. Something about the principals of Computer Caterers bothered her. She sensed that Howard had some reservations as well. That presumptuous bastard, she thought. Her mind was not so much involved with any logical analysis of Computer Caterers, as it was with showing this company of male chauvinists that she was not only as good as they were but better. Her common sense told her that these feelings were unproductive and premature. She would have to control her anger and pride if she wanted to be accepted.

It came to her as she tried to get used to thinking with someone chattering on the telephone three feet away. She called information in Chicago, got the number of Serv-Air, and dialed it.

"Could you tell me the name of the president of Serv-Air?"

"Michael McCartney."

"Is he in?"

"Who shall I say is calling?"

"Elizabeth Clark."

"From what company?"

"Baldwin Cooper."

"Please hold."

Liz waited.

"This is Mr. McCartney's secretary. He's on another line. May he call you back?"

"Please ask him to call me." She gave the woman her number. She was about to hang up.

"Please hold."

Liz held. Curt continued to chatter away, oblivious to what she was doing.

"This is Mike McCartney." The husky voice sounded as if its owner had a bad case of laryngitis. "What can I do for you?"

"We're considering putting together a financing package for Computer Caterers."

"So?"

"I believe you know the company rather well."

There was a long pause. "You might say that."

"May I come out to Chicago and talk with you about this?"

"I'm pretty jammed up."

"We're going to meet early next week to decide what we want to do on this."

"When could you come up?"

"Name a time, Mr. McCartney."

"I've got a hell of a schedule. I've got meetings all day tomorrow. Then I'll be out of town the following week."

"That will be too late." She hesitated. "Mr. McCartney, could I meet you for dinner this evening?"

She heard him laugh. "What do I tell my wife?"

"That you're having a business meeting."

She heard his rasping chuckle. "You've never met my wife." He paused. "Flights leave from La Guardia on the hour. Could you get here by six-thirty?"

She thought quickly about the one-hour time difference in her favor. "I'm sure I can."

He hesitated. "Meet me at the desk in the lobby of the Drake Hotel by seven. I'll have my secretary fix you up with a reservation."

"I'll be there, Mr. McCartney. Thank you."

"How do I recognize you?"

She hesitated. "I'm rather tall with sort of medium length reddish brown hair. How do I recognize you?"

"Look for a guy with gray hair who's probably old enough to be your father."

Curt had hung up and was listening to her.

"You're here two days and you're off to Chicago. We *are* in a hurry, Miss Clark, aren't we?"

Liz was becoming irritated with Curt's Old World style, which was just a little too smooth. She smiled ingenuously. "Maybe *we* can have a little get-acquainted dinner when *I* get back from Chicago." She looked at him evenly. "Now, Mr. Von Loutich, perhaps you can tell me how I get a ticket and some T-and-E money to tide me over in Chicago."

He started to laugh. "Call our voluptuous receptionist who makes all the travel arrangements around here. And remember, I'll hold you to that dinner invitation when you get back."

Liz felt easier now that she was doing something. It occurred to her that she had no one's permission to do anything. Howard Grayson might not regard her trip to Chicago with enthusiasm. But BC was an arena for initiative. She had that in plenty, and she was going to use it.

Chapter 6

SHE HAD HELD her breath during the wild cab ride up the East River Drive with a maniacal driver who, as he cut in and out of traffic, had told her in badly broken English that he was from Lebanon. Her pleas for him to drive more carefully were met with an uncomprehending grin. Then, after fighting the lines at the ticket counter at La Guardia, and the lines at the security checkpoint, she finally boarded American's five o'clock flight to Chicago.

I don't even have a toothbrush, she said to herself. She wondered what the hotel clerk would say when she checked in without any luggage. Probably think I'm a hooker. She laughed. The rumpled-looking, overweight man beside her tried to make conversation.

She felt hesitant about making this impulsive trip without anyone's permission. Yet she was excited, too. She had never been to Chicago before.

The flight passed so quickly that the chattering of her seat companion, who had attempted a mild pass after three Bloody Marys, seemed like the hum of street traffic. She didn't even hear what he was saying. She was looking out at the vastness of Lake Michigan with Chicago's skyline rising majestically from its western shore.

A fifteen dollar cab ride had taken her through the city, along the edge of the lake with its tall condominiums facing the white chop of waves that rolled in over the vast stretches of beach.

She walked into the lobby of the Drake, looking for Michael McCartney. It suddenly occurred to her that she hadn't the faintest idea of what he looked like. She stood still for a moment while the chill of a new thought made her wince. Suppose he doesn't show up, she thought. My God, I will have spent the firm's money to come up here, and I won't have a damn thing to show for it. Another thought made her equally uncomfortable. Suppose my hunch is wrong. How do I explain this to Howard and George?

She walked up to the reservation desk. She saw the clock behind the desk. It was 7:05 Chicago time. "My name is Elizabeth Clark. Michael McCartney has made a reservation for me."

The clerk smiled blandly and consulted his file. He was taking more time than he should.

Lord, she thought. If there's no reservation then McCartney won't show. Her anxieties began to build rapidly.

"I'm sorry, Miss Clark, but we don't have a reservation for you. The hotel is completely booked. We've been fully reserved for the next three days for over a month."

"Are there any messages for me?" she asked desperately.

"One moment."

The clerk, with the anonymous indifference of reservation clerks the world over, came back with a small white envelope. She opened it with her stomach feeling as if she had eaten ground glass.

"Meet me in the bar," the note said. "I'm the tired-looking guy with the white hair. Mike McCartney."

"Thank God," she said audibly.

"I beg your pardon . . ."

She glared at the reception clerk. "Which way is the bar?"

"Over there, miss." He pointed.

Liz walked into the dark interior of the crowded bar. He wasn't hard to find. He was sitting at the far end of the bar, nursing a drink, seemingly preoccupied with his own thoughts.

He wasn't kidding about the white hair and looking tired, she said to herself. As she approached Michael McCartney, her overriding impression was one of fatigue. He looked worn out. His hair was nearly white; his bushy eyebrows were gray. In the modulated light of the bar his face took on an almost blue-white color like starlight. He was well dressed. He saw her approaching him and got up.

"Miss Clark?" He held out a large, strong hand.

She realized when he stood up that he was tall. "Elizabeth, Mr. McCartney."

"Then you'll have to call me Mike."

"Mike it is, then."

He pointed to the unoccupied stool beside him.

"Did you eat on the plane?"

"No."

"Good. I haven't eaten either. Sorry about the hotel. I'm pretty well known here, but I couldn't get you in. They're booked solid."

"So they told me."

"I got you a room at the Palmer House."

"Fine."

"Did you check your luggage with the hotel?"

She laughed. "I didn't have time to bring any. I left straight from the office."

He looked at her with amusement. "What will you have to drink?"

"White wine."

"You want a spritzer?"

"No, just wine."

She could sense his preoccupation, but also his interest in a young woman who on the spur of the moment would fly to Chicago for a meeting with a man she had never met.

"Do you do this often?"

She laughed. "Hardly."

He paused. He was looking at her with detached analytical amusement. "Tell me, aren't you a little young to be putting together deals for an outfit like Computer Caterers?"

"Do you mean *young* or do you really mean *female?*"

He laughed. "Both."

She was annoyed. It showed.

"Now, don't get touchy. I'm just curious."

"Well, in the first place, I don't put the deals together. The senior members of our firm do that. I help to decide which proposals our principals will take a hard look at. Part of that job consists of making sure they aren't wasting their time. Or,

more important, that they aren't going to invest the firm's
capital and the capital of our banks and insurance companies
in deals that have some hidden hole in them that we'll eventually fall through."

He took out a pack of cigarettes and offered her one. She
shook her head.

"Will you be annoyed if I ask you another question?"

She smiled. "It depends on the question."

"How old are you?"

"Twenty-five."

"That old?" He was smiling. "I have a daughter who's older
than you are."

"I'm happy for you." Liz's voice had an edge to it.

"Look, I'm not trying to be a wise guy. But a girl calls me
up out of the blue from New York. She flies up to meet me in
Chicago the same day, and tells me she works for a banking
firm—"

"A venture capital firm."

"Okay, a venture capital firm. And that she's helping to put
together a deal for Computer Caterers. She walks in here looking younger than my daughter—now you have to admit that
is a little surprising."

"I guess from your point of view it is, Mike."

He hesitated. "How long have you been out of school?"

"Listen, Mike. If you want my biography I'll give it to you
very quickly. I'm a graduate of Radcliffe College, with a master's degree from the Harvard Business School." She was getting mad. "I graduated last month, and Baldwin Cooper hired
me. I have been in their formal employ exactly two days. Now,
does that satisfy you?"

He slapped the bar with his hand and started to laugh. "You
are a pistol, kid. You know that? You're a real pistol! Goddamn
it, you're all right. I wish to hell you were working for me."
They finished their drinks.

"Come on. I'll buy you dinner." He put his arm around her
shoulder. For some reason she didn't mind. She had begun to
like Michael McCartney.

They both ordered oysters and filet mignon. They skipped
dessert and were sipping Courvoisier. His original amusement
at her presumption and her youth had given way to a cordial

admiration and respect. Mike McCartney was no pushover, but Liz sensed that beneath the somewhat worn veneer there was a basic integrity that appealed to her.

"I would say your instincts are good, and you're damn perceptive. Those bastards at Computer Caterers play very hard ball. Very hard." He held up his hand. "Now, don't get me wrong. I'm no Saint Michael myself." He laughed. "But those guys are something else."

"What do you mean?"

His eyes seemed far away. He sighed audibly. "We have contracts with most of the major airlines that fly out of O'Hare. The airlines are extremely cost conscious; they have to be. In our business, we have to be very competitive, and we are. It's a damn tough business. Most of the unions we have to deal with are either controlled or influenced by the boys in Cicero."

"What's Cicero?"

He laughed. "Did they ever teach you anything about Capone at Harvard?"

"The course escapes me."

"I thought it might. When the Cicero boys really ran things in this town, you weren't even a twinkle in your father's eye. Anyway, let's just say that we have no margin in our cost structure for labor problems."

"What about the Labor Relations Board?"

He laughed again. "Come on, kid. You've gotta be putting me on. If we had to depend on the government and the National Labor Relations Board, we'd spend all our dough on lawyers and politicians. We don't have the time or money to crap around with that. We settle these things ourselves if we can." He paused. "You know a guy by the name of Leo Montelli?"

"Yes. I met him at our offices in New York."

"You know what he does?"

"I know he's legal counsel for Computer Caterers."

McCartney laughed sardonically. His expression suddenly changed. His jaw muscles rippled under the pale skin. "Mr. Montelli has some very interesting clients." Mike sighed. "Look, I'm not going to name names or go into a long song and dance with you. I will go this far, though." He pushed his chair back from the table and crossed his legs. His eyes were not on her. He was lost in his own thoughts. His voice sounded muffled and hoarse.

"The Mid Continental Airlines contract came up for renewal," he continued. "The contracts are competitively bid. We weren't the lowest bidder, but Mid Continental knew the quality of our service and our dependability.

"You know, when you have three hundred people taking off on an airliner, and the plane leaves with no meals on board, you can kiss your relations good-bye with that airline.

"Anyway, we got the contract with Mid Continental, but the lawyers were crapping around with some language. About a week before the contract was supposed to be signed, I got a phone call from my people at O'Hare. They said three of our lift trucks were out."

"I don't understand."

"The lift trucks are specially designed to raise or lower containers of food. The goddamn lifts wouldn't work." He shook his head. "I don't know how we ever did it, but we managed to get those meals to Mid Continental. A day later two of our trucks went to the wrong flight. By the time the error was caught, Mid Continental's flight to Denver was an hour late because the plane had been sitting on the ground waiting for us." He sighed.

"I got a call from Mid Con's director of ground operations at O'Hare, and the guy is going bananas, and I couldn't blame him. I tried to calm him down, but I knew that if there was one more crisis we'd be through."

Mike squeezed out his cigarette. "A couple of days later a guy shows up at my office, no appointment. Just tells my secretary he wants to see me. I hear the guy's name and I break up the meeting and tell my people to come back in a half-hour.

"The guys comes in, sits down, and tells me he hears that we've been having some trouble at O'Hare." Mike's voice was bitter with irony. "The bastard tells me how sorry he is, and then he gives me a little advice. 'Mike,' he says, 'you got a good business going here. You do a good job, but you don't leave room for anyone else. It's un-American,' he says." Mike laughed bitterly. "The bastard does have a sense of humor. 'Mike,' he says to me, 'you gotta learn to share with your friends. Now I'm not asking a lot, am I? Your friends don't want to hurt your business. They just want some of the action for themselves. That's the American way.'"

Mike McCartney shook his head as he remembered. "Then

this guy says to me, 'You let us have Mid Continental, and you keep the rest of your business. Is there anything wrong with that deal?' he says."

Liz sat listening to him, fascinated. This was a tale of the real world, not some Harvard case study.

Mike continued. "Then comes the threat. The guy says, 'Mike, if we don't land Mid Continental, we'll have to...' And he raises his hands like this and then drops them into his lap. 'You're a bright guy, Mike,' he says to me. 'You'll know what to do.' I could go on, Liz, but I'm sure you get the picture."

Mike paused. "We got a call from Mid Con's VP for operations the following day. He asked me to have lunch with him at the Chicago Club. I did. He's a hell of a guy. We like each other; I think he respects me and I respect him. He didn't mention one word about the contract; he didn't have to. When he signed the tab for lunch and shook my hand, I could see the whole thing in his face. He squeezed my arm and walked out of the club." Mike sighed. "I spent the rest of the day at the club's bar."

Liz felt his fatigue, his frustration, his resignation. It was not the resignation of a man who was beaten. Far from it. As she watched Michael McCartney run his finger around the edge of his brandy glass, she knew this was no tamed tiger. He had just made the rational decision to give a little, to avoid a lot of expensive trouble. He would fight like hell if they pushed him any harder.

"Mike, can you tell me if Montelli had any direct responsibility for what happened to your Mid Continental contract?"

His eyes came back to her, and she saw the caustic smile. "I said I wouldn't mention any names, remember?"

"Yes. I remember." She paused. "You're leaving me to assume a good deal, but as you said, I get the picture. You've been very helpful, Mike."

"Does that mean you won't finance those bastards?"

"That's not my decision to make."

"Well, for what it's worth, let me give you a little advice on a point that you financial types sometimes overlook. There is no way in hell that you can protect yourself against a crook. You can't stay up all night and watch him. A contract to him is just a piece of paper from which to begin litigation, and the longer the contract the more probable it is that a good lawyer can find a hole in it." He sighed. "There's only one thing you've got going for you in any deal—the integrity of the people involved. No matter how smart they are, no matter how capable, that contract doesn't mean a damn thing unless they are straight. In my business, I've got to do a lot of bending and looking the other way. That's just business. You know, I always laugh when those government jerks get upset because they find that some multinational has paid off an official in a foreign country to get a contract. How the hell are they *supposed* to get it? If you don't come up with the long green in the Middle East you might as well stay home. Every big company in Europe and Asia will do what they have to get business. That's the way the world has been since Adam and Eve, but that's not what I'm talking about. The kind of people I'm referring to are the amoral ones, the guys who don't have a straight bone in their body. They have no standard of ethics. The word isn't even in their vocabulary. There's only one way to protect yourself from that kind of crook: stay away from him." He looked at his watch. "Hey, it's getting late. You going to get a chance to catch up on your sleep tomorrow?"

She laughed. "Hardly. We've got a ten o'clock meeting tomorrow on Computer Caterers. That's why I was so eager to see you."

"You'll have to catch a plane out of here around six in the morning to make that." He was watching her with amused interest.

"I know. I won't even have a chance to change before I get to that meeting."

He laughed. "You're a hell of a kid. Tell me something. What made you decide to look me up? I'm curious about that."

"It was something I read in a memorandum that one of my associates wrote. He mentioned that Computer Caterers had taken the Mid Continental contract away from Serv-Air. It struck me odd that an outfit that's only been in business for three years could take a contract away from a company the size of yours, whose relations with Mid Con go back a long way. I simply had a hunch that there might be more to it, especially after I met Leo Montelli and Miles Bateman." She paused. "I'm from Maine. We have an expression up there." She smiled. "A fish stinks from the head down."

He laughed. "You are too much, kid. Listen. It's getting late. My car's in the hotel garage. I'll drive you to the Palmer House."

"No. Please. I've already taken up too much of your time."

"It's no bother. It's on my way." He looked at her with that same expression of amused admiration. "So you're a Harvard girl." He laughed. "It seems funny to say that. In my day they didn't have girls at Harvard. They also didn't have twenty-five-year-old kids who had the moxie to call the president of a company in Chicago and make a date with him for dinner." He shook his head. "Kid, I've got suits that are damn near as old as you are."

She laughed. "Mike, I wish it was your company that was coming to us instead of Bateman's. But you're a little too big to need venture capital."

"I'll tell you what, Liz—you venture your capital on Miles Bateman's company and it will be an ad-venture. He'll take you on the fastest sleighride you've ever been on. You ought to know something about sleighrides, coming from Maine."

"I do." She hesitated. Her tone became serious. "I can't tell you how much I appreciate your frankness, Mike, and your time. Next time you get to New York, call me. Let me buy you a drink."

"The next time I'm in New York, you can be sure I'll call. You're one hell of a girl, and your firm is damn lucky to have you. If you ever decide you want to live in Chicago, you let me know. Serv-Air has always got room for someone like you."

"Thank you, Mike. I won't forget that."

"That's just good business. I've been around long enough to spot a filly who can run."

She sat on the edge of her bed in the Palmer House thinking about tonight's meeting, and the one that would be held in New York the next morning.

It was nice of Mike to come to the registration desk with me, she thought. It would have been even more embarrassing coming into the hotel without any luggage, if he hadn't been there. He's a nice guy, but he's been around. I'm sure he's tough as nails when he has to be, but Mike McCartney is straight. I know it. I feel it.

She picked up the phone and dialed the bell captain. "Would

you send someone out to get me a toothbrush and some toothpaste?"

"The shops in the hotel are closed, lady."

"I understand that. Send a bellboy out in a cab if you have to, but I've got to get a toothbrush and toothpaste."

"I'll see what I can do, ma'am."

She hung up and then dialed American Airlines. The earliest flight was at 7:00. With the time difference, that would be too late. She found that United had a flight that would get her into Kennedy at 8:30 New York Time. If she wasn't held up in morning traffic, she could be at the office by 9:15.

I've got to speak to Howard, before we go into that meeting, she reminded herself. I wish I knew where he lived. She looked at her watch. It was 12:30 in New York. Too late to call anybody. Besides, she wanted to tell him in person why she came to Chicago.

She felt uneasy. How would they react to what she had done? It was the right thing to do. She was convinced of that now, but what would Howard say? He'd be mad as the devil. George would certainly be surprised, and she was afraid to imagine what Larry Baldwin and Bob Cooper would say.

She took off her suit jacket and blouse and hung them in the bathroom. She hung her skirt on a clip hanger and turned on the hot water to let the steam take out some of the wrinkles.

She was dressed only in her slip when the door buzzer sounded like a chain saw. She was startled by the sound.

She checked the peephole.

"It's your toothbrush and toothpaste, ma'am."

"Just a minute." She went to her bag and took out five dollars. He'd probably had to go out of the hotel. Damn expensive toothbrush.

She kept the chain on the door and opened it a crack. She took the package he held out and handed him the five dollars.

"Thanks, miss."

She closed the door looking at the toothbrush in her hand as if it were some kind of talisman that might ward off the disquieting spirits her impulsiveness had stirred. Tomorrow was going to be some day. She pulled down the bedspread and got into bed. She reached for the phone and left a wake-up call for 5:00 A.M.

Chapter 7

HOWARD WAS NOT in his office; neither was Curt or Arthur.

Liz went over to Mary Rawlings who was sorting the morning mail. "Do you know how I can reach Howard?" she asked her.

Mary smiled. "Good morning." She looked at Liz appraisingly. "Had a rough night?"

"Does it show that much?"

"Well, not really. You look a bit tired, but nothing some makeup won't cure."

"Is the meeting still on for ten o'clock?"

"Been moved up to eleven. Howard's at the dentist. George is on his way back from Atlanta. Curt and Arthur are getting in from Minneapolis."

"Is Mr. Baldwin or Mr. Cooper in?"

"They're both here, but they're tied up."

"Thanks."

"Hey, wait. Here are some interoffice gems for you to read and a few more forms to fill out."

"My fingers are numb from filling out forms."

"This is the last of them. The bonding company. They only want to know everything there is to know about you. Not a very trusting lot."

"Is everybody bonded who works here?"

"Everybody."

Liz took the forms and walked back into her office. She put them down on her desk and moved to the window. The buildings cut sharp shadows on the street below, the yellow beetles of taxis thrusting and surging in the flow of traffic. She watched the lights change from red to green and saw the sluice of people flowing like colored ants along the cross streets and along Sixth Avenue. Her mind no longer comprehended what she saw. All she wanted to do was sleep.

They had gathered in the main conference room. Though the room was without windows, the wallpaper gave a surprising sense of space. On it were scenes of Manhattan in the late 1700s, showing the harbors and the sailing ships on the Hudson River. Eight Sheraton chairs stood around a large circular walnut table. Yellow pads and pencils were placed before each chair. On a small Federal sideboard against the west wall was a sterling silver tea service. The room was lit by a brass chandelier.

Larry Baldwin seated himself facing the double walnut doors. Bob Cooper sat beside him. George faced them, flanked by Howard, Curt, Arthur, and Liz.

George looked tired beneath the tan he had acquired somewhere in his frenetic traveling schedule. Curt and Arthur were pale and tense from their own quick round-trip flight to Minneapolis. Only Larry and Bob seemed rested and relaxed.

Liz had the feeling that, though this meeting was important, everyone but Bob and Larry would rather have been home in bed. The thought of Peter Wells flicked through her mind. She could see him shaking his head at this group whose pace Peter would never understand; he would think it ridiculous and unnecessary. She could hear his voice in her mind: "Do you want a scholar in Western European history to come home to when you have time to fit me in between business trips?"

She remembered what Larry Baldwin had said during that first luncheon interview that seemed so long ago: "Everyone in this firm is committed one hundred percent. Are you ready to make that kind of commitment?"

She looked at the faces around the table, at their intensity. Their necessity to make the most efficient use of time was what struck her most vividly about her new career. In this meritocracy there was no room for trivia. Time pressured each of them to accelerate their efforts in a continuum of pursuit. Pursuit of what? For what? Why? If you have to ask yourself these questions, she thought, maybe you shouldn't be here.

"All right, let's get started," George said. "Liz, you act as secretary of this meeting and keep the minutes." He turned to Curt and Howard. "How many deals do we have to look at?"

"Four," Howard said. He had a stack of memoranda in front of him.

"Okay. Are you three unanimous in your recommendations about these deals? Are there any we can throw out?"

"You three," he had said. Liz felt excluded, but then, she reminded herself, she had not been a part of the firm when these deals had come in.

"We think that you, Larry, and Bob should take a look at all four proposals," Howard said.

"May I be included in this discussion?" Liz asked. The words were out before she could stop them.

They all looked at her inquiringly.

"Of course, Liz," George said. "Is there something you would like to say?"

Liz felt seasick. She spoke slowly, keeping her voice even.

"Yesterday Howard gave me a memorandum to read on Computer Caterers." She glanced at Howard who was looking perplexed. "I met Miles Bateman and Leo Montelli." She looked at Howard. "I wanted to go over all this with you, Howard, before this meeting, but you were unavailable and I was out of town."

Larry Baldwin was looking at Liz with his usual intensity, his fingers drumming in little pianissimo tattoos on the edge of the table.

"Liz, if you have something to say, say it. We have a lot to go through here," George said.

Her face was white. Her jaw muscles contracted under the almost translucent skin. "George, if I may dissent from Howard, Curt, and Arthur, I recommend that we take a firm step away from Computer Caterers."

For a moment the silence was palpable. Howard's face flushed in anger. "What! You recommend what! After an hour's reading of a memorandum that it took me nearly a month to prepare?"

"Okay, Howard," George said. "I'm sure Liz has a good reason to support what she has just said." George looked at Liz, his glance stern.

Bob Cooper looked embarrassed. Curt and Arthur seemed

to share Howard's antagonism toward this female nouveau who hardly knew as yet her way to the ladies' room. They all waited.

"Yesterday, none of you were here," Liz said.

"Brilliant," Howard murmured.

"There was no one whose permission I could ask to go to Chicago."

"You don't need permission to go to Chicago around here, Liz. We hired you because we don't have time to give permission to people. We have to rely on their maturity and good judgment. Now, what was so important in Chicago?"

"After reading Howard's memo, it occurred to me that it was most unusual for a company the size of Bateman's to take a contract away from a company the size of Serv-Air."

"It's done all the time," Howard said in exasperation.

"That may be, Howard." Her tone was growing firmer, and the obvious antagonism of the younger men was making her mad as hell. "It's true that small companies take contracts away from larger ones, but I had a hunch—"

Howard was trying hard not to explode. "You had a hunch!"

George looked at Howard evenly. His voice had an edge to it. "Go ahead, Liz."

She exhaled audibly. Her face was flushed with anger, but she kept her temper. "I decided to find out exactly how Serv-Air lost that contract." She looked around the room. The atmosphere of uneasy expectation hung like fog. "I called Serv-Air and asked to speak with Mike McCartney. I had dinner with him last night."

They all looked at her in amazement. This was supposed to be the fledgling who hadn't tried her wings.

"In Chicago?"

"In Chicago, Mr. Baldwin."

Larry was leaning on the table looking at her. "Go ahead, Liz."

"Mike," she said, looking directly at Howard, "told me the story of the Serv-Air contract." She repeated what she had learned in Chicago. As she spoke, their attention was riveted on this young woman who had been in their employ less than three full days.

She looked around the table. "Gentlemen," she said evenly, "I don't know if I have a vote as yet in what the associates of this firm recommend, but if I do . . ."

"You do," George said quietly.

"Then I recommend that we take Mike McCartney's advice . . ."

"Which was?" Howard asked.

"Which was that one should avoid dealing with amoral people."

"Did he call Bateman amoral?"

"No, Howard, he didn't."

"Well?"

"He implied that he was a crook."

Bob Cooper burst out laughing. "I'll be a son of a bitch," he said and slapped the table with his fleshy hand.

"You don't suppose McCartney's chewing a few sour grapes, do you?"

"That's possible, Howard. But not if I've read McCartney correctly. I think what he told me was true."

"Are we supposed to rely on female intuition now in accepting or rejecting deals for this firm?"

"You can rely on anything you want, Howard, but I vote to reject Computer Caterers."

Howard shook his head in disbelief.

"You know our procedures here, Liz," George said. "We prefer to have a unanimous recommendation from our associates before Larry, Bob, and I look at a deal. We will take a majority vote, but not a split vote. Three out of the four of you are going to have to recommend that we proceed with Computer Caterers." George looked at Howard, Curt, and Arthur. "Well . . . what's it going to be? We know how Liz feels. What about the three of you? Howard, are you still in favor of going ahead with Computer?"

Howard's face was grim. His voice, strained by frustration, sounded choked. "My problem, George, is that we have to rely on what McCartney told Liz. We don't know how objective he is. He might be sore because Bateman beat him out of some business."

"You said that before, Howard. How do you vote?"

Howard hesitated. "I'd like to think about that for a minute, George."

"Okay, we'll come back to you. What about you, Curt?"

Curt had been looking at Liz with an expression of measured, detached inquiry. "When you were talking to McCartney, Liz, did he make any other accusations about Bateman's people?"

Liz looked directly at Curt. "He didn't accuse anyone by name. He said he wouldn't mention any names. He did say that Leo Montelli, their counsel, has some unsavory clients."

"Such as . . ."

"I told you, he wouldn't name anyone. He said that Montelli's clients, at least some of them, came from Cicero. I asked him what that meant, and he laughed. He asked me if I had ever heard of Capone. He intimated that Montelli had broad contacts with organized crime in Chicago."

Curt tapped his pencil lightly against the yellow pad. "I'll pass on this one," he said quietly, not taking his eyes off Liz.

"That does it, then," George said. "We'll table the Computer Caterers deal. Howard, you get back to Bateman after this meeting and tell him of our decision."

Larry Baldwin had not said one word. Bob Cooper's face was a mask of compressed control.

"Let's get on with the rest of them. Curt, I believe you have the buyout figures for that veterinary supplies distribution company."

"I do." Curt motioned to Howard who had the reports. He passed a copy to each of them.

"Give us a rundown on the deal."

They spent the next two hours going over the information on each of the three remaining companies. Liz abstained from voting, as she had not had an opportunity to discuss these proposals or to read any of the material. The associates recommended all three deals to Larry, Bob, and George for their review. It was quite probable that they would reject all of them, Liz thought. Very few proposals got through this rigorous screening process.

The meeting broke up promptly at noon.

"Liz, I'd like to see you in my office at two," George said.

She had expected this. "Two, then," she said, and walked out of the room.

It was embarrassing to go back with Howard to the office they shared. He didn't say one word to her. She knew it would take him a long time to get over this. It was going to be a difficult and tenuous relationship for both of them. She anticipated a certain reserve on the part of Curt and Arthur, too.

Well, they play hardball in the big city, she said to herself, grimly. She picked up her handbag and walked to the elevators to go out to lunch.

She felt isolated from the rest of the office staff. The only one she knew even slightly was Mary Rawlings. She had nothing in common with June, the auburn-haired overly made-up receptionist. Besides, she knew that the associates did not mingle socially with the office staff. She would have enjoyed the company of Mary Rawlings at lunch, but she passed on that one. She got on the elevator; it descended forty-eight floors and spilled her out into the crowded lobby and the even more congested Avenue of the Americas.

She felt as lonely in this anonymous mass of moving color and noise as she had when her mother had driven her to Radcliffe for the first time.

She stood near the wall of the McGraw-Hill building, out of the flow of the crowd. She wasn't hungry. The scent of cooked lamb that came from the street vendors' carts nearby sickened her.

Mary had told her of a restaurant near Rockefeller Center. It sold outrageously expensive hamburgers and beer or liquor. The luncheon crowd jammed into the place until it was wall-to-wall bodies. It was almost impossible to get a table. Most of the younger office crowd ate lunch standing up.

She left the restaurant and walked to the corner of Forty-eighth Street, then east toward Fifth Avenue. She wasn't in the mood to listen to the cacophony in that restaurant. The air was warm and she decided to sit on the benches in Rockefeller Plaza and look at the flowers that splashed their spectrum of colors.

She could hear the music of an itinerant jazz band playing somewhere close by on Fifth Avenue, and the blare from the youths who carried their enormous portable radios and played rock music at ear-shattering volume.

She sat down on a bench. She was an island, isolated in a sea of movement, sound, and color. Her thoughts focused inward so that she was oblivious to what was going on. Her only awareness was the beauty of the flower beds and the tall spire of 30 Rockefeller Plaza reaching from behind the skating rink toward the warm June sun.

I haven't spoken to Peter in days, she thought. It seems like years. Maybe he was right. Maybe New York and this job aren't for me. This damn town is so huge. There are so many people. Yet no one seems to have time to talk to anyone else.

Howard had a right to be sore, but he didn't have the right to insinuate that what I did was either amateurish or improper. I think the firm is well out of that deal.

Her thoughts continued. The only place I feel in the least at home is my apartment. She smiled. I've bought one Empire scroll bed that will take me weeks to refinish. I've got a card table to eat and work on in the living room, and one reading lamp in the bedroom—plus two chairs. She chuckled to herself.

She felt herself getting hungry, but she simply didn't have the desire to endure the crowds and the noise. She looked at her watch. It was 1:00 P.M. George wants to see me at 2:00. Her face became set. He'll probably bawl me out for upsetting Howard. She got up and decided to walk over to 57th Street and spend the rest of her lunch hour in the art galleries. As she walked and looked, her mood began to change slowly to one of determination.

This town has everything, she thought, if you've got the money to buy it. By God, some day I'm going to have it! She looked up at the tall buildings, which seemed like a forest of concrete and steel. They were like an impenetrable maze through which she had to find her way, which she had to conquer.

She wondered how many millions of other people had come to this town with the same idea, only to be broken by the competition and the loneliness. Her step became firmer, and her features hardened. She brushed back her hair with her right hand in a habitual unconscious gesture. "But I'm going to make it in this town," she said to herself.

It was only the second time she had been in George's chrome and glass office.

"Sit down, Liz. Sit down." He waved her toward one of the leather chairs. Her stomach felt tight, and she knew she probably showed the tension she felt. She tried hard to relax. She crossed her legs and swung her foot in that unconscious habit of hers. She saw George's eyes follow her legs.

"That was quite a show you put on in there, Liz."

Her voice was controlled, but tinged with anger. "It wasn't

a show, George. It was an attempt to contribute something to this firm."

He raised his hand, smiling broadly. "Peace, tiger. I wasn't being critical. I meant every word I said. It *was* quite a show. That's supposed to be a compliment."

She was so unprepared for his equanimity that she floundered for a response. She could feel her face flush, and she knew he could see it.

"You did one hell of a fine job in following up on your intuition about Computer Caterers. That's the kind of initiative we want around here and don't always get. Howard should have picked up your hunch about Bateman and his crowd and followed through the way you did. Don't get me wrong. Howard's one of the best associates we've got, but like all of us, he has more work than he can handle, and like all of us, sometimes he overlooks things. That's why we have the screening process. It saves us time, money, and a hell of a lot of headaches. But we still get involved in marginal or bum deals that we have to work our way out of.

"Liz, I want to apologize for having spent so little time with you since you came to New York. I'm afraid I haven't done a very good job at helping you settle in here. I understand you found an apartment."

"Yes. In the Village."

"How is it?"

"At the present moment it looks like an abandoned warehouse, but it will come along. I'm trying to furnish it with antique pieces that I can afford to pick up, one at a time. Most of them need refinishing or repair work. I do the scraping and staining myself. The repairs I leave to a wonderful old man I found who has a shop close by. He looks out for things that have some intrinsic value but need to be fixed up, and he tells me about them."

George was watching her closely. "How's your social life?"

"Nonexistent. I spend most of my time browsing around the Village looking for things for the apartment. Occasionally, I go to a movie or to the theater or a concert."

"It sounds lonely," he said quietly.

She looked away from him. "It is."

George was tuned in to her mood. This was not the way he wanted her to begin her career at BC.

"I wanted to talk to you about what happened this morning, Liz, and then I have some other things I want to go over. First of all, I want you to know that you showed us the kind of intelligent initiative and moxie that should take you a long way in this firm. Unfortunately, you bruised some male egos pretty badly in the process."

"I'm well aware of that."

"This is a small firm, Liz, and we all have to work very closely together." He paused. "I'd like to see if you can get Howard on your side. It shouldn't be too difficult for you. It would be a lot tougher if you were a man."

"Just what are you implying?"

"I'm not implying anything. I'm telling you. Look, Liz. Let's not horse around with this male-female thing. Any woman who can't handle a man is either stupid or sexless."

"Hold on, George . . ."

He held up his hand. "Wait, Liz. Hear me out. You're a damn attractive woman, and you're smart as hell. And you've got guts. Now, that's a winning combination in any environment, but especially in a male environment. If you use your brains and your sex—"

"George . . ."

"Liz, I'm going to give it to you like it is. These Young Turks around here are all hostile toward you, because you're as smart as any one of them, and let's face it, Liz, you're a hell of a lot more attractive than Howard, Curt or Arthur."

She started to laugh. "That's not much of a compliment."

"Maybe not, but you get the idea." He hesitated.

She was smiling. She hadn't smiled in a very long time. It seemed so long ago that she had talked to anyone personally.

"Is this some new sociological theory of yours, George?"

"New, hell. It's as old as Adam and Eve. I'm just telling you to start using what you've got with these young guys and you'll have them scraping furniture for you."

They both laughed.

George put out his cigarette. "On another subject, Liz . . . I'm going to assign you to assist me in covering three companies in which we have investments. I'm a director and sit on the board of each of them. You'll become thoroughly familiar with each company, and Martha Wainright will give you all the background material you'll need. When you think you have a good understanding of their balance sheets and their product mix, get back to me and I'll set up appointments with each of them for you. I want you to meet all their key people. When you've done that, I want you to prepare a brief report on each, giving me your comments on their personnel and operations. You're going to be attending board meetings with me, as a guest of the board, so I want you to be knowledgeable. Martha has started pulling a lot of material . . ."

Martha stood in the doorway.

"What is it?" George asked her.

"It's Mrs. Hall," she said softly.

Liz watched George's face pale. "Oh, Jesus. What does she want?" He hesitated. "Didn't you tell her I was in a meeting?"

"I did. She said she had to speak to you."

Liz stood up. "I'll go and see what Miss Wainright has for me."

George shook his head in resignation. He motioned for Liz to go with Martha Wainright.

Liz walked out of his office and closed the door.

Chapter 8

WHEN SHE DESCENDED the steps of 115 Weymouth Place, it was as if a great weight had been lifted from her. Just the personal contact with George, the fact that he seemed to care about her and her career, had completely dispelled her depression. Now she had direction. She had a specific assignment, work she could sink her teeth into. Her mood had changed so completely that she had bought a bottle of California champagne to celebrate. She put the champagne in the refrigerator to chill and took out the small steak she had defrosted.

Then she went into her bedroom and changed into an old shirt of Peter's, which was covered with wood stain, and a pair of faded jeans. The sneakers she wore had long ago given way to holes, but they were perfectly adequate to work on the Empire bed, as she had been doing almost every night for the better part of three weeks. She had removed the paint and was now going over the bare mahogany with steel wool.

Tonight she planned to start reading the material Martha Wainright had given her, but after dinner she wanted to put in at least an hour of work on the bed.

She was peeling onions and potatoes when the phone rang. The phone had rung so few times since she had moved into the apartment that she was startled by its sound. It was in her bedroom beside the bed, and as she approached it she was sure it was Peter.

"Hello."

"Liz?"

"Yes."

"It's George. Am I disturbing you?" His voice sounded weary, and he seemed strangely hesitant.

"No. Not a bit. Is everything all right?"

She felt the long pause. "Not really."

"What is it?"

"Are you doing anything special?"

She laughed. "Not exactly."

He hesitated. "Would you mind some company?"

She was confused, but at the same time flattered. "George, I'd love to see you, but I'm not exactly set up to receive visitors."

"I don't care about that. I'd . . . I'd like to talk to you."

She suddenly felt a tinge of anxiety. "Is it something I've done?"

"No, no. Nothing like that. It's personal. It's got to do with me, not you. For some reason I want to talk to you. Do you mind?"

"Of course not. Where are you? Do you want me to come up there?"

"No." He paused. "As a matter of fact I'm probably not more than a few blocks from you. I'm on the corner of Broome Street and Sixth Avenue. I've got a cab waiting. I can be at your place in five minutes."

She thought quickly. My God! How could she let him see her like this? "George, I'm afraid you'll find me dressed to work on furniture."

"I don't give a damn how you're dressed."

It was so unexpected, so unlike George. Something was really bothering him.

"George, come on over. You have the address."

"Yes. I stopped to telephone because I didn't want to intrude if you had plans."

"I'll see you when you get here."

"Five minutes."

"Fine."

She hung up. She put the phone on the floor and stood in the middle of the bedroom wondering what had happened.

He could have called from uptown, she thought. He didn't

have to come all the way down here. She couldn't figure it out, but her mood of elation was quickly displaced by one of anxiety.

She waited in the bedroom where she would be able to see a cab on the street. Not many cabs came to Weymouth Place. In less than five minutes she saw the yellow cab drive slowly past her apartment.

She opened the door and walked up onto the street. The cab turned around and came back. It pulled up alongside the curb.

George handed the driver a bill and got out. He looked pale and withdrawn, but he smiled when he saw her.

"What the well-dressed career woman wears when entertaining her boss," she said.

He laughed. "I've got to admit it's different." He glanced at the steps leading down to her apartment. "That's an interesting touch."

"Yes, I think so. I'm one of the few people who can definitely state that each morning, I come up in the world."

They walked down the steps and into her apartment.

"Well, at least it doesn't have that overdecorated look."

She laughed. "I'm trying for a hint of Japanese simplicity. You know, one beautiful object on which to focus your attention. Like this card table, for example. Isn't it exquisite?"

"Definitely a collector's item."

"If you will sit down, sir, in the one chair I have in this room, I think I can scare up another chair."

She brought in a ladder-backed Shaker chair that she had refinished.

He looked at her with an expression of amusement mixed with sadness. "Are you sure you want to be a venture capitalist? Maybe carpentry is more your line."

"Sir, when I make the kind of money I hope to earn in your august firm, I assure you I don't intend to refinish my own furniture."

"Do you serve liquor in this hotel?"

"Only champagne."

She saw his surprise.

"Don't let the sparseness of the furnishings fool you. This hotel is known for its wine cellar."

He started to laugh. Really laugh this time. "You've got the cellar. Have you got the wine?"

She went to the refrigerator and came back with the bottle of champagne and two water glasses. "I was preparing a small steak for dinner. Could I interest you in sharing it with me?"

He hesitated. "Do you want to go out for dinner?"

"Do you want to talk?" she asked quietly.

"Yes."

"Then let's stay here, and I'll fix us both something to eat."

He brought his chair into the small kitchen and watched her slice onions and potatoes.

"Do you always drink champagne?"

"Only when I feel like celebrating."

"And you have something special to celebrate?"

She turned from the sink and looked at him.

"A gift from you, George."

"From me?"

"Yes," she said quietly.

"I don't understand."

She put the steak in the broiler and the potatoes and onions in a frying pan.

"I was feeling pretty down before you called me into your office today. The loneliness of this city was getting to me, and the incident with Howard didn't help. When you gave me my assignments and told me we would be working together on things that were important, suddenly I knew what I was doing here. I had work and a purpose and direction. I've always been uneasy without goals, without specific objectives to attain. You changed all of that for me this afternoon, George. I'm very grateful to you for that."

They ate dinner on the card table. The light from the single lamp reflected the highlights of her hair. Her eyes seemed darker in the poorly lit room. She was waiting for him to say what was on his mind.

"I'm sorry I bothered you, Liz."

"Don't be silly. I haven't been exactly overwhelmed with company since I came to New York. You're very welcome here, George, I assure you."

He was looking at the oversized shirt that had obviously belonged to a man.

"A little large for you," he said, pointing to the shirt.

"It's the latest from Bergdorf's."

He pushed back his plate and lit a cigarette.

"More champagne?"

"Please."

She filled his glass.

He looked around the room. "I think I might be able to come up with a few housewarming gifts."

She laughed. "I know I should say that's not necessary, but I'm afraid it's somewhat obvious that anything would be much appreciated."

"Liz, I honestly don't know what I'm doing here. I feel like a damn fool."

"For what?"

"For imposing like this."

"Don't be silly. You're hardly imposing. Something's bothering you, and if I can help, I'd be only too happy to."

He sighed. "I can't figure out why I chose to come down here."

"Because you wanted an elegant meal in elegant surroundings."

He laughed.

"George, is there anything I can do to help?"

He sat looking at her, yet not really seeing her. "Sometimes I feel like saying the hell with it all and getting out. I've often thought about it. What it would be like to sell everything, quit this rat race, buy a boat, and just take off. I'm tired of knocking my brains out to finance a woman who's milking me until I'm like a gerbil in a cage, just going 'round and 'round."

Liz didn't know what to say.

"The former Mrs. Hall, Liz. We were married for twelve years. I'm not going to bore you with the gory details. She's a lawyer, here in New York. A very successful one I might add. She's got me tied up tighter than a drum. Call it vindictiveness. Call it sadistic pleasure in making me miserable. Call it anything you want, but that bitch is really getting to me."

Liz knew that she had better just listen. She also knew that there were two sides to every story, but at the moment she felt sorry for George Hall.

"Liz, this is all off the record, of course."

She nodded.

"I guess I came down here because I wanted to talk to a woman tonight. Someone I have respect for and" . . . He let the sentence hang like smoke.

"Liz. Do you have someone . . . I don't want to pry into your personal life, but a girl like you must have a man . . ."

Liz hesitated. "In a manner of speaking, I do, George. He's a wonderful person. He's getting his doctorate in Western European history at Harvard." She sighed audibly. "We have our problems, too. My career, mainly. He needs a wife who'll stay home with the kids and be home when he arrives. He doesn't mind my working, but not a full-time commitment like this."

"Sounds like a Mexican standoff."

"Whatever that is, it sounds like we've got it." She paused. "I think we both know it can't work, but we don't know how to break it off."

"You and I should form a corporation. Marriage Unworkable, Inc."

"I think we'd have a lot of stockholders, George."

"I know damn well we would."

Their eyes met, and in his she sensed the same attraction she had seen in the small North Side restaurant in Boston. That seemed like light-years ago. Now, she saw in George a melancholy that surprised her, and to which she felt drawn.

He swallowed hard. "Liz, I'd better get going."

He stood up. "I enjoyed the elegant meal, in the elegant surroundings."

"I wish I could offer you a nightcap."

"Never mind. The next dinner is on me." He looked at her, hesitating. "Do you mind if I call you again? We can meet uptown."

"I don't mind," she said quietly.

"Where can I get a cab?"

"I'll walk you to Sixth Avenue. There should be plenty of cabs there."

"Aren't you afraid of getting mugged?"

"In this outfit?" She laughed. "I'd scare the mugger half to death."

They walked through the narrow streets to the broad area of lights that was Sixth Avenue. He held her arm as he had in Boston. She remembered being irritated by him then. She wasn't now.

They found a cab.

"It was good of you to have me, Liz."

He looked at her for what seemed like a long time. He

kissed her lightly on the cheek and got into the cab. "The next one's on me," he said.

She walked back to her apartment, puzzled and troubled by an intuitive warning.

She knew the dangers of becoming involved with George. It would isolate her further from the other three associates. It would not sit well with Larry Baldwin. But as she walked back to her apartment, the practical part of her mind, which had an unnerving way of asserting itself, pointed out to her that her sex was an advantage, as George said it was. If she could control George's reactions to her and at the same time not disaffect him, she would advance more rapidly in the firm.

She disliked herself for thinking this, but these thoughts had occurred to her. Besides, she was tired of being lonely. She wanted and needed someone to talk to, and evidently so did George.

She stood at the sink cleaning up from the impromptu dinner.

Why did he come here tonight? she wondered. He could have gone to friends, to another woman. Surely a man as attractive as George knew plenty of other women.

Something brought him down here tonight, to see me. Just me. She remembered being aware of his attraction to her the first time they had dinner together in the little Italian restaurant in Boston. She knew his attraction was there, and it made her glow. She stopped scrubbing the pan, letting the water run over her hands. He came here because he wanted to be with me, she thought. A Yankee girl from the coast of Maine. And he could have any eligible woman in New York. She realized that she had practically been talking to herself and she began to laugh. "Well, Mom, what do you think of your little girl now?"

She rinsed the pan and turned off the tap. Her mind flicked to Peter.

I've known Peter for over three years, she thought. He never would have been as impulsive as George was tonight. He's sweet and dear and sensitive, but there's a reserve about Peter. She leaned against the sink. They're so different, she thought. Peter is so reserved in that British way of his. She thought about her own reticence. I'm not like Peter, she thought, but I'm not as impulsive or as warm as George, either. He's very open and direct, action-oriented. He knows what he wants in business and he knows how to get it. But Peter is so much more difficult to read. There is a stubborn, quiet undercurrent of self-protection about him. He has his life planned. He isn't hung out on the end of a limb with the breezes blowing like George. She paused. And now, like me.

She stood leaning against the sink. She began to see an affinity between herself and George. She was flattered by his visit, floored by it. "George Hall on Weymouth Place in Greenwich Village, with Liz Clark from Falmouth, Maine." Her smile broadened as she said it. "Think of that, Mom!" The warmth of her thoughts flowed through her, and she felt happier and more carefree than she could remember. Then a new thought struck her. In three years with Peter, she had known moments of incredible fulfillment, even ecstasy. But always, lingering in the background was the shadow of sadness. George, she wondered. What would it be like with George? She dismissed the thought, but not until some tendril had probed for an answer. Don't get carried away, Liz, she thought. You hardly know the man, and as she thought about it, she knew that wasn't quite accurate.

Chapter 9

THE RAIN HAD given way to broken clouds that had become tinged with the saffron rays of the late afternoon sun. Liz had left her office to go to the firm's library to look up some information pertaining to a stock offering the firm had been a part of. As she entered the reception area she saw a giant of a man sitting reading the *New Yorker*.

"Miss Clark?" The receptionist stopped her.

"Yes, June."

"This gentleman had an appointment with Mr. Hall, but Mr. Hall telephoned and said he wouldn't be able to make it. He asked if you would see him."

The tall man stood up.

My God, Liz thought, he's a big one.

"Elizabeth Clark, Dr. Haley."

She turned to June. "Is one of the conference rooms free?"

"The small one. It's free for the rest of the afternoon."

"Thanks."

"Dr. Haley, if you'll follow me please." She felt as if she were being followed by Wilt Chamberlain.

They sat in the small windowless conference room with its circular table. The recessed ceiling lighting gave the room a warm, intimate ambience. Larry Baldwin's passion for Japanese wall coverings extended to this room as well. From the wainscoting to the ceiling were scenes of a Japanese garden and foot bridge with lily pads and long, graceful reeds.

"Charming," he remarked.

Liz was so distracted by the physical size of Dr. Haley that she was not concentrating on what he was saying. His shoulders seemed to fill the small room.

"Perfectly beautiful," he said.

"I beg your pardon . . ."

"That ink drawing of the dove on the plum tree."

Liz turned around to look at the delicate framed drawing that hung over a Baltimore table.

"That's over four hundred years old, Dr. Haley. It was drawn by the most famous of all the Japanese samurai, Miyamoto Musashi."

"Odd."

"What's odd, Dr. Haley?"

"That a warrior could create something so beautiful."

"I never thought about it that way. There are so many artifacts and paintings around this place that we could use a curator, and a guide to explain them. We're all so busy here that we forget to look at what's around us."

He paused, thoughtfully. "Beauty, violence, and indifference. You could describe a good deal of life using those terms."

She looked at him more carefully, less struck by his size, more aware of his sensitivity. She folded her hands resting her elbows on the table. She could feel him looking at her with a disturbing discernment. "Now, what can I do for you, doctor?"

"Will I be able to see Mr. Hall?"

"Not today, I'm afraid. He won't be back in the office until tomorrow."

"That's too bad. I have to return to Boston tomorrow." He smiled wanly. "I'm afraid I have neglected my institute far too long as it is. You see, I've spent a week here in New York talking to financial people, and I'm afraid I've been less than successful." He exhaled blue-gray smoke, which moved slowly toward the vent ducts in the ceiling.

"How did you come to call on us?"

"The people at First Boston suggested I try your firm. They told me Mr. Hall was the one I should contact here."

She sensed his disappointment at not seeing George. She knew intuitively that he felt he was wasting his time with her.

"Dr. Haley, perhaps I should explain how we do things

around here. I am Mr. Hall's assistant. My associates and I are responsible for screening all of the proposals that come in. We have a series of investigative procedures we go through to decide whether a deal is worth Mr. Baldwin's, Mr. Cooper's, and Mr. Hall's time. A majority of the associates have to agree on that. We have to put together a great deal of preliminary information before we can make that judgment, and certainly before we submit anything to the firm. Even if you had met Mr. Hall this afternoon, he probably would have turned your proposal over to me."

She could see that he was visibly relieved. She saw the flicker of hope come into the gray eyes.

"Now, could you briefly tell me, Dr. Haley, how you think we might be able to help you?"

He pushed his chair back from the table and turned slightly so he faced her.

"I've been through this so many times." He laughed. "I feel like an actor giving his final performance in a show that's going to close."

There was something about her, he thought, a directness, an inquiring intelligence. There was nothing brusque about her. She was feminine and appealing. She seemed so young to have this responsibility. She was the first woman he had talked to in a week of conferences. He was surprised and in a way relieved. He felt more comfortable with her than with the male financiers who seemed to look at him as an amalgam of innovative psychiatrist and inexperienced businessman. They were not attracted by the combination.

"I have an institute. Family Care Centers, Inc., in Chestnut Hill, right outside Boston."

"Yes. I know the area. I went to school in Boston."

"Where did you go?"

"I did my undergraduate work at Radcliffe, and got my M.B.A. at Harvard."

"That's very impressive."

"Let's talk about you, doctor."

"Four years ago, two other psychiatrists and I pooled our resources, borrowed some money, and bought an estate—a large Victorian house, which we modernized and brightened up. The place was almost forbidding when we bought it, not exactly the atmosphere we wanted for the kind of therapy we wished to practice. I own the majority of the stock. My original concept, which we have continued to expand, was to devote our practice to helping neurotic business executives, scientists, professional men and women, and successful artists, writers, musicians whose personal problems were interfering with their ability to do their jobs properly.

"In your jargon, Miss Clark, it is my intent to market our services to the most productive and talented members of society. It is my feeling that those who have the most to contribute are the ones who most need our help. These people more broadly influence the lives of others. I feel we can contribute more by helping society's leaders than by working only with the followers." He paused, watching her reactions carefully. "That point of view usually needs some explanation, Miss Clark."

"I think it does, doctor," Liz said evenly.

"You see, I think one has to decide how one's efforts can be most effective. For example, Mother Teresa has chosen to spend her life helping those whom O'Neill referred to as the 'misbegotten,' the castaways of life who are without hope. I'm not implying that what she is doing isn't exemplary. Far from it. She is relieving suffering and bringing comfort to thousands who would be lost without her." He paused, searching Liz's face with a professional analytical detachment. He saw the small shimmerings of hostility.

"I have chosen the opposite course, based on the assumption that exceptional skills and talents are in relatively short supply in any society. The people who expand science, create beauty, advance medicine . . . they are the motivators and the leaders, the ones who are responsible for progress."

Some progress, she thought. We've got a planet ready to destroy itself, thanks to these so-called leaders.

"I decided long ago," he went on, "that if I was to spend my life productively, I would have to select how I wanted to use my skills and training. The world is too vast an arena of suffering for any one man or organization to make a really meaningful contribution. But by helping the movers, the doers of society, I could more broadly influence the lives of others. If we can help make one brilliant doctor and one outstanding scientist more productive by freeing them from a crippling neurosis, then they can influence the lives of thousands." He paused, searching her face, seeing her understanding.

She tapped the tip of her pencil against the yellow pad. "That's an interesting point of view, doctor."

"We think so."

"How do you go about your therapy?"

"We involve the whole family. After we've spent considerable time with our patients, we often find that their problems are exacerbated by a neurotic wife, husband, or lover. Sometimes we find that the work environment imposes unbearable stresses on extremely talented and sensitive people. We try to explain those problems to management, who often work with us to make some of their most valuable personnel more contributive.

"It's too bad I can't show you the film I've brought with me. It shows very vividly what I am talking about. The old cliché about a picture being worth a thousand words is quite true in this case."

She was beginning to understand his point of view, and she found herself becoming more interested in what he was saying.

"Do you have the film with you?"

"Yes, it's in my hotel. I've been showing it to the firms I've been talking to. At least the few who were interested enough to let me get that far."

Liz thought for a moment. "Are you staying in town tonight, doctor?"

"Yes. I'll be leaving in the morning."

He watched her trying to make up her mind.

"Where are you staying?"

"At the Plaza."

"Would it be possible for you to show me the film in your hotel?"

She saw his surprise.

"Why, yes. That would be marvelous, if you could..."

"How long is the film?"

"About fifteen minutes. But I think you'll be impressed with what you see."

She thought for a moment. "I could probably make it about seven. I have a lot of work to get through here."

He hesitated. "Since you are being so generous with your time, Miss Clark, could we have dinner? We can dine in the hotel if you like, in the Oak Room."

She laughed. "Well, doctor, that's more enticing than the

lamb chop I was going to have tonight." She paused. "But I'm afraid you'll have to take me as I am. I won't have time to go to my apartment and change."

"I can assure you, Miss Clark, that you don't have to change a thing for me. I'll be delighted to take you as you are."

She looked at him carefully, realizing for the first time that she knew nothing about this man. She didn't even know if he was really a doctor. She had volunteered to go to his hotel room, to view a film he said he had, and to have dinner with him. Not particularly bright, she thought.

"Doctor, whom did you talk to at First Boston?"

"Amory Cantrell."

She asked for the number of Family Care and wrote it down along with his room number.

"I'll see you at the Plaza at seven o'clock. If something comes up, I'll call you."

She returned to her office and put in a call to Amory Cantrell at First Boston. She then called Family Care.

She pushed the pad away from her when she hung up. At least he was who he said he was. But she still had an uneasy feeling about visiting the room of a total stranger.

She reached into her file drawer and took out the checklist of information the firm required from those who sought its capital and its expertise. She turned to the stack of reports that she had to read on the companies that George had taken her to see on their last swing around the country. She inwardly groaned at the amount of material. Her meeting tonight with Dr. Haley was going to cut into her time. She'd just have to make it up over the weekend. George expected her to keep up to date on these companies, and she would soon be covering several of them on her own. George had even suggested that she would someday sit as his proxy on the board of Twenty/Twenty Security Systems, where George was a director. He was, he said, too busy to attend so many board meetings around the country. Twenty/Twenty was a computer software company in Palo Alto, which designed computer security systems to protect banks against the rising number of computer related thefts.

She took the folder containing the minutes of the last board meeting she had attended with George and started to read. She had the financials to go through which would take more time, as would a description of the new Twenty/Twenty system, which had aroused a good deal of initial interest on the part of two large West Coast banks. Twenty/Twenty Security Systems was also courting the Bank of America, the country's largest bank, and the prospects looked good.

She reached into her desk drawer for an apple. She bit into the sweet flesh of the fruit as she leaned back in her chair and began to read.

Chapter 10

SHE HAD DECIDED to walk to the hotel. The early evening air was hot and humid. I should really look terrific, she thought sarcastically, by the time I get to the Plaza. She thought again about a cab and decided against it. They were hot, slow, and dirty, and the distance was too short. She crossed Forty-eighth Street and headed east toward Fifth Avenue.

She had become so gradually absorbed in the pace of the city that she found herself walking rapidly even in the summer heat. The color and excitement of the city were now a part of her. So was its anonymity. The crowds she saw every day on the streets were now just a montage that she took for granted and then forgot. She felt like a salmon fighting her way upstream. She was no longer a spectator. She gulped meals, chased cabs, rushed to airports, ran down the long corridors certain she would miss her flight. George was giving her so much work and increasing her responsibilities so rapidly that when the weekends came she found she was too exhausted to do much other than a minimal amount of refinishing on the Empire bed and some other pieces of furniture she had bought. She was far behind on her decorating program. The apartment still looked neglected. It was.

She found herself constantly reading or writing reports. She worked on planes and in airport lounges. She attended meetings with George flying from New York to Chicago to Houston,

Los Angeles, San Francisco, and back to New York. She was becoming a familiar sight at board meetings as George's assistant, and her talent for keeping her mouth shut at the right time and contributing at the right time was winning the admiration of skeptical men whom she sensed initially wondered what George was doing flying around the country with a long-legged, attractive female assistant.

She stopped briefly in front of Bergdorf's. I've got to find time to buy some new clothes, she thought. She smiled purposefully. I'd love to be able to walk in here one day and not worry about the price of anything. She moved reluctantly away from the enticement of the windows toward Fifty-eighth Street and Fifth Avenue. She walked past the fountain and on through the main entrance of the Plaza, past the shops in the lobby. She found the bell captain's desk and asked where the house phones were.

"Around on your right, miss."

She felt a small annoyance at the "miss." She gave the number to the operator and heard the phone ringing.

"Hello."

"Dr. Haley?"

"Yes."

"Elizabeth Clark. I'm in the lobby."

"Marvelous. I'll meet you at the elevator. Come on up."

As the elevator took her to the twelfth floor, she again felt uneasy.

What am I doing voluntarily going to the room of a total stranger? I must be out of my mind. She drew some small comfort from the quick background check she had made on Dr. Haley, but she still felt disquieted. Charge the beachheads, eh, George, she thought. Do or die for dear old BC. She shook her head at her own initiative, or was it foolishness? I seem to keep running to appointments with strange men, she thought as the elevator rapidly passed the lower floors. I wonder if there's any Freudian implication in that. Maybe I should ask Dr. Haley; he's a psychiatrist. She shook her head in mock recrimination.

The elevator doors opened on the twelfth floor.

"Ah . . . there you are. It really was so good of you to come," Haley said.

She was again awed by his size. She hoped he was a gentle giant.

"Come this way. I've got everything all set up for you, to save time."

He led her to a large room. He had set up a projection screen next to the draped windows. An 8-millimeter projector with a sound track stood on the desk, which he had moved near the door. He had placed two chairs on each side of the desk facing the screen.

"May I get you something to drink?"

"No, thank you."

"Well, we might as well get started. I have a reservation for us in the Oak Room for eight."

Liz sat down looking at the blank white screen.

"Before I show you the film, I'd like to give you some background on what you will be seeing. The film is a study of one of our patients; Dr. Charles White. We film a lot of our patients as part of our therapy. As psychiatrists and psychoanalysts, we of course spot neurotic and sometimes psychotic symptoms on the first visit of a patient, but that same individual may deny those behavorial patterns. Viewing the film can be quite a revelation to the patient, I can assure you.

"Dr. White is one of our prize patients. He came to us about three years ago at the recommendation of the vice-president of personnel of an important defense contractor in the Boston area. Dr. White is one of the world's leading technical experts in the field of stable platforms." He looked at Liz who had removed a yellow pad from her briefcase and was making notes of his presentation.

Dr. Haley started to laugh. It was a rich baritone laugh that for some reason reminded her of one of those large talking trees in a Disney cartoon.

"I didn't know what a stable platform was either, Liz. It's a gyroscopic device that uses lasers to sense extremely minute changes of motion. The stable platforms are used to plot the course and direction of guided missiles, nuclear submarines, the space shuttle, and satellites. White has extended his navigational technologies to the point of sophistication where he can lock on to stars or planets as reference points, and through his guidance techniques he can direct almost anything to its mission position or target."

Liz tapped her pencil against the yellow pad. "He sounds very impressive."

"He is. Which is one of the reasons his company took the

trouble to bring him to us. And I think that is an extremely important point for you to understand, Miss Clark. The people who are referred to us by corporations such as his are usually top executives or technical people whose contributions to their companies are simply too important to be lost to crippling neurotic behavior. Since the demand for the skills of these people is so intense, we don't have the leisure to pursue traditional psychoanalytical techniques, which could take three to five years or longer. Our client companies need results a lot faster than that."

She found the phrase "client companies" a strange mixture of commercialism and healing. There was a pragmatism to Dr. Haley that irritated her. A part of her mind pointed to her own profession and she had to force herself not to make premature judgments. But the feeling stuck.

"We have put together a whole series of therapies including the traditional psychotherapies. We use hypnosis, drugs, family therapy. Also a technique we call confrontation therapy. It's a very intensive program, and very expensive."

"You want to patch them up and get them back on the line again, is that it, doctor?"

He didn't miss the sarcasm. "Yes, Miss Clark. That's exactly what we try to accomplish. These people are too important to their companies to be 'off the line,' as you put it. We try to get them to function at full capacity as quickly as possible. We're not always as successful as we would like to be, but our batting average is pretty good."

"And how does this psychological overhaul affect the personal lives of your patients, doctor? Are they happier human beings when you are finished with them? Are they more content with themselves? With their families? I assume they're more proficient in their field after your therapy, but are they equally as fulfilled in other areas of their lives?"

"The answer to that is yes. Definitely yes. When we ameliorate a neurosis, we unburden the patient not only in his professional capacities, but in his other life areas as well. He or she becomes a happier more productive human being."

"But that is not your primary goal . . ."

He looked at her carefully. "No, Miss Clark, it is not. Our primary objective is to perform the role we are being paid to perform—to get the patient to function at a higher professional level."

He looked at her steadily as he said it. He saw that she seemed hostile.

"If all this sounds somewhat businesslike to you, Miss Clark, I submit that we are no different than the orthopedic surgeon who can earn $400,000 a year if he's good or the orthodontist who might earn a quarter of a million. They perhaps are less businesslike in their approach than we are, but they are equally as interested in having their fees paid. Have you been to a doctor or a dentist lately, Miss Clark?"

"No, I haven't."

"You're fortunate. Here in New York, I would guess that a routine office visit for a general checkup, not counting the lab fees, would cost over a hundred dollars. We are engaged in far-reaching programs that grapple with the most complex problems of the human mind. We have developed a market for these programs, which we wish to expand, and that is the reason you're here tonight. But let's get back to Dr. White. The first scenes will show Dr. White as he was when he came to us— or more accurately when he was sent to us by his company. He was told that he would be forced to resign if he didn't attend our center."

"Why don't we get on with the film, then?" she said.

He walked over to a wall switch and turned off the lights. The light from the bathroom gave Liz some comfort.

The screen suddenly was filled with the interior of a large book-lined room that looked like a library, with a good-sized desk flanked by comfortable high-backed leather chairs. At the far end of the room was a sofa that looked comfortable. In the center of the room was a low coffee table with a large vase of cut flowers. The French windows looked out onto a snow-covered walled garden. The highly polished parquet floor was partly covered by a large Oriental rug. The room had an inviting air.

"That's my office," Haley said.

The door opened, and Liz saw Dr. Haley standing to one side, ushering in a frightened little man who peered tensely from side to side like a nervous rabbit.

"This way, Dr. White."

Liz was surprised that the film had a sound track.

She saw Haley towering over the thin, pathetic figure of Dr. Charles White.

"Why don't you sit down here, Dr. White?" Haley pointed

to one of the leather chairs facing the desk. White sat down hesitantly. Haley did not go behind his desk, but sat down in the chair opposite Charles White.

Liz watched the pinched face of the little man. His eyes kept darting about the room. His long, thin fingers kept moving like writhing snakes.

"Dr. White . . ." Haley's manner was quiet and reassuring. "You must be a very important man. Your company would never have gone to the considerable expense of sending you to us if they didn't need your talents very badly." He paused. "I might add, Dr. White, that we have helped many men and women who have come to us, and we are going to help you."

Haley stopped the machine and froze the frame that showed the two of them facing each other. Liz found Dr. White's obvious fear and discomfort compelling. She found herself sitting on the edge of her chair staring fixedly at this pathetic genius whose inner torments she could only guess.

"It doesn't take a psychiatrist to see that this patient is in a highly neurotic state," Haley said. "He is being confronted by a new and strange environment that he fears and does not understand. His response is to become almost incapacitated emotionally. This is a different sort of pressure for him than he encounters in his work, but the important thing to keep in mind is that this is how he responds to almost any but the most trivial pressures. We refer to his state as one of agitated withdrawal.

"What Dr. White doesn't know is that we had a long preliminary interview with his vice-president of personnel. We were given the details of his educational and work background and a description of his behavior in his work environment. We were told that he had been observed over a prolonged period drinking heavily, and with excessive variations in mood, which were attributed to his taking stimulants as well as antidepressant drugs.

"You have to understand, Miss Clark, that Dr. White's work is watched carefully by the Department of Defense. He has the highest security clearance given by the military, and as such he is subject to periodic reviews that check on his stability and the likelihood of his becoming a target for those who profit by securing classified technological information. Industrial and military espionage is widespread in this country due to the ease of obtaining information in a free society."

She kept watching the harried face of the tormented man on the screen.

"But why does the government permit a man as obviously unstable as this to be involved in classified work?" she asked.

"That's exactly the reason his company brought him to us. They were being pressured by the Department of Defense to get rid of White. Their problem was that they couldn't replace him. We were their last hope.

"Now, I want you to fix the state of Dr. White in your mind, because the film is going to show him approximately six months after he first walked into my office." He started the projector, and Liz saw the same room. This time Dr. White was lying on the sofa. Sitting beside him in a tweed sports jacket, turtleneck, and loafers was a handsome dark-haired man who appeared to be in his early forties.

"That's Dr. Paul Arnaud, a French psychiatrist who learned of our work at a seminar I gave in Paris. He became interested in what we were doing and decided to come here and see for himself. He has been with us ever since. His background is somewhat unique. He is a graduate of the Sorbonne with a degree in physics. He became interested in psychiatry and completed his medical training at Columbia Presbyterian. His special interest is in patients from the scientific community. He speaks their language and can relate to them on their professional level. He's been of enormous help to us with patients like Dr. White."

Haley started the film. Liz was transfixed by what she saw. Dr. White seemed to her to have put on weight. He was no longer the emaciated scientist with the desperate, furtive manner she had just seen. He was dressed in a well-tailored muted plaid suit. He seemed relaxed. His expression was almost beatific. He was no longer pale. The thin wisps of white hair were gone. His hair seemed fuller and darker, and it was neatly cut.

"Notice his loafers. Look at them carefully, Miss Clark." Liz looked at the Gucci loafers Dr. White was wearing but could not see anything unusual.

"Those loafers are custom made for Dr. White. If you look at the heals carefully, you will see that they are somewhat higher than the usual loafer. As a matter of fact, those loafers contain lifts that increase his height by an inch and a half."

He again froze the frame and gave Liz an opportunity to view Dr. White closely.

"Part of the core problem with most neurotics is a deeply imbedded feeling of lack of self-worth. This can manifest itself in a variety of neurotic symptoms that we can see, and some that are hidden from us. Dr. White is only fifty-five years old."

"My God. In those first frames I thought he was sixty-five."

"How old does he look to you now?"

"I would guess in his late fifties."

"What we did with Dr. White is the reverse of what happens in most clinics. We started from the outside and worked inward. We had Dr. Arnaud's assistant, whom you will see, shop with Dr. White for a new wardrobe. We had one of the best hair stylists in New York create a realistic set of hairpieces for him. We put him on a weight-inducing diet and gave him a carefully controlled exercise program to build up his heart muscle and a mild weightlifting program to reestablish muscle tone. The change in his complexion that is noticeable even on black and white film is the result of daily sunlamp treatments. It may sound trite, Miss Clark, but people who see themselves looking better begin to feel better about themselves. But of course, all of this is only cosmetics. We had to get to the core of Dr. White's problem before we could really help him on a long-term basis."

Liz couldn't take her eyes off the transformed figure of the scientist who lay on the sofa with the handsome French psychiatrist sitting beside him.

"Dr. White is in a hypnotic trance. Most people don't understand hypnosis. There is a good deal that we doctors don't understand about it, either. In a hypnotic state the patient is in a heightened state of consciousness. He will remember what has transpired unless he is given a posthypnotic suggestion to forget.

"Before we approached Dr. White's problem with hypnosis we had the usual psychotherapeutic interviews with him. These were largely unsuccessful because of the deep layers of resistance he had build up over the years. You see, Miss Clark, the mind is like a computer: it switches on during the prenatal stages of development and it never stops recording impressions. The painful impressions are repressed in the stem, or the unconscious portion, of the brain. To understand these repressed experiences, so that we can gradually expose them to the patient's consciousness, which lies in the cortex of the brain, we use drugs. These drugs affect the resistors in the forebrain and help us to make the connection, if you will, chemically, to allow us to penetrate more deeply into the areas of unconsciousness that we have to reach to find out what is really at the root of the patient's neuroses."

The projector started to roll again. She watched Dr. Arnaud fill his pipe and light it.

"Can you describe to me, Charles, how you feel now?" Dr. Arnaud asked.

Dr. White answered, relaxed and smiling, "Extraordinarily peaceful."

"Like that day at camp . . . when you were a boy?"

"Ah, yes. Just like that day. The sun was so warm. The heat from the dock warmed my back. I've never forgotten those few precious moments of pure peace. I've never had them again. It was like a religious experience."

"Were you alone?" Dr. Arnaud asked.

"There were other boys in canoes in the middle of the lake, but I was alone on the dock."

"And you enjoyed being alone?"

"Yes, I adored it."

"Would you have been as happy in a canoe with the other boys?"

"Oh, no. No." Dr. White paused. "I couldn't. I . . . I couldn't."

"You couldn't what?"

When Dr. White answered, his voice was low, tremulous. "I couldn't swim well enough. I couldn't pass the canoe test, but . . . but they permitted me to go on the dock. I liked that. But I only knew that sense of peace once. Just once."

"Did you like camp?"

"I hated it."

"Why?"

"The boys used to tease me. They'd play tricks on me. Sometimes at night they'd frighten me."

"How?"

"They would tell ghost stories. Then sometimes they would drag me out into the woods."

"Did the camp permit this?"

Dr. White shook his head. "When they found out they punished the other boys, restricted them from movies and swim periods. They took away their candy and salamis that were sent from home."

"And how did the boys react to that?" Dr. Arnaud asked.

"They hated me. They gave me the silent treatment."

"They wouldn't speak to you?"

"That's right."

"Did you ever report this to your parents?"

"Yes." Dr. White looked agitated. "I kept writing to them, begging them to take me home. My mother came to see me. She saw how unhappy I was..."

"Did your father come as well?"

"No, he was too busy. He was a petroleum engineer. He was always away somewhere on a trip." Dr. White paused, lowering his voice. "He was always away. I knew he would be very angry if I came home."

"Why?"

"Because he didn't like me. I heard him tell my mother once..." Dr. White's voice changed to a deeper pitch in imitation of his father. "'Millie,' he said, 'that kid needs some roughing up. He needs to mix it up with boys his own age. With you always mothering him, the kid's going to grow up a damn sissy.'"

Dr. Arnaud put down his pipe and shifted his position slightly. His voice remained low and soothing. Calm. "Your mother took you home?"

"Yes."

"And you were happy?"

"No. Never again. Never like those few moments on the dock. That was the only time in my life when I was truly happy. The only time."

Dr. Arnaud leaned forward slightly. "Dr. White, I want you to fix in your mind that particular day on the lake. I want you to feel the warmth of the dock on your back. Remember how blue the sky was, with the white puffs of clouds hanging like cotton candy..."

Liz saw the expression on Dr. White's face. He seemed to be infused with an inner peace that approached the tranquillity of the Buddhist stage of the middle path.

Arnaud continued talking to him in a soft monotone: "Each

time someone upsets you, I want you to think of that day on the lake. You will not be afraid of anyone at work or in your home. When you feel threatened, you will instantly remember that one particular day and you will be happy. You will react to fear and to pressure by remembering that day. Anything that disturbs you will make you recall that day. Do you understand me, Dr. White?"

Dr. White nodded, the tranquillity of the remembrance still on his face.

"You are going to awaken when I count to five and clap my hands," Dr. Arnaud told him. "You will always remember that one day of peace whenever you feel threatened."

Arnaud began to count slowly: "One. Two. Three. Four. Five." Then he clapped sharply. White rubbed his eyes and sat up. He looked relaxed. He smiled at Dr. Arnaud.

Haley stopped the film. "What you have seen so far, Liz, is a Band-Aid for Dr. White's deep-seated neuroses. The hypnotic suggestion implanted in the mind of Dr. White needs to be periodically reinforced while we probe much more deeply into his unconscious to understand the root causes of his feelings of inferiority and lack of self-worth.

"At this stage we had Dr. White on an antidepressant drug called Evadil. Like all drugs it affects people differently. In Dr. White's case, it worked remarkably well.

"During Dr. White's therapy, to get through his deep layers of psychological resistance we used injections of sodium pentothal, which induces the second phase of anesthesia, putting the forebrain asleep and inhibiting the repressive sensors that in effect hide his deepest anxieties from himself and from us.

"The problem with this drug is that it leaves the patient totally amnestic, which means that he can remember nothing he has told us. The most difficult part of our therapy is to gradually bring these anxieties to his attention and make him emotionally understand that they are the base of his neuroses. Understanding something intellectually and understanding that same thing emotionally are two entirely different things, Miss Clark."

Haley rolled the projector again. The scene moved to the garden in late spring. There was a white circular outdoor table and two white wrought-iron chairs. The table was set for lunch. Seated there were Dr. White and a beautiful dark-haired woman, dressed casually in a white angora long-sleeved sweater and a light woolen skirt. She and Dr. White were laughing uproariously.

Liz was amazed at the further change in Dr. White. He didn't look at all like the man she had seen in the first portion of the film. He looked physically vigorous now, and Liz sensed his confidence in the presence of this attractive woman.

"That is Delphine Ravenel, a psychoanalyst trained in France. She is Dr. Arnaud's assistant. She has become an important part of Dr. White's therapy, and I might add in the therapy of other men with problems similar to Dr. White's.

"You see, Miss Clark, many men with technical or scholastic brilliance are shy and inept with women. It is a reflection of their own deeper insecurities, which must be dealt with, but again we do not forget what I choose to call, the outside, the exterior personality.

"It might surprise you to learn that Dr. Ravenel is the one responsible for Dr. White's physical appearance. She took him to a good tailor for his clothes. She encouraged him to use a sunlamp and to exercise. He has actually become confident enough to ask her to dinner and the theater . . ."

"What about Mrs. White? How does she react to her husband escorting someone who looks like Dr. Ravenel?"

"Mrs. White was brought into the program long ago. She has had long talks with Dr. Ravenel. She knows exactly what Dr. Ravenel is doing, and why. She is aware that Dr. Ravenel has many more patients whose confidence she is trying to build." Haley paused. "Would you be surprised if I told you that Mrs. White is now far more conscious of her own personal appearance and has gone to a great deal of trouble to make herself more attractive?"

Liz laughed. "If my husband was being treated by a woman who looked like that, I think I might dash over to Elizabeth Arden myself."

Haley laughed. "What you are going to see next is the final phase of this film."

The rays from the projector shifted beams of light that became images of a rectangular conference room with a long elliptical table around which stood a number of chairs. Liz saw immediately that the two men who sat on the left of Dr. White seemed tense and demanding.

"This scene, Miss Clark, shows how Dr. White now responds to pressure in his work environment. This meeting was photographed by us using hidden cameras with the approval of the president of Advanced Technologies. The two men at the opposite side of the table are representatives from an aerospace company working on the cruise missile. Advanced Technologies is a subcontractor to them, and they're responsible for a crucial element of the missile's guidance system. I'll roll the film."

A large, heavy-set man, whose belly overhung a wide belt that seemed to be supporting his bladder, was speaking. He wore a wide knotted tie that hung away from his open collar. His face was jowly, and there were beads of perspiration at the edge of his streaked gray pompadour hairline. "Now, Charlie, these gyros of yours ain't worth a damn to us if we can't get 'em and keep 'em. Your return rate for failure to meet specs just isn't acceptable. Charlie, I've got Pentagon guys crawling up the damn walls. They're screaming because we're running twenty percent over budget. They don't want to listen to the fact that they keep changing their minds. Charlie, we just can't sit still for a return rate from your company that's bucking twenty percent. That won't get the job done."

Liz watched the face of Dr. Charles White as he waited patiently for the man to finish. She noticed that Dr. White rolled a yellow pencil between the thumb and forefinger of both hands, but he seemed attentive and relaxed. Liz looked for the signs of the furtive timidity she had seen in the first part of the film. There were none.

She watched Dr. White turn to his product engineer who faced the two men. When he spoke, his voice was strong and level. "Can we assure these people that the production problems we've been having with the lasers can be corrected soon?"

"Charlie," the product engineer replied, "we've sent our people down to Bell Labs on this, and we have literally spent night and day, seven days a week, trying to straighten this thing out. We've narrowed it down to something as ridiculously simple as the laser mounts. Sam," he said, nodding in the direction of the man across the table, "we have to tighten up manufacturing procedures on those mount lines. I've put the best men I've got on it, and I think I can assure you, Sam, that the next run you get from us will be up to specs."

Liz watched the cool eyes look carefully at Charles White. She saw Dr. White's jaw muscles contract and his lips narrow slightly, but there was an air of control about him that amazed her. "Sam," he said, "I'm very sorry—"

"Sorry won't cut it, doc. We have to be sure that Advanced Tech is up to this program or we're going to have to do something about it. I don't want to beat this thing into the ground, but you're running out of time."

Liz watched the face of the project engineer tighten. His whole aspect was that of a tautly drawn bow. Liz had the distinct impression that if he could have backed into a corner and sucked his thumb, he would have.

"Sam . . ." White's tone was even, almost pleasant, but Liz could hear the hint of firm purpose that seemed as pointed and as direct as the tip of a rapier. "Our specs are built into your contract, Sam, and we both know that our technology and learning curve could not be duplicated without an enormous waste of money and time. The Department of Defense would not hold still for that."

Sam bristled. "We have no intention of letting you guys screw up a four billion dollar contract."

"And we have no intention of doing so," White said calmly. "I will take full responsibility to assure you that we will have this problem licked by the time we make our next shipment of gyros."

Liz watched Dr. White rise. She saw his eyes meet those of his antagonist. She saw the look of surprise that was poorly concealed on Sam's face. She was aware that he was no longer enjoying the encounter.

"We appreciate your taking the trouble to come here," Dr. White said coolly. "We can assure you we will hold up our end of the bargain. And now, gentlemen, if you will excuse me, I have a staff meeting to get to." He turned to the project engineer. "Would you be good enough to take Sam and Mr. Johnson to the Algonquin Club for lunch? I won't be able to join you, I'm afraid. And then if you would drive them to the airport." Dr. White walked over to Sam who had remained seated. He patted the man's shoulder. "Not to worry, Sam, we'll do our part." He smiled thinly, and Liz watched the erect form of Dr. Charles White walk firmly from the room.

"Well, that's it," Haley said. He flicked on the lights.

Liz was amazed. "It's really incredible. He seems like a totally different person." Liz found herself looking at Dr. Timothy Haley with an expression bordering on awe.

"We mustn't be deceived by Dr. White's recovery. As you can see, we have certainly brought him to a level of emotional stability where he can function quite effectively. This particular meeting was suggested as a test environment by the director of personnel. He knew about the browbeatings White had suffered at the hands of that man. When we showed the film to the president of Advanced Technologies, he couldn't believe it. Neither could Dr. White when he saw it. He was just as surprised as you are right now." Haley laughed and glanced at his watch. "I believe I promised you dinner. It's eight-ten. We should be going."

Liz put her pad back in her briefcase and stood up. "Really quite impressive, Dr. Haley."

"We can talk about it downstairs."

Chapter 11

THEY SAT AT a window table facing Central Park South. The summer night was just beginning to gather the shadows of dusk, as horse-drawn carriages took the tourists for rides through the park. Liz watched the montage of taxis and people as they kaleidoscoped past the large windows of the Oak Room.

Liz was trying to form a cohesive impression of Timothy Haley, but she wasn't having an easy time. He seemed assured and relaxed and unobtrusively sophisticated. He didn't make a big deal about ordering dinner or the wine, but she knew immediately that he was well traveled, and that his manner with headwaiters and women was sure and without pretense.

Tim chose shrimp and celery rémoulade, rack of lamb Persillade, green beans, orange-buttered carrots, and a marbled mousse for dessert.

"How about a bottle of Chassogne rouge '78 if you're going to have the filet. I think you'll enjoy it," Haley said.

"Fine."

"What would you like to begin with?"

"I think the smoked salmon."

The headwaiter wrote swiftly on his pad.

"And would you like the filet mignon with peppers?" the headwaiter asked.

"Yes."

"And roasted potato sticks. They are very good."

"That sounds good."

"And for dessert?"

"I think the apple tart."

"Excellent."

The waiter relayed their order to one of the captains.

"I was telling you upstairs that you should not be deceived by what you saw of Dr. White's recovery. He certainly has improved tremendously over the frightened little man who was unable to function and who was on the verge of ruining his career. But what Dr. White really needs is about four years of intense psychoanalysis. I would be the first to admit to you that he is somewhat old to begin a psychoanalytical program. But under the mission we were given by his company, we had no time for that kind of therapy. That is really the core function of what we perform. We use a variety of innovative techniques to get results more quickly than they can be obtained by the usual psychotherapeutic or psychoanalytical methods. Since we are not allowed the time for more permanent solutions, we adopt a program we call follow-up reinforcement.

"Dr. White and most of our other patients come back to us monthly so that we can catch the first symptoms of any slipping back to former behavioral patterns. We work very closely with members of the family in this area. We check with them frequently and try to discern if the home environment continues to be supportive. Or if a wife or husband notices signs of recidivistic behavior, that person will alert us to the problem."

"All this must be expensive."

"It is."

"What does it cost?"

The wine steward came to the table and went through the ritual of presenting the wine. Tim glanced at the label and nodded. The steward opened the bottle and poured a small amount of wine into Tim's glass. Tim held the glass to his nose briefly. He sampled the wine without pretense and pointed to Liz's glass.

"Merci, monsieur."

Liz's impression of Timothy Haley was being positively reinforced. But then her pragmatism warned her that she was dealing with someone whose skills lay in probing people's minds. She wondered if they also lay in creating favorable impressions.

"What does this therapy cost, Dr. Haley?" she repeated.

He paused before answering her. "It depends on whether or not a patient needs our complete program..."

She was again put off by his use of the word "program." Nagging at the edges of her mind was the commercial language in which Dr. Haley described his work. She was again disturbed by the fact that he saw healing as a business. But if it wasn't a business, she told herself, there would be no reason for my being here.

"If we decide a patient needs our complete program, we charge a flat fee of fifty thousand. That includes follow-up reinforcement, which can continue for twenty-four months after the completion of our basic therapies, and then we sit down with the company people who referred the patient to us, and together we do a further evaluation. If in our opinion the patient can benefit from more treatment, and if the company and the patient wish to continue, then we charge one hundred fifty dollars an hour."

Liz sipped her wine.

The waiter brought their hors d'oeuvres. Liz poured a little oil on her smoked salmon and spread the green capers with her fork over the pink slices of fish.

"Isn't that pretty high?"

"Possibly for Boston. Certainly not for New York."

Liz ate thoughtfully. She could feel him watching her.

"Why have you come to us, Dr. Haley? You seem to have things going pretty smoothly as they are."

"We do. But we feel...I should say *I* feel that we can duplicate what we are doing in Boston in other major American cities and in other countries as well."

"I'm going to have to ask you some questions, doctor," Liz said.

"I was hoping you would."

"What are you grossing now, doctor, on an annual basis?"

"Approximately two and a half million dollars."

"And what is your pre-tax return on that?"

"About forty percent."

"That's very good."

"It should be better. We need a tighter administrative operation. We should be able to hold costs down to give us at least forty-five percent before taxes."

Liz looked at the gray eyes that were regarding her with an almost clinical detachment.

"What kind of a return are you getting on your investment, doctor?"

"Do you mean on our capital investment, or our return on assets?"

Liz wondered if this man had gone to business school. Maybe I haven't met enough doctors, she thought sarcastically. "I mean your return on your invested capital," she told him.

"Three of us put up a total of three hundred thousand. We had to borrow another half a million to purchase, rebuild, and equip the center. If you are asking what our return is on our own invested capital on a pre-tax basis, it's about thirty percent. It's our plan, Miss Clark, to open seven new centers in Stamford, Chicago, Los Angeles, San Francisco, Houston, and Atlanta."

Liz looked at Haley carefully. She was searching for some clue to him, something that would allow her to understand a man who wanted to franchise a package cure for emotional problems, like some sort of fast-food chain. She knew she was not being logical or fair, or even accurate, but she couldn't help it. What he accomplished seemed miraculous to her, but his approach to what he did tainted her appraisal of him, and a part of her mind knew that this conflict had more to do with her than with him.

"What do you think such an expansion will cost?" she asked.

"It depends on how lucky we are in being able to buy property. If we can duplicate what we did in Boston, buy an old estate and fix it up, we can keep our costs down."

"Have you identified properties you want to buy?"

"We have. But our plan is not to expand into these areas simultaneously. We have to recruit and train more staff, a process we have already begun in Boston. We want to move carefully. Essentially, our biggest investment will be in the physical facilities, the property. In a sense, we are very much in the real estate business. That also provides us with the tax write-offs to offset our personal income."

The waiter carefully placed their entrées in front of them.

Liz cut into her filet. "How much money are you looking for?"

"We would like a commitment for ten million but would

only take down a portion of that in the beginning. About one-point-two million to build the next Family Care Center in Stamford."

"Has anyone told you that standby fees can be pretty expensive? No one is going to commit to lending you funds for some date in the future without charging you a pretty stiff premium for that."

"That's one of the things I've learned in talking to your competitors." Haley laughed as he began eating his lamb. "I've come to realize, Miss Clark, that not only does everything I want to do seem unorthodox to people in your profession, but it also appears to be quite expensive."

She could no longer resist asking him: "How did you become interested in mixing psychiatry and business?"

He looked at her with humor. "Do I detect a slight note of hostility in that question?"

"Not hostility. Just curiosity." She realized that he knew she was lying.

"I don't know when I started thinking about medicine. I didn't consider psychiatry until my second year in medical school." He laughed. "When I was an undergraduate at Penn, I thought I was going to be a professional football player. I was All-American and had several offers. I even considered going with Pittsburgh. My father talked me out of it. He was professor of cardiology at Jefferson, and I admired him very much."

Liz was eating slowly and sipping her wine, but looking at him and listening to him with obvious concentration. As he spoke, she found herself holding her hostilities in abeyance for the moment.

"My father's whole life was his profession," Haley said.

"You keep referring to him in the past tense."

"Yes. He died when I was in medical school."

Liz's mouth tightened. "I'm sorry."

Haley sighed. "So am I. We were very close. He was an exceptional human being as well as an outstanding physician. His faults lay in not being able to share more of himself with my mother and my sister."

"He seems to have found time enough for you."

"I was different. I was a very involved, competitive kid. My own schedule at school, with athletics and extracurricular activities, was almost as hectic as my old man's. Somehow I understood his commitment and his love for what he did." Haley paused. "Unfortunately, my mother and sister didn't. My mother divorced him when I was in high school. I grew up trying to placate her, and trying to be a kind of bridge between them. My mother was very active socially. She was a Philadelphia Main Line hostess. My father was preoccupied with trying to prevent people from dying of heart disease.

"I've always thought that really broke up their marriage—their inability to tolerate the trivialities each saw in my mother's life." He looked at Liz carefully. "Do you understand what I am saying? My father thought my mother's life was useless. Unfortunately so did my mother." He paused. "She still does, which I don't think I ever fully understood until I completed my psychiatric training. Now I believe that seeking the solution to that problem may have been an unconscious motivation for my becoming interested in emotional problems."

"You said you went to Penn?"

"Yes. Both undergraduate school and medical school. My father and I agreed that, because of his position at Jefferson, it would be better if I chose Penn."

Liz paused. "You have more knowledge of business than any doctor I have ever met."

He laughed. "I read a lot, Miss Clark. Especially when I'm interested in something. You see, all my life, I've been a winner. At anything I've ever tried, I've always excelled. I hope that doesn't sound immodest."

It does, she thought, but then he's probably telling the truth.

"As I evolved the techniques that have resulted in Family Care, it occurred to me that they could be applied to other geographic areas. I knew that meant creating a fairly decent-sized business, and so I took some business courses and did a lot of reading. I'm not in your league, Miss Clark, but I have a grasp of the fundamentals." He smiled. "Six million pre-tax is what we project for the combined centers, and we think those numbers are conservative."

Liz looked at him and thought that in her very brief experience, she had never known anyone's projections to be conservative. She thought of George and began to smile.

"You're smiling. Do you doubt what I'm telling you?" he asked.

"Let's say that in our business we usually find it a good practice to cut someone's projections in half. My boss, George Hall, is somewhat skeptical about other people's optimism. He says that projections are like counting other people's money. You are far better off subtracting and dividing than adding or multiplying."

"Your boss sounds like a cynic."

For some reason the thought of Peter, rather than George, flashed through her mind. She remembered him once saying that you can't study history without becoming a cynic. Odd, she thought. We are the ones who are usually thought of as cold and pragmatic. But perhaps Peter, whose life is the study of the past, is the true cynic. He knows more about the sordid story of humanity than any of us. Odd, she thought again as she emptied her wineglass. An observant waiter refilled it for her and poured the remainder of the bottle into Tim's glass.

"You seem preoccupied," Tim said.

"It's nothing. What were you saying about George?"

"I said he sounds like a cynic."

"In our business, Dr. Haley, skepticism has to be balanced with the ability to recognize opportunities and to weigh those against risk. That is really the essence of what we do. If that leads to cynicism, and it probably does, than your description of George would have to include me and my associates."

Tim looked at her appraisingly, at the copper-colored hair whose sheen reflected the lights in the subtly lit room, at the incredibly steady eyes whose cobalt blue seemed darker in the ambient light, at the straight nose and the rather full mouth.

She was tall, erect, and slim and had about her an air of a quiet, inquiring intelligence. He knew that she was highly motivated, and he assumed she was capable at whatever she chose to do. He wondered briefly how much fire burned under that aloof exterior. He was sure that Elizabeth Clark did not involve herself with a man easily. And he was even more sure that her pride, which was an essential, visible, almost palpable part of her character, kept her out of men's beds unless there was a deeply felt relationship involved.

"How do you think your cynical boss, Mr. Hall, would regard my project?"

Liz hesitated. "I'm not sure. We are interested in medical services, but frankly, we normally look for a company whose potential growth is a good deal greater than what you have described to me."

He began to laugh. "I knew I was right to save the best till last." The busboy cleared the table, and the waiter brought their desserts.

"You mean there's more?"

"Yes, my skeptical Miss Clark, there is a good deal more. Mmmm. This mousse is delicious. I hope your tart is as good. Would you like to try a bite of my mousse?"

"No thank you."

"What I am about to describe to you is most unorthodox and would certainly be viewed by some members of my profession with derision. But if I may remind you of the film you saw upstairs, I get results with what I do. I also want you to know that we have started initial testing of what I am about to describe to you, and these tests are very encouraging. And I can assure you, Miss Clark, this market is big enough even for your Mr. Hall."

"What are you suggesting?"

"I'm not suggesting anything, Miss Clark; I'm telling you about a technique that will revolutionize psychotherapy."

Liz's skepticism was becoming harder to lick.

"Still the cynic?"

He's so damn tuned in, she thought.

"Well, you won't be a cynic when I have finished telling you about teletherapy, but perhaps you need an after-dinner brandy to go with this." He laughed and signaled the waiter.

She felt the warmth of the brandy flame through her as she watched him. The wine and the brandy had relaxed her, and she felt she was in danger of losing her objectivity. That was exactly what George had warned her against time and again. She could hear him saying it, and she smiled as his voice seemed to clang inside her head, like the warning bell above a hidden spine of rock.

"Always look for the con, Liz," George had told her. "But remember the unrealistic dreamer can be as dangerous as the con. You're trying to find the people who have the experience, the drive, the guts, and the willingness to commit their own capital up to the limit of their resources, and who are ready to work like hell to get their dream off the ground. It doesn't hurt if they're lucky either."

Was Haley one of those people? She looked at the great bear of a man sitting opposite her, with the appraising gray eyes. He was terribly sure of himself. Almost too sure. And he had an unnerving ability to see through her. Almost as if she were made of glass.

He had been watching her smile, which reflected her inner thoughts, but it left her as quickly as the shadow of a hawk. He watched her face become serious, purposeful. She was a remarkable young woman, he thought.

"We're testing teletherapy in the Boston area right now, and as I told you, we are delighted with the results we've been getting."

He folded his hands, which seemed enormous to her, and rested his elbows on the table. He looked at her intently. She felt the return of her vulnerable transparency that made her uncomfortable.

"Look for the con," she thought. She clung to that single warning of George's. She summoned all her reserves of concentration and discipline to listen to him as objectively as she could while he spoke.

"Most neuroses are rooted in feelings of inadequacy which develop further into feelings of a lack of self-worth. The problem with psychoanalysis, as I said earlier, is that it can take four to six years or longer. The patient is required to visit the analyst at least four times a week, and the cost both in money and time is beyond the resources of most people. Also, not everyone can be analyzed. The resistance may be too deep, or there may not be enough intellectual awareness on the part of the patient. People who are not intelligent cannot be analyzed.

"Psychotherapy, on the other hand, is less intensive, but it is still time-consuming and expensive."

He sipped his brandy. "Miss Clark, society in general is pretty much of a mess. All of us are neurotic in one way or another. As long as these neuroses don't interfere with our lives, our work, or our personal relationships, we can tolerate them. But when they do interfere, the patient needs help.

"Remember"—he pointed a long finger at her—"I said they *need* help. Most people who need it don't get it." He paused. "We are attempting to reach as many people as we can using the newest communications and computer technologies available. That's where teletherapy comes in. Here's how it works.

"We run advertisements in the Boston newspapers informing the public that Teletherapy, Inc., which is a wholly owned subsidiary of Family Care, is a test program for people who suspect they may have emotional problems. We ask them to send for a booklet that describes our teletherapy program. In the booklet we outline our approach and state what the program costs.

"Our subscription fee is fifty dollars." He looked at her, judging her mood. "We felt that fifty dollars would not inhibit those who were serious and really needed help."

She was watching him now, fascinated by what he was telling her, but at the same time repelled: he was conducting an ad campaign for neurotics. She couldn't hide her hostility from him; she knew that, but she didn't care. Her feelings of vulnerability were rapidly giving way to a cool, sustained anger. It was unreasonable, she knew that, but she couldn't help it.

"The whole professional community in the Boston area is up in arms about this program. We keep it separate from Family Care for obvious reasons. But Liz"—his voice was deep and sonorous though laced with a touch of humor and triumph—"it really works. We get results.

"We send our subscribers a questionnaire that amounts to a psychological profile. We put the results of each questionnaire into a computer and classify those patients—"

"You call them patients?"

He paused and looked at her evenly. "Yes, that's what we call them. Patients. What else should we call them?"

"Customers." She shouldn't have said it. It was rude.

He smiled.

Damn him, he's reading me again, she thought.

"They are really patients, Liz. We're just using a different technique to treat them. Before you judge me too harshly, hear me out."

She felt like a fool. The wine, the brandy, and now her own prejudices and inexperience had made her act like a juvenile. She choked back her self-recriminations.

"As I was saying . . ." The gray eyes smiled at her discomfort. "The computer classifies all those with compatible neurotic symptoms and problems. We then have to apply to the telephone company for a picture phone, which allows the patient and the therapist to see each other. We then arrange conference calls so that each of our teletherapists can talk individually to a particular member of the group, or to the entire group. The picture phone maintains the patient's privacy, because the patients cannot see one another; they can only see the therapist who is listening to them. Each therapist sits in front of a bank of ten phones and can observe the reactions of the entire group or of a particular individual.

"Each session is videotaped, and the tapes are played before two of our staff psychiatrists. They make suggestions to the therapist to emphasize areas they think should be more fully explored. The psychiatrists are the therapists' backup.

"We maintain a twenty-four hour hot line that is staffed by one of our therapists who can give support to a patient who may feel in need of talking to us."

Liz was fascinated by the imaginative use of the latest telecommunication equipment to approach neurotic problems on a mass basis. She knew the market was enormous. If he expanded this thing, it would be a gold mine. And he seemed to believe he was doing some good. It was hard for her to swallow, but she had to admit to herself that he probably was.

"How much does one of your telescribers—"

"Telepatients," he corrected.

"Okay, telepatients. What does this cost them, Dr. Haley?"

"We charge them thirty dollars for each telephone contact." He paused and smiled at her. "That's a great deal cheaper than the seventy-five to a hundred dollars an hour they would pay if they visited a psychiatrist."

Her mind started working on the numbers. "What do you project this test program in Boston will gross?"

"We only have seven therapists at present, each handling two forty-five-minute sessions a day. You may not be aware of it, Miss Clark, but a psychotherapeutic hour is actually forty-five minutes. The analyst, psychiatrist, or therapist needs the intervening fifteen minutes to prepare for the next patient. To be effective you have to concentrate very hard on what the patients are telling you, and I can assure you, Miss Clark, that the process is exhausting. That's why we have to limit our therapists to two sessions a day. They are dealing with a total of twenty patients each, and they couldn't take more than that and be effective."

She was listening to him in awe, as a part of her mind

admitted that what he was doing was effective and would help a great many people. But her own skepticism would not hide. She couldn't put her finger on it, but she simply did not like this merchandising of psychiatric medicine. She had mixed feelings about this enormous, appraising doctor who sat opposite her, reading her like a newspaper.

"You asked what we are grossing in this test," he said. "We're currently grossing one-point-five million a year and our pre-tax profit on that is about nine hundred thousand. Multiply that by the six centers we want to open, and we can earn pre-tax about five and a half million with just seven therapists in each center. If we double the number of therapists we could do better than ten million." He paused to watch her carefully. His eyes never left hers. His voice was low and controlled. "Miss Clark, there is so much misery and unhappiness out there that the market would always be far larger than we could handle."

She had averted her eyes, and she seemed to be tracing her thoughts on the white linen tablecloth with the handle of her teaspoon. She was calculating in numbers what her mind had conjured. Rooms full of therapists sitting in front of picture phones electronically hooked into the neuroses of troubled America.

He watched her make the quick calculations with the back of her spoon. If he had one hundred forty therapists, he'd be doing eighteen million pre-tax. That's crazy, she thought. I'm doing just what George has taught me never to do. I'm taking the man's projections and assuming they can be geometrically extrapolated.

She looked at Tim, and as she did so, she found that her mind was still caught by the image of all those therapists looking at all those picture phones. She couldn't shake the scene from her head. The numbers that kept rolling over in her mind like the symbols on a slot machine came to a staggering jackpot. She tried to keep her voice calm and objective.

"Tell me something, Dr. Haley, and please give me as accurate a response to this as you can. If I decide to look into your program, what I am about to ask you will be what I am going to look for." She paused. She was leaning forward, her elbows on the table. She continued making doodling motions on the tablecloth with the handle of her spoon.

"You said you're using newspaper advertising. What would happen if you used television?"

He waited a moment to reply. "We're running a low-budget campaign now and we have a three-month backlog of people waiting to subscribe. If we ran a television campaign, we'd be backed up for a year."

She looked directly at him. "Can you prove that?"

"Absolutely."

"Tell me something else. Do you believe you can success-fully duplicate what you are doing in Boston in the other areas you spoke about?"

His voice was calm. He sat looking at her with an appraising, clinical detachment that she found irritating. "We can do what we are doing in Boston anywhere else in the country, Miss Clark. Emotional problems are not confined to any particular geographic area. The world's leading commodity is personal misery and unhappiness."

She sat back in her chair, erect and looking at him with great intensity. Her mind had caught fire with the potential of teletherapy. "Tell me something, doctor. If you can demonstrate and substantiate what you are telling me, why has everyone else turned you down?"

He thought a while before answering her. "I wish I had an explanation for that, Miss Clark. I don't. Frankly, I have been asking myself the same question all week." He paused. "The negative reactions I've received seemed to be based on the degree of psychological discomfort felt by those I've talked to. Men in particular don't like talking about psychiatric problems. That seems especially true of financial people." He chuckled in that rich, deep bass of his. "You know, Miss Clark, I've talked to more neurotic men in the past week than you could imagine. This business of yours seems to attract goal-oriented people with highly directed, but narrowly focused personal objectives. Their whole *raison d'être* seems to be tied into the stock market and the deals they are doing. They neglect them-selves and their families. They hide their neuroses in the chal-lenge of making money."

She looked at him coolly. "And your world, doctor? What is your world about? Is it healing the sick or making money?"

He didn't answer her immediately. For the first time since they met, he touched her. He took one of her hands in his. For the first time she felt his enormous gentleness. This huge hand covering her own seemed preposterous, but his touch had the quality of restraint.

"At least I help heal the sick, Miss Clark."

He said it in such a way that it made her feel like a defensive child. She knew he was right. Who was she to criticize him for finding a way to create wealth. She didn't think he was a charlatan or a crook. If he was, she would sure as hell find that out. And he seemed to be helping people. Maybe not as effectively as he could. Maybe as effectively as he was capable of. She didn't know and really, was that her problem? Wasn't she sitting in the Oak Room of the Plaza at eleven o'clock at night because she was supposed to be finding out whether or not this was a deal worth the firm's pursuing? She wasn't supposed to be sitting in moral judgment; she was supposed to be weighing a potential investment.

She withdrew her hand from his and smiled at him. "Dr. Haley, I'm afraid I am one of those people who can't always completely separate the making of money from how that money is made. I am not one of the narrowly focused Wall Street strivers you just described. Of course, I am highly motivated and goal oriented or I wouldn't be in this business, but there's more to it for me than just making money, doctor. A lot more."

He lit another cigarette. "More brandy?"

"No, thank you."

"More coffee?"

"No. It's getting late, doctor, and I'd better be getting home."

"Where's home?"

"In the Village."

"I don't know where that is."

"It's downtown."

"May I take you home?"

"No, that's not necessary. I'll just grab a cab."

"I'd like to take you home. You've been very kind to give me so much of your time."

She smiled. "It comes with the territory, doctor."

"I really would appreciate it if you'd let me take you to the Village. I'd like to prolong this evening just a little."

She looked at him, surprised at the abrupt change in his manner into something more personal. "Doctor, I have to be on a plane tomorrow at eight-fifteen with my boss for a meeting in San Francisco. I think I've stretched myself a little thin as it is, agreeing to meet with you tonight."

"I'm sorry. I didn't realize you had such a demanding schedule."

"Demanding is the word for it, doctor."

He hesitated. "Then how shall we leave this? Do you have any interest in what you've heard and seen tonight?"

She thought she heard just a trace of anxiety in his voice. She sighed with the fatigue she was beginning to feel. "I'm interested, Dr. Haley, and I will convey that interest to Mr. Hall. I'll need his permission to go ahead."

"I hope you are able to convince him."

She smiled. "I'll try."

She got up. "Thank you for a very unusual evening, Dr. Haley." She stopped and reached into her handbag and handed him the fact sheet she had brought with her from the office. "If Mr. Hall gives me the go ahead on Family Care, I'll need the information listed on that sheet, and a lot more."

He glanced quickly at the paper. "This will take a good deal of time to pull together."

"It will take me a good deal of time to check it out, too, Dr. Haley."

He folded the single sheet of paper and put it in his inside breast pocket. "I'll walk you to the door and get you a cab."

They stood in front of the hotel entrance. The air had begun to cool, but it was still a warm and surprisingly humid night. The summer was passing rapidly.

Tim held the door for her. She turned to him and extended her hand. "If we take this any further, Dr. Haley, I'll call you and make arrangements to come up to Boston. Thank you for dinner."

He held her hand for a moment longer than she felt was necessary. "For a lot of reasons, Miss Clark, I hope we meet again."

She got into the cab. "We'll see, Dr. Haley."

She waved through the open window and watched him looking at her, as the cab pulled away down the ribbon of light that was Fifth Avenue.

Chapter 12

THE ALARM went off at 5:00. She lay there in the semidarkness of her bedroom, seeing the rectangular sliver of light beneath the bathroom door. Accustomed to the hum of city traffic, she no longer heard the noise. Only an occasional horn or siren, the everpresent sounds of the city, touched her consciousness. She was exhausted. She should never have agreed to meet Haley last night. She should have come straight back to the apartment and reread the files on Twenty/Twenty so that she would be as current on the company as possible. George was going to propose that she represent him on the board of directors. Though she felt that the other board members were impressed with her, she still felt it was too early for George to suggest something like this. But George seemed determined to let her go as fast and as hard as her talents and drive would permit. He had given her more opportunity to test her abilities than she would have had in any other business. It was what she liked most about him. That, and the little things she couldn't put her finger on. Together they formed a demanding but attractive package.

Sweet Jesus, how was she supposed to function this morning. She got out of bed and stretched and yawned. The folders. Were they in her briefcase? She pawed through her briefcase looking for the material; it wasn't there. "Oh, my God." She was suddenly wide awake. She rushed into the living room and saw the stack of material that lay in manila folders on the wall desk and on the coffee table in front of the sofa.

She flipped through the files until she came to one marked Twenty/Twenty. "Thank God." She put the file in her briefcase. George would pick her up in a limousine for the ride to the airport at 6:30. George believed in leaving plenty of time to get to airports, especially in morning rush hour traffic.

Oh, God, I can't face this today, she thought. She ran her fingers through her hair and went into the kitchen to boil water for coffee. Her head ached from last night's wine. Why do I drink it? Every time I have wine I get a hangover. My mouth feels like wet socks. I've got to brush my teeth.

She went into the bathroom and turned on the hot water. The ancient plumbing started to gurgle and bang, but the water was hot. The shower slowly brought her back to life. She lathered herself, rubbing her breasts with soap.

It's been so long since I've had a man, she thought. Her mind turned back to Peter as she cleansed her body.

It was almost three months ago, in her mother's house in Falmouth. She let the water flow over her soothingly.

Peter. My God, it's been so long since I really thought about Peter. *Really* thought about him. She felt the ache come into her mind and transform itself into a physical longing that she could feel in the pit of her stomach.

She thought of George. She had been with him on such a personal basis for the last few weeks, flying around the country meeting his clients.

He'd never made a pass. Never said or done anything that was the least out of line. But she knew it was there with George. She knew the way a woman knows. But Peter! Damn, why did every man she was attracted to always get mixed up with Peter?

Why was it that you could love someone, yet know that it won't work. Why in hell did that someone have to be the man you loved? She felt her tears mix with the droplets of water as she stepped out of the shower.

Peter is like this job, she thought. He's a full-time commitment, and I am already committed full-time. Is this going to be all that my life is about? Deals and excitement? Money and what it can buy? What about sharing and caring? What about that?

She wrapped a towel about her head and for some reason the inconsequential thought came to her about how lucky she was to have naturally wavy hair. All she had to do was dry it and brush it. Thank God I don't have to sit around in curlers. I would have had to get up at four.

She went into the kitchen and poured some orange juice. They would have breakfast—or more accurately, brunch—in flight. George always flew first class, and they always wound up drinking and eating more than they should. But she was one of those fortunate women who would never be fat. She was all legs, with broad swimmer's shoulders and well-shaped breasts. She didn't have the figure of their voluptuous receptionist, but what she did have was good enough. She had known that since she was sixteen.

She poured herself some coffee and began to feel at least half alive. They were going to fly to San Francisco and then drive to Palo Alto to see Twenty/Twenty's representatives. They would have a late lunch, and then they could relax for the afternoon and evening before they flew down to Los Angeles the following day. They would spend the next day and night in L.A. and then fly back to New York, and she would be a zombie by the time they were through.

She had to get some break in all this. She had been going flat out ever since she had arrived at BC, and it couldn't continue. Not at this pace. Not without some interruption. She was going to tell George she needed a few days to catch up. Everyone else in this place, she thought, might be willing to have a nervous breakdown for dear old BC, but I'm not one of them.

The limousine pulled up at the United terminal, and the driver took their bags out of the trunk. George never checked luggage; he didn't have the patience to wait at baggage terminals, and he was reluctant to take the chance on the airline sending his luggage to another city, or not sending it at all—and Liz had picked up the habit. They signaled a porter to take them to the checkout counter. George handed the porter ten dollars. "Take these bags through security and wait for us at the gate."

"Yes, sir," he said and hurried their tickets through seat selection.

The way George got things done was one of the main characteristics Liz admired about him. He knew how to expedite what he wanted to accomplish, and he wasn't concerned if it cost a little more. He expected service. He paid for it, and he usually got it.

They seated themselves in the wide seats of the first-class section of the Boeing 747; George gave Liz the window seat. They had been living in airplanes and hotels for the past three weeks on intermittent trips, and Liz was beginning to feel as if she spent half her life at 35,000 feet and the other half on the ground, with one city melting into another so that she could barely tell them apart. Only San Francisco remained unique in her mind. She had come to love that city.

The enormous aircraft climbed toward the high altitude of clear blue sky and bright sun over the Jersey Shore and began its vectored course toward the Pacific.

She had sensed George's mood as soon as she settled into the comfort of the limousine for the drive to Kennedy. He seemed depressed and withdrawn, and he looked as tired as she did.

The drive to the airport was strained and subdued. She had felt uneasy just sitting beside him in the car. Now that they were settled in the plane, she felt she had to say something. Her voice was soft and hesitant. "Anything wrong?"

It was a long time before he answered. "There's a hell of a lot that's wrong."

She waited. "I don't want to pry, but is it business?"

He was looking past her, out the window at the wispy clouds, seeing everything and seeing nothing. "No, business has just become a drag. I'm worn out from it. I need to get away . . . Oh, hell, I can tell you. You've probably guessed it anyway. It's the ex–Mrs. Hall. I don't know what's driving that woman, what she wants from me. It's not as if she were starving in the street or as if we had children I wasn't taking care of. She doesn't need me. She's a damn successful lawyer." He paused. "It's the alimony I owe her. She's pressing me for it, and I don't have it. I'd have to hock every asset I could lay my hands on to clean it up. I could fight the thing in court, which is what I may have to do, but that's going to cost me as much as I owe her." He turned to Liz really not seeing her, but using her as a focus for his thoughts.

"Why is it that two relatively decent people, when they finally decide they can't make it together . . . why is it they have to become enemies? I don't hate her. I don't even dislike her.

She's a hell of a fine woman. I just couldn't live with her, and for some reason that has set off a vindictiveness I never knew she had."

"Some champagne?" The flight attendant stood beside them smiling pleasantly.

"You know, I don't exactly feel like champagne right now, but how about two Bloody Marys?" He looked at Liz. "How about you?"

"I thought you just ordered one for me."

"Those two are for me."

She looked at him sympathetically. Her voice softened. "It's that bad, huh?"

"It's that bad."

She looked at the flight attendant. "Make it three Bloody Marys. It's going to be a long day."

"Would you like to choose your luncheon entrée now?"

"It's too early to think about food, miss. Come back to us a little later, okay?" He tried to manage a smile.

He lowered his seat and turned to look at Liz. "I called you last night. You were out. Late."

She grinned a very tired grin. "I wish I could tell you I was having fun, boss, but unfortunately, yours truly was hard at work for dear old BC."

"Are you pulling my leg?"

"I don't have the strength."

"What in hell were you doing out past eleven for dear old BC?"

She laughed. "I would be flattered if I thought I caught just the faint trace of concern in that remark, or do I presume too much?"

"Presume hell. Now that you have so tactfully brought it up, I was concerned."

She was teasing him, trying to get him to come out of the blackness of his mood. "I am getting just the slightest vibe that you would like to know my after-hours whereabouts."

He looked at her with a mixture of annoyance and amusement. "It's none of my business, of course, but as a matter of fact, yes. I would like to know your after-hours whereabouts. But if you feel I'm stepping out of line, just say so. But softly, please. I have a lousy headache and my rejection threshold is very low this morning."

She touched his hand with her long soft fingers. "It isn't

too difficult to keep track of me after hours," she said softly. "I'm usually in the apartment working."

"But not last night..."

"No. Last night I was working in the Plaza." She realized what she had just said and began to laugh. "Not to worry, boss. I'm not an after-hours hooker."

It was his first smile of the day. He looked at her and the fatigue in his eyes seemed to disappear. "I'm glad to hear it." He looked at her humorously. "Well, give. What were you doing at the Plaza until eleven last night for dear old BC?"

The flight attendant brought their Bloody Marys.

"Just in time." He handed a small bottle of vodka and Bloody Mary mix to Liz.

"Would you care for some fruit or cheese?"

He looked at Liz. She made a face. "If I eat another thing I'll need an operation." She was still satiated from last night's dinner.

"We'll skip it. Just keep an eye on our drinks; we may be coming back for more," he told the flight attendant.

Liz looked at him but didn't say anything. George could hold his liquor, but she knew the fatiguing effects of a long flight and the hour's drive they would have to Palo Alto. It would be a grueling day, but the time change was working for them. On the way back it would be against them, and that was the worst part. She began to speculate that if you flew frequently enough, your bioclock became so confused that the only way you could straighten yourself out was to stay in one place long enough to let your body and your mind regain their equilibrium. This was the state she and George were in now, and they both literally had to stop for a while.

"Well, come on. What was going on at the Plaza?"

She sighed, because she knew the degree of detail he would want from her. "Do you remember the appointment you had with a Dr. Timothy Haley?"

"Yeah. Some shrink tank guy from Boston."

"He has a shrink tank as you so eloquently describe it, boss."

"I don't feel eloquent."

"I know. I know." She patted his hand. Her legs brushed against his as she lowered the back of her seat and turned to face him.

"You look very attractive, Liz. Do you know that? A little washed out, but attractive."

She smiled wanly. "That's what I like about you, George. You really know how to compliment a girl."

"I only meant that you looked damn attractive but tired, that's all. What's wrong with that?"

"Nothing. Nothing."

"I'm sorry for interrupting."

"It's okay," she said softly.

They were reclining, looking at each other, aware of the invisible energy that was being generated between them.

"Anyway, Dr. Haley came in yesterday expecting to meet you, and wound up with me instead."

"I would say he had a remarkable change of luck."

He touched her hand and let his fingers rest on hers.

She told him the whole story of Dr. Haley. She watched George's interest develop. When she had finished, she could see that the fatigue had vanished from his face. It was replaced with a cautious enthusiasm that began to glow like fanned coals.

"Why has everybody turned him down?" he asked.

"I asked him the same thing. He said that most men with financial backgrounds don't like to talk about psychological problems. He implied that they had built-in layers of resistance that were difficult to overcome."

"He's right. I ought to know. I spent four years in analysis. That was one of the reasons I left my wife. I went and she didn't. There's an old analytical joke that goes, 'I can't get adjusted to the you who got adjusted to me.'" George sighed. "Anyway, what Haley said is true."

"He said that we financial types are narrowly focused and highly goal oriented. When you come to think of it, we are."

"We definitely are."

She paused, looking past him, thinking of Peter. Remembering what Peter had said on the banks of the Charles River that warm spring day that seemed a hundred years ago: "England is going to become a repository of Western culture. An island museum, a library...You can seek your roots in our antiquity. Just put your feet up by our cultural fire and warm yourselves."

"What are you thinking about?"

She hesitated. "Just something someone said to me once about people like us."

"What was it?"

She shook her head. He didn't press her. He lay back looking at her, his fingers resting on her hand.

"George, you've had some experience with this sort of thing. Do you believe the demand is really there to develop his tele-therapy at the rate he thinks he can?"

"Liz, the number of people with emotional problems is tremendous. They probably constitute one of the largest markets in this country. It's part of human nature."

"That's what he said. He called it part of the human condition."

"It is." His voice lowered. "It certainly screwed up my life before I got some help."

The flight attendant handed them their menu. "I'll be back to take your order whenever you're ready. We'll start the movie after lunch."

George took the menus and handed one to Liz. "Since we're supposed to be fed by the boys from Twenty/Twenty, I think I'll skip mine," he said. "What about you?"

"I'm not hungry either. Only let's go easy on the booze, or I'm going to fall asleep at that board meeting."

They were still turned toward each other, relaxing as they sped westward across the United States at 495 miles an hour. The pilot had announced strong headwinds and had told them the flight plan was five hours and twenty-one minutes. They would arrive in San Francisco at 10:30 and in Palo Alto by noon, as scheduled.

"Did you have a chance to review the material on Twenty/Twenty that I asked Martha to give you?"

"Briefly. I was planning to do it last night when Dr. Haley popped up." She paused. "I thought I'd get caught up on the flight."

"The hell with going through all that crap now. I'm too tired even to watch you read it. I'll fill you in quickly, and then we can talk about something else . . ." He looked at her carefully, letting his silence hang like the broken silk of a spider's thread.

"First we'll have a formal board meeting where I will propose you to represent me. I think they'll go for that. I've talked to them about it, and I see no resistance there. They respect you and know you'll be my eyes and ears in that company. If they don't like it, the hell with them. We have a right to put anyone from our shop on their board, and that someone is going to be you." He paused. "The rest of this meeting should be pretty interesting."

"What's up?"

"Nicholas Barkley's smart as hell, as you know. He built Twenty/Twenty from scratch, with our help. We're going to do a public offering of his stock. We'll sell maybe twenty percent of our position. Should make nearly one hundred times our original investment. Not bad in less than forty-eight months. And we'll do a lot better the next time around. Anyway, Barkley's got the Bank of the West lined up, and he's going to show them how to steal money from a bank."

"What?"

George laughed. "He's going to show them how their own computer security systems can be broken. Once you've done that, the rest is a piece of cake."

"You see today, in major banks, money is electronically transferred. At today's volume, if the banks didn't electronically transfer funds, they would literally drown in their own paper. Everything goes into the bank's computers. If you know how to break the security code and enter a bank's computer, you can wire funds to accounts anywhere in the world. In other words, you can steal them blind if you know how to break their codes."

"And Barkley knows how to do that?" She shifted her position slightly.

"He says he does. He'd better be able to, or he's going to look like an awful damn fool in front of the Bank of the West."

"But how can he do that?"

"It isn't easy, I can tell you. The computer software business is just people. What you're buying is their imagination and creativity. Barkley stalked the woods for the guys he's pulled together. He's gotten hold of some cryptologists from the Department of Defense and from Cambridge—"

"In England?"

"In England. All kinds of nuts. Guys who would rather work cryptograms than go out with girls."

"Sounds awfully dull."

"To you and me perhaps, but not to Barkley and his boys. They've developed a system that they claim can penetrate any bank's security computer codes."

"My God. They sound like a national menace."

"They could be if the right people didn't know who they were and what they're doing."

"So Barkley is going to show them how their codes can be

broken, and then what?" she asked.

"Then Barkley is going to sell them a system that is unbreakable!"

She sat up in her seat. "That's brilliant!"

"It's brilliant if it works, Liz. If Barkley can do what he says he can, he'll have banks standing in line from California to Massachusetts. And we'll have a very, very sweet deal, Liz. Including warrants and stock, we own over forty percent of that company. It's one of those deals you pray for and very seldom get."

The flight attendant was smiling at them again. "Have you decided on lunch?"

"We're going to skip lunch." She seemed disappointed, as if no one who flew first class should skip lunch.

"Why not bring us a couple of more Bloody Marys. Okay with you, Liz?"

"I'll have just one more. You may have to help me off the plane."

"When the movie starts, we'd appreciate your pulling down your window screen." George nodded as the flight attendant made her way toward the rear of the first-class cabin.

Their fatigue combined with alcohol had made them mutually resigned to forget about the work in their briefcases, and instead they reclined, looking at each other and knowing that something was passing between them, something silent and unspoken.

They paid no attention to the movie. They were surprised when the pilot announced they would be landing in San Francisco in fifteen minutes.

I wonder how long we can go on like this, she thought. He looks ready to explode. This business is bad enough without the pressure cooker of some avenging bitch who is trying to ruin him.

Maybe that's unfair. I don't know her. I don't know anything about her. There are always two sides to these things. But he looks so strung out. I'm strung out myself, but thank God I don't have his problems.

I wonder what she's thinking, he mused. I knew it would be dangerous to hire her. Was I kidding myself when I first saw her back in Boston? I was attracted to her the first time I laid eyes on her. How can we be almost constantly together like this without something happening? She's got everything I want. She understands what I do and wants to help me do it. She's bright as hell, and there's fire in that girl; I know it. I can feel it. She's a woman. All the B School stuff and all the go-go-go for dear old BC hasn't touched that. She's still warm and feminine and appealing. I want that girl. Does she know that? She probably does. Does she want me? What about that history guy of hers? She feels very deeply about him, and yet she says it won't work out. What about Larry and Bob and the associates? I know they think I'm showing her preferential treatment. Am I? I sure as hell would rather fly around with her than spend all my time looking at Curt or Howard or Arthur. Am I getting myself into a jam with this girl? Don't I have enough problems with Claudia? He groaned audibly.

She was watching him, trying to read his thoughts. "That bad, eh, George?"

"Liz, it's all a pain in the ass."

"Ladies and gentlemen, we are on our final approach to San Francisco where the local time is ten thirty-five. Please see that your seats are in an upright position, your safety belts are fastened, and that all carry-on luggage is stored under your seat."

George and Liz raised their seats.

"Well, kid. I guess it's 'California, here we come.'"

Chapter 13

IT HAD BEEN an incredible afternoon. Twenty/Twenty's demonstration of the new computer security system was breathtakingly dramatic.

"How did Barkley's people ever come up with anything like that?" she asked George as he looked for 101 North off the Oregon Expressway, which would take them back to San Francisco.

"Will you get my sunglasses? They're in my briefcase."

She turned, leaned over back of the seat, and opened his briefcase. "Here you are."

He took them from her. "That sun is murder."

"Anyway, how did Barkley ever pull that off? My God, it's like being able to reach inside a bank and help yourself to as much money as you want. It's unbelievable."

He turned on to 101 North, heading for San Francisco.

"Barkley approached bank security codes using the same cryptological techniques they use in breaking military codes," George explained. "I told you on the plane that he recruited some very hot types from the Department of Defense. He's even got some guys from the CIA. They raised hell with him. Gave him all kinds of flak. Barkley had to convince Washington that if he could do what he thought he could, it was a potential national disaster. More accurately, an international disaster."

She turned toward him, fascinated by what she had just

experienced. Not only was her fatigue temporarily banished by the way Twenty/Twenty had accepted her as a guest of the board, but she was impressed by what this small California company had been able to accomplish.

"It's a damn good thing Barkley's honest. He could have walked away with millions of dollars."

"When Barkley came to us with his idea, remember, it was still only an idea. Larry wanted to throw him out of the office. Cooper thought he was a stark raving lunatic. I didn't think he was a nut. He convinced me that most codes can be broken, especially where the key has to be shared by a large number of people.

"He kept talking about talent. If he could put together a small group of trained cryptologists and some far-out computer software guys who had the talent, he could do it. He could build a system that could break any bank's computer security code. If he could do that, he knew he could design and sell them a system to stop someone else from doing what he proved he could do."

George paused. "It was the screwiest deal I ever worked on. I was positive that if Barkley tried to recruit guys from the CIA and the Defense Department, they would lock him up. I can remember Barkley sitting in my office and smiling at me as if I were a hopeless idiot. I remember him saying, 'Not only won't they lock me up, but they'll help me. They don't want to see the major banks of this country exposed to the kind of larceny that could cause them to collapse.'

"I remember thinking to myself that if this guy could put together the group he's talking about, I would convince the firm to give him a shot."

She saw a sign that said Dunbarton Bridge. San Francisco, 35 miles. "But how did he do it?" she asked.

"He had some connections at Cambridge in England. Barkley was a Rhodes Scholar from Princeton, a math major who became interested in theoretical physics. Then he came back to Stanford for his doctorate. To support himself while he was getting his degree, he worked for Hewlett-Packard as a software consultant. While he was there, he opened an account with the Bank of the West. Electronic banking was really just getting started. Barkley's rather fertile imagination began to wonder what it would be like to have fun with the banks. He started this whole thing as a joke. It became a challenge to him and then an obsession. He became convinced that if he had access to sufficient computer time with the help of a few trained cryptologists, he could do it."

Liz stared out at the traffic moving with them, past the low, flat-roofed buildings of factories whose windows reflected the sun. Past small houses that tried to hide from the freeway behind dust-laden hedges and trees.

"Barkley had a hell of a time with the government," George went on. "He finally got to the secretary of defense through the president of Stanford. Barkley's a very convincing guy. He was finally able to attract two Defense Department guys and a guy from the CIA's code section in Maryland. These birds have access to classified information, and the government doesn't like to lose them. But it wasn't as if Barkley was trying to pull something on Uncle Sam. It was just the opposite. He convinced them, as he had me, that a system had to be built to defend the banks from the kind of exposure he knew they had.

"I finally talked Larry and Bob into a deal where we put up a quarter of a million, which we eventually raised to half a million. Then we borrowed a million and a half from an insurance company. The kicker was that if the insurance company converted their debentures, they'd own about ten percent of Twenty/Twenty's stock.

"Barkley and his brain trust locked themselves up in a small office they rented from the university. Stanford made them a good deal as far as computer time was concerned.

"Anyway, Barkley and his guys worked as if they were possessed. When these government fellows got their first whiff of pure capitalism, it became a real high for them. For the first time in their lives they had a shot at making some real dough, and they ate it up. When they weren't talking to bank security people, they were locked up in their office working on the Twenty/Twenty system. What you saw today was the result of four years of very hard work."

"Did we have to put up any more money to keep them going?"

"No. They were able to get some consulting contracts from the Bank of the West, who became interested in what they were doing."

"It's fascinating. Incredible, really."

He turned to look at her quickly. The traffic was getting heavier, especially in the southbound lanes. "It's what makes this business so exciting, Liz."

The signs began to read Bay Bridge and Downtown. They followed the left bound lane that said Golden Gate Bridge and got off at the Van Ness exit.

"You really know your way around here."

He smiled. "I should. I was raised in Hillsborough, which is about eighteen miles south of here. Barkley has a home there."

She was made aware of how little she really knew about George Hall. They had spent a good part of the last few weeks flying around the country together, but he had never been very revealing about himself. She was used to that. She was fairly taciturn herself. But she had the feeling that George was working hard to keep their relationship businesslike. She knew, though, that it wasn't going to work. The time was coming, she could feel it, when something would have to give. Would it be her?

Is that what I want? Is George what I want? she asked herself. It's too soon. Too fast. If the associates find out, they'll cut me to pieces. If Larry and Bob find out, they won't like it. Will I like it? Is George Hall what I want? What's the matter with me? I love Peter, but that won't work. I'm attracted to George, but it looks as if that won't work either. What is it with me?

He followed Van Ness to California Street and turned right. The car climbed the steep hills past Powell. He saw the Fairmont and turned left.

"Man, can I use a shower and a drink!" he said.

"I'll vote for that."

The doorman took their luggage, and they walked to the desk to register.

They were seated in the Skyroom of the Fairmont overlooking the darkened bay. The lights of the city were spread beneath them like scattered luminescent pearls.

He looked at her carefully as he toyed with the skewered olive in his martini. His eyes seemed dark and troubled in the low light of the room. The candle in its hurricane globe flickered yellow light at his face. He sighed audibly as he looked at her. "You feel like going out for dinner or eating here?"

"What have you got in mind?"

"If you like Chinese food we could go to the Mandarin. It's good, and the atmosphere isn't too touristy. It's on Ghirardelli Square."

She was watching him closely, aware that he had something on his mind. She was concerned about it.

He waited a long time before he said anything. When he did, his mouth was tense and he looked at her as if trying to probe her mind for his answers. His voice was low, hesitant.

"Liz, I'm wondering if we have a problem."

She waited. She didn't say anything.

"Maybe I'm the one who has a problem. I'm not sure."

She hesitated. "I don't understand, George."

He finished his martini and signaled the waitress for another. "Want some more wine?"

"I don't think so."

"How long can we go on like this? How long before I have to tell you how I feel? Before the other associates start rebelling against what they see as an obviously personal relationship? I am supposed to be giving them some attention too, you know."

"I know."

"How long before Larry and Bob . . . well, maybe not Bob, but certainly Larry . . . How long before he calls me in and wants a quiet little chat about what's going on between us?"

"I don't think you would have a difficult time explaining what has gone on with us, George. We've been working like hell."

"He knows that. They all know that. That's not what I'm talking about." He paused, looking at her, seeing her concern. Being attracted by the warm intelligent anxiety that was mixed with something detached, aloof, yet with an almost tangible femininity. A latent sensual quality that he was sure she didn't realize she had.

"Liz, let me say it for myself. I can't speak for you. But I'm getting damn tired of playing Father George. I'm not a monk. We're together more than most married people. We share the same profession. We speak each other's language. You're a very attractive woman, and I'm a man who responds to that."

He just looked at her. "When I hired you, Liz, I knew I was taking a chance. I knew this male-female thing would come up. I expected it to be a problem for the associates; I didn't expect it to be a problem for me."

He knew that wasn't quite true. He had been attracted to her from day one, and he had thought he could handle that. But now he was tired of handling it...

"George, I'm flattered."

"Don't say that. Don't give me that damn 'flattered' crap. That's a brush-off."

"I didn't mean it that way," she said.

He reached across the table and touched her hand. "I'm sorry. I didn't mean to jump all over you."

"It's okay." Her voice sounded remote, sad.

He let his hand rest on hers. "You know what we should do..."

"What?"

"Stop it."

"Stop what, George?"

His face flushed with anger. She could see it even in the candlelight. "Look, do I have to draw you pictures?"

"No, George," she said quietly. "You don't have to draw me any pictures. As a matter of fact I was wondering when this would come up."

"Why were you wondering?"

"For the same reasons you are." Her mouth became tense. "It's a shame, George, that this male-female thing has to intrude on a professional relationship."

"Has it intruded for you?"

She hesitated. "In a way it has. I'm aware of us together. You're a very attractive man. It may be easier for me because I have Peter..."

"Since when? You haven't seen him in weeks."

"It isn't always necessary to see someone, George."

"You mean you're really in love with this guy? I thought that was over. I thought you told me it wouldn't work."

She waited a long time before answering. She looked at the fog moving in over the black plain of the bay, shutting out the lights of Oakland. "George, my feelings for Peter are something special." She paused. "I don't think it will work. Peter and I can never marry. But that doesn't mean that my feelings for him have changed." Her voice became soft. "Perhaps when Peter meets someone else—but even then a part of me will always love him. You can love people in different ways, George. I don't believe that we go through our lives without finding someone we can care for deeply, but we don't have to make a marital commitment. Marriage isn't a safe where you deposit all your affections for a single person and then lock the door on everything and everyone else. I think relationships between men and women have to be more flexible than that, or we submerge ourselves, repress ourselves, and impose restrictions on one another."

"What are you trying to tell me?"

"Only that a part of me will always love Peter even though I choose to spend my life with another man."

He looked at her, watching her profile as she gazed out at the bay. "Liz," he said softly, "I told you on the plane that my rejection threshold is getting very low."

She turned toward him. Her eyes were soft and compassionate. "I'm not rejecting you, George, but I am telling you that I don't become involved easily, especially with my boss. I happen to agree with you. I think things are moving too quickly. I think it's bad policy as far as the firm—"

"The hell with the firm! I don't give a damn about the firm. I've given that firm fifteen hours a day five and often six days a week. And a hell of a lot of weekends in between. The firm has been my only real life. Work has been my life. That's all I've done. I'm getting damn sick and tired of it. I want to rest. I want to feel something for someone again and have that feeling returned. You can't make love to a balance sheet."

She watched him while he spoke. She could feel his loneliness and unhappiness reach out to her and she was surprised that she was so moved by him.

He finished his drink and signaled the waitress for the check.

"I wouldn't have this problem with Howard or Arthur."

She laughed. "I certainly hope not."

He got up and she stood up with him.

"Come on. I'll buy you dinner."

"I was hoping you'd say that soon. I'm absolutely starved."

They had eaten dinner with silent tension as an uninvited guest. The time change and the accompanying fatigue was beginning to get to them, but it was only 9:30 Pacific Time, although their bioclocks were still operating on New York time where it was after midnight. It had been a long day.

"I've never had diced squab before, especially served with rice rolled up in leaves of iced lettuce. It was a treat, George."

He paid the bill. "It's a specialty of the Mandarin." He looked at her and could sense her fatigue. "Are you game for one short side trip before we go back to the hotel?"

Her face was flushed from the bottle of Pinot Chardonnay they had drunk. She seemed tired but relaxed. She appeared less hesitant, less circumscribed by her anxieties for herself and for him. "I'm game."

"Good. I'll take you to Telegraph Hill. It's not far."

They rode the elevator from the Mandarin to street level and walked to the intersection of Bergen and North Point looking for their car.

"I have a lousy sense of direction."

"I think we turn left here, George. I think we parked near that gas station."

"It's a good thing I've got you with me. I might have to hire someone to find the car."

She laughed.

"Don't laugh. I actually had to do that once with Claudia. We were in Montreal. I left her for a meeting and told her I would meet her back at the car in about two hours. I was right as far as the time was concerned, but I couldn't remember where I parked the damn car. I actually had to stop some guy on the street and tell him my predicament. You know what he said?"

She shook her head.

"He said, 'Buddy. You don't need me. You need a priest.'"

It was out before she could stop it: "Was losing Claudia a form of wishful thinking, George?"

His laugh was laced with irony. "Maybe that should have given me a slight hint. It took me about forty minutes to find her. When I tried to explain what happened, she was mad as hell."

"She should have been."

"I guess she should have."

George and Liz found the car. He unlocked her side and opened the door for her. "Do you think you can find Telegraph Hill?" she asked.

He laughed. "I think I can."

• • •

He drove east to Columbus and turned up Lombard. As the car climbed the serpentine road that wound up to the top of the hill, she could see vistas of the city and the bay through the dark masses of leaves and the narrow separations between houses and apartments. They drove without speaking until they came to the parking area that was like an eagle's aerie hanging over the lights of the city. The enormous statue of Columbus stood black and imposing, silhouetted against the sky. They got out of the car and walked toward the low-walled perimeter of the viewing area.

"God, George, it's beautiful."

The stars had begun to prick feeble points of cold light through the rose darkness caused by the city's glow.

"There's Orion. Look there, George." She pointed at the faint constellation barely visible because of the lights of the city. "That's Cygnus, the Swan. And there. See those faint stars right there? Those are Lyra, and the bright blue-white star is Vega."

"The only one I can ever find is Polaris. But I can't see the dipper."

She laughed. "Better try looking to the north, George. You do have a lousy sense of direction. Right there. See the end of the cup. Look for the first bright star. It's barely visible."

"I've got it."

The air was soft and moist with the night breeze from the Pacific. Low patches of gray fog ghosted across the middle of the bay. She turned to the west and south to view the rest of San Francisco sprawled below her. She got up and stood on the low wall to get a better view over the tops of the trees. George stood beside her. The night breeze ruffled her hair. She felt his arm around her waist. She didn't resist; she didn't want to. He drew her toward him, and she nestled her head against his shoulder. They were oblivious to the other people who were equally enthralled at this jewel of a city spread beneath them, its lights like a million fireflies. They seemed to blend into the sky and stars. They were part of the magic of the night.

He could smell the light fragrance of her perfume. He could feel the strength and softness of her body beside him. He turned her slowly toward him and looked at her for a long time. He held her face in his hands and very gently kissed her. He felt her arms embrace him, her hands tentatively pressing against his back. "George . . ."

"Yes?"

Her voice was soft. "I think we have a problem."

He didn't speak. The pain he felt was an accentuation of the dull ache he had carried around with him for years, only now it had a focus. He could physically locate where it hurt.

"What are we going to do about it?" he asked quietly, still holding her.

She shook her head slowly, her voice as soft and as sad as the night wind. "I don't know," she said. "You're the boss."

They sat in his room at the hotel feeling a new awareness, a new frustration, a new pain. They sat silently in separate chairs, looking at each other. Finally she spoke: "George, I was thinking. Perhaps if you think it wise, I could follow up on this Haley thing. There is a lot of background work to do on Family Care and Teletherapy before I can present it to you or to BC." She hesitated. "I would be spending a fair amount of time in Boston . . ."

"With Peter?"

She looked at him with great compassion. "I would see Peter, yes." She hesitated. "It would give us time, George. It would look better at the firm. It would give me an opportunity to mend some fences with the other associates."

He looked at her for a long time before he spoke. "What would it give me?"

"A chance to find out . . . about us."

He stood up. "It's getting late."

She walked to the door. "Than it's okay if I get started on Family Care and the Teletherapy program?"

He nodded. "Make us a bundle, kid. Claudia needs the dough."

She stood in the open doorway of his room and looked at him for a very long time.

"Good night, George," she said softly. "Sleep well."

His face was a mask of irony. He held up his empty hand as if it contained a glass and did a lousy Bogart imitation: "'Here's looking at you, kid.'" She smiled sadly and very gently closed the door.

• • •

It had taken three days for her bioclock to readjust to New York time after her trip to the West Coast.

The radio alarm had sounded, and she rolled over in bed and looked at the red digital numbers of the clock. It was 7:00 A.M. She turned on the news and between commercials, the world came into focus.

She got up and went into the kitchen and automatically started to pour orange juice and prepare coffee in sonambulistic movements.

Her mind slowly fought its way out of the deep, fatigued sleep, and she began to think. Two subjects preoccupied her: George, and her relationship with the others in the firm.

She went into the bathroom and brushed her teeth. She found herself looking at her reflection in the mirror of the medicine cabinet. She had picked up some color from the sun on the Coast. She shook her head at her reflection. She stopped brushing her teeth to really look at herself, to analyze her physical appearance. She was never satisfied with what she saw.

Objectively, I guess I'm not unattractive. But my face is too long. My mouth is too large or my lips are too full. Eyes, not bad. Body, pretty good.

"Will you tell me what you're doing, Elizabeth?" she asked aloud of her reflection, gesticulating at herself with her toothbrush. "You must be cracking up." She rinsed the toothpaste from her mouth.

What am I going to do about George? she asked herself. How do I really feel about him?

She could hear the coffee percolating in the kitchen, and she could smell its aroma.

Am I attracted to him? she wondered. I guess I am. Why am I? Why the hell do I always have to be so analytical? she wondered, glaring at herself in the mirror. That's my problem, always searching for neat, precise answers when life doesn't have any neat precise answers. When am I going to learn to let things flow? Go with them instead of always trying to look ahead and plan.

She stepped back from the mirror still looking at her reflection. Still holding the toothbrush and staring at the angular face that looked back at her.

That was the core of her problem with men; she knew that. Every time she met an attractive man, she began building barriers that interfered with the relationship. Now she was starting the same thing with George. She put the toothbrush in the white porcelain holder and turned on the shower. She adjusted the water temperature until it was hot. She removed her nightgown and got into the shower.

"God that's hot!" She stepped away from the stream of water and then, as her skin became adjusted to its temperature, she backed into it. As she began lathering her body, she felt the first tracings of erotic thoughts. She was back to George.

There we were, she thought, in one of the most beautiful cities in the world on a night that only God could have painted for us, and George wanted me.

And what did I do? I wanted him. He needed me. He was reaching out for me, but oh, no. Not me. Not good old cool Liz. No screwing around with the boss for me. Right? Wrong! Who would have known? What harm would it have done?

I knew what harm it would have done, she said to herself. It would have started something I might not have been able to control . . .

Control, control. Plan, plan. My whole life has been planned. When do I stop planning and start being a woman? I want to love someone and have someone love me. Is that too much to ask?

She reached for the shampoo and began lathering her hair. She could smell its faint lemon scent.

What about George? she asked herself. Is he just lonely? Is he really attracted to me? Is it more than just a physical attraction? Now stop. Let's look at this thing objectively. There I go again. Must everything be objective with me? In this case I think it must. He's my boss. He's terribly upset with Claudia. I wonder what really happened between those two.

She rinsed the shampoo from her hair and squeezed in some conditioner.

Claudia can't be as miserable a bitch as George claims, she thought. He must have loved her once. What happened to them? Her thoughts of George led her to think about the office, and she began to feel uneasy.

I've got to reestablish some relationships at that office. George has isolated me from Curt, Arthur, and Howard, and the chill factor in that place is like the dark side of the moon. That's not good. Larry picks up everything. I'm sure he thinks George and I are spending too much time together. I can sense that he doesn't like the friction between the other associates and me. I'm doing it again, she thought, analyzing every damn thing to death. I have a morbid tendency to spoil things for myself. I worry too much, and I'm too damn logical.

She rinsed the conditioner from her hair and stepped out of the shower. She wrapped a towel around her head, quickly fashioning it into a turban, then wrapped another towel around her body. She opened the door and felt the cool, dry air from the air conditioner in her bedroom. She put on a robe and sat down at her dressing table looking at herself in the oval wood framed mirror. She removed the towel and started combing her wet hair.

I've got to do something to break the ice in that office or I'm going to isolate myself so completely that the only ones who will be talking to me are George, Larry, and Bob . . . But what's wrong with that? They run the firm.

I can't do that. Something about a house divided . . . She put down the comb and began vigorously brushing her wet hair.

I really don't know how I feel about George. I'm attracted to him. And why not? He's a very attractive man. There's something sad about him, too. It takes the edge off what might be an unbridled materialism.

She sighed, disgusted with herself. If she kept up this kind of introspection with every man she met, she would never settle for any of them. She would just work and earn money. She *was* going to earn money, lots of it. But was that what life was all about? She couldn't snuggle up to her bank account, no matter how healthy it was.

She began to blow dry her hair. I've got to do something about the associates. I'll give a party, she thought. Not a party party, but a work party. I'll let them in on Family Care and Teletherapy. I'll invite them down here to discuss it and get some of their ideas. It will accomplish several things. It will let them in on a project George specifically handed to me. That should take some of the sting out of that, if I really seek their advice. They're bright, and they might really be able to help. They've got more experience than I have. They know that. Maybe that will reduce their resentment a little. And if we can have a good time while doing all this . . . Lots of booze and a good meal . . . They'll see me cooking a meal for them. A little servility does wonders for the male ego.

She looked at herself in the mirror, smiling. You are a smart lady, Liz. That's truly inspired. I'm going to charm the asses off those three chauvinists. After all, when have only three men ever really been a challenge for a smart girl? "Come on," she said to herself as she turned off the dryer and started combing her hair. "We're going to have an ice-breaking party." She laughed aloud as she looked at herself in the mirror.

Chapter 14

IT WAS A HOT night in August, and the air conditioners in her living room and bedroom were barely adequate to keep the people at the party comfortable.

She had decided on a filet of beef as being easy and quick, but she had forgotten about the oven. The heat from the kitchen was drifting into the living room and had forced them to remove their jackets.

They stood in the small living room watching her work quickly and efficiently in the kitchen. The dining room, which was really an extension of the living room, looked festive. The table was set with a bowl of fresh flowers in the center. The candles were lit, and the wineglasses sparkled in the soft yellow light.

They watched her as she tossed the salad in the large wooden bowl. She was wearing a sleeveless aqua silk dress with a low neck and a single strand of cultured pearls. Her skin was still lightly tanned from the California sun. When she stood erect, they could see her broad shoulders tapering to a narrow waist. Her breasts pressed against the soft fabric. They watched her long beautifully slim legs. In her bone-colored pumps with their medium heels she looked even taller than usual. Not one of them could help looking at her. She saw it and felt it and glowed with the satisfaction of knowing she was being watched and admired by three men. Her particular pleasure was in the fact that she was the sole woman. She had them all to herself.

They had each brought a small gift. Curt, a bottle of fine French wine. Howard, a small ceramic cigarette box. Arthur, a pot of African violets, which particularly pleased her.

Curt stood at the edge of the dining room, watching her as she deftly timed the meal, removing the filet from the oven with the baked potatoes, and turning the burner off under the pot of sliced carrots. She looked up at him and smiled. "Not too bright of me. I should have planned a salad in this heat." The small exhaust fan in the kitchen labored ineffectively at extracting the warm, humid air.

"How did you ever find this place?" Curt asked.

"Not easily."

Howard and Arthur were drinking gin and tonics in the living room watching Curt with Liz.

Curt was almost too handsome, she thought. He had light blond hair which he wore somewhat long, and his features were sharp, well-defined, as if someone had sculptured his face. He was also urbane, very sure of himself with women, with an aloofness that she could feel, as if he were holding up one hand to keep others at bay when they came too close. She realized for the first time what it was about him that she didn't like; what she hadn't been able to put her finger on when she first met him. It was that combination of assurance in his own physical attractiveness and the cool, detached, hard core of protected self-interest that she knew was there. Curt lacked the capacity to love, she had decided—probably prematurely, and inaccurately. But that was her initial impression, and it hadn't changed in three months. She looked up at him and smiled. She placed the filet on the carving board.

"Curt, be a dear and carve for me, would you?"

"Of course." He smiled at her as if he had been asked to take the helm of a ship.

She placed the carrots and potatoes on four plates.

"Hey, fellas, this is a working party, remember?" she joked to Arthur and Howard. "Would you come in and serve the salad for me?"

"Our muse calls," Howard said to Arthur. They put down their drinks and came into the kitchen.

She squeezed past them, giving them her warmest smile. She looked directly at Howard, her fingers touching his arm.

"Would you help Curt get everything on the table and pour the wine? I'll be right back."

Howard watched her as she went into the bedroom. He acknowledged his silent envy of George. She was damn attractive, he thought, and no one had to tell him, especially him, how bright she was. Howard was still looking at her closed bedroom door when Arthur nudged him with his elbow. "Come on, champ. Orders from Her Majesty are to get dinner on the table." Arthur saw Howard's suppressed attraction. He laughed. "You want to follow her in there, chum? Forget it. That's the private preserve of our lord and master. You lay a finger on that Cliffie and I suspect Uncle George will cut your balls off, and you won't even hear them drop." He watched Howard's jaw muscles tighten as he turned reluctantly to help.

They were on their third bottle of wine. Though their varying degrees of hostility toward her were receding, there was still an antipathy toward her because of her relationship with George, which they felt was not based soley on her ability. The nucleus of their resentment remained, but it had been contained by the maneuver of this party. The wine eased their reserve.

She had seated them so that there was no head of table. She sat next to Howard, who would be the hardest to win over; she deliberately wanted him close to her. Curt and Arthur faced them from the opposite side of the small oval dining table.

They had removed their ties, and the conversation took a bantering tone. Their mood was lightened by the considerable amount of alcohol they were consuming. They were becoming collectively plastered.

"This is my first work party, Liz. I think your innovation should become standard procedure. It's a hell of a lot better than the meetings George holds."

She laughed. "Thank you, Arthur. I'm inclined to agree."

"Liz, I can't tell if you're coming up in the world or going down." Curt pointed to the legs of a woman and a man whom they could see through the living room window. The woman was standing on tiptoes, one leg bent in an *L* shape behind her. The legs of the man were pressed solidly against the one leg on which she stood.

"Someone's not having any work party out there," he said, looking out the window.

"You're damn right."

"This view of yours must give you a different perspective on life, Liz. You must be an authority on feet and legs."

They all laughed. Curt poured the last of the wine.

Howard looked at her. "Is there some latent impulse toward podiatry in your family, Liz?" Howard had turned his chair sideways so that he could see Liz more easily, and also to better observe the couple on the street.

"Look at that. What's he doing?"

"Stop panting, Arthur. You're just envious," Curt said.

"You're damn right I'm envious. That guy is trying to screw her right on the street!"

"How can you tell? All you can see are her legs."

"Yeah. And now they're both off the ground!"

Liz had turned to watch the pantomime that was taking place on the street. She couldn't believe what she saw.

"Who's got ten that says the little tart will wrap her legs around the gentleman?"

"I'll cover your ten, Curt," Howard said. "She's probably got pantyhose on."

"Put your glasses on, Howard. I don't think the lady is wearing anything under her denim ensemble."

The legs moved closer to Liz's building, pressing against her low, rectangular living room windows.

"Jesus Christ, there she goes," Arthur said, pointing toward the woman's legs, which had wrapped themselves around the man's waist.

"I don't believe it," Howard said.

Liz was as fascinated by the sexual ballet that was going on outside her window as the men were, but at the same time she was embarrassed by this male entourage who understandably had almost completely forgotten her in their absorption and incredulity at what was happening on the street.

"Howard, you just lost your ten."

The girls' legs came down slowly as her feet touched the sidewalk. Her legs trembled. The two pair of legs were now pressed closely together. The girl's legs suddenly left the ground again in another unexpected explosive leap.

"Holy Christ, there she goes again!"

They were all standing now, moving over toward the living room window.

"You can see better on the floor."

Howard and Arthur crouched on the floor looking up at the street. Curt kept looking at Elizabeth, whose face was scarlet.

"This is like an X-rated movie! It's unbelievable!" Arthur shouted.

"Hey, Curt, you've got to see this. Come on over here!"

"If you two voyeurs don't mind, I'd prefer to remain with our hostess." Curt hadn't taken his eyes off Liz. He realized that the sudden imposition of events on the street had not only interrupted her party, but had probably thwarted what was obviously a carefully orchestrated attempt at reconciliation.

"Will you two drag your corrupt minds and bodies back to the table? You're not being very gallant."

The legs started to move away.

"Aw, hell, they're going." Howard and Arthur got up.

"You owe me ten, Howard." Curt held out his hand.

"Later."

"Not later. Now. After that display of your true character I want cash on the line."

Howard handed Curt ten dollars. He turned to Liz. "Do you often have entertainment like this for your guests, Liz? If you do, we could syndicate this place and turn it into an X-rated restaurant."

"Okay, Howard, knock it off." Arthur said, looking at Liz, whose expression was a mixture of embarrassment and anger.

"I think we'd better get to the *work* part of this work party," she said quietly.

"I'm sorry, Liz. It's just . . . well, I've never seen anything like that before."

"How about the dishes? We'll clear the table for you."

"No, Arthur. Leave them. I'll do them."

"It will give us more room to work. You sit down. We'll take care of it," he said contritely.

"Come on, Liz. Let them do penance. They deserve it," Curt said.

Curt took Liz's hand and led her toward the sofa. Arthur and Howard cleared the table and stacked the dishes. When they had finished, Liz got up. "I don't think I can follow an act like that, but I did ask you three to dinner to get your advice on a deal I'll be working on." She looked at them. "What do you say we go to work?"

"Pay for our supper?"

"Something like that, Howard."

"After a floor show like that, we should pay you."

"Arthur, try to clear that puerile brain of yours. Let's hear what Liz wants to discuss," Curt said.

Arthur nodded. "You know, Curt, I'm beginning to agree with Howard."

Curt smiled. "My charm is pervasive. I can't help it."

They seated themselves around the dining table. This time, Liz sat at its head.

She looked around the table at each of them. Their collective expressions were a languid attempt at concentration brought on by three bottles of wine, and the dissipation of energy after the performance they had just witnessed. They were like three slowly deflating balloons. Liz felt like the schoolmistress on the first day back from summer vacation about to ask her reluctant class to describe how they had spent their summer. The absurdity of the scene suddenly struck her, and she began to laugh. Not a polite chuckle, but a boisterous, rolling laugh freed by the wine she had drunk. Their faces showed collective surprise, and then a slow appreciation of her abandon. They began to laugh with her, all of them, even Curt. The small room rocked as the contagious laughter spread. Liz's head was on her forearm on the table, and she was slapping the table, her body convulsed, wracked by laughter.

"Oh, God! Oh, sweet Jesus," she gasped. It was absurd trying to work after drinking so much wine, after the explosion, like summer lightning of the erotic scene on the street. Her carefully planned evening had been completely turned around, as if by a wild, unexpected shift of wind. But even in her convulsive laughter she realized that she had accomplished her purpose. The ice had very definitely been broken. Now they almost seemed like soldiers, comrades who had been under fire together. They had shared a unique experience that none of them would ever forget, and their laughter, at least for that evening, bound them together in camaraderie.

"Hear ye! Hear ye!" Liz swayed slightly as she slapped the table with her hand.

"This screwed-up meeting—"

"It was certainly screwed," Arthur shouted.

Uproarious laughter.

"It was a fucked-up meeting." More laughter.

Howard was convulsed. He hammered on the table with his fist. "Will you raunchy bastards give Madam Chairwoman a chance to speak for chrissake."

Howard stood up, holding on to the table. "Mr. Speaker, the chairwoman of the meeting wishes to speak. Will the not so honorable members of this house do her the courtesy of permitting her to do so?"

"Speak! Speak! Speak!" They started to clap and stamp their feet. She was still laughing.

"Dishonorable members. The chairwoman of this house . . . Oh, God!" She clasped her hands to her breast. The pain in her sides from laughter was like a torn muscle. "The chairwoman declares this meeting adjourned. Who wants another drink?"

They were all on their feet cheering, clapping, roaring their approval.

How she ever got them to leave she didn't know. They stumbled up the stairs singing and laughing. The cab she had called was waiting for them, the driver eyeing them with mixed emotions.

"I don't want any trouble, lady."

"Don't worry. They're fine."

Their addresses brought the driver some small comfort. They were all clustered about the cab. Elizabeth pointed to Curt. "Handsome, here, goes to Sixty-eighth and First Avenue. And this one"—she pointed to Howard—"goes to Sixty-first between Lexington and Third. And this one"—she pointed to Arthur—"goes to Brooklyn Heights." She smiled at the cab driver. "You figure it out."

"Hold it. Hold it." Arthur pushed them all aside and put his arms around Liz. "A kiss for the most screwed-up party I've ever been to."

Gales of laughter. Shouts.

"Hey, you guys better lower it. It's three in the morning. You gonna have the cops here," the cabbie said.

"Kiss. Kiss for Madam Chairwoman." They all crowded around Liz. Arthur embraced her and kissed her full on the mouth.

"Get away from my girl," Howard said and put his arms around Liz and kissed her.

"You American oafs disgust me," Curt said. He pulled Howard away from Liz and held her face in his hands and looked at her for a long time. "You're a hell of a girl, Madam Chairwoman." He kissed her on the cheek. "I'll be back for more, madam. I can assure you of that."

"Over my dead body you will."

"Get in the cab, Howard," Curt said.

They all piled into the cab, their arms waving to her through the open windows.

"Great party!"

"Best fucking party I ever went to." They all roared.

The bewildered cabbie turned quickly in the narrow street and burned rubber toward Sixth Avenue.

Liz was weak, exhausted from laughter. The street was now quiet. She entered her apartment and locked and bolted the door.

How was she ever going to go to that office tomorrow? How would they go? My God. They would never make it.

She stood in the living room looking around her, surveying the debris from the party. Well, I wanted to break the ice, she thought. It's pretty well broken now. Her mind replayed the scene of the unknown girl whose legs had suddenly wrapped themselves around her lover. She shook her head. That one unexpected moment, as violent and surprising as a mugging, had changed her relationships with the associates more effectively than anything she could have planned.

"Arthur was right. It was the best fucking party I ever had." She laughed weakly to herself and went into her bedroom for what she hoped would be five hours of deep sleep.

Chapter 15

GEORGE WALKED INTO her office and stood looking at her. She was oblivious to him standing there. She sat with her elbows on her desk, her head supported by her hands. Her hair hung like a copper curtain, hiding her face.

George watched her for several moments.

"I assume by the fact that you're sitting up that you haven't died."

She turned slowly and looked at him, her face pale, grimacing with each word he uttered as if she were recoiling from pellets of sleet. She held up one long finger against her lips. "Shush, George, please. Not so loud. I have a splitting headache."

"Are you all right? You're not sick?"

"No. No," she whispered. "I've just taken some Excedrin. I'll be okay in a while. I just need a little time."

George sat down in Curt's chair. "It must be an epidemic. I saw Howard and Arthur earlier this morning and they looked like . . ." He paused. "As a matter of fact, they looked like you. Would you mind telling me what's going on around here?"

"George, please. Softly. Softly. I've got a big bell clanging in my head."

He looked at her sharply. "What you've got looks to me like one beast of a hangover."

She nodded. "You might say that," she whispered, turning

171

away from him and resting her head against the palms of her hand.

"And those other three guys. Curt came into my office ten minutes ago looking as if he'd spent the summer in a cellar in Moscow. What is it with the associates in this firm? Have I hired a bunch of alcoholics?"

"Shhhh. Please, George. Softly."

"Liz, what in hell have the four of you been doing?"

"Party."

"It must have been some party."

She nodded. "Believe me it was."

He looked at her for several moments, trying to make up his mind if he was annoyed with her or if he felt sorry for her.

"Liz, I hate to intrude on the aftermath of your social life, but we have a problem."

She held up her hand. "Please, George. No problems this morning. I just can't handle any problems this morning."

"Liz, I'm sorry that all four of you got smashed last night, but I'm afraid that's your problem. The firm has a problem, or at least the beginning of one, so I hope you're lucid enough to listen. You don't have to respond; just listen. Make sure to sigh or something every once in a while so that I know you haven't fallen asleep."

She could hear his tone becoming annoyed, sarcastic. She couldn't blame him. This was a business office, and she was in no shape to discuss business.

Why do I drink wine? she thought. Wine gives me such a lousy hangover. Why don't I just drink scotch. Oh, the hell with it.

George's voice sounded like a bell clanging through a thick fog. "Liz, you're still conscious enough to recall that you're a guest of the board of Twenty/Twenty."

She nodded. The curtain of hair again hid her face.

"Since you'll be representing me on that board, it might be interesting for you to know that the illustrious chairman of that kooky little company hasn't been seen in three days."

"So?" she mumbled.

"So, I got a call yesterday afternoon from Sol Masters. I hope you're able to recall the cherubic and harried vice-president of finance of Twenty/Twenty."

She nodded.

"Sol sounded very concerned over the phone. He says that

our esteemed chairman Barkley hasn't been showing up at the office lately, and has been seen squiring a black TV newscaster around San Francisco."

"So?"

"So. Sol tells me this girl is an absolute knockout and that our Barkley is not only getting his name in the papers, but worse, he's fallen in love."

Liz turned to look at George, trying hard not to show her annoyance.

"Would you please enlighten me, George, as to why any of this should be part of my morning briefing? Why is any of this important? Or more to the point, why is any of it our business? Barkley's love life is his own affair."

"Not quite, Liz." George paused. "I don't have to remind you that we are working to put together a common stock offering for Twenty/Twenty."

"I know. I know," she said, unable to hide her exasperation at being told information she already knew.

"We think we can get that stock off, if the market holds at somewhere around twenty-five dollars."

She nodded.

"We're thinking of selling five million shares. That's a hundred twenty-five million dollars. We control about forty percent of the stock if we exercise our warrants. I've spoken to Baldwin and Cooper, and they want to sell twenty million dollars' worth of our shares if everything goes all right." He looked at her as she turned toward him, the sun from the window backlighting her hair. He could see the Excedrin was having an effect. She was beginning to look a little better. He knew, too, that the numbers were impressive enough to get her attention.

"Since you are now our representative on the board of that august company, I might tell you that Twenty/Twenty is one of the most lucrative deals this firm has ever had. I can assure you that Larry and Coop don't want to see anything happen to blow it."

"What could happen?"

George's lips tightened. "Liz, you know the company. You know the business they're in. Their client list, which seems to be increasing daily, includes some of the largest and most prestigious institutions in the country." He paused and gave her an acerbic glance. "How do you think it looks to the top executives of Barkley's client banks to have him photographed in the San Francisco *Post* with—"

"George, that's outrageous," Liz said, interrupting him. "Barkley's company sells a service that a great many banks buy. They are paying for the expertise of Twenty/Twenty; they won't care whom Barkley chooses to squire."

"Liz, you do have a hangover, and it's affecting your judgment. Barkley is selling computer security systems to banks. He has a very nervous clientele who know that his company can penetrate their computer codes."

"But Twenty/Twenty's sole purpose, George, is to sell the banks its system which, according to Barkley and the banks, is unbreakable."

"True. But banks get very nervous about two things: bad loans and lax security. It's only natural. They are responsible for a great deal of money that belongs to their depositors."

"Isn't all this a little undergraduate, George? I'm fully aware of the role of banks."

"And are you also aware, Liz, that it takes a long time to gain a bank's confidence, and a very short time to lose it?"

"I'm aware of that."

"And how do you think the senior executives of major banks will respond to seeing Barkley with this woman?"

"If she's attractive enough, they might be jealous."

"Will you cut that out, Liz? They won't be jealous. They'll think Barkley has gone off the deep end. Not all of them have your liberal Harvard outlook. These are some of the most conservative people in business."

"In their personal lives?"

"Their personal lives are their own business."

"I rest my case."

"Goddamn it, Liz, will you stop that! You know what I'm talking about, and you know that I'm right. I don't create the prejudices of people, but they exist. Barkley is threatening to blow a hell of a lot of work, and he'll blow our deal, too, if he doesn't stop screwing around in public. And you don't know half of it. Sol says that he punched some guy in a restaurant in San Francisco because of a remark the guy had made about his date. Sol says the woman had to use every bit of influence she had to keep it out of the papers and off the tube." George paused. "There's more."

Liz sighed.

"Well, at least I know you haven't fallen asleep."

"I'm all ears."

"I hope so, because the story doesn't get better. Sol says that Barkley has been bringing the girl back to Hillsborough. That's a big no-no. Hillsborough is definitely an all-white community. They don't cotton to blacks much."

"Are you playing *Uncle Tom's Cabin?*"

He smiled. "I thought you'd like that." He paused to look at her.

"Liz. Sol says Barkley is holding some very kinky parties in a town house he owns on Russian Hill in San Francisco."

"What's Sol's idea of kinky?"

"Booze. Drugs. And black women."

Liz paused. Her lips compressed as she thought about it. Her headache was clearing, and so was her mind. "It's a shame. An absolute shame."

"What?"

She looked at George with that cool detachment he had come to know and respect.

"That an adult as gifted as Barkley and a woman who must be bright, well-educated, and attractive can't live their lives in peace because one of them happens to have skin of a different color." She paused. "Tell me something, George. Suppose I were black. Would you have come to Harvard to recruit me?"

She watched the expression on his face change. She saw his initial shock, then the quick contrition, and just as swiftly, a truculent resistance to her questioning. He remained silent, looking at her.

"You know, George, that's something I've noticed about our firm. We have no blacks. None. How do we get away with that under the equal opportunity law?" She watched the annoyance in his eyes.

"When we find a bright person who is interested in our business, who has the social graces we need, and who ranks not lower than tenth in a business school class at Harvard, Dartmouth, Stanford, Chicago, or Columbia, we'll recruit that person, and we won't give a damn whether he or she is black, green, or yellow."

She was looking at him with those steady cobalt eyes. "Is that really true, George? If we find a black like that, will this firm hire him—or her?"

She watched his annoyance grow. "Liz, I'm not going to

spend any more time defending this firm's attitude toward minorities. I'm not interested in that, now. I'm interested in not blowing twenty million dollars."

Liz was beginning to get the point. She knew in the expedient world in which they lived that he was right. George was telling it like it was. She found herself shaking her head, her emotions fluctuating from disgust to guilt and then to shame.

Why should I feel culpable? Because if I had the guts to back up my principles, she thought as she watched the light play on George's face, I wouldn't work for a firm as prejudiced as this one. She sighed at her own involuntary acquiescence to the discrimination that was basically so tragic and so unfair. The Jews. The blacks. The Asians. Only we WASPs don't have to think about the incredible inequities people impose on one another.

He watched her face as he knew her mind was probing the ramifications of what he had just told her. He had come to understand her more with each passing week. That Yankee pride and stubbornness of hers. The integrity that everyone in the firm had come to respect. It was hard to conceive of her doing anything dishonest or unkind. And yet he knew she was no Mother Teresa. She was bright, motivated, tough, and very much a woman. But she was a principled human being, and of her many attractions, he found this the most meaningful and the most enduring.

His tone softened. "Look, Liz, I know you've had a rough night, but I want to impress on you the seriousness of this thing.

"I put you on the board of Twenty/Twenty to be my eyes and ears. In this firm you are increasingly becoming more closely associated with that company." He looked at her with affection. "Liz, Twenty/Twenty is my deal, but I don't have the time to be on deck the way you do. I've put you on that board for all the reasons you know, and"—his voice lowered— "and perhaps a few you don't know. If the deal is a success, I will get the credit for it in the firm. If Barkley blows up this deal, I could switch the focus from *me* to *you* on what would be a tremendous loss of profit for the firm."

He watched her shocked expression. It was as if he had slapped her face. He sat down at Curt's desk and rolled the desk chair toward her on its thick, transparent plastic mat. He touched her arm briefly.

"For God's sake, Liz. I would never do that to you. But we're playing hardball for very high stakes. In another firm, where your relationship to someone like me was purely business, you could get body-checked in a deal like this in a minute. In our racket, Liz, when the shit hits the fan, everyone hits the deck. All I'm trying to tell you is that with you on the board of Twenty/Twenty, if they have a problem you've got a problem."

As she watched him, listened to him, it was beginning to sink in. He was warning her, trying to protect her. And she knew intuitively that what he was telling her was true.

"What do you want me to do?"

He looked at her carefully. "When are you planning to go to New England on Family Care?"

"I was going to set the trip up for Thursday and Friday if that's convenient for Tim. I thought I'd spend the weekend with my mother. It's been weeks since I've seen her."

He waited a long time before saying it. He knew he shouldn't bring it up. "And Peter? You'll be seeing Peter?"

"Yes, George," she said softly. "I will be seeing Peter, if he can get away."

George's expression hardened. He waited a long time before he spoke. His eyes were looking directly into hers, searching for what he hoped to find. What he found was empathy and understanding. He wanted more than that.

"When you get back from Boston, I want you to go to San Francisco and find out what's going on out there."

"Isn't that a bit bizarre? Is this a venture capital firm or a detective agency? What right do I have to poke into Barkley's private life?"

His voice became harder. "Every right in the world. To protect this deal and our dough. And I'm telling you, Liz, in no uncertain terms, that you'd better damn well handle whatever is going on out there."

"But why me? You said yourself that this is your deal. You've known Barkley for nearly five years. I've known him for less than two months."

He waited a long time before answering her. He got up and walked over to the large twin windows that overlooked Sixth Avenue. He saw the crowds moving in the August heat that would be stifling by late afternoon. His mind wasn't focused on the rectangular steel and glass boxes that followed one after the other up the avenue like gigantic blocks carefully placed by some great unimaginative hand. He turned toward her. She could see his resignation and the determination with which he was looking at her.

"I want you to see Barkley because you're a woman. Barkley likes women. He respects your intelligence and your tact, or he never would have agreed to have you sit on his board. I think you can be far more effective with him than anyone else in this firm, including Larry and me." He paused. His voice still had an edge to it. "I know Barkley. He'll respond to a woman far more quickly than to any man."

She looked at him, trying to suppress her anger. "And just what am I supposed to do?"

"Find out if what Sol is telling us is accurate. If it is, then find a way to handle it."

"Are you kidding? How in God's name am I supposed to interfere in Barkley's private life?"

"I haven't the faintest idea, Liz." He paused and looked at her with taut purpose. "But you're our best shot. And Liz . . ." he paused.

"What?"

"You'd better come through on this one."

He started to leave the room but stopped in the doorway. He turned to look at her. "Have a good time in New England. That Family Care deal sounds as if it could be interesting. I'd like to hear more about it when you get back." He paused. "Maybe we could talk about it over dinner."

She felt a smoldering resentment at this imposition, this intrusion into the life of another. But the pragmatic part of her mind told her that George was right. At the moment she found little that appealed to her about George, but she knew that feeling would pass. She knew, too, that he was making her play ball in the major leagues, and she was his star rookie. It was a clutch situation, but that was what this business was all about; this game she had chosen to play. That was its perverse excitement, its lure.

"We'll see about dinner, George," she said coolly, and she watched him as he silently left the room.

Chapter 16

THERE WAS HARDLY time on the short flight to Boston for her to collect her thoughts. She scanned the *New York Times* and the *Wall Street Journal* quickly, out of habit, but her mind had not absorbed what she had read. Part of her was still in New York with George.

He seemed so strange to me, distant, she thought. Was it because I told him I would be seeing Peter? She found herself wanting to believe that was the reason for his truculence. She knew that George could be all business, that he could be abrupt and sarcastic, unfeeling. When he was like that, even his language changed. He seemed to become a different person, but then she knew she was like that herself. There was a cold-blooded side to both their characters.

Why do I feel so sad? she wondered. Am I depressed because I was disappointed in George's reaction to me? Am I that dependent on his approval? Does he mean more to me than I realize?

She wondered why she said she would *think* about having dinner with him. She wanted to have dinner with him. She wanted to be with him. She shook her head as she stared out the window at the white puffs of cumulus clouds below her. She could feel the plane slowing for its descent into Logan Airport.

Why wasn't she more excited about seeing Peter? It had

been weeks since they had been together. Why did George and Peter keep getting mixed up in her mind? Was it because they were like the two parts of her mind that seemed so conflicting? Was Peter the compassionate part of her and George the businesslike side?

The Boeing 727 banked sharply left as it rapidly lost altitude. She could see the cluster of towers of the new Boston. The morning sun reflected fiercely off the glass facade of the John Hancock Building, sending spears of light across the city that was a blend of old red brick and new concrete and steel. The tires squealed as they touched down.

Her thoughts switched to Tim who would be waiting for her at the gate. For some reason, her mind blended Tim with Barkley. How in hell am I supposed to handle that? she wondered. George, you've put me in an impossible position. What am I supposed to do? Fly out to San Francisco and have dinner with Barkley and say, Nicholas old boy, you're screwing up our deal. We've got twenty million dollars riding on you, Nicholas, and your rather peculiar choice of female companion—a black, Nicholas . . . a black, you dumb bastard. Can't you see how that looks to those reactionary bank clients of yours, Nicholas? Knock off seeing her, Nicholas . . .

How's that, George? she thought. Is that what you want me to say to Barkley? She sighed audibly as she thought of the distasteful assignment George had given her.

"Ladies and gentlemen," a voice interrupted. "For your own safety and comfort, the captain requests that you remain seated until we are parked at the gate." The mechanical voice of the flight attendant grated on her ears. She picked up her handbag and waited to join the line of impatient passengers who were anxious to deplane.

As she walked to the gate she thought of Peter. Now that I'm here, now that we are finally going to be together after all this time, why don't I feel more excited? Why haven't I ever learned to take emotional advantage of what's happening to me? Why does my pleasure seem to come in anticipating things rather than from their actuality?

She saw Tim Haley towering over the crowd at the gate area.

God, he's huge. I had forgotten how big he is.

He saw her, and his face broke into a wide grin. He looked

tan and handsome in an off-white linen jacket with an open-necked light blue sport shirt. The last thing in the world she would have thought this giant to be was a psychiatrist.

"Good to see you, Liz. Great that you could come up."

He took her elbow in his great hand and guided her through the terminal.

"You have baggage?"

"Yes."

"We'll go get it. Then what do you want to do? Check in at the Ritz first and then go out to Family Care? I've reserved a suite for you."

"You needn't have done that, Tim. A bedroom would have been fine."

He laughed, that deep bass rolling-thunder laugh of his. "Have to butter up my venture capitalist."

It grated on her. He had said it jokingly, but she knew there was some truth to it. She had to remember that this man's profession was looking into the minds of people, at times shaping their personalities. She had to make sure he wasn't going to influence the objectivity of her examination of his company.

They picked up her baggage, and he guided her to the parking area. "Have a good flight?"

"It's so short you can hardly call it a flight."

"You're right. It's just one parabolic curve. A climb and a let down."

She nodded.

They walked through the labyrinth of the parking garage.

"Here we are," he said.

Her astonishment showed. There was no way to hide it. He was opening the door of a sky blue convertible Rolls Royce. She had never ridden in a Rolls before. She knew that this car cost over one hundred thousand dollars. That was outrageous, she thought. The incredible ostentation of the car collided with every one of her conservative Yankee genes.

"You like it?"

"Why, yes. It's magnificent."

He glowed with pride. "Here, get in. We'll put the top down. It's a beautiful day."

It's going to be hotter than Hades with the top down, she thought.

She got into the car. The glove leather seats felt like human skin. Tim pressed a button and the top silently folded back. She felt herself bathed in cool dry air.

"The air conditioning. We can get the sun and stay cool at the same time."

"I knew doctors lived well," she said, "but I didn't think they lived this well." She made a mental note to find out if this was a company car. She would bet a month's salary that it was, and if it was, it said a lot about how Dr. Haley ran his company. It wasn't a good omen. It implied extravagance in the use of company funds, and that was never a good sign when you were a potential investor, as BC would be if they decided to raise money for Family Care.

If Tim Haley wanted to make an impression on her, he was certainly off to the wrong start.

The car glided out of the parking garage and into the traffic that flowed toward the Callahan Tunnel, which would take them into the heart of downtown Boston.

"This car, Liz, is an expression of my philosophy of life."

Jesus. He's reading me again. I forgot how he can do that. It's uncanny. She trembled involuntarily at his almost mystical ability to know what she was thinking.

"This car may seem ostentatious, but actually it's a very good investment. These cars are worth more used than they are new. Rolls makes so few convertibles. There is such a long waiting list for them that I could sell this car in a day and get more than I paid for it. In the meantime, I have the pleasure of enjoying its opulence." He looked at her and smiled. He sensed her reticence, her struggle to disprove his logic, which she couldn't do. But she still made a mental note to find out who owned this car—Tim Haley or Family Care.

"Why don't we go to the Ritz-Carlton first as long as we're downtown?" he suggested. "You can get settled, and then we'll go out to Family Care."

She chuckled to herself. If Peter and Mom could see me now in a Rolls convertible going to my suite at the Ritz!

"What are you thinking?" he asked.

"Just how extravagant you're making my stay in Boston."

"Relax. Enjoy it. You deserve it. Believe me, Liz, you can get used to this kind of living in a hurry."

"I don't doubt it."

The suite he had reserved for her was like the car. Too

expensive and unnecessary. It overlooked the Boston Gardens and the Common beyond. It was far too large for one person. She felt uncomfortable in it, but she had to admit that it was beautiful, with its silk upholstered furniture and the vase of bright summer flowers on the sideboard under the gilded oval mirror in the sitting room.

"Doctor, I must say you know how to make a girl feel welcome."

"We always try to please our bankers."

Well, you're off on the wrong foot with this one, doc, she thought. If you spend company money this way, how are you going to spend our money?

She kept smiling deliberately, forcing herself to create a defense he couldn't penetrate. She had to find some way of concealing her feelings from him, or she would be totally ineffective in appraising Family Care.

He waited for her while she unpacked. She noticed that there was a phone in the bathroom. She went into the bathroom to touch up her makeup and brush her hair. Then she called Peter. As the phone rang, she felt her heart begin to beat rapidly in anticipation. She was suddenly afraid he wouldn't be there. She felt herself tense with anxiety.

"Hello?" he said.

She breathed a sigh of relief.

"Peter, I was afraid you might not be in."

"I stayed around hoping you would call," he said.

"I'm glad I did."

"So am I."

"What are your plans?"

"You won't believe it, but I'm in a huge suite at the Ritz, and I was picked up at the airport in a convertible Rolls Royce."

"You're kidding."

"I couldn't believe it myself."

"And this guy you came up to see wants you to raise money for him? It sounds as if he could lend your firm some."

"That's something I've learned since I left school, Peter. Things aren't always what they seem. This potential client of ours has very expensive tastes, and that's never reassuring to a lender or an investor."

"Maybe he can afford it. There's nothing wrong with a little luxury if you're spending your own money," Peter said.

"You just hit the nail on the head, Peter. There's nothing wrong with it if it's your money. If it's the stockholders' money, that's a different story. Look, I have to run. I don't know if I'll be able to make it for dinner or not. I may have to dine with the good doctor. But we're on for tomorrow?"

"You bet your life. But I'm afraid you'll have to take my ancient Chevrolet. It'll still get us to Maine. You call me whenever you're through, and I'll come and pick you up."

"I may not finish until tomorrow afternoon."

"That's okay."

A thought occurred to her. "Peter?"

"Yes?"

"Why don't we make a slight change in our plan?"

"Doing what?"

"Taking advantage of the good doctor's generosity."

"Meaning?"

"Meaning, I'll finish up with him today, and you and I can spend the evening together here."

"You mean at the Ritz?"

"At the Ritz."

She could feel him thinking.

"Liz . . ."

"What?"

He laughed. "I think you've just made me an offer I can't refuse."

As they drove to Family Care she was distracted from her desire to savor once again being on Commonwealth Avenue with its island of grass and trees, the European facades of the town houses with their clustered pipe chimneys, and the hotels, clubs, and apartments that faced both sides of the broad avenue.

She felt embarrassed by the car. People stared at them as they stopped for each traffic light. They looked at the car and then at her and at the enormous man driving. She could see the questions on their faces. She fantasized that they might think she was some Hollywood personality. She found herself enjoying the luxury of the car and simultaneously annoyed with herself for feeling so sybaritic.

"Having fun?" Tim asked. He looked at her and grinned broadly.

"I must say, doctor, I've never driven through Boston quite like this."

He laughed. "As I said before, it's easy to get used to." He drove skillfully through the heavy traffic oblivious to the tendency of Boston drivers to make up their own traffic rules.

I wonder what it costs to have dents fixed on this thing, she thought. It must be incredible. The sun was getting warm; she could feel it on her head, but the ingenious air conditioning kept her body bathed in cool air. Remarkable, she thought. Really remarkable.

She found herself wondering if she would ever want a car like this. It didn't occur to her to think that she might not be able to afford one. Somehow she knew that she would. But if you could, she asked herself, would you? A car like this could put some kid through four years of college and graduate school. The enormity of that thought struck her, and she felt her jaw set. She was now more than ever determined to find out who had paid for this Rolls.

When they drove through the open wrought-iron gate at the foot of the curved drive, she was surprised at the opulence of the old brick mansion that was the home of Family Care. It had a curved portico over the entrance supported by four white Corinthian columns. The wide main door was made of heavy walnut panels with a carved white painted fluted fan decoration above it. On each side were leaded-glass panels curtained with a gauzelike material. The handle and lock of the main door were of highly polished brass as was a large dolphin-shaped knocker.

"Here we are, Liz." Tim Haley got out of the car and opened her door for her. She stood up and looked around. The turn-of-the-century estate was bordered by a high brick wall. She could see two wooden outbuildings, painted white, with slate roofs. There were carefully tended gardens in bloom with summer flowers. Old shade trees protected the brick walls that led through carefully groomed lawns to a large pond over which there was a small wooden bridge. She saw the silent vigilant swans swimming among the water-lily pads that spread out from the banks.

It's impressive, she thought, but then she knew that it was meant to be.

"Come over here, Liz. Let me show you something."

She followed him to the east wing of the house where they could see the gardens. Tim stood beside her, his voice low. "You see those enclaves over there?" He nodded in the direction of the serpentine undulations of the ivy-covered brick wall. Two men were seated there, talking in quiet, serious tones. An extremely attractive dark-haired woman was seated on the grass listening to another man, who was speaking to her intently. Other people were walking around the grounds or seated under shade trees in quiet conversation.

"It may be difficult to believe that what you are seeing out there is intensive psychotherapy."

She had guessed as much. "If you need psychotherapy, I can't think of a more beautiful or peaceful environment."

He beamed at her. "That's exactly the ambience we try to create here." He paused. "You can't tell the doctors from the patients."

"I've noticed that."

"No white coats around here. That's not our style." Tim took her arm and turned toward the mansion. "Of course, our more formal analytical and chemopsychotherapeutic sessions are done inside. Let's go in."

They entered a spacious main hall whose floor was covered with a handsome Aubusson rug. Liz wondered whether it was authentic; if it was, it was worth a small fortune.

The house seemed to be divided into two separate corridors off which she could see various-sized rooms. Some looked like offices, some like luxurious bedrooms. Two broad staircases led to a second floor where she saw more rooms behind a white balustrade.

"My office is over here." Tim guided her into a spacious room that she recognized from the film he had shown her at the Plaza in New York. "Sit here," he said. He pointed to a leather couch flanked by leather wing chairs. He sat in one of the chairs while she sat near him on the couch. "What are your impressions so far?" He was looking at her intently with a trace of a smile that suggested he already knew what her impressions were.

"It seems to me you have contrived an ambience that would mitigate the natural anxieties of your patients."

"That's exactly what we have attempted to do, and I think we've succeeded."

"It seems to me you have." She paused. "Where do you conduct your teletherapy sessions?"

"In the two white-painted buildings you saw. We've outgrown those facilities, but we have no desire to clutter the property with more buildings."

Liz opened her briefcase and took out her notes from their meeting in New York. She reviewed them quickly. "You said that three of you started this corporation with your own money and then borrowed funds from banks to finance and equip this center." She looked up at him. "Is that correct?"

"That's right."

"But you also said that you owned the majority of the stock."

"I do."

"What is your percentage of ownership?"

He hesitated. "I normally don't give that information, Liz."

She looked at him with a steady, objective professionalism that he found provoking. "I'm afraid, doctor, that you'll have to give me a great deal more information than you may be accustomed to if we are going to seriously consider financing your company."

She watched him recover his poise quickly. He smiled. "I own eighty percent of Family Care."

She jotted down the figure. "That seems odd to me, doctor. The three of you put up a hundred thousand apiece, and yet you wound up with eighty percent of the stock. You must be quite a salesman."

He laughed. "It wasn't quite that way. You see, my first partner—"

"Partner? I thought you said this was a corporation."

"It is. But we always treated each other as partners. My first partner was a psychoanalyst well known in this area, a Dr. George Lewis. He died of a coronary. We had a buy-sell arrangement among the three of us. My other partner didn't want to buy out his shares, so I ended up with two-thirds of the stock." He paused. "My remaining partner was not in the profession. He was head of a Boston consulting firm. You may know it—Lloyd Compton Associates." Tim smiled sardonically. "He was a good high-tech consultant, but he couldn't manage money. He needed money and sold his interest to me at what I considered a bargain price."

"So you wound up with all of the stock."

"Temporarily. I set up a stock purchase plan to attract promising young therapists and analysts. I've allocated twenty percent of the stock for people I want to attract."

She looked at him carefully. "How does your plan work, doctor?"

"Simple. The board votes to allot specific numbers of shares to individuals we feel merit the opportunity to purchase stock at current net worth per share. Since net worth increases if you have a profit—and we've been very profitable each year we have been in business—the value of our stock purchase plan is quite attractive to those we wish to reward. You see the corporation stands ready to repurchase the stock from the shareholder at current net worth, so that if the individual stays with us for a year—and most of them stay a great deal longer—they have an almost guaranteed capital gain."

Liz listened to Haley and couldn't believe what she was hearing. It was a simple but ingenious plan whose sophistication lay in its simplicity. A company's net worth will increase as long as it shows a profit, even a small one. Tim was right. The recipients of this plan were almost guaranteed a long-term capital gain whose tax rates were far more attractive than ordinary income.

"Who created that plan, doctor?"

He looked at her with that same damnably annoying omniscient smile. "I did," he said quietly.

She was really amazed at his reply, but she again fought to make herself less transparent.

"Where did you learn enough accounting to come up with a plan like that, doctor?"

He laughed. "I told you in New York that I make an effort to learn skills that will help me professionally."

She wanted to ask him if he made the same attempt to help his patients, but she knew that would be rude and inappropriate.

She saw him watching her with an amused, detached, almost clinical air. It annoyed her. This whole place annoyed her. She felt hostile toward him and what he was doing. She understood her feelings were irrational, but she could not shake them.

"This room may look informal to you, but let me show you something," he said. He went over to a door opposite his desk and opened it. "Take a look at this."

Liz followed him and was surprised to see what looked like a small operating room, complete with light green tile walls, overhead lamps, and an operating table with anesthesia apparatus. The electronic life-support system monitors, with their cathode ray tubes turned off, reminded her of dead eyes. She was surprised at this room, and this time she could not conceal it.

"I don't understand, doctor."

"I'm sure you don't, Liz." He seemed to fill up the small windowless room, making her feel claustrophobic. "You see, as I told you in New York, we don't have the time to pursue leisurely therapeutic techniques. We are often dealing with patients who have to be—"

"Back on the line," she interrupted.

He paused, looking at her without humor. "Yes, Liz. Back on the line. I believe you said the same thing in New York. It seems to me you are implying that our objective is to please the client rather than cure the patient."

She didn't answer him. She didn't have to. He was reading her again. For just a moment, standing in the small room, she felt childlike and powerless. Afraid. He looked so authoritative in this environment. So capable of penetrating her puny defenses.

I'm not neurotic, she told herself. He deals with neurotics. There is no need for me to be afraid of him. He needs my help; I don't need his. Then why am I afraid? Why do I feel helpless around him? It's ridiculous, she thought. He's just another shrink. Technically he's a shrink who thinks like an accountant. It's just that damn intuition of his. It's weird. Of course it's his training, unless I'm ready to believe in the supernatural, which I'm not.

He pointed at the equipment. "Despite your initial prejudices about our center, you can see that we care very much about what happens to our patients. This room, which our patients never see, contains the necessary equipment to prevent cardiac arrest, which can occur with the administration of sodium pentothal. As I explained to you in New York, some of our patients need help quickly to become productive again."

The adjective *productive* grated on her, but this time she had won; this time it didn't show.

Tim continued. "In cases where the patient's psychological layers of resistance may be so acute that we could never penetrate them with psychotherapy or psychoanalysis, we use psychochemotherapy. We administer the drug very slowly for a short period of time. Perhaps no more than five or six minutes.

Usually in one of the antecubital veins." He paused to look at her intensely. "We never administer the drug without an anesthesiologist standing by in this room. I might add that we have never had to use his services. Does that convince you that our first priority is the welfare of our patients?"

"I'm convinced." She smiled as she said it. She knew she was lying, but she was damned if she was going to give him the satisfaction of knowing it.

"Well, I'm relieved to hear that, Liz." They walked out of the small clinic and stood in the center of his office. "I would like you to meet a few of the staff. Dr. Ravenel and Dr. Arnaud, especially. Then I thought we could visit the teletherapy centers."

"I'll need to talk to your vice-president of finance. I'll need a lot of information from him."

"I'll arrange that for you."

She paused. "Before meeting Dr. Ravenel and Dr. Arnaud, I would like to see your teletherapy centers."

He grinned. "Can't wait, huh? Okay. If you like, we can ask Ravenel and Arnaud to join us for lunch."

She didn't want to take the time to eat lunch, but she could tell that he expected her to join him, and she felt it inappropriate to refuse. So much time is wasted eating lunch and dinner, she thought, but then not everyone had her dedication to work.

Chapter 17

THEY WALKED OUT into the hot August sun that was nearing its zenith, along the brick paths that led to the two white buildings, which looked like guest houses. She knew by comparison with the brick stables and garage that these structures must have been added relatively recently. Yet they were in keeping with the reserved elegance of the estate.

Tim led the way into a small foyer off which were several doors arranged much the same as in a hotel corridor. The corridor was well lit and cheerful. On the walls she noticed signed prints by Calder and Clarence Carter. She knew something about the value of signed prints by recognized artists.

Tim opened the first door off the left of the corridor and held his finger to his lips in a signal for her to be quiet. They entered a scene that looked furturistic. In the center of the room at a curved desk on which sat ten picture phones, a therapist was talking to a group of women. They appeared to be about the same age. Their images on the picture phones were in full color and extremely sharp. Much more so than the images she was used to seeing on television. The therapist's back was toward them, and he did not know they were in the room. Liz felt uncomfortable, intruding not only on the therapist, but on what was obviously a sensitive and intimate discussion:

"Please repeat that again for the group, Mrs. Meyers," the therapist said.

"I was just saying that I feel so vulnerable because I can't do anything. I have no skills. I've thought about getting a job. We could use the money, but I can't do anything."

Liz watched the faces of the other women who could hear but not see Mrs. Meyers. Only the therapist could see her. Liz remembered from what Tim had told her at the Plaza that all of the women could see the therapist.

"Mrs. Meyers, you raised three children. Is that correct?"

"Yes. Three."

"And you and your husband struggled to educate those children so that they would have marketable skills."

The therapist waited for a reply.

"Yes. So they could get jobs," the woman said. "I didn't want my daughters to be like me."

"Do you think any job is more difficult or more important than being a good parent?"

Liz watched Mrs. Meyers try to fight the tears she could no longer control. Liz saw the intent, anxious expressions of the other women as they heard the dialogue between the therapist and Mrs. Meyers.

"Mrs. Meyers, I want you to tell me—tell us—exactly how you feel right now."

Liz watched Mrs. Meyers burst into sobs of anguished depression. She blew her nose into a tissue and tried valiantly to continue.

"I feel like hell, doctor." Her voice was broken with despair. "I sit here in the apartment. Morris is at the office. I look at the goddamn plants, at the fish. I put the television on and listen to the soaps. Not a goddamn soul comes into the apartment. My kids, they got their own lives, their own problems. Once in a while they call. Once in a while they visit. The rest of the time I just sit. Morris sits. It's all over for us."

Liz watched the mixed reactions of the faces of the other women: annoyance, irritation, compassion, hostility.

"Are you on any medication for depression, Mrs. Meyers?"

She shook her head.

"Would you speak up for the group, please?"

"No."

"But you are drinking."

Mrs. Meyers touched her forehead with one hand. "My mother, may she rest in peace, she must be turning over in her grave."

Liz watched the kaleidoscope of expressions of the other women. Mrs. Meyers continued to wail.

The therapist now addressed all of them. The faces on the picture phone screens turn toward his voice like gulls facing the wind.

"First, I am going to ask Mrs. Meyers to see her family physician to get a prescription for an antidepressant. There are very effective drugs today that can help alleviate depression.

"Second, I want all of you to think about this: You are not alcoholics. At least not yet. You are all problem drinkers because, like Mrs. Meyers, you have negative feelings about your own worth.

"It has probably never occurred to you that the organizational and managerial skills necessary to run a home and raise a family successfully are skills that the business community will pay for when they are combined with other specific skills that you can learn.

"The problem for all of you is to find sufficient motivation in your lives to prepare yourselves for careers outside your households. You are using your homes to insulate yourselves from the challenges of the outside world. You tell yourselves you are not competent to compete in an environment filled with technically trained young people, many of whom are college graduates with one or more advanced degrees." He paused, looking at the tense, defensive faces whose expressions reflected their confusion and hostility at even contemplating the thought that, at their ages, they could think of entering a highly competitive technologically oriented society.

Liz watched him, feeling the intensity of his concentration. He's so involved he doesn't even know we're standing here.

"With your present lack of skills, you cannot compete," the therapist said, watching their expressions change. There were underlying similarities in their reactions. They all showed fear, anxiety, hostility, and despair.

"As you know, this is an action-oriented program," the therapist continued. "We told you that before you subscribed." He paused. "If you wish to remain in this program, you will have to do things that you are afraid to do."

An obese, florid-faced woman with short-cropped frosted hair spoke. "Dr. Ravensky," she said. Her voice trembled.

"I'm not a doctor."

"All right. *Mr*. Ravensky. What am I supposed to do? I

barely got out of high school, and that was nearly forty years ago. I had a lousy job working at the Liquor Control Board."

Liz watched the fleshy face break into a pathetic smile. The woman's jowls began to shake as she shook her head at the irony of it. "Ain't that something? Me workin' at the Liquor Control Board. I could drink up the whole damn place." The thought seemed to strike her as particularly ironic. "Only they ain't got no liquor at the Control Board."

"Mrs. Collins."

Liz noticed that the tone of the therapist had become strained. "We don't have any time to waste here. If you have something to say, please say it. You are intruding on the time of the others."

Mrs. Collins's face deflated like a punctured balloon. She was immediately defensive, almost cowering. Her voice was husky, almost inaudible.

"Don't get mad, Mr. Ravensky. All I wanted to say is what have I got to look forward to? Look at me. I look like a pig. What man would want someone who looks like me? Only some bum who's got no job and wants me to pay his rent. I live alone. I got a few friends." Her lips began to tremble. She tried hard to control her tears. "The weekends are the worst. Sometimes I feel so lonely that I'd like to say the hell with the whole thing and turn on the gas." She paused. "The holidays are even worse. The family invite me, if I'm lucky. I'm the fat aunt."

"Mrs. Collins." The therapist's voice was now soft and compassionate. "We're getting near the end of our hour, and there's something I must talk to all of you about. We're at the stage in the program where we must separate those of you with enough motivation to continue from those who lack that motivation." He paused. "I hope that you, Mrs. Collins, that all of you will choose to go on, but remember," his voice became authoritative. "This is not a baby-sitting service. Teletherapy is not an electronic kaffee-klatsch. Either you agree to take certain steps or you cannot go on."

Tim held one finger to his lips and started to back out of the room. He motioned to Liz to come with him, but she shook her head. She was fascinated by the montage of faces on the color picture phones, and she wanted to hear how the therapist was going to qualify those who would be permitted to remain in the program.

Tim smiled at her interest in the teletherapy session. The therapist, she noticed, was so involved with his patients that he still did not realize Liz and Tim were standing in the open doorway behind him.

"I am going to ask each of you to make an appointment next week with Aptitude Skills and Testing on Boylston Street," the therapist continued. "We have sent you their brochures; you should have them by Monday." He paused. "Those of you who are not tested within ten days of receipt of the brochures will be dropped from the program."

The women looked like a flock of frightened birds. Their responses became a confused babble.

"Wait a minute, please," the therapist interrupted. "Our time is almost up. Teletherapy, if it is going to help you, has to build up confidence in yourselves by finding out what aptitudes you have and by making sure you are willing to enter training programs to build those aptitudes into skills that are commercial." He paused, looking at every screen separately. "Otherwise," he said softly, "you are going to live your lives in despair and loneliness. You must be delivered from the womb of your apartments and your homes into the mainstream of life. You need confidence to meet and compete with other people, and you must cut down your drinking. Eventually your lives will be interesting and joyous, and you will not have to relieve your despair through alcohol. But we can't help you unless you help yourselves." He paused, his voice low but intense, the power of his own will projecting over the telephone lines to his frightened patients. He slumped back in his chair exhausted by the emotional effort he had expended during the last forty-five minutes. "I'm sorry, but our time is up." Liz watched him push a button. All the screens went blank.

Liz felt Tim's hand on her arm. They backed out of the room and silently closed the door. Her last view of Ravensky was the top of his dark, balding head resting against the back of his leather chair.

Tim looked at his watch and motioned her to follow him down the corridor. Her mind was so transfixed on what she had just seen that at first she didn't realize he was asking her to come with him.

"My God, that was like something out of a dream. All those faces," she said. "Those poor women."

She looked at her watch. "How long were we standing there?" she asked.

"Maybe eight or nine minutes."

"It seemed like a lifetime."

"That's why our therapists can only handle a limited number of sessions like that a day." Tim paused. "If the therapist is doing his job properly, he is really trying to connect himself psychologically with ten people at one time. That's a demanding and exhausting experience."

"I can understand that after seeing Ravensky in action."

Tim opened the door, and Liz found herself in the blistering heat of a Boston summer.

"This is almost as bad as New York," she said.

He laughed. "It's cooler here in the suburbs than it is in the city, but then I don't have to tell you anything about Boston."

He led her back to the main house. "I thought we could have some lunch. I've invited Dr. Ravenel and Dr. Arnaud to lunch with us. I thought you might be interested in meeting them since they were principally responsible for Dr. White's remarkable progress, which I showed you on the film at the Plaza."

Liz felt irritated about the intrusion of Ravenel and Arnaud. She wasn't interested in meeting them. She wanted to spend time with Tim and with his financial VP. She had a lot of questions to ask them, but there was no way she could gracefully suggest that she and Tim dine alone.

He guided her into a private dining room that she found astounding. The walls were covered with paintings that appeared to be originals. She could only guess their value. There were the abstractions of de Kooning. A Richard Diebenkorn showing a somber woman looking over a primitively painted landscape; she was wearing a vertically striped skirt of blue and white that Liz somehow associated with an Auschwitz prisoner. She saw a Jasper Johns and a Robert Motherwell. She knew enough about these artists to know that their paintings were valuable, and she began to wonder whether Dr. Haley had found still another way to pyramid his wealth.

Around a white and black Italian marble table stood several chrome-framed chairs with wide leather straps for seats and back. She knew from weeks of poking through dusty Greenwich Village shops and endless volumes of decorating magazines

that the furniture in the room had been specifically designed
for Tim. It was like the convertible Rolls, opulent and ostentatious, and again the thought began to gnaw at her: Do we
want to invest in this kind of person? Should we risk our money
and the money of our banks and insurance company partners?
Is this how a man lives and works who wants other people to
invest in his business? Such lavish spending was irresponsible,
unless Haley had great wealth, and she assumed he didn't, or
he wouldn't have come to Baldwin Cooper.

"Do you like paintings?" Haley asked.

"They're very impressive. I'm hardly an expert on contemporary art, but I recognize the names."

He smiled. "They have been one of my best investments.
A lot better than the stock market, I can assure you."

Here we go again, she thought. First the Rolls, then the
etchings in the main hall, and now these paintings. This man
does everything with the thought of increasing his net worth.
She could feel Haley watching her, and she felt a shiver of
anxiety run through her as she suspected he sensed her reaction.

The phone rang on the buffet near the French doors that
overlooked the lawns with their lush summer grass and aged,
dark-leaved shade trees.

He picked it up. "Yes? I'm sorry to hear that. No. It's more
important that you stay with your patient. Perhaps another
time." He hung up and turned to Liz. "Dr. Ravenel and Dr.
Arnaud have a problem with one of their patients, and they
won't be able to join us for lunch."

"That's too bad," she lied.

"Yes, I thought you might enjoy talking with them. Well,
another time."

He held her chair for her and then seated himself. A waiter,
who looked like a club steward in white mess jacket and black
trousers, appeared as if by magic.

"There will only be the two of us, Henri. Perhaps you might
bring in the wine." He turned to Liz. "I've taken the liberty
of ordering our lunch as I knew you would want to maximize
your time here."

"That was thoughtful of you, doctor. I do have a lot to go
over, and the more we can accomplish today the better."

Henri came in with the wine in a standing cooler and placed
it beside Tim. He came back with two cups of cold vichyssoise.

"This is delicious," she said. It was cool and refreshing. Exactly what she would have ordered. "Do you mind if we talk business while we eat? It will save time."

He laughed. "Not at all. I know how busy you are and how—" He paused, smiling with irony and amusement. The sardonic smile irritated her.

"Finish your sentence, doctor," she said, trying to keep her tone light without betraying annoyance.

"I was only going to remark on how purposeful you are. I would be happy to have you represent me, Liz. I can assure you."

"Thank you, doctor."

"And now for some wine. I think you'll like it."

Henri came in as if by magic, summoned by an electronic signal located under the table in front of Tim's chair.

"We'll have the wine now, Henri."

Liz noticed again what seemed to be a contradiction in Dr. Haley's behavior. She had seen it first in New York. Most men as careful and as organized as Tim seemed to be, as particular and selective about the material things with which they surround themselves, were ritualistic when it came to selecting and serving wine. Not Tim. There was no ceremony with the label and the cork, just as there had not been at the Plaza. Liz watched him signal Henri to pour the wine. Henri's only acknowledgment to tradition was to serve Tim a small taster's sample. Tim paid no attention. He nodded again and Henri filled Liz's glass.

Liz had been looking at the rug, which fascinated her. It was woven in the lumpy, interesting, distorted figures and bright colors of a Miró. But then, people hung Miró's on their walls; they didn't use them as rugs.

She sipped some wine. "That's absolutely delicious."

"I'm glad you like it. It's from the Chalone vineyard in California. They bottle a superb Chardonnay and Pinot Noir."

This is all getting to be a bit much, she thought. I've got to ask him about the rug.

"Doctor—"

"Must we remain so formal? I would like you to call me Tim."

"It takes me a while to use first names, doctor."

"It wouldn't be perhaps some vestigal puritanism, would it, Liz?"

She looked at him, determined to play his game, and not get caught. "It might be, doctor. All those cold, silent nights in Maine do take their toll, I suspect."

I'll pull his tail for a while, she thought, and she watched the gray-green eyes look at her with amused clinical detachment.

"Doctor, I'm fascinated by this rug. Is it—it couldn't be—"

"A Miró?" He laughed. "No, Liz. It's just a clever copy. I haven't arrived at the stage where I walk on money."

Score one for me, she said to herself but she kept her expression blank.

Henri came in with avocado salads stuffed with fresh chunks of lobster.

"Doctor, tell me something of the corporate setup at Family Care. For example, I've noticed a lot of improved real estate here and some valuable pieces of art, not to mention the car we drove up in." She watched him look at her carefully. He was quietly contained but expectant.

"Does the corporation own these things, doctor, or do you?"

He did not answer her directly. He continued to eat slowly, deliberately. "Does that come under the heading of things your firm needs to know, Liz? Or is this your own personal curiosity?"

Damn him, she thought. God, how this man can annoy me. She smiled, keeping her face bland and composed.

"Doctor, I think you had better understand what I'm trying to do here. I not only have to decide whether your company has sufficient growth potential to interest us; I also have to form opinions about the people who run it. Once we put our money in, and get our institutional partners to come in with us—then, doctor, it's a little late to worry about integrity and competence."

He kept looking at her steadily, his face expressionless. He placed his knife and fork carefully on the side of his plate. "Are you concerned about my integrity and competence?"

She paused before replying. "I'm concerned about everyone's integrity and competence until I have enough information not to be."

"That's an honest answer."

"I'm an honest woman, doctor."

He didn't press the point.

They ate in silence while she waited for him to answer. It was a direct, somewhat embarrassing question, but it was crucial to her better understanding of him and of his company.

"This lobster is delicious," she said.

He picked up his fork and began to eat with deliberation. He looked at her with a trace of annoyance. She could see that she had touched a sensitive nerve and that this might be the moment when he would decide that she and BC wanted more personal information than he cared to give. As she watched him, she thought he might be prepared to call the whole deal off. His mouth smiled, but his eyes remained cool and penetrating.

"Well, I guess if we are to proceed we'll have to do so on your terms. The real estate is controlled by the Haley Corporation, of which I am the majority shareholder. All of this property, the car, and the works of art you seem so interested in are owned by the Haley Corporation, which leases them to Family Care. I might add that when you check the lease agreements you will find them very reasonable, quite a bit lower than what a normal landlord or art dealer would charge."

This bird is too much, she thought, but she made no comment.

"Is there any particular reason you chose to set things up this way, doctor?" She knew the answer, but she wanted to hear it from him.

"Yes." He paused. She could tell he was struggling to overcome his reluctance to answer her questions.

"Life is full of uncertainties as well as opportunities, Miss Clark. I chose to retain the real estate and art objects and the Rolls so that I could control these assets, which are appreciating in value. Should something happen to Family Care, or to the Teletherapy program, I will still have the hard assets of the Haley Corporation to fall back on."

Liz looked up, a thought flashing through her head. "What about the agency you send your patients to for aptitude testing? You wouldn't by any chance have an interest in that, too, would you?" She looked at the enormous man sitting on her right. What goes on in that huge head of his? she wondered, and she decided that it would frighten her to know.

"Family Care owns a minority interest in Aptitude Skills and Testing. It doesn't mean anything. Their business is relatively small, but it does give us a means of ensuring the quality of their work."

Henri came in with raspberry sherbet for dessert.

"As I told you in the car coming up here, Miss Clark, I like to maximize the results of what I do." She noticed that his manner had become less cordial. "I'm a rather competitive person," he went on. "I believe I told you that, too, in New York. I don't wish to appear immodest, but I'm a winner. I always have been—in school, in college, in my profession. I think you will find after talking to members of my staff that they will tell you the same thing." He paused. "As I have said to you before, I see nothing inconsistent with that philosophy in a medical environment."

She did not reply. She looked at him without expression, but her mind raced with the conflicts he presented to her.

Maybe I should tell George I'm not right for this assignment, she thought. I can't react to this man logically. What he tells me makes sense. I can't fault his philosophy. But still, something about him frightens me. That's an infantile reaction; George would laugh me out of his office. This is my first chance to bring in a deal for the firm, and I'm going to blow it. I know I will, she thought. God, maybe I'm the one who needs a shrink.

"You realize, doctor," she said, trying to strip her mind of the thoughts that were interfering with her attempts to get a clear picture of Family Care, "that if we decide to finance you, you are going to have to convert those assets back into whatever form we decide on."

He looked at her with something close to antagonism. "I had not considered that, Miss Clark," he said evenly.

"You couldn't expect our firm and our institutional partners to invest our money in your company and let you keep the hard collateral."

"The hard collateral, as you put it, Miss Clark, I should think would be the earnings of a rapidly growing business."

Then why did you separate out the assets, doc? she thought.

"I'm afraid, doctor, that hard assets, especially *appreciating* ones, as you pointed out, are a comfort to investors." She paused. "You'll have to give that serious consideration, doctor, if you want us to raise ten million dollars for you. We wouldn't do the deal without it."

"I'll consider it carefully, Miss Clark." He paused. "Well,

who would you like to meet now?"

"Whoever handles your finances."

"That would be Arnold Goodwin. I told him you'd want to talk with him. He's waiting to see you."

"I'm going to have to ask him for some sources we can check. We'll have to ask about you personally and about the corporations you control."

"Ask him whatever you like. I've told him to cooperate with you fully." He stood up. She could never get used to his size.

"I'll take you to Arnold, and he'll bring you back to my office when you two are finished." There was no smile. His manner was aloof.

This wasn't going to work, she told herself. But then if it turned out to be an attractive deal for the firm, she would have to make it work. That was the business she was in. She wasn't paid to judge people by her own standards, she realized. She was paid to find lucrative deals. She wondered if George had these problems, too.

Chapter 18

SHE SAT IN the compact office of Arnold Goodwin, looking across the metal desk of the short, round-faced man with the full, dark hair. His summer tan looked out of place in this Spartan office. No paintings or etchings here. Just functional gray carpeting that gave Goodwin's office all the ambience of moldy bread.

He seems pleasant enough, she thought, but there's something soft about him. He just doesn't strike me as a strong man. I can't picture him standing up to Tim, and that's not good. Liz knew that every business needed a strong financial officer who could make sure that everyone stayed in line, including the president and chief executive officer. That was the ideal. In practice, it didn't usually work that way. People who run or control businesses don't like to be told that they're spending too much money or that they have to cut costs. If the financial officer has enough backbone, he or she will stand up to someone like Tim, but Arnold Goodwin hardly seemed like that sort of man.

Liz had her notebook in her lap. "Your title is vice-president of finance?"

"Yes."

"And how long have you been with Family Care?"

"A little over two years."

"And you came from—"

"From Arthur Young."

"That's a good firm." She paused. "Why did you leave?"

He smiled. He had pleasant features, and his manner was convivial; she could guess why he had left.

"Dr. Haley made me an attractive offer and I accepted," he said.

And you knew you would never be made a partner at AY, she thought.

"And where did you go to school?"

"Wharton."

She paused. "Did Dr. Haley tell you who I am and why I'm here?"

"He just told me to answer any questions you asked. I really have no idea who you are or why you're here."

Liz's face flushed with anger. That's a hell of a thing, she thought. This man is supposed to sit here and answer my questions and not know why I'm here? She also felt extremely awkward. If she handed Goodwin her business card, maybe she would be doing something Tim didn't want her to do. She'd have to clear this up with Tim before she went much further with Goodwin. But she was here, and she didn't want to waste time. She studied Goodwin carefully. He didn't look annoyed. Evidently he was used to this sort of treatment. She couldn't imagine working under such conditions.

"Here is a list of the information I'll need, Mr. Goodwin. It will take you some time to put it together, but I would appreciate your giving me some idea when I could expect this."

She watched him look over the BC checklist. He turned to her, smiling, but his eyes were serious, questioning.

"You planning on buying the company?" His tone was still light and pleasant.

"Not quite."

"Has Dr. Haley seen this list?"

"Yes."

"And he agreed to supply you with all this information?"

"He did."

Goodwin whistled. "You certainly must have charmed Haley."

"I don't understand."

Goodwin looked at her. "Miss Clark, Dr. Haley is not very confiding, especially when it comes to Family Care. The only reason I know what's going on is that I have to give the numbers to our auditors. Sooner or later I get to see about everything that's done here."

"*About* everything? Don't you see *everything?* You're the senior financial officer."

Goodwin laughed. Something furtive had crept into his manner. "I guess I see everything I need to."

"Who are your auditors?"

"They're a local firm, Goldstein and McCracken."

You can be damn sure, she thought, that if we do this deal, we'll have a national firm audit these books. I don't like the feeling I'm getting.

"Tell me something, Mr. Goodwin. Are Family Care and Aptitude Skills the only corporations in which Mr. Haley has an interest?"

Goodwin's eyebrows arched in surprise. "You know about Aptitude?"

"I know that Dr. Haley has a minority interest in that corporation. I also know about the Haley Corporation."

Arnold Goodwin looked at her carefully. "You're not with the IRS by any chance, are you, Miss Clark?" He said it half jokingly, but there was an inquisitiveness in his tone that was penetrating.

She laughed and held up her hand. "Scouts' honor, Mr. Goodwin. Your secrets are safe with me. I'm about as far removed from the government as you can get." She paused. "Does Dr. Haley have an interest in any other corporations?"

Goodwin got up from his metal-framed plastic chair. He went to his small window and looked out at the rolling lawns of Family Care, his back toward Liz. He seemed to be thinking of her question and his reply. He turned to face her, his expression defensive and uncertain. "Who are you, Miss Clark?"

She was embarrassed and angry—not at Goodwin; he was just a functionary, but at Tim who was making her go through this unnecessary embarrassment. "Mr. Goodwin, I can assure you I have Dr. Haley's full confidence and his authority to ask you these questions. I'm sorry he hasn't told you why I'm here, but I can assure you that the next time we meet, either he or I will explain fully to you just what my business is with Family Care." She paused. "I would tell you now, Mr. Goodwin, but I think that should come from Dr. Haley."

He went over to the gray file cabinets that lined nearly one whole wall of his office and pulled out a drawer. He flipped through several file folders until he found the one he wanted. He handed it to her in silence. It was labeled, "Haley Supply Corporation."

She opened it and saw several ledger sheets with different titles: Haley Linen Supply Co., Inc. Haley Fuel Oil, Inc. Haley Garden Supplies Co., Inc. Haley Medical Equipment Monitors, Inc.

She couldn't believe it. "What are all these companies, Mr. Goodwin?" Arnold Goodwin was looking at her sardonically. "Those, Miss Clark, are the corporate holdings of Dr. Haley. Nothing of importance in the way of supplies or services comes into this place that Dr. Haley doesn't own a piece of."

She was staggered, not because there was anything wrong with what Tim was doing, but because of the sheer greed of the man. But was "greed" the right word? Was it greed or just good business? Was Haley just smarter than anyone else she had met in her brief career? Or was her reaction to the healer-businessman an instinctive warning that something was wrong?

Is that what worries me about him? Liz asked herself. Is it my own ambivalence, or is it something deeper? Should I act on my negative gut reaction to Haley and just drop this whole thing? Or should I say, we've got a potential partner in a very attractive growth business who may be smarter than we are?

She sat on one of the two leather wing chairs that flanked the desk while she waited for Tim Haley to return. As she looked around his office, the contradictions that flew at her mind only increased her confusion. An office usually reflects the person-ality of its occupant, she thought. As she looked around, she remembered seeing Tim's office on the film at the Plaza. But sitting here alone, and after seeing all these etchings and the paintings, and that chrome and marble dining room of his . . .She stood up and looked around. This place looks like the office of a very successful and very conservative lawyer. Why would he do that? How many sides to his personality does this man have?

She was standing near his desk looking at the floor-to-ceiling bookshelves. Medical and psychiatric volumes were mixed with books on law, economics, business, management, and a wide variety of biography, contemporary history, and fiction. A Renaissance man, she thought.

The door opened while she was studying the titles of his books. "My tastes must seem somewhat eclectic," he said.

She turned to see him standing there, his mien controlled and formal. "They certainly are."

"I think we'd better have a talk, Miss Clark."

She immediately picked up the change in his manner as she watched him settle himself behind his desk. He pointed to one of the wing chairs. She sat down feeling the premonition that Dr. Timothy Haley had had enough of her reservations regarding him and how he conducted his business.

"I think we need a little confrontational therapy, Miss Clark." He smiled thinly, but his manner was clinical. "I came to your office," he said, "because you are supposed to be in the business of investing in growth companies. I had an appointment with your boss, Mr. Hall, and through circumstances with which we are both familiar, you were assigned to evaluate my company." He paused. His eyes never left hers. He was sitting with his forearms on his desk, his enormous hands clasped in front of him. "It is my profession and my life's work and interest to better understand the emotions of men and women. Therefore, what I am about to say to you, Miss Clark, you can accept as my professional point of view.

"When I first showed you that film of Dr. White, I saw in your manner and your conversation a certain hostility toward me and my work." She started to protest, but he held up his hand. "Please, Miss Clark, let me finish." Her face flushed, and she sat back in her chair, crossing her legs and trying hard to hide her apprehension. Your first chance to bring in a deal and you've blown it, she thought.

"Ever since I drove you up here in the Rolls—as you looked around Family Care and learned how I handle my business—I have had the impression that you don't like the blending of my profession with my business. I think that's true, Miss Clark, so let's both admit it and accept it." He leaned back in his chair, never taking his eyes from hers. She felt almost powerless, looking at him. She felt dwarfed by his size and intimidated by the authority of his knowledge and the variety of his experience. She felt diminished by his ability to read her thoughts.

"I think your problem with me, Miss Clark, lies in what you perceive as my unwarranted commercialism." He paused, and this time his smile was pure irony. "I find that very amusing, coming from you, whose career, if it's to be successful, will emanate from one of the primordial bastions of pure greed."

Her face flushed with anger. "Now, just a minute, doctor—"

He held up his hand again. "Does the shoe pinch a little, Miss Clark?" He paused. "When you implied in New York that I was more interested in money than I was in my patients—"

"I didn't—"

"You did, Miss Clark," he said quietly. "You were discrete enough not to say it, but you implied it. We both know that, so let's not waste each other's time. Miss Clark, when I say that you represent a bastion of greed, I am not being critical of greed. It is a natural human emotion that exists to a greater or lesser degree in all of us. If you substitute the word 'motivation' for 'greed,' it immediately removes the stigma from a term most people find either embarrassing or insulting. But there are different kinds of greed—greed for knowledge, greed for excellence, greed for love and affection. You can extend the list further if you wish. You can define greed as excessive need, so that it is not greed itself that is repugnant, but the excesses to which it lends itself. Therefore, it is *excess* rather than greed that in a psychological and philosophical sense we would both think of as undesirable." He paused.

She felt as if she were being led up an elliptical path by her former philosophy professor.

"If we really are talking about excess and not greed, Miss Clark, let's compare your business with mine." He paused. "Yes, Miss Clark. I call this a business, and I make no apologies for that.

"Now, let's see how Baldwin Cooper stacks up against Family Care," he went on. "Baldwin Cooper's sole purpose is to make money—as much of it, and as quickly, as it can." He leaned forward slightly. "Is that an unfair description of the goals of your firm, Miss Clark?"

She couldn't fight it. What he said was true. Rationalizations flashed through her mind, but he had cut to the heart of it. The sole aim of her business was to make money. Her jaw muscles contracted as she met his glance with a look of defiance.

"You've seen enough in your short time here," he said, "of one of our teletherapy sessions to know that we *do* perform a needed human service."

"So do we. We create jobs. Without us there would be fewer businesses operating and fewer executives and workers to run them."

"I agree, Miss Clark. That is a constructive result of what you do. But would you really equate that in humanitarian terms with what we do here?"

She found herself on the defensive again. She hesitated. "I suppose not," she said reluctantly.

"So let's speak of excess again. Who is more excessive in the pursuit of material gain, you or me?"

She felt like a pinned butterfly. He had skillfully manipulated his argument so that she couldn't win. But the worst part was that it was true. She had been critical of him because of what she had construed as his preoccupation with wealth. She was the last person to be critical of that goal. She had chosen to become part of Baldwin Cooper. Money was their game, and they played it with everything they had.

She felt exhausted. She had fought a losing battle. It was the same battle she had fought with herself at Harvard. Maybe I'm in the wrong business, she thought. But it was too late for that now. She looked at him and smiled wanly. "Dr. Haley, I surrender. You're right. I apologize."

"You have nothing to apologize for, Miss Clark." He smiled. "Life is a process of maturation. In my profession, we spend a good deal of time trying to give different insights to people whose perspectives may be colored by a variety of problems. All I have been trying to do is to give you an opportunity to look at us without the distortion of a somewhat oversimplified perspective." He paused. "You may decide, Miss Clark, that I am not a good risk or that this business doesn't meet your investment criteria. All I ask is that you make your final decision without predetermining its outcome according to your own ethical values."

They looked at each other with measured glances. His manner had softened. "Friends?" he asked amicably.

"Friends," she said, and in that moment she meant it.

He stood up. He looked at his watch. "It's three forty-five.

I've arranged for you to meet Dr. Ravenel. Unfortunately, Dr. Arnaud will not be able to see you today. Maybe on your next visit." He paused. "I've kept tonight open for dinner."

"I'm sorry, doctor, but I'm afraid I have plans for dinner."

He frowned. He seemed disappointed, as if he had been planning on it.

"That's too bad. Well, why don't we go to Dr. Ravenel's office? I'll show you the way. When you're finished with her, I'll drive you back to the Ritz."

She remained seated, still trying to find her way out of the philosophical web he had spun. She couldn't fault his logic, but a persistent tendril tickled her anxieties. "There is one thing, doctor, that we should get cleared up."

"What's that?"

"My reason for being here. Arnold Goodwin was unaware of why I was questioning him, why he should provide me with the information on the checklist I gave him. I found that embarrassing. I'm going to have to spend a lot of time with Goodwin, and I told him the next time we met he would know either from me or from you what I am doing here." She saw a flicker of annoyance cross his face.

"Until your firm has made its decision, Miss Clark, I prefer that your role not be made known to our employees or staff." He paused. "Suppose you decide you don't want to invest in my company. Then I will have raised their expectations, only to let them down."

"Dr. Haley," she said, "it will be impossible for me to work with Goodwin without his knowing my role. I can't get the kind of information I need for an analysis of your business without making him feel defensive." She hesitated. "If you don't mind my saying so, doctor, it doesn't speak very well for your confidence in Mr. Goodwin. And to be completely candid, that will be a serious point of contention at my firm."

He stood there, physically immense even in the large office. He was looking at her with the measured, analytical gaze that she found intimidating. But this was a point on which she would not yield to him. This was *her* game, not his. If she was being asked to investigate a company where the financial officer was treated as a subordinate functionary whose watchdog role was meaningless, then they had better end this right now. She watched him come to a decision. "All right, Miss Clark. You may tell

Arnold Goodwin, but no one else. There is no need to bring Dr. Ravenel into this. The rest of the staff can learn about it when and if we sign a formal agreement."

"That seems fair enough, doctor. Let's leave it like that."

She could tell he wasn't happy about it. Why? she asked herself. Is it because he's lost a round? Is his ego so large that that's what's annoying him? Or is there more to it than that?

"Shall we go to meet Dr. Ravenel now?" He looked at his watch. "We're already about ten minutes late."

She got up and took her bag, and he held the door open for her.

She followed him up the stairs to the second floor. They walked down a broad corridor where the bedrooms must have been in the original house. He knocked on a heavy wooden door, which was painted off-white. The door opened, and there sat the beautiful woman Liz had seen in the film in New York. In person she was even more attractive. She was wearing a lime green dress that emphasized her eyes, which were green flecked with brown. She wore her dark hair pulled back in a French braid, which emphasized the sculptured look of her face. Her voice was melodious in accented English. Her skin was deeply tanned.

"Ah, Miss Clark. I have been expecting you." She looked at Tim. "You did not tell me I was to have such an attractive visitor."

Liz was struck not only by the beauty and charm of Dr. Ravenel, but by her immediately apparent penetrating intelligence.

"I'll leave you two alone to get acquainted. When you're through here, Liz, Dr. Ravenel will call me, and I'll take you back to Boston." He smiled and nodded to them both and closed the door. Liz was looking out of the leaded casement windows to the shallow fishpond with the footbridge. She saw large coral and white carp swimming lazily among the small clusters of water lilies. The hot sun had driven everyone inside the air-conditioned comfort of the Family Care buildings. Even the shaded alcoves with their weathered benches were testimony to the smothering humidity and heat.

"What a lovely view," Liz said.

"Yes, it is very comforting and peaceful. The grounds are quite therapeutic when the weather is cooler." She motioned

Liz to a chair. The office was tastefully furnished with a feminine flavor but not overwhelmingly so. There was a comfortable couch. Two upholstered high-backed chairs flanked a small tiled fireplace. Framed photographs of mountains, sea, and sky gave the room a warm, inviting feeling, much like its occupant.

"Sit down, Miss Clark, please." She pointed to the chairs near the fireplace. She seated herself opposite Liz with her hands folded in her lap, leaning forward slightly, smiling, waiting for Liz to begin. With the practiced intuition of a psychoanalyst she saw Liz hesitate, not quite knowing how to begin. "I understand you are interested in what we do here."

"Yes, doctor. I am."

"Are you connected with the profession?"

"No, I'm not."

"You are from the press?"

"No." Liz was uncomfortable again, embarrassed and annoyed that Tim had put her in this position.

"May I ask, Miss Clark, what it is that you do?"

The hell with Tim, she thought. "I'm what's known as a venture capitalist. To be more specific, I work for a venture capital firm."

"And what is this venture capital? It sounds terribly impressive." Liz saw the humor in the green eyes.

"We invest our capital in companies we think can grow rapidly, and we bring in other institutional partners like banks and insurance companies."

"And you are here to look us over for that purpose?"

Liz hesitated. She remembered Tim's warning. "Dr. Ravenel, Dr. Haley does not want this known to the staff. It puts me in an awkward position."

Liz saw the humor disappear quickly from Dr. Ravenel's eyes, but she watched the practiced smile maintain itself.

"You are going to invest money in Family Care?"

"It's much too early to tell, doctor. It's an interesting business—"

Dr. Ravenel interrupted her. "Did you say business?"

"Ah, yes, I did. You see that's the way we have to look at it."

Liz saw the smile disappear. "You consider what we are doing here a business, Miss Clark?"

"I'm afraid I have to."

Dr. Ravenel hesitated. "Yes. From your point of view I can see that." Liz could sense the hostility in her voice.

"Tell me something, doctor. Don't you consider this a business?"

"I certainly do not."

Liz hesitated. "How about a specialized private professional practice?" She watched Dr. Ravenel think about that carefully.

"I suppose I could not find fault with that definition—"

"But run along business lines," Liz said.

Liz watched the green eyes flash. "I don't like that definition, Miss Clark."

"But you admit that it is accurate?"

"Yes and no."

"I believe Dr. Haley would refer to this as a business."

Liz watched Dr. Ravenel's face flush with anger. "I am thoroughly familiar with the views of Dr. Haley."

"And you don't agree with them?"

"I would rather not answer that."

Liz paused, having decided to drop the subject. "Doctor, I saw a film in New York of the magnificent work you and Dr. Arnaud did with Dr. White." Liz watched the woman's face brighten.

"Yes. That was a wonderfully satisfying case. Most gratifying."

"Have you had many successes like Dr. White?"

"Yes. I am happy to say we have."

"You say 'we.' Do you mean you and Dr. Arnaud?"

"Yes. We work as a team. As Dr. Haley may have told you, I am a psychoanalyst. Dr. Arnaud is a psychiatrist. We are interested in the emotional problems of very gifted adults." She paused. "That's what brought us here. We became interested when we read of the work Dr. Haley was doing in Boston. We met him about two and a half years ago in Paris when he was a speaker at the International Neuropsychiatric Institute's annual conference. Dr. Arnaud eventually came to the States to observe Dr. Haley's work. He became very interested in it, and persuaded me to join him here." She hesitated. "It has been an unusual, but on the whole, satisfying experience."

Liz wondered what her relationship was to Arnaud. She was an incredibly lovely and cultivated woman. She seemed to resent any implication that her work was being commercialized.

"Doctor, were you trained in France?"

"Yes. Completely."

"Dr. Arnaud, however, completed medical school here in New York, isn't that correct?"

"Yes. That's right."

"Could you explain to me, doctor, why you and Dr. Arnaud, two obviously highly qualified people, chose to associate yourselves with a little known private center rather than with Harvard, or Stanford, or Chicago? Or at a clinic like the Mayo?"

Dr. Ravenel brushed back her hair in what Liz thought was probably a habitual and unconscious gesture.

"The answer is simple, Miss Clark. We know of no one who is doing the imaginative and innovative work in psychotherapy that Dr. Haley is doing here at Family Care. It's very exciting to utilize new techniques in an environment that is not only receptive to innovation, but encourages it."

"Dr. Ravenel. What is your feeling about teletherapy?"

"Teletherapy is very experimental, and we have far too little data to make any scientific judgment as to its value as a therapy." She paused. "It does attempt to deal with three of the main difficulties in treating neurotic disorders."

"And what are they, doctor?"

"Numbers, time, and cost."

"I'm not sure I understand."

Dr. Ravenel sighed. "One of the main difficulties with treating neurotic behavior is to make therapy available to the enormous numbers of people who need it." She paused. "Miss Clark, I don't know how much you know about emotional problems, but the number of people who could use professional help is staggering."

"Why do you think that is?"

"Ignorance. Fear."

"Fear of what, doctor?"

"Fear of being thought of as unstable or different."

"When you say 'ignorance,' doctor—"

"I refer to the great mass of neurotic men and women who don't realize that they carry emotional problems like baggage weighing them down. If they could rid themselves of this baggage, they would lead happier and more fulfilling lives. These people are not only unaware that they have problems; they are equally unaware of the help that is available to them."

The late afternoon light played off the right side of Dr. Ravenel's face.

"You mentioned time and cost, doctor."

"Yes, this is very important. It is the reason that Paul Arnaud and I are here. You see, Dr. Haley has been experimenting with new psychological techniques that in theory, at least, allow us to approach far greater numbers of people at a fraction of the cost of individual treatment. That is the whole rationale behind Teletherapy."

Liz hesitated. "Doctor, hasn't the teletherapy program passed the theory stage?"

"It depends on who you talk to. If you talk to Dr. Haley or any of the teletherapists, they will tell you that is an evolving technique." She paused, thoughtfully. "I'm not sure that that is not an accurate description of teletherapy. It is an evolving technique."

"And you disapprove of that?"

She hesitated. "I don't disapprove of the concept." She paused thoughtfully. "What concerns me, Miss Clark, is that in my opinion at least, Dr. Haley is commercializing an experiment. Professionally and ethically, this conflicts with my own concept of how the technique should be explored."

"And how is that, doctor?"

"In a controlled environment. In a university."

"Does Dr. Arnaud share your view?"

"I would prefer that you ask Dr. Arnaud."

Liz got up and walked to the window and looked out across the grounds. *I don't know how to ask her this*, she thought, *but it's key. If there is something sour with teletherapy, then we don't have a deal. The rest of Family Care is too small and too specialized.*

"Doctor, I would like to ask you a few more questions. I don't wish to intrude on any confidences, but you can help me in not wasting my time here or anyone else's. I would appreciate your answering me as frankly as possible. I can appreciate a difference in views between professionals such as you and Dr. Haley. What I would like to know is this. In your opinion, is teletherapy open to criticism that might extend beyond differences in professional opinions?"

"I don't know what kind of criticism you are referring to, Miss Clark."

Liz looked at her, matching the steady gaze with her own. "Doctor, is Teletherapy, Incorporated, the kind of innovation that will stand up to national publicity? Or would it arouse such a storm of criticism that its value might be questioned?"

"Do you mean its commercial value or its therapeutic value?"

Liz looked at her carefully. "I'm afraid, doctor, that from my perspective, I cannot afford to separate the two."

Delphine Ravenel looked at her with a trace of distaste. "I suppose your main concern has to be the business aspect."

She's beginning to sound like me, and I'm beginning to sound like Tim, Liz thought.

"I can assure you that my interest, though commercial, doesn't ignore the treatment value of teletherapy." Liz paused. "Logically, doctor, you can't separate them. If teletherapy fails as a form of treatment for neurotic problems, then it will fail as a commercial enterprise." Liz hesitated. "My firm would not want to be associated with either failure."

Liz watched her think about that. She saw the reluctant acceptance of her logic. "I suppose you are right, Miss Clark. I cannot predict the reaction of my profession if teletherapy became publicized. My guess is that it would be in for a lot of critical review."

"Good or bad?" Liz asked.

"Mixed, I would suppose. There are all kinds of—how do you say it?—quacks practicing a variety of supposed cures for neurotic behavior."

"We are not interested in associating with quacks, doctor."

"I didn't mean to imply that teletherapy is a quack approach. Not at all. Perhaps I am too European, too French—"

"Meaning too skeptical?" Liz interrupted.

Dr. Ravenel smiled. "You are very perceptive, Miss Clark.

"Yes, I guess you might say I am skeptical. But not about what Dr. Haley is attempting to do. I think that quite laudatory. It is only the method I object to. The commercialization of an experiment. I have told Dr. Haley that."

"And what did he say?"

She laughed. "He said that if everyone was afraid to take a chance, we would all be reading by candlelight."

That sounds like something he would say, Liz thought. "But that doesn't answer my question, doctor. My firm will not associate itself with an evangelical effort that lacks scientific support."

"Then you had better stay away from behavioral psychology, Miss Clark. Dr. Haley is breaking new ground, and you can't break anything without creating noise and confusion."

"May I ask you, doctor, if you have reservations about teletherapy, why are you here?"

"I'm here, Miss Clark, because there is brilliant innovation in the work that Family Care does."

"And you don't consider it experimental?"

"Not in the same sense as teletherapy."

"Is that a personal judgment?"

"It must be. I'm making it."

I'm back to where I started, Liz thought. "Doctor, let me ask you this question. If Dr. Haley could raise sufficient funds to expand the teletherapy program, do you think that would be good or bad?"

The beautiful face lit up in a smile. "For Dr. Haley it would certainly be good."

"And for the patients?"

"You mean the subscribers."

"Yes, I suppose I do."

Delphine Ravenel became thoughtful. She waited for what seemed a long time before replying. "Miss Clark, there is so much unhappiness, so much neurotically sponsored misery, that anything that is not fraudulent would be of some value."

Liz decided not to ask her if she considered teletherapy fraudulent.

"Can I infer, doctor, that if you don't condemn the program, then you support it?"

"You ask questions like a lawyer, Miss Clark. Are you a lawyer?"

Liz laughed. "No, doctor. My degrees are in history and business administration."

"An interesting combination, Miss Clark. I suppose one could make a case that commercialism has in good part directed the course of history."

"I've never quite thought of it that way, doctor, but the association is compelling."

"It is an interesting speculation, is it not, Miss Clark?"

"It certainly is. But to get back to my question, doctor. Do you support teletherapy?"

Dr. Ravenel sighed. "With the reservations I have discussed. Yes, I suppose I support teletherapy."

Liz looked at her for a long time. "Doctor, I'm sure we will be seeing more of each other. Thank you for being candid with me. Oh. One more thing. I would like to make a phone call. Is there some place where I could talk privately?"

Delphine Ravenel rose. "Use my phone, Miss Clark. I am late as it is for one of my patients."

"I'm sorry I kept you."

"No bother. Nothing urgent, I assure you. Please feel free to use my office. Dial nine to get an outside line, eight if it is not a local call."

"Thank you so much, doctor." She watched Dr. Ravenel leave the room.

She didn't like to sit down at someone else's desk, it seemed like an intrusion. She stood by Dr. Ravenel's desk and dialed Peter. The phone rang only once.

"Peter?"

"Yes."

"I'm so glad I caught you."

"I've been waiting by the phone all afternoon."

"I'm sorry, Peter, but this is the first chance I've had to call you all day. I'm still out at Family Care in Chestnut Hill."

"Can I pick you up?"

"No, Peter. Dr. Haley is driving me back to the Ritz." She paused. "I can't wait to see you. It's been so long."

His voice was low. Thoughtful. "It's been weeks."

"It seems like years," she said.

"What time shall I come by?"

She thought for a moment. "It's four now. How about six? I don't know if Haley will be able to leave here right away."

"I'll see you at six. Oh—where shall I meet you? In the lobby?"

"No. Haley has reserved a suite for me." She gave him the suite number. "Just come on up, darling." She tried to control the emotions rising within her in anticipation of seeing him.

"I'll knock on your door, Liz, at six sharp," he said softly.

"See you, darling." She hung up. Her hand was shaking. The gorging of her emotions began to rise in her throat as her mind swept over the trials of their relationship.

Nothing is going to spoil this weekend, she promised herself. Nothing. I'm going to enjoy the time I have with him; every last minute. No probing. No wondering. No laments. If this business has taught me anything, it has taught me how to compress time. That's what I want to do with him. She felt her eyes beginning to mist. This weekend has got to be right. Her hand was still shaking as she picked up the phone to call Dr. Haley.

Chapter 19

SHE HAD SHOWERED and changed into a sleeveless cobalt blue silk dress with a V neckline that accentuated her tall, lithe figure. She knew that the dress almost matched the color of her eyes, that it highlighted the copper tones in her auburn hair. She knew she looked attractive; she felt attractive.

She kept looking at her watch. When will he come? God, I want him to come. It's been so long. So very long.

At the stroke of six she heard the buzzer. She rushed to the door and opened it. She could see the joy in his eyes as he stood there looking at her.

He still looks the same, she thought. Still the same tall, handsome, ironic spectator. An observer of life. An academic. Removed. Skeptical. Someone with the special secret who knows what will make him happy and what won't.

She backed into the small foyer. He closed the door, still looking at her. He hadn't touched her. "Liz, you look absolutely beautiful. I've never seen you look better." He paused. "Whatever you're doing, it seems to agree with you."

She didn't say anything. She couldn't. She moved toward him slowly. It was like the pull of the moon on the tides.

Oh, dear God, he feels good in my arms. Has it been this long? Have I missed him this much? He was kissing her with that tender reticence of his that made her love him so.

I've tried not to think about her, he said to himself. I've

tried to work and put her out of my mind. But my pace is so much less frenetic than hers. She has less time to think about us. Will she ever change? Will she ever want more than the excitement and challenge of her career?

"It's so good just to hold you, Peter. God how I've missed you."

"And I've missed you." They parted momentarily, and he gave a soft whistle as he looked about the suite. "This sure beats St. Vincent's Avenue."

"Oh, I don't know. St. Vincent's Avenue had a charm of its own."

"If it did, it was only that you lived there."

She took his hand and led him to the sofa. He could see Arlington Street and the Boston Gardens. Tourists were paddling the swan boats around the small lake. The city sweltered under a merciless sun.

"My darling," she said to him softly. She stroked his hair and couldn't take her eyes from his face. It was as inevitable as dusk and dawn. What they felt was too intense, too confused, too conflicting to verbalize. They had to plumb the depths of each other's souls. Each had to become part of the other. Even this intensity wouldn't satisfy them because in the back of their minds lurked the specter of what kept them apart. But that was for later. Now, there could be no more waiting. Now, the shadows of their souls had to absorb each other. She felt her body mold itself to his as she kissed him with all of the expectant urgency that had built inside her like a smoldering volcano. They clung to each other, her mouth to his as he lifted her off the floor with that surprising strength of his. It was like the first time on that brutally cold winter night in Cambridge when he had carried her to his bedroom, just like this. She had learned to know the exquisite choreography of his lovemaking. The ballet that infused her with a mind-breaking pleasure, so intense, that it seemed cataclysmic.

"I just want you to hold me. I don't want you to move or to do anything. Just hold me, Peter. Just hold me."

She lay in his arms. He's always been more controlled than I am, she thought. No man will ever make love to me the way he does. He's so gentle and knowing. Where did he ever learn to make love like that? I've always wanted to ask him, but I never have.

The sky had started to darken, diffusing gray shadowed light through the room.

"Did I hear you mention dinner," he said, smiling at her.

"Why does sex always make you hungry, Peter?"

"Sometimes it makes me hungry for more sex," he laughed softly.

"I hope this is one of the times, Mr. Wells, because if you think I'm letting you out of bed for dinner you're out of your mind."

"I've had worse offers."

She kicked him. "You rat."

"If it's lust for my poor body you feel, madam, may I say that the feeling is very, very mutual. Only/. . ."

"Only what?"

"Only your body, madam, is hardly poor."

She snuggled against him. "I'm glad you said that."

"If I didn't, I'd be an idiot. You're a beautiful woman, Liz."

"No, I'm not."

"Liz, I know a beautiful woman when I see one." He brushed her hair away from her face.

"Suppose I told you, Peter, that today I saw the most beautiful woman I have ever met."

"Women are lousy judges of another woman's attractiveness."

"Not this woman, Peter. She was so incredibly lovely that she didn't seem real. And she has an M.D." Liz sighed. "She can give a girl a complex. I mean it."

He drew her closer to him and kissed her tenderly.

"Where did you meet this Aphrodite?"

"At Family Care. She's a psychoanalyst on the staff there."

"Remind me to develop some emotional problems."

"Don't laugh, Peter. That's one of her functions."

"What?"

"To use her looks as a part of therapy with male patients who feel insecure with women."

He moved away from her slightly, looking at her skeptically. "Are you putting me on?"

"I definitely am not. That's one of the things she does, and it seems to work. Dr. Haley, the head of Family Care, showed me a film in which this woman was working with a very important scientist. Over a period of time she helped him regain his confidence. Even helped to pick out new clothes for him. Had dinner with him. Obviously they did a lot more for him than give him a beautiful woman who was sympathetic. But that is really part of her job."

"Well, you'll do for me, Liz."

"Not if you met her."

"Even if I met her."

"You're sweet."

"I'm not sweet, but I *am* hungry."

"You're impossible, Peter."

"If you feed me, I'll have more strength." He laughed.

"Then I'll feed you," she said. "And then—"

"And then, Liz, you're going to have a very hard time getting me out of this room."

"Even to go to Maine?"

"Even to go to Maine."

"You're all packed for the weekend?"

"I left everything in the trunk of the car," he said.

"Not very bright, professor. You'll need a shave and change."

"I know. I thought we would be going out for dinner and I could bring my things up later."

She groaned. "Oh, Peter, now you will have to get up. You're breaking my mood. I didn't want us to be apart a second until we had to leave for Maine."

"I'm sorry, Liz. But it's hardly a voyage to the car. It's in a lot near the hotel on Boylston Street."

She sat up holding the sheet over her breasts.

"Go shower, Peter. I'll order dinner. What do you want?"

He got up and walked into the bathroom. "Is this on you or on the company?" he asked.

"It's on Dr. Haley."

"Well, in that case, I'd like filet mignon and a shrimp cocktail." He turned on the shower. "How about a bottle of champagne to celebrate?"

"Now you're beginning to make me hungry," she said. She picked up the telephone to call room service.

This should fit in with Tim's idea of a sybaritic life-style, she thought. But the champagne. That might be a little much. Oh the hell with it, Liz. Live it up. Dr. Haley does.

• • •

The night sounds of the city were reduced to the occasional siren, splitting the silence with its strident urgency, punctuating their need to find reassurance in the proximity of the other. Touching. Making sure this was no illusion.

I've tried so hard not to think about him. Only a few phone calls. Scattered letters. I've tried to hide everything in work, and now it's all opened up again. A wound that won't heal. It's like waiting to be executed. Knowing that they're going to come for you at an appointed time. That's the terror and the agony. Time. Sunday we'll drive back here, and I'll fly to New York. He'll go back to Harvard, and then what? When will we see each other? What will happen when we do? Peter wants a commitment from me, which I can't give. Why? What's wrong with me? Does my career mean more to me than he does? How would it work if he came to New York? Could he put up with my traveling so much? Being with George so often? How long would it be before I had to make a choice? He wants a wife and children, a home. Am I a homemaker? His kind? Do I want that?

There is something tragic about this, he thought. We're lying here in each other's arms. She loves me. I know that. I adore her. So what's the problem? The problem, you idiot, is that you've fallen in love with the wrong girl, and she has fallen in love with the wrong man. It's that simple. Unfortunately, yes. But are you supposed to accept this? What do you do, become a Buddhist monk? Drown yourself in some psychological absinthe and moon around wailing about unrequited love? What the hell do you do, Peter? You've been in love with her for three years. There are these tearing separations and these searing reunions. But what's in between? She's always so busy. I keep calling her, and she's always on some damn business trip. I don't even bother to leave messages. What's the sense? Even if I came to New York and got a job at Columbia or NYU, when would I see her? Our lives would be so totally different. What would we have to share besides a love that is being wrecked by her damn business? When would my demands on her time begin to conflict with those of Baldwin Cooper? And what about children? It would be impossible with her career. Totally unfair to the children. And I'm damned if I'm going to become one of those husbands who winds up doing the cooking and the laundry. Do I have the guts or even the ability to break this off? Does she? Oh God, what the hell do we do?

She knew that what they had was changing. It was as ineluctable as the tides. She knew both consciously and unconsciously that she had chosen. She could feel the difference in their relationship. Peter was more withdrawn. He was building a protective layer around the irritation, like an oyster. She felt guilty for having become so involved with her career that her time for him was insufficient. He's slipping away from me, she thought, and I'm letting him go. It's like watching raindrops slide down a window. They just disappear. She turned toward him. He was staring at the ceiling. He lay perfectly still.

"What are you thinking, Peter?" she asked, her voice thick with fatigue.

"Us," he said.

"What about us, darling?" He paused a long time before answering. "I wish to hell I knew, Liz." He stroked her hair and kissed her. She moved closer to him and fell asleep in his arms.

The windows of the old Chevrolet were wide open. Hot, turbulent air blew at her face and hair. It's really hot for Maine, she thought as she lay back against the front seat while Peter drove. They had run out of things to say to each other in the cataract of inner revelations that had left them exhausted from the night.

It's horrible to even think it, she thought, but I begrudge the time I have to spend with Mom when Peter and I can't be alone. But I've got to see her. It's been three months. Her thought processes could not contain that perception. Only three months. It seems like a lifetime. It's impossible. It has to be more than three months. Peter held a steady sixty miles an hour. Her mind rebuffed the sound of tires on the hot, black asphalt; the buffeting of the wind. The monotony and heat of the turnpike was their penance.

"We should have stayed in Boston," she said.

"Your mother wouldn't have appreciated that."

"I know."

He looked at her quickly and then turned back to concentrate on driving.

There has to be an explanation for two people doing to each

other what we're doing, he thought, but I'll be damned if I can figure it out.

"I've been thinking about Mother," she said. He didn't answer.

"I'm going to tell her we want to sleep together."

He turned to look at her. "Are you crazy, Liz? That would be embarrassing for me. I couldn't sleep with you in your mother's house."

"Don't be such a hypocritical prude. My mother is a nurse. There's not much to do with life that she hasn't seen." Her voice softened, "or been through. Do you think she's so stupid or naive that she doesn't know that we've been to bed together?" She paused. "Peter, we have so little time. I'm not going to waste any of it. Mother will understand. And you'll just have to live with your embarrassment." She put her head on his shoulder. "Don't be difficult, darling."

"I'm not trying to be difficult, Liz. But I think you're underestimating your mother's permissiveness. She's pretty old-fashioned, especially where you're concerned."

"Let me handle my mother. She'll understand. She likes you. She can't understand why we haven't married."

"Neither can I." His face was set, determined, his eyes still on the road. I shouldn't have said that, he thought. What good does it do? It only hurts her and makes her feel guilty. Maybe she should feel guilty, damn it.

"Do you want me to drive, Peter?"

"No. It's okay. I'm fine."

"Then I'm going to sleep for a while. I'm really bushed." She leaned against him, her head resting on his shoulder. He could feel her hair blowing against his face. "I hope it's cooler in Falmouth," he said. She didn't answer. She was already asleep.

The small white house in Falmouth was as he last remembered it. Lifeless. Cleaned. Waxed. He remembered the artificial fruit on the unused dining room table. Even that had been dusted. He wondered if Liz's mother had any interests in life other than her job at the hospital and keeping this small house spotless. It wasn't a house as he thought of a house. It was a symbol of the past that Liz's mother had kept morbidly alive. What had happened to the three of them that had affected Mrs. Clark so permanently? He knew Liz's father had been killed in an accident. There was something about his being with another woman at the time who had also been killed. Is that possible? Could a woman like Betty Clark have allowed an episode like that to warp her whole life and affect Liz? It doesn't seem reasonable, he thought, but then, what does? It must have affected Liz, too. Maybe that's why she tries so hard to be independent.

"May I help you with anything, Peter?" Mrs. Clark asked.

"No, thank you, Mrs. Clark. I'll take care of it."

"Peter." Liz looked at him determinedly. "Please put our things in the upstairs hall. I want to talk to Mother for a minute." He avoided her gaze and went back to the car to get their luggage.

"Mother, let's go into the living room." Betty Clark followed her daughter into the darkened living room with its drawn shades and stale air. "Mother, I want to ask you something." She hesitated. This is harder than I thought, she said to herself.

"Mother . . ."

"Well, what is it?"

They heard Peter walking up the wooden stairs with the luggage.

This is ridiculous, Liz thought.

"Mother . . ."

"Will you stop saying 'Mother'? What is it, Liz?"

"Peter and I would like to sleep in the same room."

Liz watched her mother. Betty Clark's face showed little expression except for the tautness around her mouth. She met her mother's gaze with her own. "If this offends you, Mother," she said stiffly, "then Peter and I can stay in a motel."

Her mother's memory drifted back to her own past. To her constricted girlhood and adolescence. She remembered the continual censures that arose from her mother's false pride, her concern for appearance, for how things would look to others. She remembered the continual reproofs, the joylessness. She looked at Liz and swallowed hard. This wasn't easy for Betty Clark, not with her background, but she was determined not to inflict her own taboos on her daughter. They had cost her too much.

"It doesn't offend me, Liz," she said uneasily. "You're a grown woman, and you can live your life as you please." Liz started to say something. Her mother held up her hand. "Liz, I'm not being critical of what you do. I'm just—" Her voice became softer, her eyes seemed to hold something of her own past. She waved her hand at Liz. "Of course you and Peter can sleep in the same room. I'll move into your room." She smiled. "He's a little tall for your old bed."

Liz felt a wave of relief. She hadn't realized how tense she had been about what she thought would be her mother's reluctant, petulant agreement. But it isn't like that, she thought. She really doesn't mind. Liz moved to her mother and embraced her, and kissed her lightly on her pale cheek. "Mother, thank you for being so dear." She felt her mother's arms around her. She felt the intimate warmth of their embrace. They were not demonstrative people. They withheld their emotions. But the love was there, and in this rare moment of declaration it was like a shaft of sunlight.

Liz kissed her mother again and walked quickly out of the room. She could hear Peter closing the trunk of the car. She went to him. "It's all right, darling. Mother doesn't mind. She really doesn't." She saw him look at her with uneasy embarrassment. "Peter, will you stop being so silly? It's all right."

He shook his head in mock resignation. "Maybe it's a good thing we're not married. You'd be railroading me, as you've been doing for the past three years. You're a very demanding woman, Miss Clark. Has anyone ever told you that?"

"Several people."

"Who?"

"You, for instance. Come on, Peter. I want to change and go to the beach. Put our things in Mother's room. She's going to sleep in my room."

"Oh, that's just great. How do you think I'm going to feel making love to you in your mother's bed?"

"Consumed by lust, I hope."

"You're depraved," he said laughing.

"Have you got any better offers?"

"Not unless you introduce me to that female psychoanalyst you told me about."

"Over my dead body. Come on, Peter. Let's go up and change. Maybe we can persuade Mother to come to the beach."

They packed beer and sandwiches in a plastic cooler and drove to Harper's Cove. It was more crowded than ever. A souvenir stand and small restaurant had been built over an outcropping of granite that faced Casco Bay. The winter storms had badly weathered the peeling yellow paint of the wooden building. Empty plastic containers overflowed the packed garbage cans. Cigarette butts looked like flattened white bugs. Aluminum cans glinted in the sun.

"It's awful," Liz said, her voice showing surprise and disappointment.

Peter looked at the crowded beach. It's wall-to-wall bodies, he thought.

Betty Clark watched both of them. "Let's go back to the car," she said. "I know a place you'll like better than this. But first I have to make a phone call."

They walked back up the hot asphalt road studded with gravel. They saw a public phone in a battered aluminum booth.

"I need a dime," she said. "I don't have any change." Peter handed her a dime. They watched her dial and wait. They could see her speaking animatedly to someone. They saw her look of satisfaction. She opened the door of the booth. "I think we can save this afternoon," she said quietly.

They got back into the car and followed her directions through winding roads that kept opening up to surprising views of the bay. "Turn to the right and go down that hill. It's on the left side of the street," she said.

"Mother, where are you taking us?"

"Don't worry. I'm still good for something," she said.

Peter and Liz looked at each other. The remark was poignant. They both had interpreted it the same way.

"There it is."

They parked on a tree-shaded street at the bottom of a hill with a sweeping view of Casco Bay. The house on their right was large, with weathered, gray wooden shingles and white-painted trim. Morning glories climbed a white wooden trellis. The lawn was neatly cut and bordered on a stone bulkhead that faced a small rock-strewn private beach. There was a wharf with a float beside it where a rowing skiff was tethered. A small sloop rode off a mooring out beyond the fall of the tide. Windowboxes held red splashes of geraniums. The garden at the far end of the lawn was a living palette of zinnias, marigolds, and snapdragons. A white wooden flagpole stood in the middle of the lawn with the American flag hanging limp in the breezeless afternoon. The property was bounded by a low stone wall.

Betty motioned them to follow her. She opened the gate under the trellis and walked to the front door of the house.

The door opened, and a tall, lean man with a shock of unruly gray hair stood on the front steps smiling warmly at Betty Clark. She turned to Liz and Peter who had stood just inside the trellis unsure of what was going on.

"Come on and meet Dr. Halsey." They walked toward the tall man whose craggy face smiled at them warmly.

"Liz. Peter. This is Dr. Nathaniel Halsey. Nate. My daughter Elizabeth, and Peter Wells."

Liz waited as Dr. Halsey walked toward her, his hand extended. "So you're Betty's daughter. I'm very pleased to meet you." Liz shook his hand. He turned to Peter. "Pleased to meet you, Mr. Wells."

I've heard of him, Liz thought. Mother's mentioned him from time to time. He's a surgeon at Portland General. She works with him.

"Your mother tells me you were less than thrilled with Harper's Cove."

Liz laughed. "That's a fair statement, doctor."

He shook his head, his lips compressed in resignation. "This bay used to be so beautiful." He said it as if he were talking to himself. "Now the oil tankers anchor off Portland like great steel whales. We've got the tank fumes and the pollution from the oil spills." His face brightened. "But I think we can fix you up for the afternoon with a little fun.

"There's not enough wind for a sail in the sloop, but the skiff is one of my favorites. If you'll promise to keep off any rocks, you might enjoy a row out to Fox Island." He pointed to the small island with its border of dark green fir trees.

"The island's owned by Jake Pratt, but he and I are good friends. He's up in Bangor, so no one will bother you. There's a little sand beach where you can swim, and some great blueberries if you're in the mood."

Liz's face brightened. "That sounds wonderful, Dr. Halsey."

"Yes, sir," Peter said.

"Nothing to it. You kids have a good time."

"What about you, Mother? Aren't you coming?"

"No. I'll stay here with Nate. You two have a good time."

"Don't deprive me of your mother, Liz. She's the hardest woman to get to visit I know."

Dr. Halsey moved closer to Betty and put his arm around her shoulder. "Is there anything the kids need? Beer, sandwiches?"

Betty looked up at him. Her eyes held a radiance Liz hadn't remembered seeing for so long. "They're fine, Nate. They've got what they need in the cooler in the car."

"You have a beautiful house, Dr. Halsey," Liz said.

"Thank you. The gardens wouldn't have passed Margaret's inspection, but since she's gone I've had to rely on what help I can get. I don't have the time to take care of things myself."

"It looks lovely."

"Suppose I go to the car and get our things," Peter said.

"I'll fetch the oars," Dr. Halsey said. He started to walk to the back of the house, then stopped and turned.

"I'd love to have you stay for supper. We'll have lobsters and clams. A little celebration of Betty's visit."

Liz looked at Peter, then at her mother. She could see her mother's pleasure, but she could also see her about to protest.

"We'd be delighted to stay, Dr. Halsey," Liz said, looking directly at her mother. Betty Clark was between a frown and a smile. The smile came slowly with a creeping hesitation, but it came.

"Then that's settled. Betty, I'll get the oars, and then we can have some iced tea if you like. I've got some fresh cucumbers for sandwiches and some fresh tomatoes."

"You talked me into it, Nate."

They watched Peter row the skiff toward Fox Island with Liz sitting in the stern. They waved a few times and then went back into the house. "Nate. I'm not used to having a man wait on me—or anyone else, for that matter. You let me fix us some lunch."

They ate under the old maple at a white-painted circular table. The first trace of an afternoon breeze was beginning to stir the trees.

"He seems like a nice young man, Betty."

"He is."

"What does he do?"

"He's working on a Ph.D. in history at Harvard."

"He sounds English."

"He is."

Nate paused. "Your daughter is a very attractive young woman."

"Thank you."

"From what you've told me, she seems to have quite a career cut out for her in New York."

"She seems to love it."

Nate paused. "Are they serious, Betty?"

She looked away from him, out toward Fox Island where she could still see the faint outline of the skiff.

"They're very much in love, Nate," she said quietly, then almost to herself, "but I don't know what's going to come of it."

He didn't say anything. He watched her as her thoughts became directed inward.

"They both want different things out of life, Nate. Liz wants a challenging, exciting career. Peter doesn't object to that, but Liz is almost constantly on the go. They've been going together for nearly three years, but Liz is afraid to take a chance, afraid she might not make a go of their marriage."

"And what are you afraid of, Betty?" He said it quietly. He placed his hand gently on hers. "You don't have to live alone, and neither do I. Why is it so difficult for you to find any joy in your life?" He paused. "We could be happy together, Betty. I know we could."

She turned to look at him. At the craggy, weathered face and the unruly hair. She saw the blue eyes probe her own. She wondered if they had found the place where she hid her private, warped sense of shame. The place where her pride had been twisted into a cord that strangled her. Could he see all this?

He's what I need, she thought, but I can't. Do I plan to spend the rest of my life in the arid runs between that small, silent house and the hospital? Is that all I want? This man is offering me a new life, and he's a good man. What's wrong with me? She looked away from him out toward Fox Island. She could no longer see the skiff, but she felt the invisible barrier that kept her daughter and herself from uniting with the men they loved.

• • •

Liz and Peter lay in Betty's bed. They seemed strangely separated. He lay on his back looking up at the ceiling.

"God, the water was cold," she said. Her thoughts were back on Fox Island.

"No wonder they call you people 'Mainiacs.' You have to be a lunatic to swim in that water," he said.

"But it's refreshing. You've got to admit that."

"Refreshing. If that's a synonym for 'arctic,' I'll agree with you."

"You're getting soft, Peter." She snuggled closer to him. "I wish we could stay here forever."

He hesitated, his voice low and serious. "No, you don't. You'd be bored out of your mind in three days."

She didn't answer. She didn't have to. The lambent moonlight mottled the shadows on the closed bedroom door.

"What did you think of Dr. Halsey?" she asked quietly.

"He's a casting director's dream of a Yankee doctor."

"He is, isn't he?" She paused. "He seems fond of my mother."

"He is."

"Funny. Mom never speaks about him or writes about him. I heard her mention him when I was growing up, but just as a good surgeon whom she worked with."

"Did you know his wife had died?"

"No."

"Did you see him helping your mother clean up after dinner?"

"You mean supper. Up here it's supper."

"Okay, supper." He paused. "There's a lot going on there, Liz."

She didn't say anything. She had watched Dr. Halsey and her mother all evening. She could see Nate Halsey's affection for her mother. She could sense her mother's controlled, embarrassed acknowledgment of her own affection for this man of substance and character. Why doesn't she move in with him or marry him? Liz thought. They could share a life together. A good life. Why does she choose to spend her nights alone in this empty house full of all the wrong memories? As she lay there thinking, the irony of the similarity between her own relationship to Peter and her mother's to Nate didn't occur to her. But it was blatantly apparent to Peter.

Peter remained looking up at the ceiling watching the gray shadows move as the wind stirred the leaves of the old maple tree outside the window. She moved closer to him with more deliberation than anticipation. His distant manner irritated her. Maybe the associations with this room were inhibiting. But it was more than that; she could feel it. She was frustrated by the peculiar blend of desire and petulance in his manner. She had become quite skilled at arousing his interest, but did she want to? She touched him. She felt him quiver, but he didn't change his position; he remained looking up at the ceiling. She moved closer to him and began to manipulate his body, increasing her own passion as she did so. She slipped her head under the covers. They both came alive with a strange reluctance. Their bodies responded to the stimuli of sex, but their minds remained separate. For the first time they made love mechanically, and her intuition told her that the years of indecision, the months of separation, the irresolution of their basic problem—her career—had finally taken its toll.

She moved as far away from him as she could. She turned on her side to look at him. "That wasn't exactly the way it was on Fox Island."

He didn't answer her.

"Peter, what is it? What's the matter?"

He sighed audibly, not looking at her. "Do you know how many times I've called you in the past three months?"

"Not many."

"You're wrong. I've called often."

"Then you haven't left any messages."

"I stopped calling your office because you were always tied up in some meeting, or you were on a trip somewhere."

"Did you try me at home?"

"Occasionally."

"I'm not *always* traveling."

"You couldn't prove that by me." He paused. "How many times have you called me?"

A shaft of guilt speared her. She hesitated. "Not often enough," she said quietly. "Not nearly often enough."

"I rest my case."

"But, Peter, you have no idea what it's like. I'm in the office by eight o'clock. I usually have meetings or conferences with clients, or I'm working on reports. George wants me to do this. Larry wants something else. George has given me a lot of responsibility."

"So I've noticed."

"Well, what's wrong with that?"

"Nothing, if that's what you want."

"Of course that's what I want, Peter. I want to go as fast and as far as I can. What's wrong with that?" It just slipped out, but it was true.

"It's a disease that seems to affect you Americans."

She was up on one elbow looking at him, annoyed more than ever by his academic condescension.

"Don't be so damn smug, Peter. I'll admit that I get carried away by my career, but I won't make apologies for my ambition. I don't have the option to pursue your leisurely paced academic existence."

He turned toward her to protest, but her anger pushed him aside.

"I know something of what life is like in a university," she said. "I know you work hard. You're subjected to internecine rivalries and university politics. But there is no way I can explain to you the pressures and demands of our business."

"And you like that?"

"Not all the time. Sometimes I'm so tired I can hardly breathe. But, yes, most of the times I like it. What I've experienced so far I find stimulating and exciting and terribly challenging."

The moonlight, dappled by the leaves of the old maple outside the window, rested softly on his face. She could see his resignation. More upsetting to her, she could sense his aloofness.

They both remained silent for a long time. Finally he spoke. Not to her, but rather to himself. "We've been kidding ourselves that we could hold this together with you in New York, in that business." His voice was laced with bitterness and hostility. "You're in love with a career, not with me."

"That's not true."

"It is true. It's always been true."

"You know what your trouble is, Peter? There's no compromise in you."

"That's a good one, coming from you. What about you? How much are you willing to compromise for me?"

"I told you we could work it out in New York, Peter. There's Columbia and NYU . . ."

"And why should I want to come to New York? I detest

that city. It's noisy, aggressive, dirty, crowded, and incredibly mercantile."

She listened to his quiet condemnation of her city, her career, her life. Perhaps she had not compromised either, but at least she was willing to consider it. He evidently was not. For some reason, as she listened to him she thought of George. Of that night when he had come to her so deeply troubled about Claudia. He had been warm and open, and he had needed her. And God knows he understood the life she led.

"What are we going to do, Liz?" Peter said evenly.

She was too engrossed in her own thoughts to hear him.

"You are far away," he said.

She paused, looked at him intently, watching the moonlight on his face. Her voice was soft, almost as if she were talking to herself. "Has it ever occurred to you, Peter, just how far away two people can be while sharing the same bed?"

Liz and Peter stood in the lounge of the Eastern Airlines shuttle at Boston's Logan Airport, waiting for the 7:00 P.M. flight to La Guardia, oblivious of the crowds and the motion and noise of the busy airport.

I can't believe it's been less than three days, she thought, not looking at him, but feeling connected to him as she knew he felt connected to her. How can I go back and just leave him here, leave *us* here?

This is worse than it's ever been, he thought. I'm not sure I can take these separations anymore. I'm weary of being turned on the spit of her indecision and roasted over the coals of our differences.

They were standing near the gate. He was holding her hand, but they were avoiding each other's eyes.

Why don't I just say the hell with my career, she thought, and accept him, or at least take a chance that it will work out? The thought of her mother's tragic marriage edged out from the recesses of her mind. Her face tightened as she thought about Betty Clark. But I'm not like my mother. I'm willing to give it a chance. Then why don't I? she asked herself. Because I'm afraid I'll fail. I'm afraid that in time, our love won't be enough.

She felt lifeless, without hope for what she longed to have— a shared, loving life. As she stood beside him feeling and understanding in his silence, she seemed to resign herself to the probability that she was only going to have half a life. What she couldn't figure out was why she was committing herself to such an arid course, as her mother had done so many years ago. It's like some mythical curse, she thought. I've got to stop doing this to myself. There's a limit. I can't go on forever having my guts wrenched out and hoping things will change.

Their thoughts were broken by the public address system announcing the departure of her flight. She turned to Peter, and they held each other briefly. They were too reticent to display their emotions easily with a crowd of moving, impatient people watching.

"I'll call you tonight, when I get to my apartment," she said. He nodded, looking at her. She seemed to see some tragic resolve there, and it frightened her.

"I have to go now, darling." He nodded, his lips compressed. She stretched up to kiss him and started to leave. He held her hand, preventing her from going.

"I'll always love you, Liz," he said quietly. She looked at him, her eyes wide with apprehension. Her intuition told her that there was something ominous in his declaration. Her mind filled her with a cold dread that gripped her with a tangible force. She squeezed his hand hard, with anxious desperation, still searching his face for more clues.

"You'd better go, or you'll miss your plane."

She unwillingly let go of his hand. "I'll call, Peter, as soon as I get home. We'll talk, darling." He shook his head, looking at her with a heartbreaking discipline that frightened her. "Go, Liz," he said quietly. He watched her tall, slender figure move toward the gate. She stopped as she showed her boarding pass, and then turned toward him. They exchanged final inquiring glances, and then she disappeared inside the plane.

On the brief flight to New York, she lay back and let her mind roam the experiences of the weekend. She found it impossible to believe she had been gone only three days. It seemed like a lifetime. New York, her job, George, Family Care, it was as if they hadn't existed. But the practical part of her mind was reasserting itself. She knew what she was going back to— back to the small apartment in Greenwich Village, back to George, back to Baldwin Cooper. The pain of leaving Peter was raw, but the tendril that attached her to him was almost imperceptibly growing thinner with her increasing separation in time and distance. A part of her mind had discovered this small pulse of guilt-ridden awareness, and as she looked out of the window at the shoreline of Connecticut, seeing the haze-shrouded shapes of Manhattan loom above the western end of Long Island, she felt frightened, vulnerable, and miserably alone.

Chapter 20

SHE STOOD IN her living room, several steps below street level. The apartment was stifling. It would be an ugly, hot night until the small air conditioners in the living room and bedroom could cool off the late August heat. She carried her suitcase into the bedroom and turned on both air conditioners.

The city was drugged by heat. In three months her ears had become attuned to the street sounds. She stood still in her bedroom to listen. She heard the absence of noise. A strange, numb silence hung over the Village, where people stared from open windows and sat on steps in silent, dripping resignation to the oven that had become Manhattan.

She undressed and showered and washed her hair and put on a loose cotton shift. She went to the telephone and dialed Peter. The phone rang at least ten times; there was no answer. She hung up the phone, her face revealing surprise and anxiety. "Where could he be? It wasn't like him to go out when he knew she was going to call. She got up and went into the kitchen to mix herself a stiff gin and tonic. She was annoyed. No, angry.

This is ridiculous, she thought. Why should he sit near a phone waiting for my call? He's not an answering service. She went back into the living room and dialed Peter again. No answer. I'm being childish, she scolded herself. He'll be back. I'll call him before I go to bed. Why doesn't he call me? He almost never calls me. I'm the one who calls him. The thought added to her frustration and anger. He's probably out getting some air. Cambridge must be almost as bad as New York. Oh, the hell with it. I've got work to do tomorrow. I've got to get organized. She went to the small desk at the far end of the living room and got a pad and a black felt-tipped pen. She went back to the couch, and sat down and started to think.

I've got to call Arnold Goodwin of Family Care and find out when he can get me a breakdown of the consolidated financials.

I need to dictate my impressions of Family Care. I should do that tonight, but I'm too tired.

Have to see George and find out if he's still serious about my going to the Coast to see Barkley. My God, that's bizarre, she thought. How am I supposed to talk Barkley out of having a love affair? It's none of our damn business. She slapped the legal pad sharply against her thigh. Damn it, she thought. George does have a point. Barkley's affair won't sit very well with his customers. She sighed. Why couldn't Barkley have been in the fashion or film business? Then no one would care if he had a hundred love affairs. But Barkley's customers are banks. She got up and began pacing the living room. George is right. They would never sit still for something like this. But what am I supposed to do? I can't even handle my own love life, never mind Barkley's. She underlined George's name on the pad with broad dark slashes. "That's going to be some pip of an assignment," she said aloud.

I've got to call Sat-Nav and Compu-Service in L.A. and Well-Log in Houston. She wrote down the names of three of the four companies for which she had account responsibility. She monitored those three companies, along with Twenty/Twenty. Liz had to know enough about their operations so that she could spot the first signs of trouble and report it to George. That meant that she not only had to watch their finances and earnings progress, but she had to understand enough about their manufacturing and marketing to know what was going on in their factories and in the field. This was far more difficult for her to learn than just reading financial reports. Consulting engineers cost money, and Baldwin Cooper tried to avoid hiring them unless they suspected serious trouble. It was part of Liz's job to spot that kind of trouble. Fast.

I still have so much to learn, she thought. I never dreamed I would have this much responsibility in so short a time. She paused. I wonder if George has brought me along so quickly because of his feelings for me. She thought about that for a while and then shook her head. No way, she thought. George is all business, up to a point. He wouldn't risk his career for me or for anyone else. No. He must think I'm up to it. She sighed. I should have had an engineering background for this job. Look at the clients I've got. Sat-Nav makes satellite navigational systems. Compu-Serv is a computer servicing business. Well-Log makes testing and measuring devices for drilling for oil and natural gas, and Twenty/Twenty devises security systems for banks. She looked at the neat stack of technical documents on top of the air conditioner near her desk. There wasn't room in or on the small desk for the voluminous data she had to read. She had been reading product information and technical specs for weeks.

She had developed the habit of making a list of what she didn't understand. On each trip to a company she would ask the production and engineering people to explain things to her. They had been impressed with the scope and detail of her questioning, and reports began to drift back to George, unknown to Liz, that she was the best representative Baldwin Cooper had, including George. That was why George had fed her so much responsibility so fast. It wasn't because of her great legs or blue eyes. It was because she did her job as well as or better than Howard, Curt, and Arthur, all of whom were bright and capable and had been with the firm for two and a half years or longer.

The apartment was getting cooler. She made herself another weak gin and tonic and picked up the phone to call Peter. It was now nearly 11:00 P.M. He had to be in. She listened to the phone ring, her heart beating more rapidly with her increased anxiety. Where was he? This wasn't like Peter.

God. I wonder if something's happened to him. Where could he be at eleven o'clock on a Sunday night? She hung up. It's so unlike him. What will I do if I don't hear from him before I go to work? The phone rang. At first its sound so startled her that she froze. It rang a few more times before she recovered enough poise to answer it.

"Peter," she said almost desperately.

There was a long pause on the other end. "Better try again," the familiar voice said.

"George. Oh, George, I'm sorry. I—ah—thought it was Peter. I've been trying to reach him, and I can't get him." Her anxiety was very apparent to George.

"Any problems?"

She paused, her mind filling with the complications of these two men. "I'm not sure. It's not like him to be out when he's expecting a call."

George let it go. "How was your weekend?"

"We had a great time. We visited my mother in Falmouth."

George had caught the pronoun "we." He let that go as well. "What about Family Care? Does it look like anything we might be interested in?"

Her mind snapped back to business. "It might be, George; it's too early for me to tell. I've got to get their financials and a breakdown of their operations."

"Never mind. That can wait until morning. I've got you set up for ten o'clock in my office. We have a lot to go over." He paused. "Are you uncomfortable down there?"

"It's beginning to cool off a little. The air conditioners are struggling."

She could sense that this call was unsatisfying to him, that he wanted it to be more personal, but that his instincts were guiding him toward reticence. She was impressed with his prescience, and grateful for it.

"I'm glad to know you're back safely, Liz," he said quietly. "I'll see you in the morning."

"At ten," she said.

"Right." He paused. "I hope it's cool enough for you to get some sleep." He didn't mention Peter. She was grateful for that, too.

She got into bed. The apartment had cooled, and her mind had begun to accustom itself to being back in New York, to being away from Peter. George had accelerated that process. She turned off the bedside lamp. She was very tired and had decided, Peter or no Peter, that she had to get some sleep. She was nearly asleep when the phone rang. She felt for it in the darkness by her bed.

"Hello."

"Hello, queenie."

"Who is this—Peter?"

"No. It's the bloody Prince of Wales. Who the hell do you think it is?"

"Peter, are you drunk?" She sat up in bed.

"You might say that, luv, if you have an uncharitable character."

She sat up in bed. "Peter, you *are* drunk."

"That is not an illogical premise, luv."

"Peter, what in God's name have you been doing?"

"It's your torrid bloody Yank summers, luv. They'd melt the breastplate off a Horse Guardsman." He laughed. "I've been cooling off in one of the lesser Cambridge pubs."

"Oh, Peter. I've been calling you all evening. You've had me worried half to death."

"Sorry about that, luv. I just got caught up with a few of the local mates. I was trying to explain cricket to them, but I'm afraid they prefer your baseball, and the Red Sox."

Peter rarely had more than one or two drinks. She understood that she was the reason why he was drunk, but what was more frightening to her was that she intuitively understood that this minor debauch was really a decision. He had made up his mind about them, and she was frightened by her intimations of what that was.

"Peter, are you all right?"

"Probably won't be in the morning, luv."

"Is there something you want to tell me?"

"Not much. I'm going to Mom and Dad's in Sussex. Have a bit of a holiday coming, princess."

"Will you be coming back?" she asked quietly.

"Damn well better. I still have that bloody degree to get."

He hadn't mentioned anything about returning to England when they were in Maine. He had decided this tonight; she was sure of that. It was more than just the desire to see his parents. This is his first step away from me, she thought. If he does this and I just let him go, then there will be others, until one day there will be no more strings. He'll go like some slowly drifting skiff that has slipped its mooring.

She sat in bed, not knowing what to say to him. He was too drunk to hold a conversation. All she could do was what she had done a hundred times before—search her mind for answers where there were none.

• • •

She had left on a Friday and returned on Monday. Yet as she sat in George's chrome and glass office with its leather chairs and contemporary art, it seemed to both of them as if an inordinate amount of time had elapsed; it was almost as if they were strangers meeting for the first time.

He's so different from Peter, she thought, looking at the urbane, well-tailored man sitting opposite her, watching her intently. Those eyes of his don't miss much, she thought. There couldn't be two more different men than George and Peter. And yet there are similarities. They're both strong. Peter's introspective, and George is gregarious. George is of this world, she thought. Peter is outside it, an observer.

George had been watching her, seeing her thoughts turn inward. When he spoke, his voice was quiet, his manner calm but firm. He was bringing her back to business, back to his work, but he knew she had been in another world and that she was finding it difficult to return.

"When I hired you, Liz, I told you that in this business it would never be dull."

She smiled. "And were you ever right." She watched his eyes. They were serious, without a trace of humor. This was unusual for George.

"Liz, while you were in Boston on Friday, Larry called a special meeting. Bob was away. So was Curt. Howard, Arthur, and I sat in. Larry is very upset about the reports he's been getting from me on Twenty/Twenty." He saw her stiffen slightly. She knew what was coming.

"Larry doesn't take lightly a deal where this firm can sell off a piece of its action for twenty million dollars." George toyed with a letter opener. "We all came to the same conclusion. Without Barkley we could never get the stock off at anywhere near market. He punched the symbols for Twenty/Twenty, and the current bid and asked price came up on his desk terminal. "The stock's bid at twenty-five and a half. You know, Liz, that the number of shares available for trading—the float—is small. Our proposed offering of five million shares is a lot of stock for a company the size of Twenty/Twenty." George looked at her, his face concentrated with purpose, his voice very low, but firm. "No way in hell is this firm going to let Barkley blow this deal. Not when so many people are involved. His officers, employees, stockholders, and us."

He could see she was slowly coming back to him, back to his world, their world, a world they both understood.

"Is he still seeing that girl?" she asked.

George nodded.

"Is it worse? What's he doing?" she asked.

George sighed. "It's what he's *not* doing. He's not minding the store. A company that sells sophisticated computer security systems to banks is really selling the capability and integrity of its people. Sol Masters tells me that he's spending most of his time trying to keep Barkley's key marketing guys from leaving." George paused. "What's worse is that he's beginning to get some dangerous feedback from the banks."

"What kind of feedback?"

"You know. The genial lunches that end with, 'Oh, by the way, Sol, we hear Barkley's not around as much as he used to be.' Then the long look and the knowing pause. Sol's been fielding too many of these remarks lately. It's getting out of hand, Liz."

She sighed. "And all of you have elected me to go out and get Barkley back on the straight and narrow."

"We don't expect miracles, Liz," George said. He leaned forward, his elbows resting on the desk. He was holding the letter opener with both hands, flexing it nervously. His face was backlighted by the gauze-draped window. "Larry and I and the associates think that you will be able to get closer to Barkley than any of us could. You might even be able to approach his girlfriend. We could never do that." George sighed. "Liz, this is absolutely top priority. I'll have the associates cover anything else you're doing, but I want you to go to San Francisco and handle this thing. I don't care what you have to do or what it costs or how much time it takes. It has to be done."

Her face was grim. There was no point in trying to equivocate with him. The firm had come to a decision. They had chosen her. If she didn't do it, her career at BC would take on a very flat profile.

"You realize, George, that I may not be able to bring this off. I resent our intrusion into Barkley's private life, and I have some comprehension of the degree of hostility I'll be facing from this woman, who may just happen to be in love with

Barkley. Did you, Larry, Howard, and Arthur consider the possibility that Barkley might be in love with her and she with him?"

George seemed uncomfortable with the thought. "No." His eyes looked away from her.

She thought for a moment. "Has Sol Masters given you any reason to believe that this is Barkley's way of rebelling? You know how antiestablishment Barkley is. He's a brilliant academic beatnik who enjoys tweaking the noses of people like you and me. Has Sol suggested that Barkley is on some kind of kick like that?"

"No."

"Well, if Barkley is not playing games with us, George, then there are only three other explanations for his behavior. One: He may be infatuated with this woman, or so physically attracted to her that he has lost his perspective. Two: It may be the forbidden fruit syndrome. Men like Barkley could very easily be attracted to a beautiful and intelligent woman who was black because he knows that she presents him with a societal taboo, and that would appeal to someone like Barkley. Three: He may love her, George." Her voice softened. "And if he does, nothing we say or do will make any difference to him. And if this woman loves him, it may be easier to deal with the banks than with the two of them." She looked at George evenly. He was still flexing the letter opener. He was looking at her analytically, but with discernible admiration.

"You're our only shot, Liz. If you can't pull this off, we may have to withdraw the stock offering and get someone into Twenty/Twenty who can rebuild its credibility. That will take time, and who knows what the market may be like by then? The market is right for us now, Liz. This is a hell of a shot to blow." He sighed and stood up. He moved to the front of his desk and leaned against it, looking at her as she watched him. The diffused morning light played softly over her face. She looked at him evenly, her expression one of intense distaste.

"George, I'm not trying to be argumentative. If the firm wants me to go, I'll go. But all this makes me wonder what kind of business we're in . . ."

"We're in the deal business, Liz," he interrupted. He held up his hand. "Wait, Liz. Let me finish. I said we're in the deal business; that means the people business. Once you get through

the basic analysis of finance, production, and marketing, everything else depends on management. In fact, everything depends
on management." He pointed his finger at her. "You give me
a company with plenty of money and lousy management and
I'll show you a loser. Give me an undercapitalized company
with good management, and I'll show you a winner." He paused.
"You can always get money, Liz. It's a hell of a lot harder to
come by knowledgeable people with integrity, whom you can
depend on." He moved away from his desk to the windows
and turned around to look at her. "Liz, Barkley is the quintessential problem and opportunity of the venture capital business.
He's a genius whom we've been able to control up to now.
Now he's gotten away from us, and we've got to get him back.
If we can't, Liz, if we don't . . . I should say if you don't, then
we will have blown the single most profitable deal this firm
has ever had."

"When do you want me to go?" she asked quietly, her voice
tingled with a mixture of resignation and exasperation.

"Just as soon as possible." He paused. "I know this is distasteful to you, Liz. It is hard for me to ask you to do it. I'm
not trying to pass the buck to you. I believe—we all believe—
that Barkley will be more resistant to us than he will be to you.
You must have noticed this. Along with his intellectual swinger
image, Barkley has a certain courtliness, or maybe it's just a
deference toward women. I'm not sure which, but it's there.
I've noticed how he reacts to you. Barkley has an empathy
toward you that he could never have with me. That's why it's
got to be you, Liz."

"What pretext do I use to see him?"

"Tell him you want to go over the stock offering with him."

She shook her head. "Too impersonal, George." She thought
for a moment, biting her thumbnail as her mind ranged over
the possibilities. This can't be a business trip. I've got to see
him for some personal reason, maybe something in which I
need his help. She looked up at George. "Barkley lives close
to Stanford, doesn't he?" George nodded. "Suppose I tell him
I have an English friend who is completing his doctorate at
Harvard and would like to do research at Stanford and get a
taste of life on the West Coast before returning to England."
She saw the quick shadows of enmity in George's eyes. "It's
personal enough, George," she said softly, "and innocuous

enough so that Barkley wouldn't suspect anything. It would
get me in, George," she said quietly.

He looked at her a long time with controlled irritation. "I
guess it would," he said.

She stood up and moved closer to him. I want to touch him,
she thought. But I can't. Not here, not now. I want to tell him
that I understand him a lot better than I understand myself.
He's annoyed because I suggested using Peter. That was stupid
of me.

He stood there looking at her, his mouth a rigid line. How
the hell am I ever going to get her to give up this Peter guy?
he thought. Maybe she won't. Maybe she can't. She's been
going with him for three years. There's something standing in
their way. She's told me that. Liz couldn't be happy with some
egghead. Two years and the ivy would strangle her. She needs
challenge and room and space. She needs to run. He can't give
her that. I can.

They stood close together, looking at each other, not touching, their eyes searching for something to hang on to, something
to begin with. "That might work, Liz," he said, his voice low
and tense.

She looked at him for a long time and nodded, turned and
walked slowly toward the door. She stopped and looked back
at him. She could feel the intensity of his control. "I'll try,
George." She paused, struggling with her own confusion. "I'll
call you from San Francisco," she said. He hadn't moved from
the window.

"Call me at home, at night," he said. "The time difference
will make it easier for you."

She nodded. "Yes, that's a good idea. I'll leave as soon as
I can arrange to see Barkley."

"Do you want Howard to follow through on Family Care?"

She shook her head. "No, George. I'd rather do that myself.
There are too many complexities there that I want to sort out.
Besides, I don't think Dr. Haley wants to see any more in-
quisitors. He's a very contained and private person. It would
be a mistake to send someone else in there now. It's too soon."

George had not taken his eyes off her. "I'll see you before
I leave, after I've set up the trip," she said. "And I'll call at
night, George," she said softly, and walked out of the room.

Chapter 21

SHE HAD HAD five and a half hours in flight to think about her life, her career. She had the drive in from the airport in her rented car. Now she was unpacking in the quiet of her hotel room, three thousand miles from home, alone.

As she moved about her room at the Fairmont, eighteen floors above Nob Hill, she saw the saffron sun begin to paint the waters of San Francisco Bay. From her room she could see the bleached surfaces of the buildings of Oakland. She was in one of the world's most beautiful cities, and yet she felt depressed.

She sat down on the bed and looked at the telephone, trying to decide whether or not to call Barkley. She hadn't been able to reach him from New York, but Sol Masters, with whom she had spoken, said he would make sure that Barkley called her. Her instincts told her to wait for his call.

Traveling by yourself for business is so lonely, she thought. People who don't do it think you're having a ball. She laughed sardonically. If you're not busy working or meeting with clients and prospects, then it's empty hotel rooms and eating alone. God, how I hate to eat alone. Maybe it's different for a man. They seem to be always on the make. I could spend every waking hour making love if I chose to. They all make passes. They all want to get you in the sack, and they're all married. Don't any of them have any sense of commitment, or after a while, do they just get tired of reading a book or watching television or writing reports, alone. She got up and walked to the television set, which had an AM-FM radio. She turned the FM on and found a station that broadcast what she had come to think of as dentist music. It was the best she could find, so she let it play. She needed sound in the room, even dentist music.

Is this the way I'm going to spend the rest of my life? she thought. Is this what I wanted when I came to New York? She knew she was depressed because she was alone, but she was also depressed because she hadn't the faintest idea of how she would accomplish what she came out here to do. So much depended on her, and it all seemed so intangible. My God. They're sitting back there in New York waiting for me to perform some kind of miracle with Barkley, and I haven't a clue as to what to do. This ruse about Peter will get me in for openers, but then what do I do?

She decided she wanted a drink and would go up to the Sky Room and kill some time. She had just started out the door, when the phone rang. For some reason she felt the chill of anxiety.

"Hello."

"Liz? Nicholas Barkley. I'm sorry you've had such a difficult time reaching me. Sol tells me you want to see me on a personal matter. Nothing serious, I hope."

"No, Nick. Not at all. It's something I thought you might be able to help me with. I hope it won't be an imposition."

She could hear his ebullience over the phone.

"Liz, I'd like to do anything I can." He paused. "Do you have any plans for tonight?"

"As a matter of fact, I don't. I was dreading a boring evening alone."

He laughed. "One of Uncle Nick's keystone philosophies is that attractive, intelligent women should never be alone, and never bored."

"Nick, that is kind of you, but I don't want to intrude."

"You won't be intruding, and I can guarantee you won't be bored. We're going out to dinner, and we would like you to come with us. I want you to meet Germaine."

"Nick, I really don't want to be a fifth wheel."

"Stop it. Do you want a date? I know some very attractive

guys who would be more than delighted to fill out a foursome."

She laughed. "That's kind, Nick, but I don't want a date. If you think I won't be an intrusion, I'd be delighted to dine with you and Germaine."

"Great." She could almost feel his enthusiasm over the phone. "I've told her about you. She's looking forward to meeting you."

"Me, too. When do you want me to be ready?"

"We'll pick you up at the main entrance at seven. We'll have some dinner, and then we'll get a little party going at my place." He laughed. "I don't think you'll have to worry about being bored."

"Sounds great, Nick. I'm looking forward to it. I'll see you at seven." They both hung up.

Well, she thought, Barkley has quite an evening planned. I'm going to get a very fast introduction into what Sol has been talking about.

She showered and skillfully applied blusher and eye liner to accentuate her best feature, her eyes. As she sat before the lighted mirror in the bathroom, she tried to evaluate her looks. She had never believed that she was really attractive, and yet she knew that men responded to her. She really could not understand why.

If I only looked like Delphine Ravenel, she thought. Imagine having that woman's looks and brains, her educational background. Oh, well, she said to herself, this is what I've got, and this will have to do. A part of her mind that denied her any hypocritical modesty reminded her that Peter and George seemed to find her attractive enough. The thought pleased her as she blended several shades of lip color in quick, practiced strokes with a small pointed brush.

She went to the closet to choose a dress. It was usually cool in San Francisco in the evening, and she decided to wear a black light wool dress with a low neckline that she knew would accentuate her tall, lithe figure. She had brought a silk burgundy shawl to drape over her shoulders. She decided to add the single string of natural pearls her grandmother had given to her mother, who in turn had given them to her when she graduated from Harvard. She looked at them around her neck in the critical light of the bathroom mirror. They had the soft patina of age, the luminescence that was unique to natural pearls. They were the only valuable thing she had ever owned. They were precious to her because they were the only really valuable possession of her mother. They were also a link to her past, a reminder of her grandmother's rambling clapboard house in Kennebunk with the carefully tended flowerbeds and neatly trimmed lawn. She could see her grandmother—a tall, spare woman whose eyes were the color of her own—come out on the porch to greet her on one of her parents' infrequent visits. The pearls were a continuum, and they reminded her of who she was and where she had come from.

At seven o'clock she stood waiting under the portico of the Fairmont. She draped the shawl more closely around her shoulders; the breeze coming from the bay was cool and damp. She had been waiting for about ten minutes when a white Jaguar pulled into the semicircular drive in front of the hotel. She noticed Barkley immediately. Sitting beside him was a light-skinned black woman. The doorman opened the door and Barkley got out and walked toward her, his face beaming. The full tea-colored beard and thick, compact figure always made Barkley look to her like a hybrid of a theatrical personality and a hippie academic. Her associations were accurate. Barkley was an engaging mixture of both.

"Liz, it's great to see you." He extended both hands. "Come. I want you to meet Germaine." He opened the door of the Jag and Liz got in the back. Germaine turned around and smiled at her.

"Nice to meet you, Miss Clark. Nick has told me a good deal about you. I'm glad we'll be able to spend some time together."

"I'm looking forward to it," Liz said.

She's very attractive, Liz thought. And that's a stunning dress she's wearing. It looks like silk. That black and white slashed pattern is very Freudian. I wonder whether she realizes that. She looks like she might have been a model.

Barkley drove one block north to Sacramento and turned west. "This is one of our best restaurants, Liz. I think you'll enjoy it." They drove past Lafayette Park, past the Pacific Medical Center. She was familiar with the city but had never been in this section before. As they drove, the lights of the city began to welcome the night like fireflies. Barkley pulled the car up to what looked like a private home with a black iron grill gate whose scroll work was intricate and arresting. They walked up a flight of stairs and entered the foyer of a small, elegantly furnished dining room whose walls were painted a soft coral. The chandeliers scattered light on the hand-cut crystal. Yellow tea roses in blue teardrop Japanese vases graced each table. A solicitous head waiter greeted Barkley with the familiarity of a frequent guest. They were seated in a select corner table where they could observe the room.

Barkley's mood was effervescent. Germaine's was pleasant but subdued. Liz felt that Germaine was sizing her up, and wondered what those soft, dark brown eyes like luminous reflecting pools were seeing. Liz felt ill at ease, like an intruder, but Barkley was preoccupied with the special pleasure of escorting two attractive women to one of San Francisco's best restaurants and anticipating a delectable dinner.

Liz caught an occasional glance from the other tables. The diners were a conservative group, the men dressed mostly in dark suits and an occasional blazer; the women had that particular look of San Francisco chic, which lacks the brashness of New York, but is more arresting for its tailored reticence and sophistication.

Barkley had been studying the menu and closed it quickly. "May I ask you ladies to let me order for you?" They both nodded.

"Liz, do you prefer meat or fish?"

"I'll leave it entirely in your hands."

"Good. Jerry prefers fish, and so do I. They have a specialty here: scallops mousseline with smoked salmon. It's absolutely delicious. It's served with sautéed cucumbers and a dandelion and Bibb salad. And the wine. I prefer a cabernet sauvignon 'seventy-four from the Beaulieu Vineyards. Georges de Latour Private Reserve." He looked up at Liz who was visibly impressed with his knowledge of cuisine and wine.

"I didn't realize you were such a gourmet, Nick."

Germaine looked at Liz with a thin, resigned smile. "Nick is a genius at everything. I thought you knew that, Liz."

"I knew he was at physics, math, and cryptography, but I didn't know his areas of expertise included food."

"He's a fabulous cook, Liz," Germaine said. Barkley beamed.

"It's a small talent. I simply love good food, liquor, and

beautiful women." He laughed and leaned toward Germaine and kissed her cheek. Liz could feel the stares from the table nearest them. Barkley was oblivious. He couldn't have cared less.

He extended his private rebellion to the way he dressed. He wore a light brown plaid suit that seemed to vibrate in the elegance of this intimate room. They make quite a pair, Liz thought. They have to be aware of it. Liz suddenly felt very warm toward both of them for ignoring the silent criticism and prejudice that she sensed all around them. Barkley motioned for the wine steward.

The meal was an experience.

"I don't think I've ever had more exquisite food in my life," Liz said.

"I'm glad, Liz." His face, which appeared fuller because of his beard, and was tanned by the California sun, seemed to wrinkle into a hundred smiles. He was like a compact pixie, delighted by everything around him. His ebullience was contagious. Liz felt it. Germaine seemed quietly moved by it. She took Barkley's hand in hers and squeezed it affectionately. Her eyes seemed to envelop Barkley in an all-encompassing understanding that was deeply intimate and touched with wisdom.

She watched Barkley look at Germaine with a glance that was so completely innocent, almost childlike in his awareness only of her, that Liz had her answer. He lives in his own world, she thought, and he either doesn't see how people react to the two of them, or he doesn't care. Can he possibly be so naive as to think it doesn't matter?

Liz's thoughts, as she watched them, were interrupted by Germaine.

"Nick has told me that you attend board meetings of his company. Is it possible that I am dining with two geniuses? You look so"—she hesitated—"so young, Liz."

Liz laughed. "I'm afraid there's only one genius at this table, Germaine." She pointed at Barkley.

He smiled. "Liz is a remarkable young woman, Jerry." He chuckled. "I must admit that I thought she was a little young myself until I came to know her better." His expression became serious. "She has a rare talent, Jerry. She listens thoughtfully and never offers an opinion or suggestion that isn't backed up by an equally rare commodity, common sense." The smile came back. "George tells me she is a real Yankee, the genuine article.

Proud. Independent. Intelligent. And unremittingly honest."

Liz's face flushed. "Don't believe it, Germaine. George isn't used to having a woman work for him."

"But Nick tells me you were a Baker Scholar at the Harvard Business School. That's quite an accomplishment."

"Germaine, since I began working at Baldwin Cooper I have discovered that almost everything I learned at Harvard has almost no application to what I'm actually doing."

"You can't be serious," Germaine said.

"Yes, I am. Aside from some of the analytical techniques I was taught, what I believe Harvard did for me was to give me a disciplined thought process for solving problems. I suppose if I had chosen a manufacturing company or a service company, I might be in a better position to utilize what I had been taught. But in an entrepreneurial firm like Baldwin Cooper, what I need is an ability to find people with qualities no university can provide: imagination, experience, judgment, a knowledge of people, and the guts to back an opinion when everyone says it's crazy, when others say it won't work. They'll never be able to raise the money, people will say. Their big competitors will eat them alive. And then despite all that, they mortgage their houses, hock their cars, work ninety-hour weeks and—if they're lucky, and they have to be lucky, to quote George—they may make it. The odds are astronomical that they won't, but they have enough faith in themselves to risk everything in spite of the odds." She pointed to Barkley, her voice low, filled with admiration. "That gentleman who is sitting quite close to you has done it all. He's done what they all said was impossible, and very soon, we are going to help him become a very wealthy man."

She could feel Barkley's serious appraisal of what she was saying, and then his grinning denial. "She's giving me too much credit, Germaine. What I did was not that difficult. It wasn't that I was so bright. It was just that the rest of them were so opaque. Look, enough about me. They have a strawberry and rhubarb tart here that is out of this world. Are you game?"

Liz looked at Germaine. "Nick is determined to ruin my figure. What about you, Liz?" Germaine asked.

"If it's anything like the entrée we just had, I'm afraid I can't refuse."

"Good girl." Barkley turned to Germaine. "You're not going

to resist temptation, are you? That may be brilliant for the body, but very niggardly for the soul."

Liz laughed. "That certainly blows Calvin out of the water. Where I come from, temptation is rarely thought of as good for the soul."

"That's Nick's private philosophy. It's like everything else about Nick. He doesn't think like anyone else does. He's a very complicated man, Liz," Germaine said.

There's something about her, Liz thought, that's very strong. She doesn't miss a thing. She has a quiet air about her, yet she is determined. She's quite a woman.

"Waiter," Barkley said. "Three strawberry tarts and"—he turned to them both—"and brandy?" They both nodded in agreement. "Three Napoleon brandies."

Barkley pulled out a package of Camels and offered them each a cigarette.

"See what I mean, Liz?" Germaine said. "The man is impossible. He smokes two and a half packs a day of unfiltered cigarettes. I've been trying to persuade him to at least use filters."

"Is that part of the temptation, Nick, that's good for the soul?" Liz asked. Her voice was low as she looked at him with just a trace of humor.

"You're catching on remarkably quickly, Liz. Yes. In a way I guess you might say that. I am as aware as anyone of the statistics on cigarette smoking, yet I like the taste of unfiltered tobacco. Since I am going to die at some point, I can't see why I should curtail my pleasures for the sake of postponing the inevitable."

"I told you, Liz, that he was an original thinker."

"I don't think there's anything particularly original about the devil take the hindmost. People have thought that for centuries."

"But Nicholas Barkley lives it. You'll see," she said quietly.

"Now, now. No cutting up Uncle Nick. If I had listened to all the fools who've been telling me what I should do, what I shouldn't do, but most of all, what I *couldn't* do, the three of us would not be sitting around this table. Liz wouldn't be here because I'd probably be head of the math department of some university, and I wouldn't own a company for Baldwin Cooper to finance. You, my dear, wouldn't be here," he said to Germaine, "because, quite frankly, I wouldn't be able to afford you."

"I *beg* your pardon," Germaine said.

"No offense, dear. You earn an incredible salary. I couldn't afford to buy you a single dress. Not at a thousand dollars a crack, I couldn't. You'd soon get tired of the academic life, Jerry, and though you might add a bit of color to the president's teas, I doubt if I would ever make dean with you as my wife."

Liz was shocked, but Germaine simply laughed. "He's outrageous. Or perhaps eccentric. I don't know. But whatever this genius is, he sure as hell is the real article. This is my main man, Liz. Crazier than hell, but he's the one and only."

The wine, the dinner, the brandy had relaxed them. They were still aware of the occasional frigid glances from the other tables, but even Liz had relaxed into quiet disregard. The hell with them, she thought, and it suddenly struck her that that is what Barkley and Germaine had had to come to a long time ago. A disregard of hypocrisy, jealousy, and deep unyielding prejudice, hidden, like a quiet subterranean river flowing deep under earth and rock, but flowing. Continually. Never stopping. Implacable. Ineluctable. Forever. Screw it, Liz thought. Her eyes came back to Barkley, who was looking at them both with pride, satisfaction, and pleasure.

He has a sort of magnetism that's irresistible, Liz thought. This is a great big kid. A genius who has discovered life's cookie jar. His pleasure is contagious. It's not hedonism; it's a personal discovery, an inner joy. She laughed to herself. And George expects me to bring Barkley back to the straight and narrow. He might just as well ask me to bring back Mount Rushmore. Her thoughts sobered. But what happens if I don't? She had no answer for that.

"What are you smiling about?" Barkley asked.

"Just some private thoughts," Liz said. "Nothing important."

"Well, then, if you ladies have supped well, the night is young. I suggest that we go back to my place."

Chapter 22

THE NIGHT AIR felt good to Liz as they walked to the car. It was cool but not uncomfortably so. Barkley drove quickly, as if impatient to get home. He turned north on Buchanan and then east on Union. As they approached the Russian Hill section, Liz could see the luminescent spire of Telegraph Hill overlooking the bay to the northwest. It seemed to rise like a giant tapered candle out of an island of shadowed trees. Barkley pulled up in front of a white two-story house with a large bow window that seemed to encompass the left side of the house, covering both the upper and lower floors. A white chimney poked skyward from an undulating terra-cotta tiled roof. She could see to the northeast the lighted pointed spire of the Trans-america Building and the cluster of sparkling buildings of the financial district including the monolith of the Bank of America building, which rose high above the city, its lights dwarfing the string of broken pearls scattered along the waterfront of Oakland across the bay. They got out of the car and waited for Barkley to unlock the front door of the house. Liz could hear Dixieland music out on the street. Barkley opened the door and motioned her to come in. She was so surprised by what she saw that at first she couldn't move. She turned to look at Barkley, her face revealing her incredulity. Both Barkley and Germaine were watching her with uncritical, amused curiosity.

Liz found herself in an immense semidarkened living room whose depressed center was a rectangle of connected sofas and scattered white shag rugs. She recognized this as a conversation pit, but it was so large that it seemed to belong in a theater, not in a house. There were, she guessed, at least fifty people in the room.

Liz looked at the balcony on the second-floor level, which ran the entire length of the room. She saw several doors in the muted light. She suspected they led to bedrooms. She looked around for the bow window she had seen from the street, but realized that it was covered by a large tapestry that looked like a Miró. The long wall to her right was lined with mirrors that reflected the kaleidoscopic lights from moving spots recessed in the ceiling.

"Come on in and meet some of the beautiful people," Barkley said. Liz realized that the Dixieland music she had heard on the street had stopped; she was now hearing sophisticated jazz. A pianist, a bassist, a drummer, a guitarist, and a sax player were almost hidden at the far end of the room.

My God. The smell of pot in this place could lay you out. She kept looking about the room as if she were watching a movie. She couldn't believe what she was seeing was taking place in front of her.

Several couples were making love on the shag rugs, oblivious to everyone else. Their languid, drugged movements were slow, as if they were swimming through mayonnaise. Liz saw that several of the other men and women were naked. It's like something out of Dante, she thought. My God, I can't be seeing this.

Barkley guided Liz to the steps leading down to the conversation pit.

She started to resist. "Really, Nick, this isn't my style."

"Don't be silly. No one here is going to ask you to do anything you don't want to, and if you don't like what you see, then just don't look at it. These people are quite extraordinary. They are artists, writers, musicians. Some are businessmen, educators, lawyers, doctors." He smiled. "You might find it amusing to try to guess who does what. It will surprise you, I can guarantee you that." He paused. "Here people can do what they like, but they know I won't tolerate unkindness, rudeness, violence, or brutality. Here, my friends can bring whom they like, do what they like, forget who they are, if they wish. Forgetting, even for a brief period, is what this is all about, Liz. I'm sure it hasn't escaped your attention that it's a rather cruel and unjust world out there. Here, no one judges, no one is permitted to interfere with or criticize anyone else. When they leave here, it is to their advantage, if they wish to return, not to spread the word around about what goes on here. Outside, people are hardly charitable toward our point of view."

Barkley took Liz and Germaine by the arm and led them down the steps into the pit. "Let's sit here," he said pointing to a long section of sofa that was unoccupied. Barkley removed his jacket and tie. Liz and Germaine were facing him. Germaine's knees touched Barkley's. He held her hand. Liz watched a black man who must have been nearly seven feet tall get up and walk to a long bar behind which a bartender was mixing drinks.

Barkley was watching Liz closely, his face wrinkled in amusement at her surprise and shock, which was bordering on panic.

"Nick, this is absolutely unbelievable!"

"Liz, I'll admit it takes some getting used to, especially for someone from the East, from Maine."

"Good Lord, you're right about that. I don't see how you keep this place from being raided."

"We have had our problems from time to time. Drugs mostly. I try to discourage the hard stuff. No heroin. No cocaine. Sometimes we do have transgressors, but I try to convince them they are jeopardizing the group."

"The group," Liz said incredulously. "What is this you're running, some kind of cult?"

Barkley laughed. "No, it's not a cult; it's an idea."

"I told you Nick has some unusual ideas," Germaine said. "This is one of them."

Barkley searched the pocket of his jacket. He handed a joint to Germaine, who accepted it without comment, and then offered one to Liz. "It's the best grass there is, Liz." He paused. "Have you ever smoked pot?" She hesitated. She knew she must appear stiff and prudish, but she couldn't help it.

"A couple of times. I want to be at least partly in control of what goes on in my head." She noticed a young couple walking toward them. They both seemed exuberant at the sight of Barkley. Their faces were almost radiant even in the dimly lit room.

"Nick, it's great to see you." The young man extended his hand. Barkley took it, his own face reflecting his pleasure at seeing them. "Nick," the woman said, and bent down and kissed him lightly on the cheek. "Hi, Germaine." They moved to her and the young man kissed her.

"This is Tony West," Barkley said, introducing the young man, "and this is Eden Summer. And this," Barkley said, "is Elizabeth Clark from Maine and New York." Barkley smiled. "I think Liz is undergoing culture shock. I'm trying to get her loosened up a little, but it isn't easy." Tony laughed.

Liz thought him good-looking. His auburn hair was carefully cut but longer than she was used to. He wore faded jeans, an open-necked shirt, and sandals. The girl had on an Indian madras dress with a jeweled belt, and it was obvious to Liz that her full breasts were unrestricted by a bra. But Liz had to admit that there was something appealing about both of them. They sat next to Barkley, who offered them each a joint. Everyone was smoking but Liz.

"How about a drink, Liz?" Barkley asked.

"I could use one," Liz said.

"I'll get it," Tony volunteered. "What'll it be, Liz?" he asked casually, looking at her with amusement. "Don't worry, Liz. You'll get used to this. You'll get so hooked on this place that you won't be able to stay away."

"Tony's right, Liz," Eden said. Liz looked at the blonde with the shoulder-length hair and full body. "When Tony first introduced me to Nick's place, I couldn't believe it either, but now I'd rather come here than any place in San Francisco."

"About that drink, Liz." Tony was standing.

"Scotch and soda, please."

"Coming up." He walked across the conversation pit toward the bar.

Liz could feel all of them watching her. She felt like some sort of living conscience, a judgmental presence, and she sensed that they all understood that. For some reason she felt guilty about her attitude and yet annoyed with herself for feeling guilt. These are a bunch of freaks. Bacchanalians. Barkley can dress this up any way he wants to, but this is kooksville, she thought.

The grass was having its effect. The blonde sat down beside Barkley. She started to unbutton his shirt. Liz looked at Germaine, who seemed relaxed yet attentive, aware. Liz watched Eden's fingers flit like butterflies over Barkley's bare chest. Liz couldn't believe it. Her eyes went from Germaine to Eden. Is Germaine just going to sit there and let that blonde make love to her man? Christ, Liz said to herself, this is a nuthouse.

"Don't worry, Liz," Germaine said. "I know how to keep Nick happy."

Tony came back with Liz's drink. "Here you go, Liz," he said handing her the glass. "Put that away, and I'll show you around."

Eden kissed Barkley and sat up. She lay back against the sofa, brushing her hair away from her face. She inhaled deeply on the joint, then squeezed the roach out in a glass ashtray.

Tony sat down beside Eden.

Barkley seemed sublimely relaxed. "I was trying to describe to Liz what this place is all about." He laughed. His speech was beginning to slur as he'd had too much to drink. "It's an idea. An idea about freedom."

"That's right," Eden said. "Freedom. Where else in this whole lousy world can you be yourself? Not just yourself like when you're alone. But deeper. Much deeper. Into your unconscious. Let it out. Nobody tells you this is wrong. You can't do that. You can't feel that. If I want to make love to Nick, then I will. But I've got too much respect for Germaine for that. Too much respect." Her speech was beginning to slur as she got high.

"I'm glad you said that." Germaine laughed. Liz finished her drink quickly. My God, that must have been pure scotch. She started to get up and stumbled forward. Tony, who had begun to get up as she did, caught her.

"What did you put in that drink?"

"Scotch, Liz. Just plain scotch."

"How about the soda?"

He smiled. "Very little soda, doll." He took her arm. "Come on, let Tony show you around this place."

He held her arm as they walked across the conversation pit. Her tolerance for alcohol had always been low, and she found herself leaning hard against Tony to keep from stumbling. Smoke hung in the air like fog. The somnambulistic couples seemed to move like slugs.

It's like some crazy dream, she thought. The dancing, the colored lights, the mirrors, the bodies, the music. This can't be happening to me. I'm going to wake up and find I'm in the Fairmont and that I've overslept and missed my dinner date with Barkley.

"Whoops. Easy, doll. Tang must have gone a little heavy

on that sauce." Liz stopped and held on to Tony, but still managed to push herself away from him slightly.

"Would you do me a big favor, Tony?"

"You've got it."

"Stop calling me doll. If there is one noun I can't stand, it's doll."

"Noun. My, my, we are specific, aren't we?" He paused. His face spread into a broad grin. "Okay, babe. Whatever you say."

Liz looked at him evenly. "Babe runs a very close second to doll."

He looked like a grinning Cheshire cat. She expected him to disappear any second and leave only his smile.

"What would you like me to call you?"

She leaned against him as the room became a kaleidoscope.

"Hold on, tiger," he said laughing. He led her to the bar. He helped her onto a stool and sat beside her. She was leaning on the bar, her head moving slightly from side to side.

"What would you like me to call you?" he asked her again, lifting her chin and turning her head toward him.

She heard his voice, but she was on an enormous roller coaster. She climbed slowly to the top, and then she plunged to the bottom with sickening speed. The room became a montage of lights and sound as the alcohol in her bloodstream played with the stability and perception receptors in her brain. His voice became a distant gong. A clanging warning that she was dangerously close to the edge of her self-control.

"What do you want me to call you?" the voice repeated.

"Try using my name," she said thickly, as she fought against her increasing disorientation. She was trying to look at him, but he kept slipping in and out of focus.

The grin of the Cheshire cat, she thought. And I'm Alice, and this is fruitcake land.

"Meet our heavy-handed bartender, Liz. Dispenser of tonight's joys and tomorrow's hangovers." He pointed to a handsome Chinese who was busy mixing drinks.

"He doesn't have any shirt on," she said, peering over the bar to see if he was naked. He wasn't.

"Tang Yu Ta." Tony pointed to the tall lithe Oriental whose oyster-colored skin seemed to glisten in the recessed lighting above the bar. Tiny droplets of perspiration reflected like beads on his full jet-black hair. Tang smiled at Liz as he served the waiting line of Barkley's friends, one of whom was a woman holding the thin stem of an empty champagne glass and looking at Liz with an expression of unconcealed interest. The woman held her eyes like a snake.

"Who is that woman, Tony?" she asked. "The one with the champagne glass?"

"Oh. So that's what turns you on."

"God damn it! That doesn't turn me on." Her voice was too loud, and she could see heads turning to look at her. The woman's stare had turned to ice.

"My God." Liz turned around to survey the room from the perspective of the bar. "It looks like junkie night at Madison Square Garden," she said, again too loudly. Tony squeezed her elbow. "Take it easy, Liz. Everyone here is very mellow, and we don't want to upset that mood."

He was looking at her. The Cheshire grin had disappeared. His expression was becoming taut, bordering on irritation.

She saw Germaine walking toward her.

She's the only one in this place who doesn't look as if she's playing in a Fellini movie.

"Liz, I came to say good night," Germaine said. "I have to leave. I'm not up to Nick's schedule. I have a show to do every night at six. Got to get my beauty rest."

Liz was beginning to be more in control of her body and at least partly in touch with her mind. "Where's Nick?"

"He's talking to some people."

Liz hesitated. She was feeling out of place and uncomfortable. She wanted to get out of this nut house.

"I'd like to come with you, Germaine."

Germaine smiled. "I thought you might feel that way. That's what I told Nick, but he wants you to see more of this place, and he'd like to spend a little time with you alone." Germaine laughed. "I think you'd better plan on sleeping late tomorrow."

Liz looked at Germaine, at the beautifully sculptured head with the straight thin nose and slightly flared nostrils. The dark pools of her eyes. The modeling of the muted light on the high cheekbones. The broad shoulders tapering to a narrow waist. The firm breasts pressing against her black and white silk dress.

"I'll call you tomorrow, Germaine. Maybe we could have lunch."

"I'm afraid I have a very tight schedule, Liz."

Liz edged off the stool so that her back was to Tony. She

took Germaine's arm to steady herself. Germaine laughed.

"A little rocky? Tang does have a heavy hand."

Liz's voice was hushed. "Germaine, I have to see you to-morrow. It's very important. It concerns Nick. I'd like you to keep that in confidence."

Germaine's eyes narrowed. Liz saw caution, the thin edge of hostility, the quick passing shadow of anxiety. She looked at Liz, measuring her, trying to determine what difficulties this young woman was going to bring into her life. She held up her hand and motioned to Tang.

"A piece of paper and pencil, Tang."

Germaine leaned against the bar and wrote down a telephone number. "Call me here at eleven o'clock." She turned to Tony West. "Nick would like you to give her a quick tour and bring her back to him."

Tony bowed in a mocking response. "As my master wishes." He turned to Liz. "Come on, Liz. Are you sober enough to complete the grand tour?"

"I may need a little help, but lead on." She turned to Germaine, who was looking at her carefully. "I'll call you, Germaine." Liz paused, caught by the dignity of this woman. "I really enjoyed having dinner with you and Nick."

"So did I," Germaine said, and turned and walked toward the pit with that fluid movement that seemed like water flowing over smooth stones.

"Here, take my arm." Tony guided Liz away from the bar and across a portion of the dance floor toward the mirrored walls. Liz noticed that the music had stopped and the musicians had moved to the crowded bar. The couples had left the dance floor and were moving toward the bar, up a flight of stairs to the conversation pit. Suddenly the room seemed enveloped in sound. It washed over her, engulfed her in waves of rhapsodic music. She clutched Tony's arm. "My God. That's Brahms' violin concerto."

"You know your Brahms."

The music was incredible. It seemed to come from every-where in the room. The fidelity was beyond anything she had ever heard. It was better than being at a live performance. She was seized by the desire not to move. To stand there on the abandoned rectangle of dance floor, in front of the mirrors that were now reflecting a mauve light. She felt as if she were on stage looking out at an audience who seemed as much drugged by the sweep of the strings as by the grass and liquor that had preceded this audio fantasy.

"Tony. It's—it's—" She stood there clutching him.

He put his arm around her. "The words you are looking for don't exist."

She looked at him, seeing him really for the first time.

"Tony, I don't want to move. I just want to stand here and listen."

"I'm afraid my instructions are to show you around this rather remarkable house and then bring you back to Nick." She was genuinely sorry.

He walked to one of the mirrors and pushed it. It opened to reveal a narrow rock path at the end of which stood a small Japanese teahouse. She saw two Asian couples dressed in breathtaking silks going through the intricate ritual of the tea ceremony. Tony closed the mirrored door. She was startled, surprised. The scene shown so briefly seemed like a frame of film being exposed to the light for a second before the shutter came down behind the lens. She knew that the film of her own mind would always hold that picture. The contrast between the magnificent Western European music that was enveloping her and the quick exposure to the Asiatic scene she had just witnessed left her feeling disoriented.

Tony opened the next mirrored door. She saw a short path leading to a small pool set in a glen of grass and stone. Two couples were lounging against the sides, their skin opalescent under the ultraviolet light. They were listening to Brahms from speakers located behind a small waterfall that fell over a wall of dark rock between junglelike plants. Liz's eyes were fixed on the trancelike languor of the bathers as they listened to the concerto.

The mirrored doors became a series of projected slides in her mind. Snapshots. Candids in full color. She could not assemble the visual impressions into tangible experience. They were optical surprises like dissembled sequences in a dream.

"Let's go to the second floor. We may find a lot of locked doors up there." He winked at her.

Upstairs she met with a similar series of surprises. The few doors that were unlocked showed an eclectic selection of bedrooms: modern, Victorian, Renaissance, Japanese.

The effect of these rooms, lavishly detailed with appropriate drapes, upholstery fabrics, furniture, paintings, each authentically reflecting a period style, left Liz incredulous.

Her brain was slowly returning to normal. I'm getting my head back, she thought. She turned to Tony. "You haven't mentioned anything about yourself, Tony. What do you do? Why are you here? What kind of a place is this? Is all this real? Am I going to wake up and find I haven't been in Wonderland after all?"

He laughed. They were standing on the balcony overlooking the conversation pit. She could see Barkley in the center of a large group of people. They sat in various postures, their faces bathed in mauve light, enraptured by Brahms.

"I run an advertising agency here in San Francisco," he said quietly, looking at her with an interest and perception she hadn't been aware of before. "I think Nick would like to tell you about the rest. Let's go down and see him. The concerto is almost over."

They joined the group in the conversation pit. Liz looked around at the strangers whose faces showed an absorption she had never seen in a concert hall.

The magic of Brahms had ended, and the mood of the music began to give way as people got up, walked toward the bar, began to talk in low, muted voices.

"Ah, there you are, Liz," Barkley said, smiling. Liz tried to figure him out. He was like a guru, presiding over this place. A high priest dedicated to what?

"Tony gave me a brief tour," she said. Tony was sitting on the steps of the pit facing Barkley. Liz sat on the sofa, in the newly vacated space at Barkley's side.

"Tang went a bit heavy on the sauce, Nick," Tony said. "I think we ought to speak to him about that. I was wondering why the liquor bills seemed to be running higher than usual, when I looked over your last letter." Tony paused. "If Tang is laying it on like that to the heavy grass burners, it could be dangerous."

"I spoke to him about that," Barkley said, "but maybe he needs another reminder. He gets very busy back there. I can understand how his hand can slip." Barkley turned to Liz. "I know you want to talk to me, Liz, but it is getting late, and I have to drive to Hillsborough. Maybe we could talk on the way back to the Fairmont."

She had lost all track of time in the looking-glass unreality of Barkley's house. She had also forgotten why she had come three thousand miles. She was like a bird who had flown into a window and had been stunned—able to recover, gathering its faculties, but stunned.

She glanced at her watch but couldn't see the time in the semidarkened room. Barkley watched her with a look of wry amusement. He took her arm. "Come on, Elizabeth, let's go. I'll drive you to the Fairmont."

She opened the window and let the cool air blow on her face as Barkley drove. There's so much I want to ask him. I want to ask him if it was all real. Was I in a room with mirrors that rotated and exposed one surrealistic impression after another?

"Liz, tell me. What did you think of what you saw tonight?"

She noticed as he drove that the street sign said Valparaiso and then watched Barkley turn south on Powell. The spire of Telegraph Hill watched over the entrance to the darkened bay. The lights of the city gave the sky a soft rose glow. The cool air was bringing her back.

"What did you think about tonight, Liz?" he repeated.

"Really, Nick, it was all so unusual, so completely unexpected that I don't know how to respond to it. All I have are questions."

"Then ask them."

"What is it all about? Is it your house? Do you live there? Who are those people?"

"Whoa. Take it easy. I can only answer one question at a time." He hesitated. "The property belongs to me, but I don't live there. I spend time there, but I live in Hillsborough. As for your question, 'what is it all about?'" He paused thoughtfully. They were approaching California Street. She could see the tower of the Fairmont with its lighted external elevators looking like electronic beetles climbing up the side of the building.

"Barkley House, that's what we call it, is *an idea*. You see, as I said in the restaurant, I wanted to provide intelligent, attractive people, people I liked and with whom I felt comfortable, with a place they could come to, where they could feel free to be themselves in a literal sense. Where they could leave their inhibitions at the door, so to speak, and seek the emotional relief of creating and living their own fantasies without the burden of guilt."

"Forgive me, Nick, but who pays for all of this? Is it run

like a club? Are there dues?"

He pulled the Jag into the crescent-shaped drive in front of the Fairmont. The doorman opened the door of the car.

"Nick, I know it's late, and that you have a long drive, but couldn't we have a nightcap in the Sky Room? There's so much I want to know about what I saw tonight." She paused. "I know that Barkley House is very important to you, and I would like to understand what you're trying to do."

He looked at her appraisingly, measuring her sincerity. "Okay, let's have a quick one in the Sky Room and then I have to go."

"Shall I put your car in the garage, sir?" the doorman asked.

Barkley gave him five dollars. "Keep it out here. I'll be back in about forty minutes."

They entered the capsule elevator, and Liz watched the city expand beneath her as they rose toward the top of the tower. The Sky Room was one of her favorites, that and the Top of the Mark. She could see the whole city spread out before her, flashing its lights at the darkness. She could see the area of Russian Hill and Telegraph Hill where they had just come from.

"It's a magnificent city, Nick. It's my favorite in the States."

"It's everybody's favorite, Liz." He motioned to the circular bar that revolved slowly around the tower giving a 360-degree view of San Francisco. "You get the feeling of being like a bird up here, free."

"I was explaining to you in the car that Barkley House is expressly designed to give its guests the kind of freedom without guilt that most of them can't achieve even in their own homes. Their inhibitions and conventions won't permit it. But I have created a place where there is no norm of behavior. My guests create their own norms and find out a great deal about themselves in the process. It's a kind of psychotherapy without the psychiatrist." He paused. "I don't mean to say that my purpose was to create a psychotherapeutic environment, far from it. But my friends have told me that their experience at Barkley House has given them far deeper insights into themselves than anything else they have ever known."

"But it must cost a lot of money to run Barkley House. If I'm not being too inquisitive, who pays for all of this?"

Barkley laughed. "My conscientious monitor. Always concerned with the balance sheet." Barkley motioned to the bartender. "What will you have, Liz?"

"Just a glass of white wine."

"Make that two."

"I bought the property, which has turned out to be a very good investment. I thought you'd be happy to hear that."

She laughed. "As a matter of fact, I am."

"I paid for the original layout of the house, but as more and more of my friends wanted to spend time there, the expense became too great, so I let them decorate the upstairs rooms to their own taste, which they paid for. I send out a letter once a month telling how much we've spent on liquor." He paused. "Notice, I didn't say a *bill*. I said a *letter*. I don't send bills to my friends. They send me checks as they feel they can, and usually it more than covers the liquor bill. We don't serve food, so that's not a problem. I bear all other expenses." He watched her as she silently computed what he had just told her.

That has to be heavy, she thought. The band, the lights, the visual effects. It gets cool in San Francisco. Heating that place must cost a small fortune.

He looked at her with analytical amusement. "You noticed, Liz, how quiet everyone was. With all that grass and liquor around, you'd think we'd have a lot of discipline problems. We don't. One of the reasons is that they never know when I'll walk in. If I see or hear anyone being rude or hostile, or just simply unpleasant, I ask them to leave. I won't tolerate anyone who threatens the ambience I've created for Barkley House. In my absence, Tang takes care of any troublemaker." He paused. "As I told you, I don't permit hard drugs. Grass is okay, but that's where it ends."

"Have you had any trouble with the police?"

"A little, but they can't hang you for smoking grass in your own house. Besides, most of my friends are well known and highly regarded people in this city. The cops have a lot more to worry about than my guests smoking grass. We're not a restaurant or a club; this is my house. What I do there, as long as I don't disturb my neighbors or break any laws, is my business."

What about smoking grass? she thought. That's illegal in most states. I'm sure it is here. Barkley must have some good connections at City Hall. It's a strange hobby, she thought, and a darn expensive one.

Barkley had barely touched his wine. "Liz, I really have to be going. But before I do, maybe this will help you to understand." He paused trying to organize his thoughts. "Everything has come very easily to me. I don't mean that I haven't had to work hard, I have. But for example, I was in M.I.T. at fourteen. I had a doctorate from Stanford when I was barely twenty. I have a very successful business, as you know, and I'm only thirty-two." He chuckled. "When you get finished with this underwriting, Liz, I'm going to be worth nearly forty million dollars.

"I'm bored, Liz. There's nothing left for me to do. I'm experimenting with ideas I've had for a long time. One of those ideas concerns personal freedom and how few of us ever really get a taste of it. Even if we have the money to tell everyone to go to hell, most of us are still bound by our anxieties and our inhibitions. I wanted to find out how people would respond in an environment designed to let them be themselves physically and psychologically. It's really very interesting to watch."

She looked at him for a long time. He could feel her analysis. He's not a nut or a guru, she thought. He's brilliant, and he's bored, and this stimulates him intellectually.

"Liz, I really have to go. It's nearly three o'clock in the morning." Liz got up. Barkley left a bill on the bar. They walked toward the elevators. "You know you're welcome at Barkley House any time, Liz. From what I could see, Tony West would be more than happy to show you around."

The elevator stopped at her floor. "Thank you for the most unusual evening of my life, Nick." She didn't know why, but she kissed him lightly on the cheek before she stepped out of the elevator. The doors closed silently behind her.

She was so completely exhausted that she simply undressed and got into bed. Her mind was numb. It had stopped. Turned off. She was asleep almost instantly. The phone, when it sounded, had to pierce through to her consciousness like a drill opening a bank vault. She heard the insistent bell with a growing awareness and irritation that some idiot was calling her at—

What time was it? The phone rang determinedly. She was really mad now. Who the hell would call at four-thirty in the morning? Her eyes gradually focused on the large red numerals of the digital clock beside her bed.

"Hello," she barked into the phone. "Who is this?"

"Where have you been? I've been worried sick about you. You said you'd call tonight."

"Is that you, George?"

Long pause. "I'm sorry, Liz. I just couldn't leave for the office without knowing you were all right."

She could sense his concern over the three thousand miles that separated them. Her irritation vanished.

"George, I'm sorry. I just left Barkley about an hour ago. I haven't had time to call. I was so exhausted. I just wanted to sleep."

His voice sounded relieved. "I was really worried, Liz." He hesitated. "I hate to have you out there alone."

"I'm a big girl, George. Really. You don't have to be concerned."

"Well, I am concerned, damn it. Can't you understand that?" Long pause.

Her voice softened. "Yes, George. I can understand that." She could hear him sigh over the phone. It was a frustrated, exasperated sound. "Look. I'm sorry I woke you at four-thirty in the morning. I really am."

"It's okay, George," she said softly, and as she said it it struck her. Who else would be so concerned about me other than my mother? Peter? Her mind went swiftly to Peter. She was sure of his love, but on what terms? On Peter's terms, or were they her terms? Would Peter have called? Would she have called him? *But George had.*

"Go back to sleep, Liz. Call me when you can."

"I've got a lunch date with Barkley's girl."

"Have you met her?"

"I spent the evening with the two of them."

"How does it look?"

"For whom?"

"What do you mean, for whom? For us. The deal. Is Sol's concern justified?"

Long pause. "If the banks find out what's going on out here, we don't have a deal."

Very long pause. "That bad."

"George, I'm so tired. I'll explain later. It's only bad depending on your point of view. From Barkley's perspective it's fine. From what we know of Barkley's clients, I would say it's disastrous."

"Can you fix it?"

She sighed. "As of now, I haven't the faintest idea how I can."

"That sounds reassuring. It should make my whole day."

"I'm sorry, George."

"So am I." He hesitated. "I'm sorry I'm not there with you." His voice softened. "Liz, I miss you."

It was the first time he had said that to her, he realized. From that first interview at Harvard which seemed like a year ago, he had always kept a certain distance between them. Now, nearly a quarter to five in the morning, three thousand miles away, he was telling her something.

"I miss you too, George," she said softly. She didn't know where it came from. She only knew that she had said it. She was as surprised at herself as she was at him.

She had been sitting up in bed. She lay down on the pillow holding the phone close to her. She began to feel a warm sense of contentment, a feeling of peace. Something had surfaced in her life that was beginning to fill it.

"Go back to sleep, Liz, and get home as soon as you can."

"I will, George." She felt languorous, like a stroked cat. She wasn't alone anymore. Why had she never felt like this about Peter? She loved Peter, but she couldn't have him because their lives were incompatible and they both realized that it wouldn't work. But George. Did she love George?

Right now I feel his nearness and his concern and his protectiveness. Do I want that? Do I need a man to make my life complete? Haven't I spent my whole life learning to be independent?

"George, I'll call you later. I've got to get some rest." She paused. "I'm anxious to come home," she said softly. She hung up the phone and rolled over on her side and clasped one of the pillows to her. She slipped back into sleep at peace. A quiet, reassuring, comforting peace. It had been a long day in a short life.

Chapter 23

NOB HILL WAS whipped by a brisk breeze, which blew across an azure sky. The flags in front of the Fairmont crackled. Liz left the hotel, letting the cool air refresh her. Did I really go to Barkley's house last night? she asked herself. Did George really call? She was still confused about last night, but with the thought of George's call she felt a warmth spread through her, comforting coals fanned by the wind that caressed her.

George's call, at least, was real, she said to herself as she stood there. With every bizarre thing that has happened to me since I came out here, that call was real.

She looked at the sun sparkle on the surface of the bay and watched a cable car clang its way up California Street, with tourists festooning its open sides. She stood in front of the hotel lost in thought.

Germaine had said to meet her at a restaurant called Davignon's. She remembered Germaine's voice when she called her office. Liz had waited while a harried secretary found Germaine. Germaine sounded guarded, almost like a stranger. Not hostile, but wary.

What was she afraid of? Did she suspect something? She must. I told her I had to see her, that it was important, that it concerned Barkley.

Liz motioned to the doorman who signaled a cab for her.

● ● ●

The restaurant on Battery Street was dimly lit, with banquettes against the walls. It gave Liz the feeling of exploring an underwater grotto while wearing a dark red face mask. The mâitre d' guided her to a banquette in a rear corner of the room where she saw Germaine. She was wearing her shoulder-length hair loose, whereas last night she'd had it pulled back into a tight bun. Liz liked the bun style better. This was more theatrical, but less classic. It didn't do justice to the sculptured planes of Germaine's face.

"I'm so glad you could make it, Germaine. I know how busy you are."

A quick smile. Swizzle stick stirring the Manhattan in nervous little circles. "It's okay, Liz. But I am pressed for time. I've got a really tight schedule today."

"I'm glad we can spend a little time together," Liz said as she sat down. The waiter came over.

"You want a drink, Liz?"

"White wine, please."

Germaine nodded to the waiter. "Give us a little time. Then we'll order."

She's nervous and defensive, Liz thought. I've got to reach her. I've got to find a way.

"Liz, I'm no good at small talk. You've got something on your mind concerning Nicholas and me, and I'd like to hear it from you now, and straight. No beating about the bush. Nick and I have had enough of that. I know you're close to his company, and I know you're not out here for your health. So if you've got something to say, get it out." Her antagonism glowed like a neon sign.

She hadn't been like this last night, Liz remembered. What had happened to turn her around?

Germaine's eyes were averted from Liz. She was staring at her drink. Liz could sense that for a moment she had slipped away. Liz hesitated. She didn't know how to begin.

Germaine's mind was back in New Orleans in the little wooden weathered frame house with its unpainted gray siding that stood near the edge of the Intercoastal Waterway near Lake St. Catherine. She was eleven years old. She spent the murderously hot, humid afternoons of late spring and early summer in the shade of the sagging porch watching the rich folks in their fancy yachts on their way from the Gulf headed north for blessed cooler and drier air. She remembered her silent, bitter envy, and her vow to be like them; like that white woman who stepped off her yacht on to the rotting bulkhead at the edge of Germaine's family's land. She asked Germaine if her parents had a phone. Germaine remembered the immaculate white shorts the woman had worn. How carefully her hair had been set. Even in the excruciating heat her face was skillfully made up. The boat was air conditioned. It was nearly twenty years ago, and yet she remembered it as if it were yesterday. The woman had been impatient and irritable.

"You don't have a phone?"

The quiet dark averted eyes. The low, embarrassed voice. "No, ma'am. We don't have no phone."

"It's so annoying," the woman said. "Our ship-to-shore isn't working, and my husband has to make an important call." The woman was beginning to perspire. Germaine, at age eleven, had made a solemn vow. Someday she would have what that white woman had. She would never be white, but she had a lot of white blood in her. She could see that each time she looked in a mirror. She had fought every inch of the way in the intervening years to get what that woman had. She had never lost the hostility toward whites, but time had taught her to hide it. Only with Barkley had she ever felt at ease. In Barkley she had found a man truly without a sense of color. Barkley might be an eccentric, but he had touched her with his ingenuous sincerity, and she had slowly fallen in love. But Liz had brought back those days in New Orleans, and though Germaine knew she was being unfair, she couldn't keep the hostility out of her tone and manner.

"Germaine, how much do you know about my firm's involvement with Nick?"

Germaine toyed with her swizzle stick. "Nick doesn't tell me much about the business. Frankly, I'm not that interested. We each have our own careers, and we try and keep business out of our personal lives."

"Are you aware that my firm is arranging a multimillion-dollar stock offering for Twenty/Twenty?" She paused to let that sink in. Even in the darkness of the room she could see the startled look come into Germaine's eyes, the look of a frightened doe.

"Are you aware, Germaine, that Nick's net worth after that

offering will be increased by nearly forty million dollars?"

Liz looked at her evenly. If she wants it straight, Liz decided, she's going to get it straight.

Germaine was incredulous. "I heard him say something about that last night, but I thought he was kidding. My mind isn't used to those kinds of numbers. I make a damn good living, but what you're talking about isn't real to me."

"It may not be real to Nick either, Germaine." Liz had her attention. The hostility had given way to wide-eyed interest.

"Germaine, do you know what Nick's company does?"

"Of course. They make computer safeguard systems for banks."

"That's right. I don't have to tell you that banks are incredibly conservative. They have to be. They are legally responsible for other people's money."

Liz could see Germaine stiffen. The flag of defensive hostility was up and waving.

"Germaine, you've asked for it straight, and I'm going to to give it to you that way." She paused, watching Germaine's lips compress, the thin muscles ripple along the delicate but determined jawline.

"Look, Liz, I don't think you're a racist, but people like you are irritating."

"Now, wait a minute, Germaine—" Liz could feel her anger rising in response to what she considered untrue, unkind, and unjust.

Germaine waved a tired hand. "Now let's not have a fight." She smiled and reached out and touched Liz's hand. "I don't know what kind of a world you come from, but I can guess. I'm sorry if it hurts you to hear the truth, Liz. One of the hardest things for us to deal with is the ignorance of well-meaning people like yourself, Liz, who like to *explain* things to us." She reached into her bag for her cigarettes, lit one, and inhaled deeply. The smoke hung between them in an acrid cloud.

"Why do you think Nick has spent a fortune on Barkley House, Liz? Because he's bored?"

"That's what he told me," Liz said.

"That's what he tells everybody, but he's not bored; he's angry. He's angry about us and he's feeling something inside himself because of that. It's a new experience for him, and it hurts like hell."

"I don't understand."

"I'm sure you don't."

Liz waited. Germaine motioned to the waiter. "We'd better order, Liz. I've got to get back to the station."

"I'm not very hungry, Germaine."

"Neither am I. How about a salad and some wine? Do you like crab?"

"I love it."

"It's rock crab and it's light and good."

"That sounds fine."

Germaine motioned to the waiter. "Two crab salads and a carafe of white wine." The waiter left quickly.

Germaine looked at Liz. "Do you know what Nick's real name is?"

Liz was confused. "I don't understand. His name is Nicholas Barkley." She watched Germaine shake her head with a persistent amused automation.

"No. Nicholas Barkley has played another joke on all of you. His real name, the one his parents gave him, which he had legally changed, was Nathan Bauchenstein. Nicholas Barkley is a German Jew." She paused. "In reality, of course, he's neither German, nor Jewish. He's an atheist and an American. He's like me, with one major exception. Barkley can change his name to any damn thing he wants, but I can't change this." She tapped her skin. "That's the difference, and until Barkley met me, he never really understood. He does now."

I wonder if George and Larry know that Nick is Jewish. The way those two check out an investment they would have to know, but Germaine is right. That wouldn't make any difference to them, but his association with this black woman would.

"When did he begin Barkley House? Was it after he met you?"

Germaine hesitated. "I've known him a long time. Yes. It was after he met me."

He most love her very much, or he must have a real desire to get even, Liz thought.

The waiter brought their salads and poured their wine.

I've got to be straight with this woman. She's too smart to hand her any line. Liz's mind raced with the importance of this luncheon. She knew that if she couldn't get Germaine on her side, Barkley would blow the deal, for himself and everyone else. She could feel Germaine watching her.

Liz put both hands on the edge of the table. She leaned forward concentrating her energies and her will like a compressed spring. "Germaine, I told you I was going to give it to you straight, and I am." She paused. "My firm has a substantial interest in Twenty/Twenty, and we stand to make a great deal of money on our investment once the stock offering we're working on comes to market. Our investment is smaller than Nick's, but it is very significant to us." Liz paused. "We're afraid that if word gets out about his rather unusual hobby, he could see a good many of his client banks look for their security systems someplace else."

Germaine started to speak. Liz held up her hand.

"Wait, Germaine. Let me finish. This has nothing to do with your relationship with him, although I certainly don't have to point out that would raise a lot of eyebrows with Nick's clients. But that's not what worries me." Liz paused. "Germaine, you're a newswoman. You know better than I what the media would do with a story like Barkley House. That would hit the wire services and make news all over the country. How would the directors of Nick's client banks feel about Barkley House?" Liz paused, her mouth grim, the intensity of her conviction palpable.

"Try to see this from their side, Germaine. Every director of every bank is responsible for the investments of the bank's shareholders and depositors. These banks handle billions of dollars every day. They transfer enormous sums of money electronically, by computer. Penetrate their computer system and you can transfer ten or one hundred million dollars faster than you can wind your watch."

Liz could feel Germaine's attention. "Suppose Barkley House became front-page news. And then suppose, just suppose, that one of those banks had a penetration of their Twenty/Twenty system. Can't you just see the stockholders standing in line to sue the bank, its officers, and the directors?" Liz paused. "That's the first thing those banks will think of if Barkley House becomes news. And if you were in their shoes, you'd react the same way." Liz touched Germaine's hand. Her voice softened. "Are you beginning to understand that this hasn't anything to do with racial prejudice? Barkley House may be a wonderful sociological or psychological experiment. It may be a way for

Nick to thumb his nose at society. God knows what he's doing certainly has an intrinsic validity, but unfortunately the world isn't very open-minded about such things." Liz hesitated, her voice soft with compassion.

Germaine's hostility had drifted to thin smoke. "What can *I* do about all this?"

Liz took a deep breath. "Germaine, is Nicholas Barkley in love with you?" Long pause. Very long pause.

"What's love?" Germaine asked.

"I don't know. Caring, I guess. Caring more for someone else than you do for yourself. Maybe that's love."

After another long pause, Germaine said, "He cares."

"Does he care enough to listen to you?"

"What makes you think I care about him?"

"I just assumed."

"Well don't assume, Liz. He and I have a very complex relationship." She paused. Her voice softened. "But I do care." She looked at Liz evenly, her eyes filled with her own confusion, bitterness, and pain. "I care."

"Enough to get him to listen to you?"

"I thought we'd get around to that. Look, Liz . . . Nick is a mule. If you've got it in your head that I could talk him out of Barkley House, forget it."

"Can you point out the danger in it for him?"

Long pause. "I guess I could do that."

"Would you?"

Germaine heaved a deep sigh of weariness, fatigue, frustration. "I guess so."

Liz looked at Germaine for a long time in the muted light of the restaurant.

"It's not only money, Germaine. There are a lot of people whose jobs depend on Twenty/Twenty. A lot of people who have worked hard and loyally for Nick. This is a chance for some of them to be rewarded for years of work. This stock offering is what they have been counting on. They don't deserve to have everything blow up in their faces." Liz paused. "Have you met Sol Masters?" Germaine shook her head. "I have a lot of contact with Sol. He's financial vice-president of Twenty/Twenty." Liz paused. "He's been with Nick from the beginning. In the early days Nick was so tied up with the technical side of Twenty/Twenty that he left the money entirely to Sol. Sol

is a loyal and caring friend. This stock offering would make
Sol financially independent. In the early days, Nick was liberal
with stock for the people who helped build his company. He
owes them more than just a pat on the back. What I'm saying,
Germaine, is not too different from what we have been talking
about. We've been talking about injustice and racism. Some-
body has to point out to Nick that he, of all people, should not
contribute to being thoughtless, uncaring, or irresponsible to
those who helped make him what he is." Liz paused. "Do you
think you can make him understand that?" Liz watched the
pools of dark eyes search inwardly.

Germaine's voice was soft. She seemed to be reaching inside
herself, touching something important. "I'll try, Liz. I'll give
it a shot."

Chapter 24

LIZ SAT ON the edge of her bed in the Fairmont and wondered why all hotels placed phones near a bed instead of on a table where you could draw up a chair and comfortably get some work done.

She dialed Sol Masters and looked at her watch. It was 3:30.

"Sol? This is Elizabeth Clark."

"Liz, where are you?"

"I'm at the Fairmont."

Pause. "I assume you had an interesting evening."

"You might say that, Sol. It's one of the reasons I want to talk to you."

"Shoot."

"Sol, I know how busy you are, but this is terribly important." She hesitated. "I want to talk with you, privately, but I don't think I should come out there. Can you come here? We could have dinner in my room where we won't be seen or interrupted."

Sol chuckled. "That's the best proposition I've ever had. What shall I tell my wife?"

It annoyed her. "I promise not to break up your marriage, Sol."

"Now why did you have to spoil my evening by saying that?"

"Sol, will you come?"

"I'll have to cancel a few things. My wife will be sore as hell. We have a weekly bridge game, and she'll have to look around for a fourth."

"I'm sorry, Sol, but I have to see you."

"I know," he said solemnly. "I'll be there."

"Thanks. When do you think you'll get here?"

"Around six."

"Good. I'll see you then." She hung up.

She looked at her watch. It was 6:45 in New York. She put in a call to George. For some reason as she listened to the phone ringing, she felt a sense of expectancy. She realized that he wasn't in, and now she felt disappointed. A little tendril of misgiving began to curl its way through her mind. She got up and looked out the window at the bay. A gray overcast sky blocked the sun.

She saw whitecaps on the water, sailboats racing from Sausalito heeling sharply in the wind.

I wonder where he is, she thought. I wish he were out here. I miss him. Is there any reason for that? He's kept me so busy since I came to New York that I've never really had time to think seriously about him. But that phone call last night. He *was* concerned. It's hard to think of anyone as preoccupied with business as George being concerned. She turned from the window. George is lonely, she said to herself. He's also attracted to me. I've felt that from the first day he came to Harvard to interview me. She sat down in the upholstered chair near the window and let her thoughts roam. He's an attractive man. He's strong and caring. He's tried to sublimate anything between us. She paused, astonished by the paths her mind was taking. Do I really feel anything important for George, or is he someone I'm using to further my career?

There are advantages to being a woman in a man's world; I won't deny that. But there's more to it than that with George. We speak the same language, share the same interests, and we're both alone. She shook her head as she thought about it. I'm not even thirty and I feel as if I've been alone most of my life. She thought about the house in Maine. It wasn't a home; it was a house. Although she had to admit that up until her father was killed it used to be fun. She used to wait for him to come home from his business trips. She missed him terribly when he was away. He would hold her and kiss her. They would walk down the street together. In the winter there was always snow, and he would cuddle her as they walked. He'd take her out for a hot chocolate. She used to hate to let go of his hand. He'd sit across the Formica table, and she'd look at his face. His eyes seemed always to be apologizing, as if he were ashamed of something. But she could feel his love for her. It was as warm as the mug of hot chocolate. After the accident, the house dried up, and her mother dried up with it. Why? Was she so warped by pride that she would turn into a recluse?

Her mind shifted to Dr. Halsey. He obviously is interested in Mother, she thought. They've known each other a long time. He seems like a fine man. He certainly could take care of her. Why doesn't she want to make a new life with him? Am I going to be like that? Am I going to cast off the men in my life like mooring lines and drift, always on my own? Always alone.

A shaft of late afternoon sunlight pierced the cloud cover and glistened off the gray wind-whipped surface of the bay. She moved from the window and picked up the phone and dialed Peter's number. The phone drilled endlessly. He wasn't in. I don't seem to be having too much luck with the men in my life, she thought. Her mind turned to what she would wear for her dinner with Sol. Nothing too dressy, but not too businesslike either. She settled for a dark blue wool skirt with an off-white wide-collared silk blouse. She placed them on the bed and looked in her suitcase for her blue and red checkered scarf, which she found and laid beside her other things. She wanted to set just the right tone for this meeting. She wanted to appear attractive, yet not too attractive. She was almost getting used to meeting men in hotel rooms, but not quite. There was always the underlying question that lurked in her mind; what does he really want from me, and what do I want from him?

Sol Masters was punctual. At exactly six o'clock her doorbell rang. She looked through the peephole and saw the thin figure through the distorted view of the fisheye lens. She opened the door.

"Sol, it's good to see you. I appreciate your driving in all the way from Palo Alto."

"It's okay. Glad to do it. It's not often I get an invitation to dinner with one of our guests of the Board, especially one as attractive as you. You look great, Liz."

"Thank you. You've made my day. It's been a little arduous."

"Oh? I'm sorry."

"Not to worry. I hope we've accomplished something. Did you manage to square things with your wife?"

"She may talk to me by New Year's. No, I'm kidding. She was annoyed, but she understood."

"Did you tell her you were meeting me?"

He hesitated. "I think, to quote myself accurately, I said, 'one of our directors.'"

Liz felt a flash of annoyance, but she buried it. What the hell, she thought. It's always going to be the same. "How about a drink?"

"I could use one," Sol said. "It's been one of those days."

"What would you like?"

"A Bloody Mary."

"Want to make it two? Room service is a little on the slow side."

"Make it two."

Liz picked up the phone and dialed room service. "Would you send up two menus with the drinks . . . Yes, that's right, three Bloody Marys." She hung up. Sol was still standing.

She pointed to a small circular table near the window. One chair was beside it. "We can move the one in front of the desk," she said. Sol moved it. They sat down at the table, not strangers, not friends, but aware that each would have to depend on the other.

"Sol, we have a lot of ground to cover so do you mind if we get on with it?"

"That's what I'm here for."

She looked at the thin balding man in front of her with the neatly trimmed spade-shaped beard. He's polyester, she thought. Probably straight out of business school where he majored in accounting. He probably thinks Hegel composed the Hallelujah Chorus. But he's bright and he's honest, and I think he is a real friend of Nicholas Barkley.

"Last night, Sol, I saw Nick's house."

Sol sighed. "I thought you might."

"First he took us to his favorite restaurant."

"He likes to go there," Sol said. "It's one of the best in town."

"But it's very racist. If Germaine wasn't a well-known television personality in San Francisco, I doubt if they would have let her in the place if they could have avoided it. She was very uncomfortable all through dinner, and I was uncomfortable for her." Liz paused. "That was thoughtless and unkind of him. Why did he do such a thing? If he cares for her, as he seems to, it doesn't make any sense."

"It does if you know Nicholas Barkley. He doesn't give a damn about what anyone else thinks. Nathan Bauchenstein becomes Nicholas Barkley. What the hell? It's a free country. It's done all the time. Change your name. But he forgot one thing—the bastards never let you forget."

"That's odd. That's what Germaine said to me at lunch, but she was talking about color. She said, 'He can change his name, but I can't change this,' and she pointed to her skin.

"Tell me, Sol, is Nick's relationship to Germaine just an elaborate protest, or does he really care for her?"

"I don't see much of Germaine. I'm not a part of his private life. He separates his business associates from his social life. I really don't know how he feels about Germaine. It may be his way of telling everyone to go to hell, or he may really care about her. I just don't know." Sol paused. "But I do know one thing. Your firm better bring this stock offering to market soon or he is going to have a hell of a time financially."

"How do you mean?"

"I mean, just how do you think he is financing that house of his?"

"I was wondering about that."

"I thought you might."

"It was one of the things I was going to ask you." She looked at the small man whose face was tanned by the California sun, but whose eyes looked harried and burdened.

"He has spent nearly two million dollars on that property. It cost him nearly a million to buy it, and he's put nearly another million into furnishing and running the damn place." Sol looked at her grimly. "Would you believe with mortgage payments and operating expenses that place costs him over forty thousand a month to operate?"

Liz gasped. "You can't be serious."

"You're damn right I'm serious. I had one hell of a fight with him over it. At first he wouldn't show me the numbers. I told him if he didn't trust me enough to give me the numbers I would have to resign. I wouldn't have cared if he hadn't borrowed company funds against his stock to pay for that nut house, but he did. He owes the company nearly two million dollars. If you don't come through with this stock offering, he's going to have to sell a lot more of his stock privately at a deep discount. It will cost him control of the company."

"Does George know any of this?"

"Yes."

The doorbell rang.

"There are our drinks." Liz got up to let in the waiter, who put the drinks on the table. He handed menus to Liz and Sol.

"Sol, let's order now. It will save some time."

They looked over the menus. "I'll have the vichyssoise," Liz said, and the fillet of sole, sautéed, spinach, and coffee." The waiter made quick notes on his pad. Sol was looking at the menu the way he might look at a financial statement.

"Shrimp cocktail," he said. "New York steak, medium. Baked potato with sour cream. Tossed salad with Russian dressing."

The waiter left.

"Sol, you say George knows about Nick's indebtedness."

Sol nodded. "George knows. He's concerned about it, but as long as Nick was backing those loans with his own stock, George felt a little easier. But George warned me that I was to pay particular attention to the company's cash flow. If Nick got too far into hock and was threatening the company's cash position, George would have had him cut off. He and Nick had a hell of an argument about it, but George was adamant. He said he'd bring it to the board if necessary, and the board holds the majority of the stock."

George never mentioned this to me, Liz thought. I wonder why? "Sol. This is important," she said. "Does George know about Barkley House?"

"Liz, that's a part of Nick's private life that he shares only with those he is close to on a personal basis. Even I have never been invited into the damn place."

"Then why did he show it to me? You've been his friend and confidant for a very long time."

"I can't answer that, Liz. I know he likes you and respects

your intelligence and thoroughness. He also likes good-looking women."

"Sol . . ."

"No, I'm serious. He probably would not have shown you the house if you hadn't been a woman and if he wasn't attracted to you. There's an advantage to being a woman when you're dealing with men." He smiled as he said it, sipping his Bloody Mary and watching her with his troubled dark brown eyes.

The doorbell rang again, and the waiter rolled in a table with burning cans of Sterno beneath stainless-steel-covered dishes that kept their food hot. The waiter set out their dinner for them and turned automatically to Sol.

"Will that be all, sir?"

"You'd better ask her. She's paying the bill."

"I'm sorry, miss."

Liz reached for the check. "Don't worry about it. It happens all the time." She signed the check and wrote the waiter's tip on it.

"Should we have ordered some wine, Sol?"

"Not for me. I'm fine."

They ate slowly, each aware of the problems of the other.

"Sol, I'm going to have to report our conversation to George."

"I know that."

"I'm not so sure we can bring this deal off unless we can find some way to disassociate Nick from his hobby. His loans will have to be in the audited figures in the prospectus."

"Of course," Sol said.

Liz's face was grim. "Sol, I'm concerned about the after-market. If news of what he's doing gets out and he's lucky enough to hang on to most of his clients, then we'll still be at risk if anyone penetrates Twenty/Twenty's security system. If that happens the stock will drop like a stone, and if lawsuits follow, as I think they will, we'll all spend a fortune defending ourselves against class action shareholder suits. Can you see us trying to defend a business whose product is to safeguard money, run by a man who owns a place like Barkley House?"

She was eating her fish, her eyes searching Sol's. She paused. "Sol, a major scandal like this would seriously damage the reputation of my firm. That's about all a venture capital firm has got when you get right down to it—a reputation for judgment, intelligence, and integrity. Larry and Bob and George have spent years building relationships with our institutional investors. If Baldwin Cooper is involved in a bizarre scandal, which is what the media would make of all this, it will ruin us."

Sol ate quietly, occasionally looking up at her. He didn't say anything for a long time. When he finally spoke it was as if he were talking to himself. "You know, Liz, Nicholas Barkley is a great salesman. He's able to project his enthusiasm so that you get caught up in it. I got caught up in it. I was a young accountant fresh out of UCLA working for Cooper Ross here in San Francisco. I had a good job. I liked my work and thought I had a good future. Nick and the group he had put together at Stanford were looking around for seed money. Some of the banks in town were interested in what he was doing and backed him with some Small Business Administration loans. He needed a financial man. His guys were a bunch of geniuses who couldn't keep a checkbook balanced. The banks insisted that they find someone to mind the money while they were building the Twenty/Twenty security system. I met Nick at a party. Two total strangers. But he's an easy guy to get to like, as you know. He told me what he was trying to do, and I was fascinated by it. Accounting firms, even in those days, were well aware of the potential danger of computer theft."

He paused and chuckled to himself. "Now, my old firm is selling a service that's supposed to protect its clients against just that, but it's a joke. There are so many ways to get into a computer that it's almost impossible to protect yourself completely from someone who wants to get you, and who has the technical knowledge to do it. That is unless you're a Twenty/Twenty client."

"You mean no one has ever broken a Twenty/Twenty system, Sol?"

Sol shook his head. "Not one of our clients has ever had a penetration." He paused. "To be completely accurate, there have been attempted penetrations, but one of the beauties of the system is that if you try and break it, it identifies you. It's like calling up a bank and giving your name and address and announcing that you're going to rob the bank." He sighed and put down his knife and fork. "When Nick and I first met, he had spent four years working in a rented dump of a building in Palo Alto using Stanford's computer facilities. He had corraled a group of guys who were really far out. They were cryptologists, puzzle freaks, mathematicians. They had knocked their brains out twelve to fourteen hours a day, seven days a week, for nearly four years, yet they could never come up with a code system they couldn't break. They caught the attention of the Department of Defense, mainly because Nick had recruited one of the top cryptologists who worked for the CIA. They gave him a very hard time until he convinced them that what he was trying to do had specific military and intelligence applications. They eventually wanted to fund him, but he was smart enough to say no. They raised hell about that, too, and tried to prevent their key code cracker from joining Twenty/ Twenty." He looked at Liz, not really seeing her as he ran through old memories.

"I'm still not sure if the CIA guy wasn't eventually allowed to go with Nick to keep an eye on what he was doing." He sighed. "Who the hell knows? Anyway, they kept coming up with systems that were always flawed. Everything they created they could eventually penetrate. When I finally agreed to join his company, they had just created the Twenty/Twenty system, and they were off and running. Nick told me how it came to him." Sol Masters turned to Liz, his eyes focusing on her but still not seeing her. Looking beyond her, back to that time in his past when it had all begun for him, when he stopped being a humdrum accountant and became a participant in an exciting new business that was about to explode.

"I was the first one he told about it. He came into my office and sat opposite my desk, leaning back in his chair, his fingers laced behind his head—you know how he does that . . . His face looked like a Halloween pumpkin, a smiling one. All he said was, 'Sol. I've got it.' I didn't know what the hell he was talking about. He got up, smiling that great jack-o'-lantern smile of his, and he came over to my desk. He looked at me and clapped me on the back. He said, 'Sol, I'm going to make you a wealthy man.' And he just walked out of my office. That was only four years ago. And he did it. He gave all of us generous stock options and bonuses." Sol's eyes returned to Liz. He was seeing her now. She could feel the force of his frustration and anger. "Do you know that I'm worth over a million and a quarter. That's on paper. If you don't get this stock to market and this deal blows up, if the company blows with it, I'll be lucky if I can sell my stock at all." He paused. "Sure there's plenty of sharks out there who would love to buy Twenty/Twenty, but if they can get it for a dollar a share rather than twenty-five, they'll be delighted, and that's just what's going to happen if Nick blows this deal." Sol Masters pushed himself back from the table and reached for his second Bloody Mary. "You tell me about what Baldwin Cooper stands to lose. Well, if you'll forgive me, Liz, I can't weep for Baldwin Cooper. I'm too damn sorry for Sol Masters, who's spent nearly five years trying to finance these kooks and keep them out of the bankruptcy courts. Now comes my payoff, and that bearded lunatic is going to blow it for himself . . ." He looked at Liz. "And for your firm and for me." He put his drink down and got up from the table and walked over to the window. Liz watched him as he gazed out at the fog coming in over the bay.

He turned and looked at her. "I'll never get another shot like this, Liz. You know that."

She sighed. "Sol, there has to be some way we can reach him. Make him understand what he's doing."

Sol's expression was bitter, his voice hard with irony. "Suddenly the son of a bitch is a philosopher. He has *points of view*. Only he's not like anyone else. He has to build a living laboratory. Maybe that's his problem. He's spent so much of his life in a lab he thinks the whole world is just another computer screen. A new circuit design or a systems code. Now he walks down off the mountain with a few bucks in his pocket and he becomes the Socrates of the pothead set. Maybe it builds his ego. Maybe it's a heavy trip for him. Maybe he is bored . . ."

She watched him as his face became a mask of anxiety. His voice shook. He stood facing her, but not seeing her. His rage had separated him, made him a ghost in his own body.

Suddenly she was afraid. This wasn't the Sol Masters she knew. He looked as if he were freaking out. I wish to God George were here, she said to herself.

"I don't know what the hell to do with him, or myself," Sol said. "He needs a shrink. Either that or a hard kick in the ass to bring him back to reality." His voice lowered. "All these years, and now's my chance to really score, and I'm going to crap out. All because of some lunatic who wants to experiment with *freedom*." His voice dripped with sarcasm. He shook his head. He looked at Liz for a long time. She still had the feeling that he was talking to himself. "You know, I'm almost ashamed to say it, but there are times when I've actually fantasized about killing the bastard."

"Sol, stop it. That's ridiculous."

"I know it's ridiculous, but the thought has occurred to me."

"I wasn't going to tell you this, Sol, but I had lunch with Germaine today. She's going to talk to him."

"He won't listen."

"He might. I think he really loves her. She's a very impressive woman."

He moved from the window and began pacing. His frustration and rage were palpable. "George will never allow this deal to go to market once you've told him how things are out here. He'd be crazy to."

He's right, she thought. George will pull the plug on this. If I were George, I would, too.

"There's not a damn thing you can do," Sol continued. "We're dealing with a nut. A psycho. The guy is off his rocker."

Sol was pacing the area in front of the window, so absorbed in his own torment that he again seemed unaware of her presence.

"I never had any pretensions," he said, as if to himself. "I wasn't the brightest guy at school, but I wasn't the dumbest. I was never really outstanding at anything. I knew that. All I wanted was a job where I could work with numbers. With numbers you don't have to be a star. Not good-looking. Not a great stud. Not a macho guy. Not great with women. Not sensitive, poetic, or artsy-craftsy. Not anything but accurate. Careful. Willing to put in the time. Make the numbers come out right and don't make mistakes. That's what I could do. Not very glamorous, but it pays well, and nobody gives a damn if you're the captain of the football team, or you look like me. I understood all of that. I never had any high hopes. I knew my limitations and I was happy living with them. I was with a good firm. I was doing a good job, and I was advancing and making good money. People respected my work..."

She watched him as the film of his mind played out the scenes of his life. She was drawn to his almost total introspection by a mixture of morbid fascination, her own fear of the potential for emotional combustion that filled the room like methane gas, and some latent empathy for this thin man with the balding head and spade-shaped beard whose life seemed to be coming apart in front of her.

She sat on the edge of the large bed trying not to appear upset, but she was. She was growing increasingly afraid of Sol's instability.

Sol stopped pacing and turned toward her, his eyes and his mind somewhere in another time frame.

"I never wanted to be anything but what I was. I was satisfied. How many people do you know who are satisfied? Well, I was." He paused. "Then this bearded jack-o'-lantern from Stanford comes into my life, like some genie let out of a bottle. He fills me full of a whole lot of garbage I really don't believe and, quite frankly, don't care about. I'm satisfied. But he keeps at me. You know what kind of a salesman Barkley can be. But the bastard's a charmer, and he followed through, but he took the one thing away from me that left me wide open. Totally vulnerable." He paused looking at her, really seeing her now. "Liz, he took away my contentment, my peace with myself, and he gave me *hope*. I never wanted hope. He told me he would make me rich. I never dared to dream that one day I might be rich. Me, rich. Why? I have nothing special. I don't have the imagination or the drive to be an entrepreneur like Barkley, and I don't have the ambition to want to be president or chairman of anything." He was holding his hands out, wringing them in front of her, in an attitude of pleading and confession. "He said he would make me rich, and I realized that he might just be able to do that, without me having to do anything more than I've ever done, just keep the numbers straight."

He's going to kneel, Liz thought. The poor half-demented man is going to kneel.

But he didn't. He stood there, an incongruous supplicant in front of the blank eye of the television set, in front of the broad sweep of gauze drape that softened the mist-shrouded lights of the financial district spreading out from the lower end of California Street. He stood there like a defrocked cleric about to beg for absolution.

"No man has the right to break inside you and give you hope. No one." His voice shook, and tears streamed down his face, glistening in the soft light of the room. "I didn't want it, Liz. I never cared about money. I just wanted enough to be comfortable. I never dreamed of being rich." His voice rose, confused, high-pitched. "But he did it! The son of a bitch did it! He made me rich, and now he's going to blow it all away! I never wanted it!"

She stood up, thrusting aside her fear at the sight of him weeping. She put her arm around him—she was several inches taller than he was—and spoke to him softly. "Sol, sit down." She pulled him gently beside her, and they sat on the edge of the bed. He was weeping freely now. His emotional dam had burst. She drew his head to her as she would have comforted a child. She stroked the back of his neck as his sobs were muffled against her breast.

"He gave me something I thought I could never have, Liz. I buried it in the bottom of my soul. He found it and took it out and handed it to me..." She felt his hands gripping her shoulders. "Liz. Now I want it! I don't want him to take it back! I've got it in the palm of my hand, and he's going to blow it away! The son of a bitch is going to blow it away!"

She held him close to her, amazed at the total metamorphosis of a human being she thought she knew and understood. Like a young mother with a frightened child who had bolted to her warmth and protection from the dread of some terrible nightmare, she found herself in the incongruous position of cradling a forty-two-year-old accountant in her arms, in her hotel room, three thousand miles from home.

Chapter 25

SHE SLEPT THE sleep of the totally exhausted. She had been emptied emotionally by the challenge that confronted her, which seemed impossible to overcome. Dealing with Sol's torment, spilling out in agonized frustration, had drained the last of her reserves. She had barely been able to undress as she got into bed at four o'clock in the morning.

Slowly she heard it. Deep within the layers of sleep it sawed at her consciousness, dragging her awake. She moaned and turned over in bed trying to block out the sound. "No, for God's sake no," she mumbled aloud. She tried pulling the pillow over her head to obliterate the ringing of the phone. "Oh, dear god, this is the end." The insistent phone rang on, demanding her response. Her hand groped toward it, knocking it from its cradle to the floor. She stretched, reaching for the phone, groping for it around the feet of the night table. "Hello," she said, her voice thick with fatigue and sleep.

"Liz, is that you?"

"What's left of me. Who is this?"

"Nick Barkley." His voice was restrained and cold. She could sense that even through the pall of her fatigue.

"Nick, what time is it?"

"Ten-thirty."

Liz was incredulous. She hadn't slept this late since she could remember. She sat bolt upright in bed clutching the phone, a cascade of thoughts running through her mind.

I haven't called George, she thought. It's one-thirty in New York. He'll be furious.

"Liz, are you there?"

"I'm here. I'm here. That is my body is here. I'm not sure where my mind is."

"I'm sorry to awaken you." The voice still very cool, restrained. "I want to talk to you about something that very much disturbs me, Liz."

Her anxieties were now successfully fighting off the resistant layers of sleep. "Nick, I'm sorry to sound so awful, but I didn't get to bed until nearly four." Long pause.

Silence from his end.

"Nick, you said you were disturbed about something . . ."

"I am disturbed, and I might add, Liz, disappointed as well."

"I'm afraid I'm not with it. You're upset and you're disappointed." She hesitated. "With me?"

Pause. "With you, Liz." The tone was flat.

She was stunned and hurt. "Why are you upset with me?"

"I just hung up after talking with Germaine. She told me all about your concerns." He hesitated. "Really, Liz, I thought you were above that kind of subterfuge. If you had to say something, why didn't you say it to me? Why did you have to spin that tale about wanting to see me about a personal problem?" He was becoming more agitated. She could hear his anger and disappointment. "Liz, one of the things I most admired about you was your honesty. There are a lot of intelligent people, but not too many people with the kind of integrity I thought you had."

She felt like a thief who had been caught with stolen goods. She had known this might happen; she had told George that it would. The firm had placed her in an impossible position. She couldn't tell Barkley that it was BC's idea to send her out here; that would sound juvenile and weak.

"Nick, please listen—"

"I think I've done enough listening for one morning, Liz. Now I want you to listen. You and your firm have built up some homemade anxieties about how I live my life and conduct my business. If those fears are not completely ridiculous, they are not far from it."

She was sitting up in bed, clutching the phone, terrified that she was blowing the most important assignment of her very brief career, a career that she sensed might be not only short but terminal, as far as BC was concerned. It all seemed so damned unfair. She had wanted no part of any of this. She had told George what could happen, and now it was happening.

"I tried to explain it to you the other night, Liz. I thought you understood." He paused. "There are some things in life— a good many as far as I am concerned—that are more important than money. I told you I was serious about Barkley House. I've spent a great deal of money on it, as you are well aware." He paused. "You may think the comparison farfetched, and perhaps it is, but I am trying to do socially—emotionally, if you will—what the Advanced Institute at Princeton is doing scholastically and scientifically."

She tried to choke back her laughter, but it just slipped out.

"If that sounds farfetched to you, Liz"—Barkley's voice was as cold as ice—"let me see if I can penetrate your skepticism. The Advanced Institute allows highly qualified scholars in various disciplines to pursue their work in a contemplative environment, free from financial worries." He paused. "Would you agree with that?"

She had to force herself to take him seriously. "I would."

"In other words, the Advanced Institute gives its members the freedom to do what they want." He hesitated. "It may come as a surprise to you, Liz, that many of the people who visit my house are highly accomplished in their own fields—in the arts, science, medicine, literature, music, theater. You name it, we've got it. They may not be Nobel Laureates, but many of them are gifted, talented people." Long pause. "I explained to you the night before last that I consider it important to give these people a particular kind of freedom, freedom from themselves." He paused. "You may not feel that that is important, but I can assure you they do. For many of them it has been an experience of discovery, and they will tell you it has been one of the most important experiences of their lives. Liz, I am not going to sacrifice this for money."

"Nick." Her voice was firm. She was wide awake now, and she could feel stirrings of anger and resentment. "I am not going to argue philosophy with you or debate the worth of what you are doing. I am not a judge of other people. Neither is George, or Larry or Bob. As a matter of fact, we are not quite as stuffy or judgmental as you might believe. We are seriously looking at the possibility of financing a number of psychiatric centers run by a psychiatrist whose ideas are as innovative and original as your own. As a matter of fact, you two should get together. You'd enjoy each other. You have a lot in common. But that's not the point." Her voice betrayed her frustration and anger. "The point is that if you're serious about what you are doing, you certainly have a peculiar attitude."

"In what way?"

"Don't you see, Nick?" She was going to roll the dice for the whole stack of chips. "If you're serious about what you're trying to do with Barkley House, you're jeopardizing everything by not being realistic." She took a deep breath. "You owe the company nearly two million dollars. If we don't get this stock issue off for you, the board is going to force you to repay those loans. It will cost you control, and you won't have the money to finance your experiment or whatever you choose to call it." She hesitated. "The other night you said to me that it's not a very kind world out there. Well, it isn't. You also told me that all your life you have been lucky, that things have come easily for you, that you're bored. Well, I haven't been at this game very long, as you know, but I've heard enough about people who have outrun their lucky streaks, and you are setting yourself up to do just that. If we get this stock off for you, we are still vulnerable, all of us, if anything happens to the Twenty/Twenty system, if there's a penetration. Then it will all come back to haunt you and us. The best motives in the world won't explain Barkley House. I'm afraid you're comparing it to the Advanced Institute might seem a trifle presumptuous to most people. Nick, this is one time you can't stick your hand into life's cookie jar and not get caught." She sighed. "Look, I don't have to tell you this. You don't control the board. They are going to vote on my reactions to what I've seen out here—George's reactions to what I report, actually. If they decide to do this deal, they are going to want some assurance that you will separate yourself in some way from Barkley House. If I can't bring them back that assurance, I'm afraid one of two things will happen. You'll either have no deal and lose control of Twenty/Twenty or"—she hesitated— "You'll lose control of Twenty/Twenty after the offering. It won't go down any other way."

There was no response from the other end of the line. She had blown it. She had given it to him straight, and she had blown the whole deal right out the window. Sweet Jesus, she thought, I should have gone to work in a bank.

"Do you have time for lunch?" he asked her.

She was taken completely by surprise. "Yes. Of course."

There was a long hesitation, and when he spoke again his voice was tired, resigned. "I'll pick you up at noon in front of the hotel." He hung up. She was left with the silent phone in her hand, which reminded her that she had to call George. She looked at the digital clock. It was ten-fifty. Nearly two o'clock in New York. She dialed George's number.

"Mr. Hall's office."

"Martha, is George available? I'd like to speak to him."

"He's in conference, Liz, but he left instructions to put you through if you called. Hold on, I'll tell him you're on the line."

Liz waited, her mouth set, her thoughts grim. The whole damn thing was going downhill just as she had predicted. She couldn't figure out why Nicholas Barkley wanted to see her again. She had told him everything he would have to do, and he showed no signs of being willing to compromise.

"Liz, you finally decided to call."

She was not in the mood for sarcasm. "Look, George, I got to bed at four this morning after Sol Masters practically had a nervous breakdown in my hotel room. I've just hung up from Barkley after he bawled me out for about fifteen minutes for not being honest with him. And added to all that I had no alternative but to tell him the truth."

"It sounds as if you've been having a jolly time." He paused. His voice turned serious. "Do we still have a deal?"

"I'm not sure."

"Well, that's certainly comforting. Do you think you could be a little more enlightening?"

She sighed. "George, it's impossible to explain unless you've been out here. I'm not even going to try over the phone. In summary, I just got finished telling Barkley that, after I report to you what has been going on out here, he'll have to disassociate himself from what he's doing here or you would decide—" She paused again. "George, I don't want to sound presumptuous, but it's just common sense how you would react to this thing."

"Go on," George said.

"Well, I told him you would probably do one of two things. You might decide not to do the deal, in which case he will lose control of Twenty/Twenty."

"Why would he lose control?" George's voice had risen slightly. She could hear his anxiety and surprise over the phone.

"George, not now. Just take it from me that if we don't do this stock offering Barkley will be out as chairman and chief executive officer. If we do the deal, after what I tell you, I would bet that the board will exercise control and remove Barkley."

"That sounds less than reassuring." She could feel him trying to control his annoyance and frustration. "Sounds as if you've been busy."

"George, I'm sorry things have gone badly, but there isn't much else that I can do." She hesitated. "There is one thing I don't understand."

"What's that?"

"After I told Barkley the realities of his position, he invited me to lunch and then hung up. I've got to get dressed soon. He's picking me up at noon." She hesitated. "I can't figure it out. He was so angry when he first called me that I found it hard to believe it was Nicholas Barkley. Well, I've found out, George, that jolly old Barkley is neither old nor jolly." She paused. "As a matter of fact, George, I don't think any of us really know him."

"I thought I did," George said solemnly.

"So did I, but since I've been out here, I've been introduced to a side of him I don't think either of us knew or suspected."

"Liz, I don't know what's really going on out there. Larry and Bob are very anxious to hear your report. So am I. Have lunch with Barkley and find out if there is some way you can get him to see the realities of what you've been telling him." George paused. "I'm assuming that your assessment of how the firm would react to whatever it is he's doing is very probable."

She caught the emphasis on the phrase *very probable*.

"Make arrangements to fly back here tomorrow," George went on. "I'll set up a meeting with Larry and Bob for the following day. We'll listen to what you have to say and decide what we're going to do. In the meantime, try to get some rest.

It sounds as if you've been keeping some odd hours."

"You might say that," she said.

"Liz, I've missed you. I'm sorry I dumped this on you, but all of us felt—and I did, too—that you would be the best one to handle Barkley."

"I haven't been very effective."

"The day isn't over, Liz. You've still got another shot at him. You might tell him we've lined up Dean Merrill as the managing underwriter and they've already put the selling syndicate together. The SEC has okayed the registration statement, so we're ready to go. The market's strong. Dean Merrill tells us the selling group is hot for the stock. They think it will move to a premium very quickly." George paused, his voice softened. "Liz, it'll be a holy Jesus crying shame if Barkley blows this deal. Everything's right for it. Everything."

She sighed. "George, I can only try. I'll do everything I can. You know that."

"I know." He paused. "You'll really be wrung out by the time you get back to New York." He hesitated. "Suppose I buy you dinner. I'll meet you at the airport. Tell Martha when your flight comes in. We'll have a nice relaxing evening. What do you say?"

She could feel the warmth and the interest in his voice. "Sounds good. I've felt like a stranger in a strange land out here. It was fun when we came out here together. Now it's just lonely."

"It's lonely on this end too, Liz," he said quietly. "I've missed you very much."

Barkley was unusually quiet on the drive to Sausalito. They had hardly exchanged ten words. Liz's thoughts were a montage of confusion. She felt very drawn to George, and that made her feel guilty about Peter. She hadn't heard from Peter since the phone call the previous week.

Nicholas Barkley's white Jag sped along Route 101 across the Golden Gate Bridge over the blue of the bay toward the wooded hills that overlooked the Gateway to the Pacific.

She was growing increasingly annoyed by Barkley's silence. She didn't know whether this was some game to see who would speak first, but she was damned if she was going to give in to him.

But I'm trying to sell him, she thought. He's not trying to sell me. Jesus, she said to herself, this is awfully trying. I've got to make the effort. I've simply got to, but my God, it is infuriating!

The car turned off at the Sausalito exit, and she finally knew where they were going to have lunch. Barkley drove slowly through the crowded street. She could see the masts from the yacht club and then the yachts themselves. He pulled on to the wooden planked parking area of Horizons. The attendant opened the door and handed him a parking receipt.

"I hoped that you would enjoy this, Liz." It was the first full sentence he had spoken since they left the Fairmont. The hostess guided them to an outside table. The sun was warm, but a breeze from the bay made it cooler.

"You can get a real sunburn out here, Liz. Would you rather eat inside?"

She could feel the sun already hot against her face. "Nick, it's beautiful out here, but I do burn easily. Maybe we'd better eat inside if you don't mind."

They moved indoors to a window table where they could see the yachts with their white sails against a cloudless sky. San Francisco glistened in the noonday sun across the bay.

Barkley ordered an expensive Sauvignon, and after they had drunk half the bottle they both loosened up a little. They ate slowly, quietly, the hostility that had separated them had begun to disappear.

"Tell me, Liz. Exactly what do you mean when you say I should disassociate myself from Barkley House?"

She thought a long time before answering him. He was giving her another chance. "Before I answer that, I want you to know that I've spoken to George. I haven't told him very much; that can wait until I get back to New York. But he had a message for you. He wanted me to tell you that the stock offering is ready to go. Dean Merrill is going to be the managing underwriter. They have the selling syndicate formed, and Merrill says they're hot for the stock. The SEC has given the go-ahead on the registration statement. About all that's left is for you to sign the underwriting agreement. George said it would be a holy Jesus crying shame to blow this deal. Dean Merrill told George that the stock should move to a premium very quickly."

She looked carefully at Barkley. "Now, to answer your question about disassociating yourself from Barkley House. There are a lot of ways you can do it, but the end result is the same. You have to build a wall between yourself and Barkley House."

"Such as . . ."

Liz thought for a moment. "You could put the property in trust, establish a foundation to fund it, and have an administrator and staff run it. That way you would insulate yourself from a good part of the kind of criticism that would cost you control of Twenty/Twenty."

She watched him think about this. Her peripheral vision saw the reflection in the large picture window of boats that seemed to be sailing toward the area of bay she had been watching. She would expect the boats to appear in front of her, but they didn't. It was an optical illusion. She wondered whether all of this with Barkley was an illusion. Would he disappear like those mystical yachts, taking her problems and the firm's with him. Not quite, she thought. The tea-colored beard and the pumpkin face remained opposite her.

"And what is my alternative, if I don't accept your suggestion?"

"I can't speak for the firm, Nick. They are waiting to decide what to do after I get back. I don't know what their decision will be, but my guess is—" she hesitated. Her voice became soft with compassion. "My guess, Nick, is that the board will vote you out."

"And the stock deal. Will they go through with that?"

"I simply don't know." She looked at him steadily, unable to read him. He sat like Buddha while the gulls soared over the blue diamonds of water and the phantom illusory yachts sailed into the reflection of the window overlooking the bay.

"I'll think about what you've said, Liz."

"Nick, I've got to tell them something in New York. They're going to ask you to sign an underwriting agreement with Dean Merrill very soon. They'll want a commitment from you before they do that." She hesitated. "What do I tell them when I get back to New York?"

He looked at her with a cool detachment. "Tell them I'll think about it," he said. "Tell them just that."

George had just hung up from talking to Liz, when his intercom buzzed. "Ms. White is here; she wants to see you." For the moment he was stunned. In the five years since he and Claudia had been divorced, she had never once come to his office. He had a meeting in fifteen minutes. God, what now? he thought. He got up and walked out to see Claudia sitting chatting with Martha. She stood up as he saw him.

She looks so thin and pale, he thought. She can't weigh more than a hundred pounds.

"Claudia, it's good to see you. Won't you come in?" He felt embarrassed at his formality in front of Martha.

"It's good to see you, too, George," she said, as she walked into his office. George pointed to a chair at the circular conference table. His anger was coming quickly to the surface. She's going to ask me for the damn alimony I owe her. Christ. That's all I need.

She settled herself in her chair and looked at him carefully. "You really do look well, George."

"I don't know how. This business is enough to kill ten men."

"But you've always loved the excitement, the pace, the challenge. You wouldn't be happy doing anything else."

"I'm not so sure. I think I could get to enjoy a little less pace and challenge. I'm tired of problems." He sighed. "I think I'm tired of a lot of things." She smiled wearily. Her expression seemed a mixture of sadness and irony as if she knew something, had some special secret, some wisdom that belonged to her alone. As he looked at her he realized that there was something very different about her. She was always thin and pale, but now she seemed almost gossamer, as if the slightest wind would blow her away. But it was more than that. She had a certain tranquillity that was completely strange to him and, he knew, foreign to her.

"George, we had some rare moments together, didn't we?"

He was caught off guard by her question. "Yes, Claudia, we had some really good times." He hesitated. "Would you like some coffee?"

"No, thanks, George." She looked at him carefully, studying his face. "The years have been kind to you, George. You've become better looking as you've matured." She laughed her brittle laugh. "Women don't seem to do as well as men as they grow older."

His intercom buzzed. "Mr. Binder is here, Mr. Hall."

"Tell him I'm tied up. I'll be with him in a few minutes."

"Not much time to reminisce, is there, George? As a matter of fact, in both our worlds—mine in law, yours in banking—we never had much time for anything but work, did we? Not even for a child." He didn't answer. He couldn't. For some reason, seeing her like this, this pale surprise with whom he had shared a part of his life was making him feel insecure. Guilty.

She sighed. "I have something to tell you, George. I chose to tell you in your office because I thought it would be less emotional here, and quicker. A more clinical environment, if you will, with no long scenes of anguish." She paused, looking at him with a kind of peace and contentment that he found unsettling. "I'm going to die." She said it quietly without any trace of theatrics. His face turned dead white. He was struck absolutely speechless. He tried to say something to her, but nothing would come out. He sat there transfixed, unable to comprehend what she had told him.

She spoke quietly. "The doctors have given me, at the most, six months. With treatment, surgery, chemotherapy, I might possibly be able to beat this disease for a few years, but I have no intention of allowing them to cut me up, dose me with radiation, and put me through hell with drugs. I'm not going to die that way, George. I'm going to die with some dignity. But before I do that, I'm going to do some things I want to do." She paused. "I have a lot to make up for, George." She seemed to be talking not to him but to herself. "College, then law school. Always the top of my class. Working like hell to become a partner. I haven't had a lot of time to think about anyone but me." She looked at him wistfully, her eyes moist with regret. She repeated it. "We did have a few good times, didn't we, George?" She paused. "But those seemed to blow away like dried leaves. Funny." She put on a determined smile. "But you are busy, so I might as well tell you why I'm here. I've resigned from the firm and sold off most of my assets. I've accumulated a good deal of cash, which I intend to use in various ways. You know, George, my life has been so self-centered that I'm faced with dying and with the knowledge that my life has not been very meaningful. No one wants to die without feeling that their life has had some purpose." She smiled wryly. "George, I don't want this to sound like *A Christmas Carol*. I'm not being dragged around by a threatening ghost showing me how selfish my life has been, but in a way, I do feel that I owe some debts that I've never paid, and I want to make up for some of that as quickly as I can. I want to do something, a few things that are really worthwhile. Pay my dues as it were. You know there's one thing about dying, George; it does have a way of focusing one's attention."

He couldn't believe what he was hearing. "Claudia, for God's sake. It's not like you to give up without a fight. You've always been a winner."

She shook her head. "Not this time, George. You see, one of my closest friends recently died of cancer. I watched her go through the whole dreadful therapy. I don't want to die like that. If I had one of the less terminal forms of course I would fight it. They can do wonders with a lot of variations of the disease, but unfortunately, what I have is very far along, George."

My God. What is she telling me? My ex-wife comes into my office out of the blue and sits there quietly and tells me she's going to die. This is insane.

"Dying isn't so hard, George, once you've learned to accept it. In fact, in many instances, it's far easier than living."

"What can I do, Claudia? How can I help you?"

"There's just one way, George. Some of the things I want to do are going to cost a good deal of money. I want to set up a series of medical scholarships for the study of oncology. Cancer. That's how I'm going to fight this thing, George. I'm not a wealthy woman, but I can do something. I came here to ask you if you would consider paying me some of the money you owe me so that I will be able to contribute more."

He was choking. He found himself wanting to speak, but he couldn't. His eyes began to mist looking at the pale, thin woman whose body was being devoured while she sat there. This was the woman he had called a bitch. This was the woman he couldn't live with—or was it?

She could see him struggling with his emotions. "George, I know how you live and what your business is like." She smiled that same wan smile. "After all, I should. I know you're not very liquid, that you're tied up in a lot of lock-up deals. All I ask is that you do whatever you can." She paused, looking at him evenly. "And soon, George. Soon."

His mind raced over the inventory of his assets. He could

sell his apartment, but that might take time. He had some investments he could sell but that would strip him of any liquidity he had left. It suddenly came to him as if it had always been there. "Claudia, the firm is about to close a deal, a big one. I've got a fairly good piece of that. We've got some problems with it, but if we can get it off, I could give you a good-sized chunk of money."

She looked at him with the appraising, cynical look he had come to know so well, but then her expression changed, it became softer, more understanding.

"George, do whatever you feel you can do." She started to rise.

"Wait, Claudia. You can't leave like this. Is someone staying with you? Who looks after you, for God's sake? Are you living alone? I just can't let you walk out of here to fight this thing by yourself."

She looked up at him. She seemed almost gossamerlike except for the aura of strength that emanated from her. She had always been a strong woman, but it had been a self-centered strength that lacked the compassion he now saw in her.

"I don't live alone, George. I have a marvelous housekeeper who takes very good care of me. I have a few close friends who are kind and attentive. And I'm so busy setting up this foundation of mine, creating these scholarships, that I don't have very much time to think about myself."

She moved toward him and touched his forearm with the tips of her fingers. Her eyes searched his face. He felt as if he were going to crack in half as he looked at her. What the hell had happened to them? he thought. Why had he never seen her like this before? *Was* she like this before? He had thought of her as such a bitch for so long. Was she? Had she been, or was it he that had been a selfish, uncaring husband who spent his life chasing a buck? He stood looking at her, not knowing who he was or what he was.

"Claudia—"

"I hope I'll hear from you soon, George." She opened the door and walked quickly past Martha Wainright's desk. He closed his door and walked to the windows that overlooked the Avenue of the Americas. The crowds looked like multicolored ants. He couldn't see them clearly; his eyes were misted by the impact of Claudia's visit. She had come back into his life like a dream, and she had left the same way. He couldn't accept what she had told him. A part of him wanted to believe that she had never appeared at all; that what had just happened had been only in his imagination.

My God, he realized she's only forty-one. The thought staggered him. I wonder how long she's known about this, he thought. She's got guts. Jesus Christ, has she got guts. He turned away from the window and just stood there. His office blurred before his eyes. Colors and shapes merged through the tears. He wiped them away with his handkerchief, then sat down and stared at nothing. "Holy sweet Jesus," he said. "Of all the no-good bastards, crooks, thieves, and bums who walk this earth, why does it have to be her?"

Martha instinctively knew that something was very wrong. She fielded his phone calls, all except one. As he sat there his intercom buzzed. At first he didn't hear it. It buzzed again, but he didn't move. The door opened gently, and Martha stood there, shocked at how stricken he looked.

"George," she said quietly, "Larry wants to talk to you. He's very insistent."

George groped for the telephone. He was still staring straight ahead, seeing nothing. His voice was a husky whisper.

"Yes, Larry."

"George—what's the matter? You sound terrible."

"Nothing. I'm okay."

Larry's voice was full of anxiety. "You really don't sound like yourself, George. Are you sure you're all right?"

"Fine, Larry. Really, I'm okay."

"When is Liz due back?"

"Tomorrow."

"What time?"

"I don't know. She's supposed to call Martha with her flight number."

"Can you reach her?"

"I can try."

Larry's voice was hesitant, uneasy. "George, are you sure you're okay?"

"I'm okay, Larry, really. I'm fine."

Larry's voice was still suspicious. "When Liz calls in, tell her to come straight to the office. Bob will be on deck. I want you here, too."

"What about Howard, Curt, and Arthur?" George asked.

"I've talked that over with Bob. We've decided that we want to keep this at the top level of the firm." Pause. "We've been talking to Dean Merrill's syndicate department. They're anxious to have Barkley sign the underwriting agreement and get this deal off. The market is strong, and their dealer group is hot for the stock." He paused. "If we have to cancel this deal with Merrill, we'll have a hell of a time getting them to lead another offering for us. We can't afford to antagonize Merrill."

"Let's not get up too big a head of steam, Larry. Let's wait for Liz."

"Let me know when she's getting in."

"I'll call you, Larry." George hung up.

Chapter 26

LIZ LOOKED AT the three of them—George, Larry, and Bob— staring at her with a fixed, anxious interest. She had passed the point of exhaustion. She didn't know whether she was on her first, second, or third wind. Fatigue was a physiological state which she had long passed. She had slept fitfully on the flight. Her mind had turned off, stopped. On the plane she had had two scotches, but she had not eaten. She didn't want food; she wanted sleep, but she could never sleep soundly on an airplane. She had landed in New York and taken the long cab ride to mid-Manhattan in a state of suspended animation. She had been surprised when Martha told her that George would not be meeting her at the airport. But now, seeing the look of anxious suspense on the faces of Larry and Bob, she was pulled out of her somnambulance and, calling on some unexpected reserves, she found herself surprisingly alert. What she couldn't fathom was George. He had been distracted when they met in his office. His whole manner was tight and controlled, almost distant, reserved, emotionally preoccupied. She thought it must be the Twenty/Twenty deal, but she still felt annoyed and disappointed at the lack of enthusiasm in George's greeting. As she looked at him sitting opposite her at the large circular conference table, he seemed aloof from what was about to take place.

"Liz, we apologize for making you come in straight from

the airport, but we had no alternative," Larry said. "Bob and I have been talking to Merrill's syndicate people, and we are under great pressure to move ahead on Twenty/Twenty. We need a report from you so that we can quantify the risk. Why don't you begin?"

She told them quietly but with precision exactly what had transpired on the Coast. She watched the expressions of disbelief cross the faces of Larry Baldwin and Bob Cooper. George kept looking at her with a tight-lipped intensity that made her feel uneasy, as if in some way she was letting him down.

"Liz," Larry interrupted, "let me see if I have this straight. Are you telling me that Barkley is financing a sociopsychological experiment with money he borrowed from Twenty/Twenty using his stock as collateral?"

"Yes."

"And your description of what goes on at that place is accurate?"

"It's accurate, Larry. I was there."

Bob Cooper exploded. "Did you tell that crazy son of a bitch that he stands a good chance of blowing this deal?"

"At length, Bob." Liz paused. "I had lunch with Barkley yesterday. I pointed out to him that he was risking loss of control of his company as well as a substantial personal financial loss."

"And how did he respond to that?"

Liz looked at Bob Cooper evenly, her voice controlled. "He said he would think about it."

"He'd think about it!" Bob roared. "Jesus H. Christ, that son of a bitch had better do a hell of a lot more than think about it!" Bob Cooper's face was the color of a boiled lobster. He was furious. "This crazy bastard is going to blow this for all of us. I never heard of anything so unbalanced in my life! This is the most profitable deal we've ever had in this firm. We nursed this lunatic with money and business know-how. This deal can *make* this firm! It can make it for all of us!"

Liz could see that Larry was looking at his partner with barely contained irritation. She watched the small, intense man looking at her, measuring, weighing, calculating, searching for some way out of their dilemma.

His brain almost seems to smoke at times, she thought. Larry was famous for his incredibly quick creative mind that could come up with solutions that eluded his own partners and his competitors. It was one of the main reasons for his success. Liz knew he was desperately trying to find a solution to what appeared to be an insoluble problem.

"Liz, do you have any idea why Barkley is doing this? Why does a man go out of his way to make his own life more difficult? More than that, why does he set himself up to lose control of his company and suffer great financial loss?" Larry paused. "That is not the act of a rational man, Liz."

Liz sighed. "Larry, let's go back a few squares and start with Germaine Fontenant."

"Who's she?" Bob asked.

"She's a network TV newscaster in San Francisco."

"You mean Barkley's girlfriend," Cooper growled.

"I mean, Bob, that Germaine has a master's degree from UCLA and is a very intelligent, attractive, elegant, interesting woman. She is a major public personality in San Francisco."

Liz was letting her anger at Bob's prejudice show and she knew this was bad business. "Bob, Germaine would be a compliment to any man. She is a remarkable woman."

"How close do you think they are?" Larry asked.

"It's difficult to tell. Both Barkley and Germaine are complex personalities. I had lunch with Germaine, and I tried to impress upon her that Barkley's hobby—or experiment, or whatever you want to call it—stood a good chance of ruining him."

"How did she react to that?" Larry asked.

"At first she was resentful, hostile. But gradually she began to see the rationality of what I was telling her."

"Did you ask her if she'd talk to Barkley?"

"Yes, Larry, I did. She agreed to talk to him, and she did. Barkley nearly tore my head off afterward. It took me a long time and some very frank conversation to get him cooled down."

"Liz, do you think there is a psychological element to this that we're overlooking?" It was the first time George had opened his mouth since the meeting started. She looked at him, still sensing his preoccupation.

"I do, George." She paused. "This is just a theory of my own, and it may be totally incorrect, but it's the only explanation that I can come up with that makes any sense to me."

"Let's hear it," Larry said.

"I had the definite impression when Barkley took Germaine and me out to dinner that he took some special delight in flaunting the conventions of society. He took us to one of the most exclusive restaurants in San Francisco, a place where he must have known Germaine would be uncomfortable." She hesitated. "I was uncomfortable for her, and I asked myself, if a man really loved a woman would he subject her to this?" She paused. "I am absolutely positive that if Germaine were not a public personality that restaurant would have found an excuse to deny Barkley a reservation. The atmosphere literally bristled with hostility on the part of the guests. I looked around at the people there. They were all conservatively dressed. The men in dark suits, the women, very chic in that understated San Francisco way. Barkley in contrast was dressed in a brown plaid suit. He stuck out like a sore thumb. I was actually embarrassed at the way he looked. Then it all came to me. He had brought two women to this place, one black and one white— a combination he knew would be offensive, and he deliberately dressed in a manner that he knew would violate the convention of this restaurant."

"You mean," Bob Cooper said, "that he was telling them all to go to hell, in a figurative sense."

"Exactly, Bob." She paused. "I kept asking myself why? It came together for me when I saw Barkley House. I said to myself, here is a man who is defying society. He's getting even for something, perhaps whatever persecution he feels he suffered being a Jew." She hesitated. "There's another side to this. I felt that Barkley was actually experimenting with his conception of personal freedom. It's not as farfetched as it sounds. He has spent his whole life in a laboratory. Now put the two concepts together. If you accept the fact that Barkley has some deep-seated resentment for whatever reason that makes him want to flout the conventions of society, then that would be at least a partial explanation for his attraction to Germaine. God knows if I were a man I wouldn't need any such rationalization; the woman is attractive enough in her own right as a woman regardless of color. But if you extend that thesis to Barkley's interest in that house of his, it at least offers some explanation for what seems like irrational behavior. He may very well be interested in experimenting with his ideas of personal freedom. He said to me that he was practicing psychiatry without the psychiatrist." As she said it, she stopped as an idea struck her. They could see the expression on her face change.

"What is it, Liz?" George asked.

Larry was looking at her with intense interest. He was hunched forward, his forearms resting on the table, his body as taut as a drawn bow.

Liz was collecting her thoughts. "It's just an idea, Larry, but it might just get us out of this hole." Liz turned to George. "George, let's take this thing apart and look at it logically. Where does our greatest risk lie? Not during the offering. We're ready to go to market as soon as Barkely signs the underwriting agreement, and I believe he'll sign. He needs the money to repay those loans." She paused, looking around the table. "Our greatest risk is in the after market, if someone should penetrate the Twenty/Twenty system and Barkely's activities become public knowledge through the publicity that could be attached to such an event." They all nodded, waiting for her to go on. "That gives us a little time to try and get Tim Haley and Barkley together."

"Who's Tim Haley?" Larry asked.

Liz looked at George. "Do you want to explain it, George?"

"No. Go ahead. You're doing just fine."

"Dr. Timothy Haley is a psychiatrist who runs a unique institution in Boston called Family Care. Simply, it is a psychiatric center specializing in the emotional problems of key executives and scientific personnel. Haley's techniques are very innovative and quite successful."

"How do you know this Dr. Haley?" Larry asked.

"He came in here looking for financing to expand his centers and a program he is engaged in called teletherapy." She explained what teletherapy was. "I've visited Family Care and am in the process of having Dr. Haley put together the information we need to evaluate his company."

"And just how is Dr. Haley going to help us?" Larry asked. "Barkley would resent any suggestion of psychiatric help."

"He would, Larry. You're absolutely right," Liz said.

"Then I don't follow you, Liz," Larry said.

She took a deep breath. She looked at George knowing how exposed she was in front of the two senior partners of the firm. She knew this meeting would decide a great many things about her capacities in the minds of Larry Baldwin and Bob Cooper, and she was also George's protégée. She didn't want to make him look bad by suggesting some half-baked idea that wouldn't work.

"I'm not suggesting that we put Barkley and Haley together in a patient-doctor relationship. I'm suggesting that we stroke Barkley's ego by legitimizing his so-called experiment with a professional like Haley." She paused. Her mind raced with the possibilities. Her eyes became bright with the prospect. "You know it just might work."

"Liz, I'm afraid I'm still not with you," Larry said.

"Let's analyze this," she said looking around the room at the intense questioning faces. "Both of them need us. Haley wants us to raise money for him. Barkley needs this stock offering to get him out of a hole and to give him the kind of money to pursue his interests, however bizarre we think them to be. Tim Haley would be interested in what Barkley is doing." She paused. "I could make him interested. If we told Tim in confidence that we have to build some kind of legal wall between Barkley and his hobby, Tim would understand that. If Tim can help make Barkley less of a risk, then if anything blows up after the stock is out, we're all insulated."

"Make that clearer, Liz," George said.

"When I was in San Francisco, I suggested to Barkley that he needed a foundation run by trustees who would be sympathetic to what he was trying to do, but who would separate him and Twenty/Twenty from any personal connection with Barkley House."

"How did he respond to that?" George asked.

"He didn't. He thought about it. Just let it hang in the air."

"What makes you think Dr. Haley can be persuaded to do this for us?" Larry asked.

"He needs our help," Liz said. "I could intimate that we would look at Family Care with as much attentiveness as possible."

They all looked at each other, and then back at the twenty-five-year-old woman who had been in their employ less than four months.

"Liz, I want to commend you on handling a very difficult job with tact and finesse." Larry paused. "If you'll excuse us, I want to talk to Bob and George alone. If we choose to follow through on your idea about Haley, George will get back to you today. The sooner we start this thing the better."

She stood up, her fatigue coming back to her like a long rolling wave. The excitement of the meeting was over for her. She felt emptied, drained. She looked at them briefly, not knowing their real reactions, wondering how they would evaluate her presentation after she had left the room.

When she had gone, the conference room was silent, each man lost in his own thoughts. Their faces reflected the yellow light from the large brass chandelier. This room with its wall coverings of scenes of old Manhattan had known many an intense moment. That was the nature of their business, but this was their biggest potential deal.

"She's a damned impressive girl, George," Bob said.

"Amen," Larry said. "How old is she, George?"

"Twenty-five."

Larry shook his head. "If we're not careful, she'll soon be running this firm."

"Maybe some day she should," George said seriously.

Larry was drumming his usual tattoo with his fingers on the edge of the conference table. He had pushed his chair back so that he seemed almost separated from them. "I'll tell you how I see this, and you can give me your reactions. I don't think our chances of pulling this deal are realistic with all of the interest Merrill has generated with the selling group. It would just about finish our relationship with them. It's taken us years to build that, and I for one don't want to risk it." He looked at George and Bob. "Do you two agree with that?"

They both nodded.

"Then if we aren't going to pull this deal, Liz is right. Our risk is in the after market." He sighed audibly. "Do you have any better suggestions than this Haley fellow? I don't know a thing about him." Larry looked at George. "Do you, George?"

George shook his head. "I've never met him. I only know what Liz has told me."

"Then we have to rely completely on her?"

"Do you have a better idea, Larry?" George asked.

Larry, who was usually as quick as sparked gunpowder, was silent. Finally he looked at Bob, then at George. "I'm inclined to go along with Liz's suggestion, but I want it clearly understood, George, that she is not to commit this firm to anything with Family Care without going through our usual screening procedures and, of course, she's not to act without the approval of the three of us."

"She knows that," George said.

Larry turned to Bob Cooper. "Bob, do you agree that we should let Liz try to bring Haley and Barkley together?"

"I don't know if she can do it." He paused. "Even if she can, we don't know whether this Haley can persuade Barkley to separate himself and Twenty/Twenty from this lunatic asylum he's running."

"Have you any suggestions, Bob?" Larry asked, his voice reflecting his tension and impatience.

Bob's lips were compressed. The heavy head with its full gray hair was a mask of frustration. "I don't know what the hell else we can do."

"Then are we agreed that we try Liz's plan?"

Bob and George nodded.

"Let's hope to God she's right," Larry said.

Liz sat at her desk so utterly exhausted that the file folders and correspondence which had piled up in her absence might have been building blocks. Her mind simply refused to function. Coming back from the Coast was always tiring for her, but she usually planned it so that she arrived in New York late enough to get a good night's sleep before coming into the office. They had made her come directly into the meeting from the airport. Somehow she had caught her second wind and was able to respond to their questions clearly and with the precision demanded by Larry. Now, her second wind had dwindled to a zephyr. She sat there like a zombie.

Curt walked into the office and looked at her cynically. He sat on the edge of his desk, his long legs crossed, his English bench-made shoes polished to a high gloss. "So we are going to do the Twenty/Twenty deal, eh?"

She looked up at him, really not seeing him, not even hearing him, looking through him.

"Liz, if you don't mind my saying so, you look a bit ragged. What have they done to you on the West Coast? What's happened to our Madam Chairman?" He paused, looking at her carefully, seeing her sitting there almost immobilized, staring at the work that had piled up on her desk with a trancelike stare that made him drop his glib manner. His tone was now genuinely concerned.

"Really, Liz. What's wrong? Is there something I can do?"

She shook her head. "I'm so damn tired, Curt, that I feel as if I'm going to faint. My mind has just stopped. Turned off. *Finito*."

The phone rang on her desk. She didn't move. Curt picked it up. "Hello?"

"Who's this?"

"George?" Curt asked.

"I was calling Liz, Curt."

"She's not here, George. She'll be back in a few minutes. I'll have her call you."

Liz was looking at Curt in surprise. It was not like Curt to show concern for someone else.

"Would you tell her to come to my office when you see her?"

"Right." Curt hung up. He had not taken his eyes off Liz, and he could see her look of appreciation at his understanding. "I thought you could use a little time to pull yourself together." He paused. "Was it rough in there, Liz? Did they give you a hard time?"

She shook her head. "No, Curt. Thanks. I appreciate your concern. It's just that they've had me going flat out ever since I took this job and I guess it's finally caught up with me. I've got to get away, get some rest. I simply have to."

"We all do, Liz. This business will chew you up pretty quickly if you let it. We all take short but frequent vacations. You've got to, to recharge your batteries. You can't work seventy and eighty hour weeks without some break."

She thought of Peter. He had warned her of this. She thought how he would view her life if he could see her. She could visualize him shaking his head, intimating that she had all the wrong values. "Look what it's doing to you," he would have said. And what would I say to him? she thought. How could I explain a life like this to Peter?

"Look, Liz," Curt said. "Why don't you throw a little cold water on your face and do whatever you ladies do to make yourselves so radiant for us?"

He's back to that sophomoric male crap again, she thought. If Curt could only forget how good-looking and worldly he is, he would really be an attractive man. The hell with it, she thought. I've got enough men to worry about without including Curt.

She got up slowly. She smiled briefly at Curt, picked up her bag and headed for the ladies' room.

George was standing behind his desk. His back was toward her as she entered his office. His door was open, and Martha Wainright had told her in a quiet, concerned voice to go right in. Liz thought it strange that Martha had silently closed George's office door. She stood there for a moment convinced that George did not know she was in the room. The two of us must be a couple of zombies, she thought.

"George . . ." she said softly.

He turned around very slowly. His manner was one of such preoccupation that she was unnerved by it. She had never seen him like this. Looking at him, she forgot her own fatigue.

"George, what's the matter? You look as if you've seen a ghost." She sat down in one of his leather chairs. "All through the meeting I felt there was something very wrong." She paused. "What's the matter?"

He looked at her, his eyes seeing, yet not seeing her. His voice sounded like an echo in a cave. "I've got a very serious personal problem, Liz." He paused, looking away from her. "It just happened out of the blue, like a car accident or a mugging. One minute you're okay, the next you're lying there bleeding all over the sidewalk."

"My God, you haven't been in an accident?" She felt a chill of fear cut through her.

"No. I'm speaking figuratively. I'm okay. It's just my life that has been turned around." He looked at her for a long time. "So much depends on this Twenty/Twenty deal for me, Liz." He was almost imploring her to tell him that it would work out, that everything would be all right. She suddenly realized that he needed her, not as just a business aide but as a woman, and she felt more drawn to him than she ever had been before.

She stood up and went over to him, her exhaustion forgotten. She touched his arm lightly with the tips of her fingers. "George," she said softly, "what is it? Something's happened to you while I've been away. I can feel it." She hesitated. "Share it with me, George. Let me help you."

He wanted to take her in his arms and hold her, but not here, not now. He wanted to stop all this pretense and tell her he loved her, but the ambience of his office wouldn't let him.

"Will you have dinner with me tonight?" he said so softly that his voice was almost a whisper.

"Yes, of course I will."

He wasn't looking at her. He was staring straight ahead, seeing nothing. He was like a shell-shocked soldier. "I'll pick you up at your place around seven-thirty," he said, "if that's all right with you."

"That will be fine, George." She didn't know what to do. She wanted to touch him, to hold him, to comfort him, but she knew this was not the time or the place. She shared his reticence. "I'll be waiting for you, George," she said softly, her fingers touching the soft flannel of his sleeve. She stood beside him for a moment, looking at him with growing concern.

"Seven-thirty," she said, and walked quietly out of the room.

Chapter 27

THEY SAT IN the rear of the small restaurant on Bleecker Street, oblivious to the chatter of the other diners, the movement of waiters, the sound of the ancient air conditioner as it labored overhead. It was one of Liz's favorite restaurants in the Village, famous for its seafood, but they were not interested in food. They had drunk a bottle of wine and poked listlessly at their stuffed flounder. Slowly George began to open up.

"It was like a dream, Liz. I knew it couldn't really have happened, that I was going to wake up and it would be all over. But it wasn't a dream. Claudia walked into my office—stepped back into my life. It's something I've imagined, I said to myself; I've been working too hard; she'll disappear." He looked at Liz, the candle of the table reflected pinpoints of light in his dark brown eyes that now seemed almost luminescent.

"Liz, the women to whom I was married walked into my office out of the blue and told me she's going to die."

"Oh, my God, George!" She reached across the table and held his hand.

"I feel like such a crumb, Liz. I've been calling her a bitch for five years, ever since we've been divorced. I thought she was selfish and materialistic and just one royal pain in the ass. And she was. But when she sat in my office, she wasn't the same woman I married. That's what was so strange. Claudia

seemed totally different to me, the way some people do when
they have had a deeply felt psychic or religious experience.
She wasn't the hyper, driving, complaining woman I had come
to know." He paused. "Look, Liz, I'm no Prince Charming
myself. It certainly wasn't all Claudia's fault. We were just
two people who shouldn't have married. But there she was
sitting like some pale, thin ghost who had discovered some
kind of inner peace. She had made a pact with death." He
stopped and looked at Liz. "Do you know why she was there?"
Liz shook her head. She was holding his hand now, leaning
across the table, looking directly into his eyes, trying to find
something within her that she could give to him that would
ease his pain.

"She wanted money. Not for herself. She said she wanted
to do something worthwhile before she died. She said she felt
her life had been self-centered and meaningless. Jesus. How
do you think that made me feel? We both have led pretty much
the same kind of lives. She was wrapped up trying to become
a partner in her law firm, which she became. She was so busy
with her practice, and I was so busy with my work, that we
literally didn't have time for one another. On the weekends we
were so exhausted trying to catch up on things around the house
that we began to isolate ourselves from each other. Gradually
our relationship began to dry up, the way leaves do in the fall."
He squeezed Liz's hand. His voice softened. "One day, we
found that they had all just blown away."

He signaled the waiter and ordered brandy.

"She's resigned from her law firm and liquidated most of
her assets to set up a small foundation for the study of oncology.
She wants me to give her whatever I can." He paused. "I've
got some liquid investments in stocks and I have the apartment,
but that's about all I have that's not locked up." He looked at
her searchingly. He was having a difficult time retaining his
control. "Liz, she's only forty-one! Forty-one, for Chrissake!
Liz. I've got to help her in some way. If she can face death
with the kind of character she showed me in my office, I'd
feel like the world's biggest heel if I couldn't do something for
her." He sighed. "That's why this Twenty/Twenty deal is so
important to me now. I've got a good piece of that and I could
really help her. That's why this deal has got to come to market."
He looked at her searchingly. "Liz, if we go with Twenty/

Twenty, how big a risk do you think we're taking?"

She thought she had answered that question in the meeting, but she could see by looking at him that he wanted her assurance that everything would be all right. She desperately wanted to give him that. She guessed that what George had found so traumatic about Claudia's visit was what it had revealed about his own life. Was that, too, as meaningless, as arid, as dead as dried leaves?

When they left the restaurant the early September night air was still hot and humid, a legacy from August. The city's glow obliterated all but the brightest stars that shone directly overhead. They walked southeast on Bleecker Street and then turned left and walked along Christopher Street across Seventh Avenue toward Waverly Place. They walked in silence, each deeply involved in their own thoughts. But there was a communion between them, a new empathy, a recognition of need.

His mind went back to the first day he had seen her at Harvard. Some intuition then told him of his attraction for this young woman, but he had rationalized that he could submerge that, placate it, handle it. It had been almost a year since that other day in September when he first saw her. Since then he had tried to walk around the void of his life, not daring to look at its vacuum, covering its emptiness with work. Claudia's announcement had caused him to focus on his own loneliness and the need to fill the emotional void that lay silent and painful beneath all his striving. Work was no longer enough. It was a pathetic substitute for a human relationship. He put his arm around Liz's waist, and she put her's around his. They were oblivious to the lights, the traffic, the people, as they crossed Seventh Avenue.

They approached Liz's apartment without exchanging a single word. They walked down the steps and opened the door. He came in. She had left the air conditioners on, and the apartment was comfortably cool. She put her bag down on the small hall table. He took her arm and turned her toward him and looked at her for what seemed a very long time. He drew her to him and felt her arms around his neck, her body molded to his. They kissed each other hungrily as if the year of disciplined separation had been lifted by a new awareness each had for the other. A new tenderness and understanding had been growing through the winter of their association.

There seemed to flow from George a magnetism she had sensed that first day in Cambridge. She felt his hands move over her body. The barrier of her own reserve crumble under the mutual rising of their passion. They both wanted to go into the bedroom, but they were reluctant to let go of each other even for a few seconds. She finally withdrew her lips from his, and they undressed as if possessed. She was bathed momentarily in light. He could see her slender shoulders, her long legs, her firm breasts. She flicked off the light. It was like a slide projected. She stood there silently in the muted darkness. Slowly she raised her arms toward him, and he moved quickly to her. He could feel her soft cool skin beneath his fingers. They moved to the bed ignited by the fires that had been banked within them for so long.

She lay satiated with her head on his chest. The silk of her hair touched his face. He kissed her hair softly, over and over with great tenderness. They tried to find ways to get their bodies closer as if nothing would suffice but a complete emulsifying of each into the other.

They could hear the whir of the small air conditioner in the bedroom, and the wail of a siren. They could hear laughter and the voices of a couple on the street walking past the apartment, and the distant hum of the endless traffic on Seventh Avenue.

"I love you, Liz." He had said it so many times tonight.

"And I love you," she said softly. Her mind turned to Peter.

It was as if he could read her thoughts. "What about Peter?" he asked quietly.

She thought for a while. "A part of me will always feel something very special for Peter. You have to know that, George." Her arm was across his chest, her fingers moving lightly, caressing the side of his face. "Peter and I in a way must have been something like you and Claudia. You two, from what you've told me, probably never should have been married," she said softly. "Peter and I somehow understood— at least I understood—that if we married it would never work. We felt very deeply about each other, but there comes a time when you want some resolution, when you want to solve a problem or give it up. At least that's the way I feel."

"How do you think he feels?"

"I don't know." She laughed quietly. "You've kept me so

busy that I haven't had a lot of time to devote to Peter. He's in England for the summer with his parents." She paused. "George, what are we going to do about the firm? Eventually Larry and Bob have to find out about us."

"Let them."

"But what about Curt and Arthur and Howard? They certainly will be resentful if they think our relationship has become serious."

"That's their problem. Right now I have a suggestion for the two of us."

"What?"

"We're both burned out. The summer's over, and we haven't had a day's vacation."

"You're suggesting . . . ?"

"I'm suggesting that after the Twenty/Twenty deal goes to market, you and I go away someplace."

She moved so that she could be closer to him, but that was impossible; she couldn't get any closer.

"Oh, George, do you think we really could? Even if it's just for a few days."

"I don't want it to be for a few days, I want a real vacation."

"But what will Larry and Bob—"

He kissed her into silence. "Will you let me worry about the firm? Where would you like to go?"

She thought for a while. "George, I really don't care. All I want is some sun and a chance to relax. I don't care where it is."

He was silent for a while. "Have you ever been to Switzerland?"

"I've never been to Europe."

He thought for a moment. "If we don't have any trouble with Barkley signing the underwriters' agreement, we should be able to get that stock off next week. If the offering goes as well as I think it will, everyone is going to feel very, very healthy. Larry and Bob will make a bundle from that deal, and I won't do too badly. I'll be able to give Claudia a substantial sum of money. Larry will let me take it out of my account when he knows what it's for." He paused. "You and I will pack our bags and head for a villa in Switzerland. We'll take a week, maybe ten days. How does that sound?"

"It sounds marvelous. But before we go, I think I should

get up to Boston to see if I can get Haley started with Barkley."

His silence was long. "And Peter? Will you be seeing Peter?"

"If he's back from England, I think I should. I owe it to him to tell him about us."

George lay very still. She could almost read his thoughts. *He's wondering if Peter will try to talk me out of this. If we'll make love.*

"George, if we are going to build something worthwhile between us, Peter can't become a ghost. My mother has lived with ghosts all her life, and it's ruined her. You and I have a lot to learn about each other. Whatever life has in store for us, I want to face it openly and together." She paused, raising herself up on her elbows and kissing him tenderly. "If we can't manage a life together, George, we're a lot better off alone."

She sat at her desk looking briefly at the Twenty/Twenty red herring—the preliminary prospectus sent to the members of the selling group and the selling shareholders. The final prospectus would be sent to the purchasers of the stock. Larry, Bob, and George were listed as selling shareholders, as were Barkley, Sol Masters, and a number of others. She knew that the managing underwriters had placed a limit on the amount of stock that could be sold by the founding shareholders, of which Baldwin Cooper was one. That was to ensure that the offering would not look like a bail-out if the ones most responsible for founding the company were allowed to sell all their stock. Larry, Liz noted, was selling twenty percent of his holdings, or 160,000 shares. At $25.00 a share, Larry would gross $4 million pre-tax. Bob was selling 120,000 shares worth $3 million, and George was selling 25,000 shares worth $625,000.

This is the business to be in, she thought. But she knew how much they had all risked and how hard they had worked and how long it had taken before they could cash in some chips. She hoped to get a piece of a similar deal one day herself. For some reason, the thought caused her to look at the Family Care folder. *That could be my deal,* she thought, but she wondered whether she was too new in the firm to be allowed a piece of the action if the deal ever came to fruition. They probably wouldn't let her have it.

She opened the folder and was surprised to see how little

information it contained. There was nothing in it except the notes from her two meetings with Haley. Where was all the material she had asked Arnold Goodwin to send? There was nothing. She had been too busy to follow up on Goodwin, but she hadn't thought that necessary. The information she needed shouldn't have taken him more than a few days to put together. She buzzed Mary Rawlings.

"Yes, Liz."

"Have you given me all the information that has come in on Family Care in Boston?"

"Never heard of it."

"You mean you've had nothing from them at all?"

"Zilch. Zero."

"Thanks, Mary." Something was definitely wrong. People like Tim Haley who were interested in raising money normally cooperated with potential lenders and investors. She couldn't understand it. A small knot of anxiety began to form in her stomach. Suppose Tim won't help us with Barkley? Suppose he wants to back out of this deal? But why would he? she asked herself. He's talked to a dozen firms trying to raise money. Could he have found someone else? Damn it. I should have kept in closer touch with Tim . . . Her phone rang.

"Liz." It was George. "I've just come from a meeting with Larry and Bob. We've been talking to Merrill's West Coast people. They want to wait awhile before marketing the stock, and we agreed. That will give you a little time to see Haley."

"George, I was just about to call Arnold Goodwin, Haley's financial VP. I asked him for a checklist of material nearly a month ago, but he hasn't sent me a thing."

"That's unusual. Could Haley's enthusiasm for us have cooled?"

"Something's cooled, George."

His voice lowered. "I certainly hope it isn't you."

She still glowed from the memory of last night. "It's not me, George," she said quietly.

"Can we have dinner tonight?"

"Let me fix you something at my place. How about shrimp and lamb chops? They're easy and they don't take very much time."

"You sold me. I'll bring the wine."

"About eight, George. That will give me a little time."

"You've got yourself a date."

She hung up. My lover at night; all business during the day. She dialed Arnold Goodwin's number, and his secretary put her through.

"Elizabeth Clark, Arnold. I haven't received anything from you. Have you sent the material I asked for?" She could sense his uneasiness over the phone.

"No, I haven't, Miss Clark."

She was annoyed. "Any reason, Arnold?"

"I'm afraid you'll have to take that up with Dr. Haley, Miss Clark." He was being very formal and evasive.

"Is Dr. Haley in?"

"I don't know. I could have you transferred to his office."

"Would you do that?"

"Certainly. Hold on." He sounded relieved.

She heard the bass voice come on the line. It was another unusual side of Tim's very complex character. He answered his own phone. He never used a secretary to take his calls if he was in his office. It was the exact opposite image of a man who drove a sky-blue convertible Rolls Royce.

"Liz, good to hear from you. I thought we'd lost you to the West Coast."

"I felt like that myself." She hesitated. "Tim, I haven't received any of the information I need from Arnold Goodwin."

Now it was his turn to hesitate. "I wanted to talk to you about that, Liz."

"But, Tim, we can't do a thing to help you until I have that material on your company." She paused. "I am assuming you're still trying to raise capital?"

"Your assumption is correct."

"Then I don't understand, Tim."

"Liz, we need to talk about this."

She was trying hard to control her temper. She needed him now almost as much as he needed her.

"Can we talk about it now?" she asked.

"I really don't think that would be appropriate, Liz."

She remembered that with Tim, you didn't want to give an inch or he would take the whole yard. "When do you plan to be in New York again, Tim?"

She could almost feel his reluctance. Something was wrong, but she hadn't the slightest idea of what it was.

"Liz, I'm terribly busy here. We have so much going on. I had no plans to come to New York."

"Would you like me to come up there?"

"Could you?"

"I guess I could." She paused. "It will have to be soon though."

"Could you make it this week?" he asked.

In an intuitive flash she realized that Tim would have less of a psychological advantage away from his own base, his center of control. She would need every advantage she could get in dealing with him. The insight sharpened her and she realized that she had to try and get him to come to New York. She would have to play him like a trout. She remembered how clever and intuitive he was.

"If you don't come up this week, when will you be able to make it?" he asked.

"Not before the end of the month, Tim."

"That's nearly another month gone," he said quietly. "That's too much time, Liz."

Jesus he's maddening, she thought. "Tim, I'm really whipped. I've got work coming out of my ears, and I'm leaving for Europe in a few days."

"That doesn't give us much time."

Instinctively she knew she had to get him to concede to her. With Tim you had to deal from psychological strength. "Is it possible for you to get to New York Friday evening, Tim? As I recall, I owe you a dinner."

He laughed. "That's a very tempting offer, Liz." She could feel him hesitate. "I suppose I could fly down and come back in the morning."

She sighed with relief. "Shall I make a reservation for you at the Plaza? We can do a repeat of our first meeting."

He laughed again. He was developing some enthusiasm for the idea. She couldn't figure out if it was the prospect of seeing her again or if he had some other motive. With Tim, she never knew.

"Let's do that, Liz, only the dinner is on me. If you'll set me up at the Plaza, I'd appreciate it."

"I'm grateful, Tim." She paused, remembering the sky-blue Rolls convertible. "Do you want a suite?"

"Yes, I'd prefer one."

"If you don't hear from me, you'll know I've made a reservation for you. If I have a problem with the Plaza, do you have a second choice?"

"How about the St. Regis?"

"Fine. I'm sure I can get you something in one or the other."

"Good. Then I'll look forward to seeing you tomorrow night, shall we say about seven-thirty?"

"That sounds good, Tim."

"See you tomorrow, Liz."

She hung up. It wasn't much, but it was a small victory. She remembered the last time she was with him in Boston he seemed to be able to read her. She would try not to be so transparent this time. Not only was he a trained psychiatrist, but he also had a probing inquisitive cynicism that she found disturbing. As she sat back in her chair, biting unconsciously on a yellow pencil, she thought about Tim. Her last impressions of him were coming back. For some reasons she could identify and some that were more amorphous, he made her uncomfortable. More important, she didn't trust him. More perplexing, she didn't know why.

She suddenly sat straight up in her chair.

"Lamb chops," she said aloud. "I've got to buy lamb chops and shrimp. Oh, George," she said. "When we get to that Swiss villa, I don't want to move." She thought about that for a moment and smiled. "Well, at least not between breakfast and lunch."

Chapter 28

NEW YORK WAS in the clutches of a late summer heat wave. Some of the humidity of July and August had been wrung from the air, but the first week in September was still hot and uncomfortable.

The battered yellow Checker cab lurched its way north on the Avenue of the Americas, known to all New Yorkers as Sixth Avenue. Liz stared mindlessly out of the window as the hot air of the cab blew at her face. They passed Herald Square at the intersection of Broadway and Sixth Avenue at Thirty-fourth Street. She was too young to remember the George M. Cohan lyric, "Remember me to Herald Square." The lights of the city were on, welcoming the quickening nights of early fall. She had become accustomed to the noise, the pace, the sounds and smells of the city; its color, compression, excitement, challenge; its dirt, its beauty, its ugliness and violence; it had all become a part of her. She had been thrown into the torrent that was New York. She had been tumbled by its rapids and had nearly foundered in the tumultuous whirlpools of its competitive demands. Here was the biggest, the best, and the worst of everything. Here was the ultimate challenge. Perhaps you had to be a little crazy to want to live and work in this city that was a catastrophe waiting to happen. Two inches of snow, and the city was a madhouse. Con Edison blows a generator, and ten thousand people are trapped in buildings. Switches freeze in the winter and trains are an hour late. Subways carry hundreds of thousands of people in conditions that rival those of over-crowded prisons. But as the driver turned east on Central Park South and then swung south into the Plaza's entrance drive, she knew that after New York, every place else would be dull. Cleaner, safer, more reasonable, and livable, perhaps, but dull by comparison. Because she was a small-town girl, she under-stood this. She also understood that at some point in her life, she would have to find a retreat in the country. She couldn't live in the killing urban bustle of New York without watering her roots occasionally. She had to get to some place where she could review and renew her perspectives, uncover old values and polish away the tarnish of New York's cynicism.

She paid the driver and walked up the steps of the Plaza, past the Palm Court, toward the Oak Room where she was to meet Tim Haley.

He was seated, his back toward her as she entered. She had forgotten how big he was. His shoulders were enormous. She remembered him telling her that he had played football for Penn, and had been an All-American.

"Dr. Haley, I presume..."

He turned and saw her and stood up. She was nearly five ten, but he towered over her. "They do grow them large in Pennsylvania, doctor?"

He laughed and held out an enormous hand. "Liz, it's good to see you."

"I appreciate your coming down, Tim."

"My pleasure." Liz sat down, and Haley signaled the maître d'.

They were seated at the same table where they had eaten dinner on his first visit. She wondered whether that was co-incidence or whether he had arranged it. For some reason, as she watched the gathering dusk begin to shadow the trees of Central Park, she felt uneasy about this meeting; so much depended on it.

"Do you want a drink, Liz, or shall we wait for the wine?"

"I'd rather just have wine, Tim."

"Good. So would I."

The maître d' came over to their table.

"Would you like something from the bar?"

"No. Please send over the wine steward."

"Very good, sir."

They were left briefly alone.

"For someone who is so whipped, as you put it, you look remarkably attractive, Liz."

"Why thank you, doctor. I might say the same for you. For someone who is so busy, you have a remarkable tan." He laughed. "Clean living and exercise, Liz. Actually, just tennis in the sun at Family Care. I play a couple of sets every day. I'm one of those people who has to exercise. I have an overly active mind, and I find the only way I can get a good night's sleep is if I exercise every day. On the weekends, I run."

"Well, whatever you're doing, Tim, keep it up. It looks good on you."

The wine steward, complete with silver chain around his neck and a large symbolic key to the wine cellar, stood smiling at them. Tim looked over the wine list.

"Red or white, Liz? Or should I ask fish or meat?"

"Meat, I think. I feel like a good filet."

Tim handed the wine list back to the steward. "Let's have the 'seventy Margaux. That's a good dry Bordeaux, Liz. I think you'll like it... Now tell me, what have you been up to in California?"

She shook her head. "If I hadn't lived through it, Tim, I wouldn't have believed it."

He looked at her with those penetrating analytical gray-green eyes that, from their first meeting, she had found strangely disturbing.

"It's hard to know where to begin," she said. "We have a client that is coming out with a rather large underwriting, at least large for us; about one hundred and twenty-five million."

"That's large."

"Yes, it is. Our firm owns a significant percentage of the stock."

The waiter came. Liz knew what she wanted without looking at the menu. "Half a dozen cherrystone clams. A filet, medium rare. Spinach. No potatoes." She thought for a moment. "I'd like a Bibb lettuce salad with that, please."

Tim looked at her and handed his menu to the waiter.

"I'll have the same thing."

The waiter started to leave. "Would you tell the wine steward to bring our wine now."

"Very good, sir."

Tim sat back in his chair. "Now, what's all this excitement about this California company?"

It was happening too fast. This wasn't the way she wanted it. She wanted to draw him out first and then gradually get around to the real purpose of this meeting.

"Tim, let's talk about Family Care. The California thing is so bizarre that I'd like to forget it for a while."

"You've excited my curiosity. I'm interested in the bizarre. It's probably a good definition of some of my patients."

"Our client in California *should* be one of your patients." It had just slipped out. It was like a ball of string that had fallen on the floor and was unwinding before she had a chance to stop it. "Tim, it's not important—"

"One hundred twenty-five million isn't important?"

"You've got a point."

"Don't be so reticent, Liz. What is this bizarre problem of yours that I sense has you more than just a little upset?"

There he goes again, she thought, reading my mind. She began to feel as vulnerable and as transparent as she had the last time they were together.

"Tim, you're right. I am upset about this, but we're here to talk about Family Care. It's been ages since I asked Arnold for the information I need, and I haven't received a thing from him. When I called him, he said you would explain." She looked at him steadily. "Why hasn't Arnold sent me the information, Tim?" She paused. "I've spent a fair amount of time looking at Family Care and have decided it's worth showing to the firm. But I have to develop a lot of information for a very complete report on your company which the partners will study before making their final decision. I can't do that without the information I asked Arnold to put together." She hesitated. "You said on the phone that you were still interested in raising money."

"I am."

"Well, if you're going to raise it through our firm you're going to have to come up with that information."

She watched his face become set; his eyes avoided hers.

"It's not the information you asked for that's troubling me, Liz."

"Well, what is it, Tim?"

He was being evasive, but she hadn't left him much room in which to maneuver.

He spoke slowly and carefully. "When you visited Family Care, you said that a lot of the separate corporations, the ones that hold the real estate, and some of our aptitude testing centers; the laundry service and the landscape company—"

"They are all separate corporations controlled by you," Liz said.

"Well . . ." He hesitated. "I only own a minority interest in the aptitude testing company."

"But you control the others."

He nodded. "Do you remember what else you said, Liz? You said that I would, in effect, have to put those holdings back into Family Care."

"That's right. You can't expect us or our institutional partners to invest in a company whose assets are withheld from us. We would want you personally as fully committed as possible to protect our investment. That only makes sense, Tim. Why should we invest our money in your cookie jar, when you have removed most of the cookies and stashed them away out of our reach?"

"Not all the cookies. You'd be investing in Family Care and Teletherapy, Incorporated. That's where the money is."

"That's true. But it's not just the money, Tim. We require that all of the entrepreneurs we back commit themselves to the limit of their resources." She smiled at him ruefully. "It has a tendency to focus their attention on performance."

The waiter brought their clams.

"I don't know of too many venture capital firms that approach things differently, Tim," she said. "Why should they? Why should anyone risk more than you are willing to risk? It doesn't make any sense."

He drank the juice from his empty clam shells before he spoke. "And if you agree to raise this capital for me, I'll have to restructure my personal finances, but you're going to wind up owning a substantial part of my company." He paused. "How much stock is Baldwin Cooper going to get in Family Care?"

"That depends on how much money we have to invest, how much outside capital we have to bring in, and our assessment of the risk we're taking."

The waiter brought their entrées. Tim Haley always makes

me feel uncomfortable, she thought. I'm paranoid around this big shrink.

They both cut into their steaks.

"How much stock does Baldwin Cooper own in that California company?" he asked.

"Forty percent."

"Forty percent! Jesus Christ! And you tell me you have a problem out there. What's the stock selling for?"

"Somewhere around twenty-five dollars."

His face seemed to pale under its tan. "How many shares are being sold?"

"Five million."

"You're not serious."

"I'd better be. The offering is going to be made next week."

"And you've got a problem? If my arithmetic is any good, Baldwin Cooper will own fifty million dollars' worth of stock."

"That's true, but we're only selling a portion of our holdings."

"My heart bleeds for you."

"You don't understand, Tim. We backed this company when it was only an idea. Larry Baldwin and Bob Cooper didn't want to touch it. George Hall had to twist their arms to get them into it. For years, BC never made a dime on the investment, and on many occasions stood to lose not only their own money but also the money they had raised from institutions. Our relationships with banks and insurance companies depend on our success. Our backers don't like to lose money. This particular deal nearly died several times. It's only because of one very eccentric genius that we were able to ring the bell." She paused. "Tim, in our business, every once in a while you get to ring a very loud bell, if you're lucky and if you're good enough. This is the biggest bell we've ever rung."

"And I assume, the most profitable."

"I can't comment on that."

He looked at her with cool appraisal that she sensed held some hostility. She wasn't sure, but her intuition told her that a lot was going on in the mind of Dr. Haley.

"Just what sort of gold mine has your eccentric genius found?"

"He's the chairman and chief executive officer of a company called Twenty/Twenty. Ever hear of it?"

"As a matter of fact, I have. I read an article about them

in one of the business magazines; I can't remember if it was *Forbes* or *Fortune*. They're in the computer security business. They have some special system."

"Right. Their clients are major banks. As you probably know, computer security is one of the most crucial problems affecting bank operations. Crack their codes and you can literally transfer millions of dollars to your favorite Swiss or Caribbean bank faster than you can close a door. Very simply, no one has ever been able to penetrate a Twenty/Twenty system. The banks around the world are becoming Twenty/Twenty customers and the company really is a gold mine, as you put it."

"So what's the problem?"

She sighed audibly. She knew she had aroused his interest, but how far he would go to help her she didn't know.

"Our eccentric genius has decided to experiment with *freedom*." She looked at him appraisingly. She could see he was waiting for her to explain. How much should I tell him? she wondered.

"It seems that Nicholas Barkley, the CEO, now has the money to support his pet philosophy. He believes that most gifted people—or most people, for that matter—are never really free. They are constricted by the confinements of society, the conventions of daily life, both personally and in their professional and business lives. He says that they are never free of inhibitions, or simply, never free at all.

She watched his intensity grow. He was leaning on the table with his forearms, looking at her with a piercing inquiry.

"Nick owns a big house in the Russian Hill section of San Francisco. The house, which he calls Barkley House, is designed to accommodate large numbers of people. The whole idea behind the place is that Barkley's *friends,* as he calls them, can come there, socialize, smoke pot, drink liquor, dance, fondle one another, and make love. Very simply, they can leave their inhibitions and their hang-ups outside the door and be whatever they want to be." She looked at him carefully. "Barkley says it's psychotherapy without the psychiatrist."

She could see that he was intrigued.

"I don't understand. Where's your problem?"

"Our problem, Tim, is not with what Barkley is doing, but how he would be perceived by his clients, the banks, if what he was doing was made public. You see, Tim, most banks have an aversion to eccentricity, because it's not reliable, and reliability is what banks are all about. People have confidence in a reliable company. And the whole banking system depends on the depositors' confidence. Undermine that confidence and the system collapses."

"Explain your anxieties further. I'm beginning to understand, but I'd like to hear more."

"I've been to Barkley House, Tim. It looks like something out of a Fellini movie. It's bizarre. It may be therapeutic, but it's a time bomb that can ruin him and, quite frankly, jeopardize our investment and everyone else's." The memory of Sol Masters breaking down in her hotel room in San Francisco stopped her cold.

Tim thought for a while. "Aren't all of you being just a little paranoid? Surely what the banks are interested in is that the Twenty/Twenty system works, not Barkley's private life."

"We understand that, Tim." She looked at him coolly. "Yes, you may be right. We may all be a little paranoid about this offering." She hesitated, looking away from him. Her voice reflected her thoughts, which seemed far away. "As long as the system is never penetrated, we're okay."

"So . . ."

Her eyes returned to his. She looked at him evenly for what seemed a very long time. "We're worried about what will happen if the system fails."

"But you said it was the perfect system."

"No. I said it had never been penetrated." She paused. "Tim, in our business, we're used to problems. We try to anticipate them if we can. We know that there is no such thing as perfection in anything." She paused. "Tim, you deal with people's emotional imperfections all the time. Isn't there a risk factor there? In human error?"

"So what you're really saying is that this system can be penetrated."

"We don't know, but if it is penetrated, can you see the publicity and the lawsuits we would all face if it became public knowledge that the man most responsible for guarding hundreds of billions of dollars in the world's major banks runs a house that, to say the least, is a little strange." She saw his preoccupation, the intensity with which he was listening to her. She knew how bright he was. She wondered what he was thinking.

"Tim, it would be the worst publicity in the world. You don't need facts to kill a stock. Rumor and innuendo can do that just as effectively. This kind of publicity would send the price of Twenty/Twenty stock right through the floor."

He seemed totally engrossed in what she was saying. She wondered if the psychological implications of what Barkley was doing interested him.

"Do you know how the system works?" he asked.

"No. Obviously, that's something the company doesn't wish to publicize." She paused. "As you now know, we have a very real interest in insulating Barkley from publicity..."

"How can you do that?"

"Well, as an example, Barkley could form a foundation managed by trustees who could be responsible for investing funds in projects they saw fit to support. One of them could be Barkley House. It's thin, I admit, but it does insulate Nick somewhat."

"I'd like to meet Nicholas Barkley," he said quietly. "I think this man is doing something that is unique, not bizarre." He paused. He was looking at her so intensely it made her uncomfortable. "Barkley's preoccupation with personal freedom I find absolutely fascinating. Has he had any psychiatric training?"

"He's a physicist."

"Then I find him even more interesting."

Liz hesitated. "Would you like to go to the Coast and meet him?"

"Yes."

She tried not to let her elation show. "I think that someone with your background and interests would hit it off very well with Barkley. As a matter of fact, I've mentioned you to him; not by name. I've said that we have a potential client who probably would share his interests."

The waiter brought their coffee.

Tim's thoughts seemed to turn inward, then flip back to her again. "Would you arrange an introduction for me? Tell him I am very interested in what he's doing. Play down the executive rehabilitation programs we're involved in. Talk to him about our teletherapy program. My guess is that he'll find it interesting, because it applies technology, which is his field, to psychiatry, which is mine."

She hesitated. She needed more from him. "I'd be delighted

to put you two together, Tim, but I have to ask a favor of you."

He didn't say anything. His face was expressionless except for those probing, calculating eyes.

"We need someone to persuade Barkley that he is putting everyone at enormous risk: his employees, his directors, and himself."

"And, of course, Baldwin Cooper." He said it blandly, without expression or comment, but she could hear and feel his sarcasm.

"Yes, he's putting us at great risk as well."

He was silent for a moment. "I can't promise to dissuade him, partly because I agree that there is a sound psychological basis for his project." He thought for a moment. "Of course, from a purely monetary point of view, I can understand your anxiety." He paused reflectively. "I have to find out how messianic he is."

"Barkley does not control the board of Twenty/Twenty, Tim. We do, with the outside directors." She tried to restrain her anger. This big shrink with his self-importance was rubbing her the wrong way again. "We don't *care* how messianic Barkley feels. If he continues to expose us to this kind of risk, the board will force him out as chief executive officer. It's as simple as that." She saw the briefest flicker of anxiety in his eyes. It passed as quickly as it came.

"Let's get back to Family Care for a moment, Tim. I can't do anything for you unless Arnold Goodwin gives me the information I need." She was taking a chance, giving it to him straight like this, but she sensed that the intensity of his interest in Barkley would support her directness. She looked at him inquiringly. "What do you want me to do, Tim? Shall I put Family Care on the back burner for a while?"

He didn't answer her for what seemed a very long time. His large hands flexed unconsciously on the white linen tablecloth. "My problem, Liz, is that I have to decide what I am willing to give up in order to obtain the backing of your firm." He paused, his voice modulated. His eyes seemed to look right through her. "I don't like giving things up, Liz. I am an acquirer, a builder, a collector. I don't like parting with what is mine."

He's a greedy bastard, she thought. He wants to own everything and use other people's money to buy it. "I can understand that, Tim. It's not an uncommon feeling. But you're going to have to give up some ownership to do what you want to do." She paused. "That decision is up to you."

He smiled at her, a chill professional smile. "Well, are we all through? Had everything you want? A nightcap, perhaps?"

"No, Tim. I'm fine. It's getting late and I want to get back." He stood up and held her chair for her.

"I'll get you a cab."

They walked out into the warm soft night. Beyond Grand Army Plaza, Fifth Avenue was throbbing with pulsating, horn-blowing taxis; its lighted store windows and towering rectangles of segmented lights reached up into the city's haze.

"Wait here a minute," he said, and walked over to one of the long black limousines parked near the entrance of the hotel. She saw the driver shake his head. Tim walked to the limousine behind it and talked to the driver. She saw him hand the man a bill. He turned and motioned for her to come to the car. The driver held the door open for her.

"Tim, what's going on?"

He smiled. "This good fellow is waiting for his boss, who will be in the hotel for some time. I suggested he might like to make a little money driving you home, and he agreed."

Liz shook her head in amusement. "It certainly beats a cab," she said.

Tim went around to the other side and got in the back seat of the car. She was surprised and a little uneasy.

"Where to, miss?" the driver asked.

"It's in the Village. Go down Fifth to Washington Square. I'll show you from there."

They settled into the back of the limousine, and Liz wondered what other little surprises he had in store for her this evening.

"I thought I'd ride down with you and you could tell me a little more about Barkley."

She could hardly refuse. But there was something calculated about what he had done; it was what she disliked most about him. The only real emotion he had ever displayed was his sybaritic enjoyment of driving her out to Family Care in the blue Rolls convertible. She remembered how he had reveled in the opulence of the car and the attention it drew, especially with someone his size behind the wheel. Barkley at least had a sense of joy about him, she thought. Tim was always the planner. She sensed with him there would always be a separation between the humane and the expedient. She wondered if he had ever loved anyone. He had once talked to her of his father with a certain affection, but what about a woman? Had there been a woman in the life of Dr. Haley, or had he been too busy being an All-American achiever, a builder, a collector? Was there a woman in his collection? She couldn't picture it. There was no warmth in him for a woman; at least she had been unable to find it.

The big car moved more quickly as it passed Thirty-Fourth Street. The cold chic of upper Fifth Avenue had given way to the more staid office buildings of lower Fifth Avenue. The lights seemed softer, more subdued. There was less traffic, fewer people.

Tim turned so that his legs were stretched toward her side of the car. He wasn't trying to be cute. He was just so tall that even in the rear seat of a limousine he seemed cramped for space.

"You're very quiet," he said.

"I was just thinking."

"I hope it was about Nicholas Barkley. If I'm going to help you, you're going to have to give me as much insight into him as you can."

She turned toward him. She could see the memorial arch at the entrance to Washington Square.

"I'm afraid I've given you all the insight I have on Nicholas Barkley. My contacts with him have been pretty formal. I've met him mostly at board meetings. You don't get to know someone very intimately at a board meeting." She lowered the glass partition and spoke to the chauffeur. "Turn right here and cross Sixth Avenue. You'll be on Waverly Place. Make a left on Christopher Street and a right on West Fourth. It's the first street past Charles on the right. One-one-five Weymouth Place."

The chauffeur nodded. Liz saw Tim's surprise at the sudden change in neighborhoods. The squat grime of the Village seemed an unlikely milieu for Elizabeth Clark.

Her eyes avoided his. I wonder if he's going to want to come into the apartment? she thought. I wouldn't like that. She gave an involuntary shudder. Something about him frightened her. She didn't know what it was. Maybe it was his remoteness, that clinical manner of his that seemed incapable of emotion. Oh God, I don't know what's wrong with me when I'm around this shrink, she thought. He makes me feel so damn vulnerable.

The big car turned into the semidarkened Weymouth Place. The single struggling tree near the end of the block seemed an anachronism amid the three-story apartment buildings with their black spiderlike fire escapes and their flat roofs that sprouted the clustered reeds of TV antennas.

"You live here?" He was incredulous.

She laughed. "Pull up right there, driver." She smiled at Tim.

"I sleep here, Tim. I live on airplanes and in the office. I rarely even eat here anymore. I haven't had the time to make this a home the way I wanted to."

The chauffeur got out and opened the door. His expression was one of practiced disinterest.

Tim got out and held out his hand to help Liz. "Which one is yours?"

She reached in her bag for her keys. She pointed down the small flight of steps.

"You're kidding."

"I kid you not, doctor. The residence of Elizabeth Clark."

He looked around the street. "Is it safe here?"

"I've never had any trouble." She smiled. "I take a lot of cabs."

The chauffeur got out of the car and opened the door for her. Tim got out of the car with her.

She held out her hand. "Thanks, Tim, for dinner and the luxurious ride home."

"But can't we talk a minute? Aren't you going to invite me in?"

"I'd love to, Tim, but I've got a busy day tomorrow, and I have to be in the office at seven-thirty. I've got to get some sleep." She was determined not to let him come in. She started to walk down the steps to her door when she remembered something. She turned to look up at him, towering above her, backlighted by the dim streetlamp. His face was in shadow. "Tim, one thing that might prove helpful: Barkley has a girl-friend, a TV newscaster in San Francisco. Her name is Germaine Fontenant. I don't know how deep their relationship is. She's a remarkable woman."

He didn't reply. He just stood there looming above her, like a dark monolith.

"I'll put Family Care on hold, until I hear from you or Arnold. Oh, I'll call Barkley in the morning and tell him you'll be in touch with him."

He remained silent. She opened the door and gave him a little wave. Then she closed, locked, and bolted it. She found herself shaking as she leaned back against the door.

"This is ridiculous," she said aloud. But as she heard the limousine drive off, her feeling of relief wasn't ridiculous; it was very real.

As the car drove Tim back to the glitter of upper Fifth Avenue, he stretched himself diagonally across the back seat of the limousine so that he would have maximum leg room. His mind was oblivious to the kaleidoscope of lights, sound, people and vehicles that moved through the city whose rhythm and beat never stopped. His face was rock hard, his eyes cold and remorseless.

They'll open up everything, he thought. They'll want to know where every asset is buried. They'll talk about the importance of full disclosure. "We have to comply with the regulations of the SEC," they'll say. He laughed audibly, a cynical laugh. They want to know where everything is hidden, he told himself, so that they can get their hands on it. They want to steal from me the way they stole from Barkley. Well, I'm no Barkley, and I'll be damned if I'll help them put their hands in my pockets.

The car approached the entrance drive of the Plaza. It made no difference to Tim that Baldwin Cooper's interest in Twenty/Twenty was not theft but a legitimate investment, whose rewards were commensurate with the risk inherent in financing. Tim would never see it that way; he couldn't. He was a possessor; he had to have it all. He slammed the car door never once looking back at the chauffeur. He strode through the lobby, his face an intense, brooding mask. They're not going to screw me, he thought, as he stood in front of the gilded elevators. No one screws Tim Haley. He got into the elevator. He was alone. That was the way he liked it. He felt comfortable alone. When he was alone he was in control, and Dr. Timothy Haley by nature and by instinct had to be in control.

Chapter 29

THERE HAD BEEN so many planes that the night flight to Zurich seemed like just a continuation of what she had been doing all summer long. But there was a difference; they both felt it. There was their mutual exhaustion, and their growing elation and understanding, a comprehension that kept unfolding like time-lapse photography now that they were finally getting away for a badly needed rest. There was also their awareness and new sensitivity to each other, and the small revelations that, in combination, focused their insight and drew them closer together.

They landed at the airport in Zurich in midafternoon and collected their luggage, cleared passport control and customs, and were standing in front of the car rental agent whose English showed just the slightest trace of her native Swiss Deutsche.

"We're going to the Schöllenen," George said. "I'll need a map." Liz stood by his side. The agent smiled at him.

"It's lovely there," she said. "Too early for skiing although at this time of year you could get some snow at the higher elevations. Will you be near the lake?"

"Yes," he said. "We won't be skiing. Just resting."

The agent gave him a knowing smile. "Passports, please, and your U.S. driver's licenses."

A long line had formed behind them, but it was orderly.

Liz looked around at the quiet efficiency of the Swiss. The schedule announcements were made in well-modulated German, French, and English. The building glistened; it was almost antiseptically clean. There was no rushing, pushing, shoving. No surly porters or predatory cab drivers. All was quiet and functioned as smoothly as one of their fine watches.

"Slightly different from Kennedy," she said.

He laughed. "That's the understatement of the age."

Liz sat with the map in her lap looking at the strange names of the little towns and villages they would be passing through.

"We have to follow this road south past Kilchberg, through Zug."

She laughed. "What a name, Zug. Oh, I see. It gets its name from the lake, the Zuger See."

George was watching the road. The sky had been gray with low rolling clouds, but the wind had risen and there was an occasional shaft of sunlight.

"I hope we're lucky with the weather," he said. "It should be good this time of year. Cool in the mountains, but great."

"Who did you say owned the villa?"

"Kurt Ahlwardt. He's a director of the Gneistbank in Zurich. He's been in a couple of deals with us."

"It's generous of him to let us use the place. Have you been here before?"

"No. Never. I just hope his caretaker speaks English. My German is nonexistent." He looked at her. "How about you?"

She shook her head. "Just French. I doubt if that will do us much good here."

They were winding higher through the mountains. Some of the peaks were obscured by the low clouds. Mist hung in the valleys. The little towns they passed through seemed unreal, like collections of doll houses. The churches clung to the emerald green hillsides with their turnip-shaped towers; the stark gray stone Germanic architecture was arresting, but not beautiful. Villages appeared, occasionally surrounded by small farms, their white-walled houses with weathered wooden bracings and steeply pitched overhanging snow roofs seemed isolated and lonely.

They had driven around the southern edge of a small lake past Goldan, then south along the Stäter See; through Brunnen and Flüeli. She had never seen mountains before, not real mountains. As the car climbed and twisted to the higher elevations, they became part of the sky and the earth all at once. Gray mist obscured portions of the road, then suddenly they were in clear air more a part of the sky, like some great soaring mountain hawk. The heights seemed dizzying. They turned into the Oberal Pass going west to the Schöllenen.

"I'd forgotten how beautiful these mountains could be," he said.

Liz was awestruck. "They seem to rise all around you. The clouds misting and parting make it so ethereal."

The change from New York had been incomprehensibly sudden and contrasting. This was what George meant by "getting away from it," she thought. "My God, George, it's magical."

"It's incredible. Liz, would you reach into my breast pocket and take out our airline tickets? Ahlwardt's directions are in them."

She twisted around in her seat as the car bumped over the frost-heaved road. He reached up with his right hand and pulled her head toward him and kissed her quickly. The car lurched and she fell against him laughing.

"George! The road—" She found the tickets and the white piece of paper on which Martha Wainright had typed Kurt Ahlwardt's instructions to Das Haus des Adlers: The House of Eagles.

"He says, 'Once you have the lake in view look for a gravel road off to the right. There will be a wooden sign in the shape of a cross at the intersection of the main road and the gravel one. Follow the gravel road five kilometers, and you will see a small cottage on your left. This is the home of my caretaker, Frans Schiller. He has the key to the house. He will provide you with climbing boots and gear if you don't have them and will act as your guide should you wish to climb. If you are not an experienced climber he will be glad to give you some instruction. Frans has stocked the larder with everything you should require during your stay. His instructions are to serve you in any way that he can. Frau Schiller will cook for you if you wish, and attend to the house.'"

She turned to George who was smiling as he looked quickly at her and back again to the narrow rutted road. They had left the gravel behind. The road they were now on bisected towering cliffs thick with dark fir trees. Liz felt momentarily cut off from the majesty of the mountains. She realized as they came closer to the long sapphire of the lake that the sense of wonder she had experienced when they were driving through the mountains was returning. The road, which now was little more than a hiking trail, approached what seemed like a broad meadow filled with white tufted sedge. They drove with the lake still in view, rising higher with the circuitous road.

"Can this be it?" George asked. "This isn't a road; it's not even a good cow path. I'm damn glad this isn't my Mercedes."

"We should be seeing the cottage soon."

"Who says?"

"I says."

"What makes you such a Magellan?"

"I looked at the odometer when we turned off at the cross. We have about half a kilometer—"

The trail road turned sharply left, and there on the side of the mountain was a small white cottage that seemed sculptured into the hillside overlooking the lake like a sedentary white bird.

"That has to be it," she said.

George was concentrating on keeping the Mercedes on a track that was little more than a twisted depression of packed meadow grass.

"If you wanted to get away from things, George, I think your friend Ahlwardt has accommodated you."

"If this is the cottage, where the hell is the villa? I don't see another house anywhere."

"Maybe it's a myth. Maybe Ahlwardt is just a great practical joker."

"Swiss bankers are not practical jokers."

They drove up to the white cottage with its dark overhanging snow roof. They saw a small barn and two other outbuildings and a fenced area beside the house.

"Let's find Herr Schiller," George suggested.

They got out of the car and were surprised at the thin, dry cold air. They had been insulated in the carefully controlled cabin of the car. They were stung by the chill sharpness of the quiet mountainside on which they found themselves. Liz looked down at the lake. The stillness was almost total, except for the sighing of the wind.

"Hello there."

He had come from behind them. They both turned in surprise.

"You are Herr Hall and Fraulein Clark?" His accent was Swiss Deutsch, but he seemed much younger than she had imagined, in his mid-thirties, perhaps. His face was deeply tanned with sun wrinkles about his eyes. He wore a thin gray woolen shirt despite the cool temperature. His eyes were a light blue and his hair the color of summer wheat.

"You are Herr Schiller?" George asked.

"Ja. Herr Ahlwardt has instructed me to make your stay as pleasant as possible."

"We're very grateful, Herr Schiller."

"I would like you to meet my wife." Liz saw a woman with flaxen braids wrapped neatly about the crown of her head. She wore a spotless white apron over a long dark blue skirt. For some reason, Liz thought, the Schillers seemed too attractive and too young to be living such an isolated life in these mountains. Frau Schiller walked confidently toward them and extended a lean, tanned hand. "A pleasure to have you with us, Herr Hall and Fraulein Clark. Would you care to come into the house for a cup of coffee or a glass of beer?"

"That would be pleasant—"

"Trudi," Schiller said, interrupting George, "I think we had better get them settled before dark. It's getting late and the light is short."

Liz couldn't get over the feeling that there was a story behind this couple. Ahlwardt must have selected them very carefully. She was sure that they were not typical Swiss farmers.

"I'll get the truck. We'll leave your car here, Herr Hall. It's a bit of a rough ride to the villa."

Liz watched Schiller walk to one of the outbuildings. She turned to Frau Schiller and saw the quiet look of appraisal.

"I'll come up to cook dinner for you," Frau Schiller said, "and take care of the house."

Liz looked at the young quiet woman whose composure was arresting. Liz understood that whatever Frau Schiller did, she would do it well and with the least possible intrusion. The two women had silently taken each other's measure and found that they liked what they saw.

They heard the sound of an engine and saw a small pickup truck come from the farthest outbuilding.

George opened the trunk of the Mercedes and took out their luggage. Schiller got out of the truck and transferred their bags to the back of the pickup.

"I will see you later," Frau Schiller said and waved pleasantly at them as the three of them got into the front seat of the truck.

They bounced along in the direction of the tallest mountain.

"The one nearest us is Mount Dammastock. Behind it over there"—Schiller pointed—"you can see the Eiger and the Wetterhorn." The mountains stood immutable and awesome with the snow on their peaks reminding Liz of bald eagles.

"Where is the house?" George asked.

"You can't see it yet. We have to climb higher and around that curve. Then you can make it out, but from there we must take the tram. We are too far to see the tram."

"I didn't realize you had to reach the house by tram."

"Ja. There is no other way to get up there, except to climb." He laughed. "I'm sure you don't want to do that." He paused. "They had to build the tram before they could build the house."

The westering sun was touching the mountains with its gold.

"It's so beautiful, George. I can't get over it. I've never seen anything like it."

"Wait until you see the view from the house, Fraulein Clark. It is really breathtaking. You will get to see a lot of these mountains during your stay here. I have brought up several pairs of climbing boots."

"I don't think we will be climbing, Herr Schiller."

"You'll need them to get to the lake. The tram will take you up and down the mountain but you will be a lot more comfortable in good sturdy boots."

"There it is," Liz said excitedly. She pointed to the west. "No wonder they call it the House of Eagles. My Lord, how did they ever build it up there?"

Schiller laughed. "It was very difficult and very expensive, but I think it was worth it. Herr Ahlwardt thinks so, and I believe you will, too. The house is really extraordinary."

As they approached it, it seemed to sit on its own aerie like a great white bird that grew larger as they drew nearer. Now they could see the thin spiderlike cable of the tramway. Below the house in the saffron light of the waning sun were tall fir trees that seemed edged with fire. Above the tree line, the rock of the mountain and the cap of snow glistened in the sun's fire. Cut into a ledge near the upper level of the tree line was the house. They could see it now distinctly with its long French windows.

The tram car was surprisingly large. George helped pass up the luggage to Schiller.

The car jerked as Schiller set it in motion. "You just push this button to start it; this one to stop it. The motor shuts off automatically when the car is docked on either end. There is a radio here in this rack." He pointed to a wall-mounted unit. "It is set to a frequency in my house. If there should ever be a problem while you are in the car, just pick up this mike and depress this button. When visitors are at the house one of us is always at home." He paused. "There is another radio in the house connected to the switchboard in Schöllenen. You can call anywhere in the world or simply to our house if you need anything."

They were suspended in midair over the fir trees that seemed to reach up for them menacingly. The crags of rock threatened as the car climbed higher toward the house. Liz felt frightened as the cable car began to sway in the wind.

They left the tram and stood on the stone terrace of the house, with its waist-high wall looking at a view that took their breath away. The mountains seemed to thrust above them scraping the sky. Golden clouds blew about their peaks torn by the rising wind, which sounded like exhalation, a sighing lonely sound that made Liz more aware of their isolation and their nothingness in comparison to the sweeping grandeur all about them.

"George, I feel like an eagle up here." She looked around her in every direction. I feel so incredibly insignificant amid all this." She turned to him. They were leaning against the stone wall. He had his arm around her, drawing her close to him. "Do you feel that way too?" she asked.

"How could I feel any differently?" he said. "Here we are among these mountains that have been here for millions of years. They have stood silently watching this poor demented species we belong to evolve until we can now incinerate the earth." He paused. "But these mountains will endure. No matter what cruelties, what absurdities humanity commits." He looked at her and brushed aside her hair, which was blowing across her face in the wind. "How could anyone feel anything but insignificant up here?"

The most surprising feature of the house was its indoor swimming pool. Liz couldn't believe it. "How did they get the water up here, Herr Schiller?"

"They didn't. They melted snow and pumped it in. When the level of the pool gets low from evaporation, new water comes in from holding tanks embedded in solid rock. No one could believe Herr Ahlwardt when he insisted on having a heated indoor swimming pool, but the engineers and architects found a way to do it. You might be interested to know that everything, including the pool, is heated by wind-generated electricity. In case of a power failure, there is a backup solar storage system."

George shook his head. "I'm glad I didn't have to pay for this place."

"This obviously is the living room," Herr Schiller said. "Off there, the dining room. There are two bedrooms and baths on this floor, plus the pool and of course the kitchen. There are two additional bedrooms and baths on the second floor."

Liz looked around her, at the long French windows that overlooked the terrace. The living room was white. Deer antlers hung on the walls with crossed swords with corrugated blades. The furniture was of gleaming oak with chrome and glass tables. The floor was of stone with scattered Oriental rugs. There was a large fireplace already laid for a fire.

Her reactions to the house were mixed. She was awed by the ethereal majesty of its view, but somewhat put off by the coolness of its interior, and the lethal-looking swords and the antlers of hunted stags. She heard Schiller tell George that the swords were for beheading. Liz shivered as she looked at them.

Frau Schiller had come up in the tram and cooked their dinner. She had prepared sauerbraten which Liz had never tasted and found delicious. For dessert she had baked strawberry tarts. She lit the fire, unobtrusively cleaned up in the kitchen—just as Liz had known she would—and came into the living room to say good night.

"Is it safe to use the tram at night?" George asked.

"You have to get used to it. What is more difficult is the ride back in the car. You really have to know the road, and be very careful." She paused. "We suggest to all Mr. Ahlwardt's guests that they not leave the house at night without my husband as their guide."

They walked out on the terrace with her where the wind blew cold and strong, sweeping the night clouds in front of a rising moon. George and Liz shivered in the cold.

Frau Schiller got into the cab and put on its interior lights. It looked so small and vulnerable in the threatening night. The wind moaned as it whipped across the swaying cable. Liz clutched George's hand.

"Are you going to be all right, Frau Schiller?" she asked. "Must you go back?"

"I'll be fine. You two should go into the house. You're not dressed warmly enough to be out here."

They went back into the house and watched the tram descend the mountain swaying in the strong night wind.

"That thing scares me," Liz said, her arm tight around George.

"You don't have to worry. If I know Ahlwardt, that tram has been designed to take some pretty strong winds. Schiller told me about the wind velocity gauge up here." George pointed to a set of instruments near the door leading to the terrace that measured wind direction, velocity, outside air temperature, and barometric pressure. "When the wind gets too strong they don't use the tram."

"In a storm, you could be here for days," she said looking at him with a suggestive humorous glance.

He smiled at her. "Maybe, when our ten days are up, we'll have a storm."

She moved closer to him. He turned her toward him and put his arms around her and held her tightly against him. They kissed long and passionately. It was as if from their very first meeting when he had come to recruit her at Harvard they were destined to be on top of this mountain, on this night.

"Let's move in front of the fire," he said quietly.

He took the large lounging cushions and spread them on the floor. The fire crackled and gave them comfort as they listened to the disturbing sounds of the wind blowing about the house.

The firelight made the stag antlers cast eerie shadows on the wall.

"Let's go into the bedroom," Liz said. She didn't want to tell him that she felt frightened in this room.

They got into bed under billowing down quilts.

"Just hold me for a while, George. I just want to feel you close to me." She paused. "This house, this place, these mountains, they're all so strange to me. I feel as if we're on some other planet looking down at earth. It's a little frightening."

"You're not disappointed?"

"No. It...well, it just takes some getting used to."

He held her as close as their bodies would permit. He was experienced enough to know how to orchestrate their love-making. He had discovered the passion that lay carefully concealed behind her sometimes-aloof manner. He discovered to his silent delight that once she was aroused she became insatiable in her need for fulfillment. He smiled to himself as she raked him with her nails, as the strength of her young body seemed to want to devour him. She writhed on top of him, moaning, exalting in her passion until she was spent. She lay in his arms panting, exhausted.

"You're one hell of a woman, Elizabeth Clark." He laughed quietly as he said it.

She was all over him again kissing him, rubbing against him, thrusting her breasts toward his mouth.

Christ, he said to himself, talk about still waters...

They lay looking up at the ceiling, wondering what each had done to the other's life.

"What are you thinking about?" he asked her. She hesitated. "You're still not frightened by the house?"

"No, it's not the house."

"Then what is it?"

"Claudia."

She could feel his body tense. "What made you think about Claudia now?"

"I don't know."

He sighed.

"I'm sorry, George. You asked me."

"I know." He stroked her hair and kissed her with great tenderness.

"It seems so unfair, George."

He didn't speak for a long while. "Who ever suggested life was fair?" He paused. "Do you feel guilty being here with me because of her?"

She hesitated. "A little."

"I can understand that, but it doesn't make a lot of sense," he said.

"I know," she said.

He paused. "When we get back, I'm going to go to Larry and ask him to let me take a piece of my share from the Twenty/Twenty deal. I want to do that for Claudia." He drew her to him and kissed her. "It's nice of you to care, Liz," he whispered. They fell asleep in each other's arms, listening to the sighing of the night wind.

Liz had decided that she did not want Frau Schiller to bother with breakfast or lunch. She would cook those meals herself. Frau Schiller could prepare dinner for them, except for their last night; she wanted to do that herself.

They spent their days hiking around the lake. There was a small sailboat that had not yet been taken out of the water for the approaching winter. Herr Schiller made arrangements for them to use it, and they bundled up against the increasingly cooler days, sailing the little sloop in the gusty late autumn winds.

On the fifth day of their vacation, they hiked along the edge of the lake to a place they had found that gave them a view of the mountains as well as the lake. The scattered trees that surrounded the peaceful glade protected them from the wind. They packed a lunch of cheese, bread, fruit, and wine. Frau Schiller gave them some pressed meats she had made herself, whose German names they couldn't remember or pronounce. They sat on a fallen log eating quietly, feeling at peace in their isolation, and yet aware that each passing day and night, which had filled their bodies and their minds with love, was making them aware of questions for which they had no answers.

Liz put down her sandwich and looked at George. "I don't like to bring this up, George, but I've been thinking about it almost since we got here."

"About what?"

"Us."

"What about us?"

"Where are we going? Obviously, when we get back to the firm, things can't be the same."

"Why not?"

"Because everyone knows we're away together."

"So?"

"Oh, George. Don't be so dense. Larry isn't going to put up with his managing partner having an affair with a junior associate."

George stopped eating and looked at her coolly. "Is that what we're doing, having an affair? I thought there was something about love involved in all this."

She moved over to him and kissed him. "George, I didn't mean it the way it sounded. It came out wrong."

"I sure as hell hope so."

"I meant what are we going to do about it?"

He smiled. "When a woman asks a question like that she's usually thinking about marriage."

"I'm not thinking about marriage. At least not yet."

"Why not?"

"Because I want to concentrate on my career first. I'm not sure I'm ready to settle down and have kids."

"Then you don't have to have kids."

"But sooner or later I'll want to, George."

"So what's the big problem?"

She stood up and turned away from him. "You men can be so damn obtuse at times."

He got up and put his arms around her and turned her toward him. "Liz, what is it? What are you trying to tell me?"

"I'm trying to tell you that I want it all, and I can't have it."

He looked at her tenderly. "No one can have it all, Liz."

She backed away from him. Her eyes snapped angry sparks. "You damn men can have it. You can have a career, and you don't have to worry about children."

"What are you getting so worked up about? Plenty of women have careers and children. What's wrong with that?"

"I grew up with a mother who had to work," she said. "I can remember how lonely it was after my father was killed. I would come home from school to an empty house." She paused. "And when my mother had to work nights I remember how frightened I was being left alone in the house. It was no damn fun growing up with a working mother, I can tell you that, and I swore that I would never do that to my kids."

He wanted to draw her to him and hold her, but he knew that this perpetual dilemma of hers was too important to her. It was a rehash of her problems with Peter. "Liz," he said softly, "I do think you have a problem that you are going to have to resolve sooner or later."

She was standing in front of the tall evergreen. The lake sparkled in the sunlight behind her; the mountains soared until their peaks were obliterated by the clouds.

She looked at George evenly. "What would you say my future is at Baldwin Cooper?"

He laughed despite himself. "I would say if you keep going the way you are, you could wind up running the firm." He paused. "I think Larry feels the same way, Liz. You're on the fastest track of any one of the associates. If you bring in this Family Care deal and it takes off, I think you could be a vice-president next year."

"And how would the other associates feel about that?"

"I don't care how they feel. Howard is going to be promoted to a VP after January 1. Don't tell him that. Curt and Arthur will get to be VPs when Larry, Bob, and I think they've earned it. You should know that our shop is strictly a meritocracy. You don't win points for longevity; you win points by being a winner. And if I've ever seen a winner, Liz, it's you. If you want to know what track you're on in the firm, I can answer that one real fast. You're on the express track, clear to the end of the line."

"And what am I supposed to do, give that up?"

"Who's asking you to give it up?"

"Someday I'm going to have to."

He moved toward her and took her in his arms. "Liz, you know something I've learned in this life . . ." He paused. "I've learned some of it from Claudia."

"What?"

"That there's no use trying to plan too far ahead. Not much sense in trying to peer through the mist. Things have a way of moving in their own direction; they develop their own momentum. They work out one way or another. It's best to take one day, one thing at a time, Liz. Look, darling. I understand why you're tormenting yourself, perhaps a lot better than you think I do." He paused. "Come sit down beside me." He moved to a tall fir tree and sat down. "Come over here," he said softly. Liz sat beside him. He pushed her gently down until she was lying on her back, her head in his lap. She was looking up through the thick boughs to the interlaced patterns of clouds and sky.

"You're the first woman I've ever worked with as a colleague, Liz," he said softly. "I've know what it's like to live with a woman who has a career. I married one." His voice seemed reflective, far away. "I'm not trying to say that marriage and a career for a woman isn't a difficult assignment. It is. It was one of the things that helped ruin our marriage. But from my own experience, Liz, from what I have seen of my friends who have done it successfully, it can work." He stroked her hair gently, his voice was filled with empathy. "It isn't easy, Liz. It's damned tough—especially, as you point out, when children come into the picture. You do give up something. The children give up something as well. But it all depends on your motivation. You can create a *quality* of time for children that is more important than just being *around* for them. You can teach them love and self-reliance without having to feel guilty because you can't be with them continually. As they get older and go to school they begin to be separated from you regardless of how much you want them to be with you. And when it's time for college, they're gone. If you've spent all your time just taking care of them, what do you do with the rest of your life? How do you make it fulfilling?"

She reached up for his hand and squeezed it hard. She brought his fingers to her lips and kissed them softly.

"What makes you such an authority on children?" Her voice held a trace of humor.

"Claudia and I thought a great deal about having children, but as things began to go downhill for us, we mutually agreed, not in any formal sense, just quietly within ourselves, that ours was not the kind of marriage in which to raise a child."

She held his hand as she lay looking through the boughs of the fir trees at the wind-rushed clouds passing in front of the sun. She could hear the sounds of birds and the sighing of the wind in the trees.

She had never known George like this. Never known this prismatic reflection of a side of his personality that she had guessed was there, but in the compressed time frame of their business lives George had only rarely revealed the understanding and empathy he was capable of feeling and expressing.

There is something strong and reassuring about him, she thought. He understands what's been tearing me apart with Peter, but with Peter there is no solution. Just the same old trauma of occasional meetings that always seem to end in an increasing frustration, with each of us digging deeper into our own personal positions. We keep building stronger and stronger barriers. There is no give. That's what happened to George and Claudia. Would it happen to George and me? I don't think so. George has learned a lot, the hard way with Claudia. He knows and shares the problems of my career. With George it might just possibly work. Does he want children? I think he does. Her mind drifted back to Peter. There's no real empathy there. I thought there was, but there isn't. Peter and I would be another George and Claudia. God, she thought. I had to come four thousand miles to really see Peter and me.

"How about some more wine?"

She turned toward him and looked at him as if she wanted to study every feature of his face. She put her arms around his neck and drew herself up so that she was half reclining, half sitting in his lap. She kissed him with great tenderness. Her voice was soft and revealing.

They finished their lunch and their wine. They hiked back to the tram car. The sun was hidden behind gray afternoon clouds. As they looked up at the house, they saw that it was almost submerged in mist. The tram car pulled them toward the lowering clouds, which seemed to creep down the sides of the mountain covering the tops of the trees, separating them from the earth.

A few moments later they let themselves into the house. They had just put down their hiking gear when the radio telephone buzzed. "Probably Frau Schiller asking about dinner," he said and picked up the phone. The line crackled with static.

"This is the overseas operator. I have a person-to-person call for a Mr. George Hall."

"This is he."

Liz looked at the sudden change of expression on George's face. She could see his concern.

"Go ahead, New York."

"George?"

"Larry?"

"I'm glad I was able to reach you, George." Long pause. "George, we've got a hell of a problem."

Liz watched George's mouth set.

"What's the trouble, Larry?"

Long pause. Larry's voice was grim. "Barkley's been arrested." George's face turned dead white. Liz, who had been sitting near the fireplace, stood up and came over to him. She put her arm around his waist.

"For what, for chrissake?" George asked.

"For transferring fifty million dollars to a Swiss bank account from the First Manhattan Bank."

"You can't be serious."

"George." Larry's voice sounded flat and metallic over the thousands of miles separating them. "Your vacation is over. I'd like you and Liz back in New York as soon as possible."

"Larry, I can't believe it."

"Believe it. Just get off that mountain and get back here. When this news gets out, we're going to have lawsuits coming out of our kazoo. We'll have every member of the selling group calling us and asking what the hell is going on. It will hit the fan, George." He paused, his voice dropping. "The firm may not be able to survive this. Please just get here as fast as you can." Larry hung up.

George turned to Liz, his expression as stunned as if he had been pole-axed. "Holy Jesus Christ," he said softly. "They arrested Barkley for transferring fifty million dollars from First Manhattan to a Swiss bank."

"George. For God's sake, how could they have arrested Barkley? He would never do a thing like that." She watched him as he turned away from her, his face as white as the belly of a flounder.

"There's goes the ball game," he said, talking mostly to himself. He turned to her slowly, his voice sardonic. "You wanted to know about your career. By the time we get back, we may not have careers to worry about." He shook his head. "I can't believe it. I knew Barkley was a kook, but I can't believe he's a crook."

"He's not, George."

He turned to her, his eyes flashing annoyance. "What the

hell do you call a guy who has just stolen fifty million dollars?"

They stood looking at each other speechless.

"Oh, George." She rushed to him and threw her arms around him, the tears filling her eyes with mist. "Why? It doesn't make any sense. Barkley is worth a fortune after that stock offering. He doesn't need any money." She clutched him tightly.

He stood there holding her, both of them lost to their private agonies. All they could hear was the sighing of the wind.

Chapter 30

TIM HALEY HAD done a good deal of thinking about Nicholas Barkley. His meeting with Liz in New York had convinced him that he had been right in his assessment of Baldwin Cooper. They would extract too high a price for financing Family Care. He had made up his mind that he was not going that route. He had never let anyone take advantage of him, and from what Liz had told him of how Baldwin Cooper had financed Twenty/ Twenty, he wanted no part of that; they wound up with 40 percent of the company. People always tried to use Tim Haley, but in the end, he used them. He smiled as he thought of it. He had a gift for using people. It was an insidious talent he had developed, but it had served him well. No one got too close. No one really knew. He played his own game, and— he smiled as the thought flicked through his mind—he always won.

He had spent several days after his meeting with Liz trying to piece together the idea that had slowly become a plan. He sat at his desk aware, but not really seeing, the fall flowers flash their yellows, reds, and pinks in their carefully tended beds along the brick wall that bordered the grounds of Family Care. The old maples that brooded over the lawns of the estate had already begun to change color.

He got up and began to pace his office in intense concentration. He stopped and smiled in final resolution. He walked to his desk and picked up the phone. He placed a call to Nicholas Barkley at Twenty/Twenty in Palo Alto at the number Liz had given him.

"This is Nicholas Barkley. What can I do for you?"

"Dr. Barkley—"

"Just Barkley."

"Yes. Well, ah . . . This is Dr. Haley. Liz Clark suggested I call you." Tim could feel the hesitancy at the other end of the line. "I am a psychiatrist in Boston. I head the Family Care Institute, which is involved in some very innovative approaches to psychotherapy. Liz is looking into the possibility of financing my institute." He paused. "I'm aware of what a splendid job Baldwin Cooper did for Twenty/Twenty. I have a copy of the prospectus on my desk."

Tim had read every line of that prospectus, and he thought Barkley was a damn fool to have given up 40 percent of his company to Baldwin Cooper years ago when he was hungry for financing. "Liz also told me about certain interests of yours, Mr. Barkley, which is the reason for my call. You see, as a psychiatrist, I am interested in guilt and inhibition. Those are two of the most formidable problems we face in therapy." He paused. "Your sponsorship of the house on Russian Hill is really quite close to some of the work we are doing here." He had to go very carefully now. "The fact that you as a layman have gone so far as to create a physical environment whose purpose is to mitigate guilt and inhibition is something I find quite fascinating." He could sense the change in attitude as Barkley's tone became more congenial.

"I'm flattered, Dr. Haley, but I don't want you to get the wrong impression. I am not conducting psychological experiments. Far from it. My motivations are philosophical, not psychological."

"That doesn't change my interest in what you're doing, Mr. Barkley." He paused. "May I come to San Francisco to observe the reactions of people to Barkley House?"

Barkley's response was open and immediate. "I'd be delighted to meet you, Dr. Haley. Name a time that is mutually convenient. I would like very much to have you observe what I'm trying to do here. I'd like your evaluation. Frankly, I never thought of this as having any great psychological implications. To myself and my friends, it is simply a refuge from the conventions and hypocrisies of society." Barkley paused. "We're not another nutty California cult, Dr. Haley. Some of the most productive people in the city are members of Barkley House." He hesitated. "Frankly, doctor, we've become so popular that there is quite a waiting list."

Haley was looking at his calendar as he spoke. "Would it be convenient if I came out on the twenty-seventh?"

Barkley looked at his schedule for September. "That seems fine for me, Dr. Haley."

"Fine, then. I can meet you in Palo Alto."

"No need for that," Barkley said. "I'll pick you up at your hotel. Where will you be staying?"

"At the Stanford Court."

"Give me a ring when you get in. My secretary will know where I can be reached."

"Good. Look forward to seeing you, Mr. Barkley."

"Me, too." The voice seemed jovial and genuine.

Tim hung up. He got up from behind his desk, and as he did so, he started to laugh softly to himself. "I always win," he said, rubbing his hands together, relishing the new excitement that flowed through him like an electric current. "They're all so damned stupid," he said aloud. "This Barkley is supposed to be so brilliant. He lets Baldwin Cooper sucker him out of forty percent of his company." He paused. "Not me." His jaw hardened with determination. "No bunch of Wall Street pirates can take Tim Haley like that." He stood up looking out at the gardens through the French windows. He didn't see the glory of the late fall day with its sharp, clear light. His mind roamed more commercial ground. As he thought of it, his face broke into a sardonic grin. "It should be so easy," he said aloud. "So damn foolishly easy." His face reflected his satisfaction with himself, and he strode quickly from the room.

Tim Haley had made arrangements to rent a Rolls Royce during his stay in San Francisco. He would have liked a convertible, but was unable to get one. He had settled into a large suite at the Stanford Court on California Street, just east of the Fairmont and the Mark Hopkins on Nob Hill. He thought about the message, which the room clerk had handed him when he checked in. It read: "I am giving a small dinner party at my home in Hillsborough." There were detailed instructions as to how to get to the house, with Barkley's telephone number in case Tim got lost. Dinner was to be at seven o'clock. Tim unpacked, showered, and dressed. He had packed a dark blue blazer, which he planned to wear with a red cashmere turtleneck, gray flannel slacks, and tasseled loafers. The outfit was just informal enough, he thought, not to be too eastern. He was very sensitive to first impressions, and he wanted to make sure that he would be viewed as not an instant Californian but as someone who was conservative without being stuffy. His clothing was as carefully contrived as everything else about him. Dr. Timothy Haley left very little to chance.

He drove holding a map of the city and Barkley's instructions on his lap. He had decided that the simplest way for him to get out of the downtown area would be to take Van Ness south and pick up the 101 Freeway south and follow that to Hillsborough. He watched the road signs carefully and had little trouble following Barkley's directions. He got off 101 turning west toward El Camino Real. He crossed the boulevard looking for Crystal Springs Road. He had to turn north off Crystal Springs and look for Sherman Way. Barkley's house was 421 Sherman Way.

As he approached the house, which was on the rise of a hill, he saw that it was unlike the conventional California structures around it. Distinctively Japanese in character, it was surrounded by a lacquered bamboo fence that left only the wavelike gray ceramic tile roof visible from the street. The carefully pruned trees looked like pieces of living sculpture. He parked the car and walked through the gate. He was struck by the authentic Japanese garden in which he found himself, complete with bonsai trees in large stone pots. Each rock, each stone, each plant was part of an aesthetic whole, a unique complex of form and style that evoked an almost instant serenity. Tim was visibly impressed. The house itself could have been transported intact from Japan. The clean, simple lines; the sliding doors with their translucent panels. He pulled a rope attached to bells that made a soft tinkling sound within the house. The front door slid open, and Tim peered down at a bearded round-faced man who looked up at him in surprise.

"Dr. Haley?"

Tim smiled and extended a massive hand. "Nicholas Barkley, I presume."

"Nick to my friends. Come in." Tim found himself in a living room of almost Spartan simplicity. The polished wooden floor was partly covered with immaculate straw mats. Magnificent Japanese screens depicting snow-covered mountains and stark winter trees separated the living and dining rooms. Soft recessed lights in the ceiling fell on exquisite urns and jars whose glazes of plum and emerald had been fired by the hands of master craftsmen. Flat cushions were scattered in the center of the room. In the gathering dusk, Tim could see the pond with its stone bridge and the carefully positioned trees, through the large sliding glass panel that made up one wall of the house. Each perspective uncovered a new surprise to the observant. To those lacking in aesthetic appreciation the house could appear barren and cold. There were some concessions to Western demands for comfort, however. A long dark brown sofa faced the carp pool and gardens. The dining room contained a table and simple black lacquered chairs for those who found it more comfortable than sitting on mats on the floor. Long tapered candles glowed on the dining room table.

Tim saw an attractive black woman dressed in a kimono. Could this be the newscaster Liz mentioned? he wondered. Beside her stood the quintessential California girl. They were holding long fluted champagne glasses, talking to each other as Tim walked into the room behind Barkley. The women turned and looked at him in surprise. A young man in an open-necked shirt with full, carefully styled hair stood beside the California girl. They stared at Tim as if he were from another planet. Their surprise was understandable. In this house with its low, beamed ceilings, Tim seemed to fill the room. Barkley began to laugh as he made the introductions.

"This is Dr. Haley. I told you I expected a distinguished visitor from Boston." Barkley turned to the black woman. "Dr. Haley, this is Germaine Fontenant."

Germaine held out a slim hand. "Good evening, doctor."

Tim saw that her eyes seemed to reflect the soft light of the room like black pearls. They were intelligent and inquiring eyes, he thought. He guessed they had seen a good deal of life and pain.

"This is Eden Summer, doctor."

Tim looked at this sensual young woman whose eyes seemed to be savoring him like ripe fruit. Her hair was a blond cascade falling to her shoulders; her blouse was cut low enough to demand attention. The thigh-high slit in her print skirt revealed long slender legs.

"My, my, doctor," she said, her voice a fluid contralto, "I had no idea they made them so big in Boston."

Tim smiled at her. "I'm afraid they made me in Philadelphia."

"Down girl, down," the young man said. He held out his hand to Tim, looking up at him with an amused expression. "I'm Tony West, doctor."

Barkley rubbed his hands together briskly. Tim had been a surprise both to him and to his guests, and Barkley liked surprises. "Doctor, what would you like to drink?"

"Scotch if you don't mind." Tim paused. "If it's a malt scotch, I would like it neat, Nick."

"Good. Good. I like a man who respects good liquor. I happen to have an excellent malt, and neat it is."

Eden looked bewildered. "What's a malt scotch, and what's 'neat'?"

Tim started to explain, but Barkley shrugged him off. "Doctor, as a psychiatrist, you'll find this out for yourself soon enough, but our perennial ingenue, Miss Summer, has spent enough time in England and Scotland not to need very many lessons in scotch whiskey." He looked at Eden and wagged his finger impishly. "As a matter of fact, doctor, this young woman needs very few lessons in anything. She has a mind like a steel trap. She graduated from Berkeley magna cum laude with a major in math."

"You're too kind." She smiled at him knowingly. "I majored in math because I detested writing papers."

Barkley rang a small silver hand bell and a butler came into the room. Barkley ordered Tim's drink.

They ate slowly, their conversation somewhat forced in the presence of the stranger who was a psychiatrist. Tim was used to that. There was a natural reticence in the company of a psychiatrist. Most people felt vulnerable, emotionally naked. But several bottles of wine had slowly done their work.

"Nick, this wine is superb," Tim said.

Barkley glowed. "A man with a connoisseur's palate. I'm very pleased, doctor."

"Please—call me Tim."

"It's a rather special California Pinot Noir, Tim, from the Chalone vineyards in Salinas. It's one of my favorite California wines."

Eden lit a joint. The musk-sweet smell drifted over the table. "Anybody want a drag?"

They all shook their heads. "Later," Tony said.

She continued to smoke quietly.

"You know what I was thinking, Nick?" Tony said. "This dinner party represents a small stockholders' meeting." Barkley laughed heartily. "Ah—my loyal friends," he said.

"Nick, I'm serious. Everyone here is a Twenty/Twenty stockholder, with the exception of Dr. Haley."

"Oh, no," Tim said. "I'm afraid you're going to have to count me in too, Tony. I'm also a stockholder in Twenty/Twenty." Tim smiled. "My only problem, Barkley, was I couldn't get enough stock. My broker could only get me five hundred shares."

"That's more than my broker could get me," Tony said. "I was too embarrassed to call Nick."

"It wouldn't have done you any good. Dean Merrill was responsible for allocating the shares. I had nothing to say about it," Barkley said.

"I read the prospectus quite carefully, Nick," Tim said. "I was intrigued by what it did not say."

"I'm not sure I follow you, doctor."

"I wish all of you would just call me Tim. I would feel more comfortable."

Eden's manner had become languid, yet her eyes never left Tim.

"The prospectus was naturally vague about how the Twenty/Twenty system works," Tim said.

"Well, Tim," Barkley said, "you can't expect us to put that in a prospectus."

"Of course not, but it is fascinating to think you have created an impenetrable computer security system. I'm somewhat familiar with computers, and from what little I know about them, I am surprised such a system could be devised."

Barkley looked at Tim with an amused analytical respect. "You're absolutely right, Tim, an impenetrable system is impossible to create, with the exception of the one-time pad."

Germaine had said practically nothing all evening. Like

Eden, she was preoccupied with Tim Haley. She sat quietly, forming her own impressions of this enormous doctor of the mind. She was a trained newswoman, and she knew how to listen.

"What's a one-time pad?" Tony asked.

"It's a very simple but unbreakable code device used by the espionage crowd," Barkley said. "In a one-time pad, only two people know a prearranged key to a particular code. The key and the code are used only once and then destroyed." Barkley paused. "But Dr. Haley—I mean, Tim—is right when he says that no code system has ever been created that can not be broken. We proved that when we developed our system. Some of the best cryptologists, mathematicians, and just plain brilliant people spent years with me trying to create a computer code security system that couldn't be broken." He looked around the table and laughed. He raised his two hands in a gesture of capitulation. "To my stockholders here present, I report that it couldn't be done. We were never able to come up with a code that we couldn't break." There was a long silence.

"I don't understand that, Nick," Tim said. "How can your own system be impenetrable if all codes can be broken?"

Germaine lit a cigarette with a long onyx and gold butane lighter. She sat opposite Barkley. She looked at him guardedly.

Barkley chuckled. "You know, my dear friends and stockholders, it came to me in the middle of the night. For years we had beaten our brains out and gotten nowhere. Then one night I awakened from a sound sleep, and the solution was in my head. It was like the chemist who founded organic chemistry. He did the same thing. He awakened one night and jotted down on a piece of paper the benzene ring. It was the real beginning of organic chemistry."

"I'm fascinated, Nick," Tim said. "Tell us what happened."

"It was really very simple. I discovered we were looking at the wrong problem the wrong way."

Eden's interest was languid, but it was there. Germaine had heard it all before, but Tony and Tim were intensely interested.

"Once I realized that sooner or later any security code could be broken, it occurred to me out of the blue that the solution to our problem was to *identify* the person who broke the code, not to try to devise an unbreakable code." Barkley looked around the room, realizing that all of them were interested, even Eden who was now high on pot and wine.

"You see, I knew that our principal market for a superb computer security system would be the banks. It doesn't take a genius to figure out that institutions handling billions of dollars on a daily basis would pay almost any reasonable price to safeguard their cash and securities. Today, with the electronic transfer of funds, enormous sums of money are shifted around the world by computer." He paused, looking at the faces in the flickering candlelight. "If you can enter the computer illegally, you can transfer millions of dollars to your own numbered account in a Swiss bank as easily as closing a door." Barkley paused. "Our system simply identifies the person who orders or initiates that transfer. That was my solution." He looked around the table. "If I gave you the codes to enter the computer system of, say, the First Manhattan Bank, would anyone of you do so for the purpose of illegally transferring funds if you knew you would be immediately identified and caught?" He looked around the table again. "That was the key. Identification." He paused, smiling. "See if any of you can guess what I came up with, as to how to identify a computer thief." He watched their faces, paying particular attention to Tim. "Can any of you guess? Anyone?" There was a long thoughtful silence. They all shook their heads.

"What's the one thing that absolutely identifies someone? I'm not referring to blood type or dental records. Those would be of no use to us."

"Fingerprints," Tim said.

"Right." Barkley's laugh was boisterous. "Something as simple as fingerprints was our answer."

"But you can dermabrade fingerprints, Barkley," Tim said.

"Yes, you can. But in our system the potential thief would first have to get the correct daily code from our computers, and then the fact that his fingers were dermabraded would immediately identify him or her."

"What does 'dermabrade' mean?" Tony asked.

"Dermabrasion is the surgical removal of a person's fingerprints."

Tim looked puzzled. Germaine was watching Tim with professional interest. "I don't understand, Nick," Tim said.

"You say your system is partly based on fingerprint identification, yet it works with someone who has no dermatoglyphics—"

"Hey wait, doc. You're going over my head," Tony said. "What are dermatoglyphics?"

"They're the ridges on the fingers that form prints," Tim said.

"Yes. And our system works whether they are present or surgically removed." Barkley looked at them all again to make sure they were interested. He rarely discussed business outside his office, but he could tell by their faces that they wanted to hear it all. They were all investors, and he knew that could be pretty stimulating. Nothing like having a piece of the action to quicken the pulse.

"All right, you stockholders, now pay attention. This is why you bought your stock, which I'm happy to report closed tonight at thirty-two. About a twenty-eight percent increase in your investment in a little over two weeks. Not too bad, eh?"

"Not bad at all," Tim said. "I hope it keeps on going."

"Well, as I was about to explain to you before we got sidetracked by the great god gold, the Twenty/Twenty system"—he extended his arms as if to embrace them all—"*our* system works like this. Visualize several circles or rings, if you will, one inside the other. Now, in the center of the inside ring visualize a great deal of money, a treasure chest, if you will. Each ring is a protective wall limiting access to that ring alone by a specific computer code." He paused. "These rings symbolize access to various levels of the bank's computers on a need-to-function basis. An employee of the First Manhattan Bank, who needs to use the bank's computer for legitimate recordkeeping tasks receives a daily code number from our computers in Palo Alto. That number changes every day. That employee cannot get access to the bank's computer until his or her thumbprint is optically scanned by a specially designed laser that sits alongside the computer terminal. These lasers read the actual ridges on the thumb. If the ridges are removed by dermabrasion, the employee will be denied access to the computer, and an alarm system will alert the bank's security people. Now let's say we get to the next ring, closer to the ability to transfer funds. These codes are changed every four hours, and use of the computer requires laser scan. Finally, we get to the inner ring, to those officers who are authorized to transfer funds. Our computers in Palo Alto change those codes every three hours. Someone trying to break the bank's computer security system would have to know the correct code, and his thumb print must be on file with us in Palo Alto and in the bank's computer memory. Otherwise the computer will not transfer the funds and will identify to the bank's security people the individual who is attempting theft." Barkley paused. "It's really not very complicated. It is based on the oldest application of crime prevention: You won't do it if you know you'll get caught." Barkley looked around the room. "Everybody understand?" He pushed back his chair. "Let's go into the living room. Anyone care to join me in a brandy or a cordial?"

"Brandy for me, Nick," Germaine said. Tim and Tony nodded in agreement.

"A Drambuie for me," Eden said huskily. She rose unsteadily and lurched against Tim. She looked up at him provocatively, her eyes slipping in and out of focus as she clung to him. "Hold it, big boy. Stop moving about the damn room. I'm—I'm a little high, you know."

"I know," Tim said quietly.

"You do?"

"I do."

She tipped her head back, looking up at him, her long hair flowing behind her like a yellow waterfall. Her breasts rose and fell as she breathed heavily. The combination of pot and liquor was having its effect.

"What makes you such a damned know-it-all, doctor?"

He didn't reply. He had to keep her from falling. Germaine came to his rescue.

"Put her on the couch, Dr. Haley."

Tim lifted Eden effortlessly and placed her on the couch in the living room facing the lighted garden and the carp pool. The small, twisted trees were lit so as to give a striking effect of contrasting shapes and shadows. It was as if they were looking at a living painting. Tim had to admire Barkley's taste.

Germaine stood smoking, looking at the gardens, then glancing back toward Tim. She had said practically nothing all evening. "Barkley tells me you run an institution in Boston that takes some innovative approaches to psychotherapy."

"That's right."

"What is it that you do, doctor? Nick told me you share his interest in Barkley House. Why?"

Tim looked at the tall, distinguished-looking woman in her kimono. For some reason the outfit did not look contrived. She had a controlled grace, and yet there was something probing and guarded in her manner. He knew he had not won her acceptance, and he did not understand why. Usually his carefully contrived manner—that of a capable professional blended with a relaxed, athletic maleness—made him attractive to women. But not this woman.

He told them about Family Care and the teletherapy program, and they seemed genuinely interested. Even Eden, who was working off her high, listened with attention.

"I've got a great idea," she said. "If Tim is so interested in Barkley House, why not go there tonight? The evening is still young."

"Maybe for you, Eden, but I've got to get some sleep. Otherwise the circles under my eyes are going to make tomorrow's six o'clock news." Germaine shook her head. "I'm going to stay here and drive into the city in the morning."

"I've got to get home, too. I'm really beat," Tony said. "I've got a hell of a day coming up tomorrow."

"Then, doctor," Eden said, "I suggest you drive me home, and on the way we'll stop off at Barkley House."

Tony shook his head and laughed. "You'll never get a better offer, doctor. You'd better take her up on it."

Tim seemed uncomfortable. "I'll drive Eden home, Nick, but I would like to discuss Barkley House with you in some detail. That's why I came out here." He paused. "Let me call you tomorrow."

"I'm afraid I'm completely booked up tomorrow, Tim. Sorry."

"Then let's set something up for Saturday. I'll call at your office tomorrow and see if we can put something together. When would be a good time to call?"

"Try me just before lunch."

"I'll call you then." He looked around the room. "Good night, everyone." He shook Tony's hand. "It's been a pleasure, Tony." He turned to Barkley. "I'll talk to you tomorrow." He tried his most persuasive smile on Germaine. "I hope we see each other before I go back to Boston, Germaine."

She didn't extend her hand. Her smile was forced, her eyes

cool and appraising. "I hope we meet again too, doctor."

Tim looked at her, trying in vain to find a reason for her reserve.

Eden put her arm around Tim's waist and looked up at him knowingly. "Come on, doctor. Give a girl a hand. My legs won't work the way they are supposed to."

She leaned against him as they all walked out into the moonlight. They noticed the Rolls parked at the curb. Barkley and Germaine stood in front of the house watching Tony and Tim walk to their cars, Eden leaning heavily against Tim.

"He looks like an oak tree," Germaine said quietly. She turned to Barkley. "Your doctor friend has expensive tastes." Barkley kissed her cheek tenderly.

"He's not the only one, my dear." He tugged the edge of her silk kimono. They both laughed as the headlights of the two cars probed the night. Tim lowered the window of the Rolls and waved.

"Let's go inside, Nick. I'm getting cold." They walked to the gate; she stopped. She turned and looked at the red taillights of the Rolls as it disappeared down the hill. She remained silent.

"I thought you were cold, darling."

"I am," she said quietly.

Barkley caught the uneasiness in her tone. "What's bothering you, Germaine? You've been like a sphinx all evening."

"I don't know what's bothering me, Nick." She took his hand. "Let's go in. We both have a long day tomorrow."

They locked the sliding panels at the entrance of the house and those that overlooked the garden. They turned out the lights and for a moment stood in the darkened living room looking at the garden. They heard the ice-crystal tinkling of the wind chimes that hung on the dwarf Japanese maple. As they watched, the moonlight's luminescence dappled the wind-roughened surface of the carp pool. A night cloud threw the garden into deep shadow. Barkley felt Germaine's hand squeeze his tightly. He could sense her fear and consternation. They turned slowly from the moonless garden and sought solace and comfort in each other's arms in the still house where the music of the wind chimes had fallen silent.

Chapter 31

As THEY DROVE down Sherman Way, Tim saw the lights of the San Mateo Bridge to the southeast. He remembered the bridge from the map. He could see the running lights and flashing strobes of the aircraft making their approach pattern to San Francisco's international airport, which lay ahead to the northeast.

"You're very quiet, doctor."

He could smell the scent of jasmine as she leaned against him.

"I'm sorry, Eden. I didn't mean to be."

She moved closer to him, leaning her head against his arm. "I've never ridden in a Rolls before. Do you always drive a Rolls?"

"I have one back in Boston. I've become accustomed to the car, and I suppose it has become an expensive habit." He felt her hand on his thigh. It was like a charge of electricity. He was enormously attracted to Eden, but his instincts told him to slow down. For some reason, he could see the dark eyes of Germaine watching him—appraising, probing, suspicious. He was trained to observe people and to listen to and interpret what they said. He remembered that Germaine had said almost nothing all evening. Strange for someone who was a public personality.

"What are you thinking about, doctor?" Eden's hand moved provocatively up and down his thigh.

"I was thinking of how beautiful your city is, Eden."

"It turns you on, doctor?"

"Yes. It really turns me on."

Long pause. "What else turns you on, doctor?"

He swallowed hard. "You do," he said quietly.

She laughed and snuggled closer to him. "I'm glad to hear it, doctor. Maybe we can work on that a little."

They were on 101 North. Candlestick Park was off to their right. They could see the lights of the Bay View area to the northeast as they rapidly approached the intersection of 280 and 101. The Rolls was its own silent, compact, temperature-controlled world.

He felt her hand touch him. He moved uneasily.

"Doctor, you're so big," she said teasingly.

He swallowed hard. He wanted to take this woman back to the Stanford Court and show her just how big a doctor he was, but he couldn't.

"Eden, we're on a freeway doing sixty-five miles an hour. This is a hundred-thousand-dollar automobile, not to mention the two of us." He almost ground his teeth in repressed desire. "You're a lot more distracting than you realize."

"You're sweet, doctor." She withdrew her hand. "All right, I don't want you to wreck this gorgeous car."

She combined her undisguised eroticism with a perceptive intelligence. Barkley had said she had a mind like a steel trap. It wasn't her mind that interested Tim, but he couldn't take a chance on her. He was sure it would get back to Germaine and Barkley, and that could upset things. He would have to control his carnality, which at the moment was approaching orbit.

"You'll have to start giving me directions," he said.

"Follow the signs that say Golden Gate Bridge. We'll get off at the Van Ness exit. We'll take Van Ness north to Vallejo. I'll show you from there."

They stood in the entranceway of Barkley House. Tim looked at the same scene Liz had seen, but his reactions were totally different. To him it looked like a large disco. He couldn't have cared less about the people in the conversation pit and on the dance floor, or about the colored lights or music. He wasn't astonished at the smell of pot that hung thick in the air or the casual sexual behavior.

"What do you think of it?" Eden asked.

"If I understood what I was looking at, I'd know how to answer that."

Eden had sobered up on the drive back. She took his hand and led him to the bar at the other end of the room. They had to walk down and through the pit to get there.

"Tang, I've brought you a big one. All the way from back East."

Tang laughed. "So I see, Miss Summer." Tang was busy mixing cocktails.

"Tang, meet Dr. Timothy Haley. He's a psychiatrist, so be careful." She turned to Tim. "Name your poison, doctor."

"Just a glass of white wine," Tim said. Eden looked at him carefully. "Is that therapeutic or prophylactic?"

He laughed. "Both."

"I have a feeling this isn't going to be a fun evening."

"I've enjoyed it so far," he said.

She swept the room with her hand. "That's what this place is all about, doctor. It's Barkley's fun house. In a world full of hypocrisy and bullshit and guilt, enter Barkley's fun house and leave it all behind. You can come in here with a gay if that's what you like, or with no one. You can make love in one of the rooms." She pointed to the doors on the balconied second floor. "Or just relax in the teahouse or in the garden pool." She pointed to the large mirrored doors, which reflected the kaleidoscopic lights. "Step through one of those looking glasses, doctor, and you're in Wonderland." She looked at him appraisingly. "I thought you were interested in this. You came nearly three thousand miles to see this, doctor." She peered at him almost mockingly. "You don't seem very interested."

He knew he had to squash that impression; that would certainly get back to Barkley. "Eden, let's understand something. In the first place, I'm extremely interested in what Nick is attempting to do here. But as a psychiatrist, I am used to the eccentricities of human behavior, and what's more, I'm trained not to reveal my reactions. Regardless of how bizarre something might appear to a layman, I view human behavior as objectively as I can and try and discern the reasons underlying what might seem abnormal or bizarre to the untrained."

"I knew this wasn't going to be a fun evening, doctor." Her face reflected her boredom. "Here we are in the Sodom of San Francisco; you with an apparatus like King Kong, and you're giving me Psych One lectures that bored me when I was a freshman at Berkeley."

She was making fun of him, and with an ego like Tim's that could be dangerous, but unfortunately, she had caught him at one of the few times in his life in which he had to submit in order to succeed.

"Eden, I'm very attracted to you. You know that." He hesitated. "But in a sense I am Nick's guest. You're his friend." He paused. He lifted her chin with fingers that were surprisingly gentle for so large a man. "This is the wrong time and the wrong place for us, Eden." He paused. "But I promise you this. When I get back to Boston, I'll keep a round-trip ticket waiting for you any time you choose to use it." He drew her head to him and kissed her with more passion than he would have wished. "And if you will come to Boston, we'll do a lot more than review Psych One."

Tim couldn't sleep. He was restless with unfulfilled desire. He was anxious about accomplishing what he had come out here to do. Jesus Christ, he thought, I wish she were with me now. He punched the pillow with a massive fist. What a waste of a real woman. The first oyster-gray light of dawn spread over the bay before he fell asleep.

The bay sparkled as the large sloop picked up wind and began to drive powerfully toward Treasure Island. Alcatraz was off their starboard bow. They could see the red spiderwork of the Golden Gate Bridge to the west.

"This is absolutely splendid," Barkley said, turning to Tim who was at the helm. Germaine sat on the high side in foul-weather pants and a woolen sweater. She had wrapped a light green scarf around her head.

"I told you on the phone when you suggested this that I wasn't a good sailor," Nick said.

Tim smiled. "I know. But I think I told you that if it's a sense of freedom you're after, I can't think of anything like sailing to take you out of yourself." Tim looked at the large

genoa and wondered if he had too much sail on. He called to
the young man on the foredeck, the son of the sloop's owner.
At the Saint Francis Yacht Club, Fulton Prescott, Jr., was
known as a good competitive sailor, like his father. Tim felt
lucky to have the boy aboard and to have been able to make
arrangements for the sloop.

Barkley turned to Germaine who was staring at the sweep
of the bay as the sloop began to heel and the lee rail seemed
only inches above the sun-diamond water.

"Isn't this marvelous, Jerry?" Nick asked.

Germaine didn't move her head. Her face was composed.
She seemed pensive.

"What's the matter, Jerry?" Nick pressed. "Don't you think
this is thrilling? What a glorious experience!" She turned to
him with the soft, compassionate look she seemed to reserve
only for him. She smiled at him the way she would at a child.
She was not patronizing, just discreetly protective. "It's beautiful, dear." She held out her hand to him, and he moved toward
the cockpit and sat beside her with his arm around her.

"Winch in that starboard genoa sheet a touch, will you,
Fulton?" Tim had to shout as the rising wind and the pitching
of the big yacht into the high chop of the bay carried his voice
astern. As he pointed the bow between Treasure and Alcatraz,
he wondered if he would have to reduce the size of the jib.
That wind must be gusting to thirty, he thought, and he had
up a full main genoa. Probably have to come back on the main
alone, he said to himself.

Tim turned the sloop over to Prescott and turned to Barkley
and Germaine. "How are you two doing? Want some soup?"

"Aren't we lunching on Angel Island?"

"We are, Nick, but we've got a good stiff sail before we
get there." Tim paused. "I'd like to talk to you for a few minutes
below, about what I saw the other night with Eden. After all,
that's why I came out here."

Barkley seemed reluctant to leave the excitement on deck.

Tim had to squeeze sideways down the aft companionway
to go below. Barkley held on to the grab rails and gingerly
made his way to the horseshoe-shaped dining area where Tim
waited for him. Barkley saw the green water through the ports
race by the ship, and for the first time since he came aboard,

he felt a tinge of fear. He realized that only the thin skin of this fiberglass hull stood between them and the cold water and treacherous currents of the bay.

They sat opposite each other, Tim facing the lee side. Barkley felt uncomfortable sitting on the lee side but he would rather look up at Tim than at that rushing water. Tim smiled at him with contrived warmth.

"Anything I can get you? Soup? A drink?"

Barkley shook his head. He had felt fine on deck, but not below. The pitching motion of the boat, the compactness of the cabin, which was large to a sailor, but would seem claustrophobic to a landsman, had quickly changed Barkley's mood. He was rapidly becoming seasick.

"Everything all right, Barkley? You're getting a little green around the gills."

"I don't know why," Barkley said, "but as soon as we came below I began to feel awful." He looked at Tim. "I want to lie down." Tim motioned to a berth on the high side.

"Take that one; you'll be more comfortable up there." Tim helped Barkely onto the berth.

"Jesus, I feel as if I'm going to vomit."

"Just lie back and try to relax. I'll get you a bowl from the galley just in case."

"I really feel crappy. It came on me just like that. I told you I was a lousy sailor."

"Nonsense. You'll feel better in no time."

Tim saw Germaine coming down the aft companionway.

"What's going on?" she asked.

"Barkley has a touch of *mal de mer.*"

"He looks green. He's only been down here for a few minutes. How could this have happened so quickly?" Germaine said.

"Seasickness is part physiological and part psychological, Germaine." Tim paused, looking at her steadily. "I believe I can help cure his sickness, certainly for today, and perhaps for some time."

"How?" She was watching him closely—alert, suspicious, disbelieving.

"Hypnosis. I've done a good deal of work with hypnosis and quite successfully." He could see her reluctance.

"The procedure is quite simple. I will put him in a trance

and instruct him to feel well. When he awakens he won't know what happened if I instruct him not to recall it. Afterward, he should be able to enjoy the rest of the sail."

She looked at Barkley whose bilious complexion and sheer misery left little room for decision.

"Well, Nicholas," she said, "are you willing to let Dr. Haley hypnotize you?" They could hear the water hissing past the speeding hull.

"Oh, God, let him do anything. He can shoot me if he wants to. Anything! I never felt so miserable in my life."

"I guess that's it, then, doctor."

Tim looked at her quietly. "I'll have to be alone with him, Germaine."

"Why? I've seen people hypnotized in groups."

"That's exactly the reason. I only want to treat one of you for seasickness. If you're susceptible to hypnosis, you could wind up in a trance, too. You don't want that, do you?"

She lit a cigarette and toyed thoughtfully with the lighter.

He was sitting on the edge of Barkley's berth. She was standing, holding onto the edge of the upper berth.

"All right," she said. "How long will you be, doctor?"

"It shouldn't take more than twenty minutes."

I don't trust that big son of a bitch, Germaine thought. I don't know why, but I've got a bad feeling about him, right to the marrow of my bones. She turned slowly and climbed up the companionway to the cockpit.

Tim could feel the boat charging through the bay. He went aft and told Fulton to reef the genoa. He came back to Barkley, who lay quietly on his back, his hands over his eyes. Tim closed the doorway to the forward cabin.

"Now, Nick, I want you to look at this brass doorknob." He pointed to the knob. His bass voice was soft and soothing. "Are you looking at the doorknob?" Barkley nodded.

"Now I want you to think of a warm day in the valley. You are lying on the grass. You can feel the warmth of the sun filtered through the leaves. You can smell the scent of the flowers, hear the drone of the bees. The sky is a deep blue with white, puffy clouds. You can hear the buzz of insects, the call of birds. Everything is warm and secure and peaceful. You want to sleep. You want very badly to sleep. Your eyes are getting heavy. You are falling into a deep, restful sleep."

Tim watched Barkley. His eyes had closed. "Your arms and legs feel heavy. You can hardly raise your arm." Tim paused. "Now raise your arm." Barkley tried to raise his right arm, but it fell lifelessly back on the berth. The ship heeled sharply, and Tim moved closer to Barkley to make sure he wouldn't roll out of the berth.

"Can you hear me, Nick?" Barkley nodded. He was entering a deep trance. Tim waited, watching him carefully. He wanted to make sure Barkley was completely ready.

"Now I am going to give you instructions, which you will obey. Move your right index finger to let me know you understand." Tim watched Barkley's finger move up and down.

"I am going to ask you some questions which I want you to answer." Barkley nodded. "Can you transfer funds from the First Manhattan Bank without them knowing that you are using the Twenty/Twenty system?"

Tim watched Barkley's brow wrinkle in thought. Then he saw the smile. "Yes," Barkley said softly.

"How?"

"I have access to all the thumbprints and computer codes stored in our memory banks in Palo Alto. I can use someone else's thumbprint and access identification code number to enter First Manhattan's computers."

"Can you transfer funds?"

Big smile. "I can transfer funds. Any amount."

"I am going to call you. I will use the code word 'Janus.' Whenever you hear that name you will instantly and accurately obey my instructions. I will direct you to transfer fifty million dollars from the First Manhattan Bank to the FHB Swiss Deutsche Bank in Zurich. I will give you the account number when I call. Do you understand?" Tim paused. "Say you understand."

"I understand."

"And you will immediately obey my instructions to the letter."

"I will immediately obey your instructions to the letter."

"And you will have no recollection of this conversation when you awaken."

"I will have no recollection of this conversation when I awaken."

Tim shifted his position slightly. "When you awaken you

will not feel seasick. You will think of yourself as standing firmly on solid ground. You will feel well, and you will enjoy the rest of the sail."

"I will feel well and enjoy the rest of the sail."

"I am going to count to five and then clap my hands sharply. One. Two. Three. Four. Five." Tim's clap sounded like a pistol shot.

Barkley sat up and rubbed his eyes. He looked around, surprised to find himself in the cabin. The sloop was heeled over sharply to starboard, and he could see the rushing blue-green water moving swiftly past the hull.

"What am I doing down here?"

"You were feeling a little seasick, and I thought you would be more comfortable lying down."

Barkley stood up, holding on to the edge of the overhead berth.

"But you feel fine now, Nick."

"Oh, yes. Never better. That little snooze must have been just what I needed."

As they started toward the companionway, they saw Germaine coming down. She looked at Barkley and immediately noticed the change in him. Gone was the bilious complexion. He looked cheerful. His eyes were bright, and his natural ebullience had returned.

"I want to go on deck," he said cheerfully. "This boat is really going like hell, Tim."

Tim smiled at Germaine and shrugged. "It's really very simple." She watched them climb to the deck. When they were out of sight she went to the top berth above the one in which Barkely had lain and reached for her lighter. It wasn't there. She stood on the lower berth and searched for it, raising the long narrow foam-rubber mattress.

"Where the hell is it?" she said aloud. Her hands moved carefully over the entire berth. Nothing. She looked on the cabin sole, on the lower berth. She couldn't find it. She had put it on the top berth. If it fell off, it should be on the floor, but it wasn't. She moved to the companionway and climbed up the stairs. She was facing the cockpit. Tim was at the helm; Barkley was looking toward Treasure Island with the binoculars. The wind was really up, and she had to shout as the yacht tossed spray aft over the doghouse as it raced across the bay.

She cupped her mouth with her hands. "Anybody seen my lighter?"

Tim shook his head. Barkley lowered the binoculars.

"The onyx one?"

"Yes."

"I haven't seen it, Jerry."

She backed down into the main cabin, holding the grab rails.

I've got to find it, she said to herself. She fought to keep from falling as the sloop clove the wind-whipped waters of San Francisco Bay.

Chapter 32

THE FLIGHT HOME had been an amalgam of apathy and intro-spection. The unreality of their idyll in Switzerland seemed to diminish with each passing mile as they flew westward over the black Atlantic.

Liz found herself wondering if they had ever actually been in that aerie of a house in the mountains of Switzerland. Had it really happened, or had it been a dream? They had flown high above the dark sea, saying little, feeling mostly their mutual apprehension, and now the incredible sight of Man-hattan at night had left them numb. It was only an incandescent reminder of the trials that waited them.

Liz sensed George's preoccupation. They had said little since Larry's phone call reached them in Switzerland. Why this reticence? she wondered. Why this inability to commu-nicate? She wanted to blame George for it, but she realized that she, too, was reluctant to speak. She was frightened by their isolation from each other, but George's depression had infected her, and she lacked the energy to overcome it.

The cab ride to her apartment with George holding her close to him was an experience in jolting exhaustion.

"You sure you don't just want to move into my place?" he asked.

She shook her head. She didn't really know why, just some intuitive feeling that they both were going to need their own privacy to marshal their resources for whatever lay ahead. This struck her as an odd way to feel about the man she was thinking of spending the rest of her life with, but it was instinctive, and she had learned to go with her instincts.

They had said good night in the small living room of her basement apartment. They had held each other tightly.

"I don't want to go," he had said huskily.

"I don't want you to, but if Larry calls you at home..." She paused. She didn't have to spell it out. She was doing the thinking for the both of them.

After he left, she stood in the living room of the silent apartment, hearing the street sounds of the restless city. Day and night had their separate sounds, their identifiable momentums, but one blended into the other. It never stopped. It seemed hardly possible that yesterday the only sound they had heard was the crackling of the fire and the sighing of the wind as they held each other under the down quilt in the Alders, on another planet in another time.

She began to unpack. She busied herself with little things. She turned on the radio to create sound. She boiled water for tea to begin her accommodation back to what was familiar. When she finally got to bed, she couldn't sleep. She stared at the shadowed ceiling, watching its darkness fade into a dove gray as the city began a new day.

At ten o'clock the next morning the phone rang. She must have dozed off.

"Liz, I just heard from Larry. He's called a meeting for two o'clock." He paused. "Have you seen the paper this morning?"

"I just woke up. Larry wants a meeting on a Saturday?"

"Get a copy of the *Times* and look at the business section."

"What's it say? Is it about Twenty/Twenty?"

"Read it, Liz. It will give you some preparation for the meeting." He paused. "How do you feel?"

"Like a visitor from another planet." She paused. Her voice was low and tremulous. "George, I can't believe we were really in Switzerland yesterday, on that gorgeous mountain, and now we've come crashing home to something like this. I feel as if nothing is real, as if parts of me are still on the mountain and some of me is here. I feel unglued."

"You're not the only one. When you come back from Europe, the adjustment is difficult enough, but this is something else." He paused. "Read the paper, darling. I'll see you at the office at two." He hesitated. "Want to have some lunch?"

"I think I'd better prepare myself for this meeting. You make it sound ominous. Is there something I should know?"

"All I know, Liz, is what I've read. I'm sure there are a lot more details that the papers haven't picked up."

"I'll see you at the office at two." She paused. "I missed you, George. I don't like sleeping alone anymore."

"I missed you too, Liz. I think we should stop this foolishness and live together."

She hesitated. He could hear the anxiety in her voice. Was it indecision? Had she still not made up her mind, not made a commitment?

"I'll see you at two, George." She hung up.

She had read the article in the *Times* a half-dozen times. It was all so incredible, so bizarre, so outrageously theatrical that it was like the worst of the television soap sagas. She held the folded business section in her hand, walking back and forth from the kitchen to the living room dressed in her satin robe, her hair uncombed, her slippered feet making soft scratching noises against the old parquet floors.

Is this possible? she thought, mulling over what she'd read. Or is it a Hollywood script? If it is, it's a damn poor one.

Now let me get this straight. Yesterday, Friday, Germaine went on her six o'clock show and gave the facts about Barkley's arrest as she knew them.

Tim took them sailing. She paused. What the hell was he doing out there? And why was he sailing? I didn't know he could sail.

Then Barkley got seasick, and Tim hypnotized him, which cured his seasickness. All of this Germaine reported on local television. A few days later, Barkely was arrested for transferring fifty million dollars to the FHB Swiss Deutsche Bank in Zurich. She paused. My God! George and I were in Switzerland not more than sixty miles from Zurich at the time! She held the paper in her left hand and brushed her hair back from her face with her right hand. She kept paraphrasing, interpreting, stopping, then going back to the column to find a sentence that she sought to reinterpret; to understand. Her mind simply refused to absorb what she was reading. It was simply too insane.

Barkley was identified by his own system, she thought, looking farther down the column. But Germaine had been suspicious of Tim and had planted her lighter, which held a recording device, on the berth above Barkley. When she went to find it, it was gone. Liz's finger moved down the column. It was discovered only yesterday beneath a grate in the cabin sole. The lighter's tape reveals Tim giving instructions to Barkley to transfer funds when Tim activates a posthypnotic suggestion.

Give me a break, Liz said to herself, raising her arms in a gesture of total exasperation. And Germaine is supposed to love Barkley. Liz sat down on a chair, her face pale. It's absolutely impossible, she thought. Germaine knows what this kind of publicity can do to Twenty/Twenty, and yet she tells all in living color on television. I've got to be dreaming. This can't be happening. It's a lousy script. Any director in his right mind would throw it out. She let the paper fall on the small Persian rug. Barkley had been arrested and released on his own recognizance. Tim was being sought by Interpol. It was no dream. It was crazy, incredible, screwy. She was getting mad as she thought of the implications. She hadn't had time to think these through, but some awareness was beginning to seep in. No wonder Larry wanted to hold this meeting on a Saturday. She got up slowly and walked into the bathroom and turned on the shower. She moved as if she were walking through mayonnaise. The time change and the unreality of this craziness with Barkley were more than her mind could handle. She let the hot water soothe her. Her thoughts became congealed until their complexities increased to the point where her mind simply turned everything off. Sheer fatigue had ground her to a halt.

Liz entered the conference room and saw that they had all arrived before her. She was surprised to see Howard there. George, Larry, Bob, and Howard were seated around the circular table on the Sheraton chairs. Eight chairs were grouped around the table; four were empty. Yellow pads and pencils were placed before each chair, including those that were empty.

It had been some time since she had been in the windowless room with its brass chandelier and its wall coverings of scenes of Manhattan with sailing ships clustered about the wooden piers.

"Hello, Larry," she said quietly. Larry Baldwin nodded and motioned her to a chair.

"Bob." She tried a weak smile as she looked at Bob Cooper's grim face, full gray hair, and meaty hands.

"Hello, Liz." His bass voice was husky.

"Howard." She looked at the tall young man with the serious expression. He was looking down at the table, his eyes averted.

"Good to see you, Liz."

As she sat down, the unreality she had felt ever since Larry's phone call had pulled her and George off their mountain in Switzerland persisted. Her bioclock was completely off. Half her mind was in Switzerland, half in New York. She wasn't prepared for the grim faces sitting around the table. The men looked as if they were attending a wake. George seemed as taut as a drawn bow.

Larry, as always, was the force center from which everything radiated, a thin, wiry man with a narrow face, quick, probing eyes, and fingers that drummed constantly on the edge of the table. Liz had forgotten how intense he could be.

"Well, now that we're all here, shall we get started?" Larry leaned back in his chair and looked at Liz. His expression was a mixture of anxiety and annoyance.

Why do I get the feeling that this is not a congenial atmosphere? Liz thought. She had to force herself to keep from smiling ironically. This was no time for even a hint of flippancy.

"George, as soon as we got word of Barkley's arrest, I sent Howard out to California. He has been with Sol Masters almost constantly, and he's seen Germaine. He flew in this morning on the red-eye." Larry paused looking around the room. "Howard is in the best position to fill us in. Go ahead, Howard."

Howard was numb with fatigue. He sighed audibly. "I saw Germaine's broadcast. If I hadn't seen it, I wouldn't have believed it. That woman is a pro. She must have the station's lawyers climbing the walls, and the police may raise hell with her for suppressing evidence, but she told her story carefully and supported it with facts. Later, Sol Masters filled me in on the details." Howard looked around the room. "I checked with the head of the department of psychiatric medicine at UCLA. He told me that what Tim did was medically feasible. Tim couldn't know, of course, that he had run into bad luck. He would have gotten away with this. The banks, as you know, would rather lose money than admit that their computer security systems had been penetrated. Anyway, Tim called Barkley from Zurich." Howard paused. "We know that because the control board operator at Twenty/Twenty logged the call. When Tim used the code word 'Janus' to activate Barkley's posthypnotic instructions, Barkley behaved in textbook fashion. He ran a computer search of suitable officers of the First Manhattan Bank until he found one who was in a position to transfer large sums to banks around the world. What Barkley didn't know, what he couldn't have known, was that the man he had selected, Anthony Crane, had been transferred that same day to another job within the bank. Because the Twenty/Twenty system is so thorough, it is standard procedure for the personnel department in any of its client banks to run a computer sweep on any person who is transferred or dismissed before a new computer access number is given to a replacement. That's how they picked up Barkley's transfer. When they found that Crane had not made such a transfer, even though his thumbprint identification and access code was correct, the bank immediately got back to Twenty/Twenty. Twenty/Twenty's procedure, in a case like this, is to sweep its own computers. In order to reach the main computers at Twenty/Twenty, you need exactly what a bank needs, an access code and a thumbprint. When they ran a check on those, they came up with Barkley. That's the story." Howard paused and shook his head. "Look, I know Germaine didn't do us any good by going on the tube with this thing, but if it weren't for her, Barkley would still be locked up, and Tim would have gotten away with this totally."

Howard paused. "I went into this in some detail with Sol Masters. Sol asked Germaine why she went on television with this. Her reasons make sense, at least to me. Germaine thought it better to air the whole thing as quickly and as factually as possible. She felt that if she told the story the way it actually happened, without letting other reporters blow things out of proportion and distort the facts, she would be doing Barkley and herself a favor. In the end, I think she was right."

"How much did Tim actually get away with, Howard?" George asked.

"Barkley transferred fifty million into FHB in Zurich, but

Tim only withdrew fifteen. Every cop in Europe is looking for him. The Swiss have frozen the remaining funds in the account and will transfer the balance back to First Manhattan. The bank has posted a half-million dollar reward with Interpol."

Larry turned to Liz. His voice was inquisitorial. "Liz, how well did you know Dr. Haley?"

"I met him on several occasions, and as you know, I went to Boston to see his company, Family Care."

"Did you make any investigation into his background?"

"I hadn't reached that stage, Larry. I was trying to get the necessary financial and operational data from his VP of finance, an Arnold Goodwin."

"And did you get it?"

"No, I found that puzzling. The last time I saw Tim in New York, I told him that if he wouldn't furnish us with the information we needed, we couldn't do anything for him."

"So, in fact, Liz, you knew very little about this man."

She looked at Larry evenly. "You might say that."

"Did you ever notice anything peculiar about him?"

"No, not peculiar." She hesitated.

"What is it?" Larry asked.

Liz sat back in her chair, recalling the times she had been with Tim. "He made me uncomfortable."

The room was silent. She could hear the heavy nasal breathing of Bob Cooper.

"How did he make you feel uncomfortable?" Larry asked.

"I could never put my finger on it. He had an uncanny ability to read me, to know what I was thinking. But I put that down to his being a psychiatrist, and a very innovative one."

"Howard told us that Germaine Fontenant used the adjective 'suspicious' frequently in her telecast. She was suspicious of Haley although she couldn't give any reasons why, either." Larry looked at Liz incisively. "Were you ever suspicious of Dr. Haley, Liz?"

She thought about this carefully. "No, just uncomfortable." She paused. "And I can't define what I mean by that."

Larry looked around the room at the tight, drawn faces. He turned back to Liz. His fingers had stopped drumming on the table. His voice was low, calculating, intimidating. "So you suggested that we send a sociopathological psychiatrist to California to help us with our most valuable investment."

Liz exploded. She slammed her fist down on the table. Her face turned scarlet with rage. "Now just a minute, Larry—"

"Liz, hold it." It was George.

"Hold it to hell. I refuse to sit here in this kangaroo court because two nuts got together and involved this firm."

"Now wait a minute, Liz," Larry said.

"No, Larry, you wait a minute!"

They had fired her temper at a time when her fatigue was so great that it affected her judgment. It all got to her: the destabilizing time change, the months of enervating travel and pressure, the lack of acknowledgment for what she had contributed to the firm and what she could contribute in the future, the lack of personal consideration for her as a human being. "In the first place, George put me on the board of Twenty/Twenty. I never asked for that assignment. And in the second place, it was you"—she pointed at Bob and Larry— "and you and you"—she fought to control her rage—"and you, George—every one of you asked me to go to San Francisco and see what I could do with Barkley. I told you it might all blow up in our faces. I told you we had no right to interfere in Barkley's personal life, but you all sat around as if the world were coming to an end. You wanted a solution. There wasn't any. I said Barkley needed a shrink, and I suggested Haley." She paused. She was so angry she was shaking. "And all of you thought it was brilliant. How was I supposed to know Haley was a psychopath? Maybe he's not; he could be just a plain crook."

"But you were the one who suggested he get in touch with Barkley," Larry said quietly.

"Yes, but—"

"Liz, in this business we have to rely on one another's judgment. We don't have the time to analyze everything ourselves. We're a team. We relied on your judgment, your knowledge of Haley. You suggested a course of action without any prior investigation of a man who could, and did, do us irreparable harm. You jeopardized this firm and subjected us all to the gravest possible danger."

"Now, wait a minute, Larry. That's going too far," George said. "You're accusing Liz of an action that we all precipitated. If one of us is to blame, it's me. Liz reports to me; she's my responsibility."

Bob Cooper didn't like confrontations. He had spent his

whole life in this business, and he knew that when everything hit the fan you had to duck quickly to get out of the way. He felt Larry was being unfair, and he said so. "Wait a minute, George." Bob held up a meaty hand. He turned to Larry. "Larry, I think you're riding Liz too hard. I agree with her. She only did what we all agreed was the best thing to do at the time. She couldn't have foreseen anything like this—"

"I don't agree," Larry coldly interrupted. "Liz was the only one of us who had ever met Haley. She herself said that he made her uncomfortable—"

"As I told you, Larry," Liz interrupted, "he made me uncomfortable, but I couldn't give you a reason why."

"Then you should have found out why, Liz, before you suggested that Haley meet Barkley."

"Larry, you're being unreasonable," George said, his voice edged with anger and frustration.

Liz looked at him. She knew he was fighting desperately to retain control.

"I'm not being unreasonable," Larry insisted. "I'm presenting the facts the way I see them. Liz knew Haley far better than any of us. She saw him twice in New York and once in Boston. If he made her uncomfortable, there must have been a reason for it. It was her duty, her obligation, to this firm to find out what there was about Dr. Haley that bothered her. I will not accept the excuse that she couldn't put her finger on it."

This is it, Liz thought. This was the realization of the foreboding she had felt when Larry called them both off the mountain in that other world a light-year ago. She had thought she felt dejected because George's depression was rubbing off on her. How could she have possibly dreamed that this whole fantastic affair would suddenly turn on her and go for her throat like a crazed animal? She looked at their faces; all but one, Larry, would not look at her. The room was silent. She thought she could hear the beating of her own heart. She got up slowly, with great dignity. She turned to Larry. Her voice was controlled.

"Your accusations are unfair and untrue, Larry," she told him. "But you seem to have made up your mind. I assume there has to be a sacrificial lamb and I'm it." She was intensely aware of the room, the wall coverings. She had actually thought that one day she would run this place, and she had been on her way, but the fates had intervened. She had fallen off a cliff, or was it a mountain?

"Larry. Bob. George." She looked at Howard, whose eyes were riveted on the table in front of him. "I've enjoyed working for Baldwin Cooper, and I've learned a great deal—especially today. I wish you gentlemen every success." Her carriage was as erect as a sergeant major's as she walked out of the room.

George started to get up and follow her. "George, please remain seated," Larry said. He turned to Howard. "Would you mind leaving the three of us alone, Howard?" Howard rose and left the room without a word. He went straight to Liz's office. He saw her standing at the windows looking out on Sixth Avenue.

"Liz..."

She turned slowly. The tears had streaked her cheeks; they glistened in the incandescent light.

"Oh, Liz." Howard walked over to her. He wanted to hold her, to comfort her, but there was a distance between them; there had always been. "Liz, it's so damn unfair. Larry's dead wrong. He'll see that. Bob and George will make him see."

She shook her head. Her lips trembled. She couldn't answer him because she couldn't talk.

"Listen, come with me and I'll buy you a drink. They're going to be in there a long time, Liz. It isn't as bad as it looks, believe me. You're too much of an asset to this place."

It prodded a memory. "What's my future, Howard? Where am I going in this firm?" She had asked George that in an enchanted glade in Switzerland with the sun glistening off snow-capped mountains in the distance.

"You're on the fast track, Liz."

She remembered George saying that. "You're on the express track cleared to the end of the line." Had he said that three days ago or three light-years ago? In another life? In a dream?

"Liz." Howard stepped closer and touched her arm. "Let me buy you a drink. You look as if you could use one."

She managed a weak smile. She nodded and picked up her bag. She still couldn't talk. She touched her face and motioned for him to stay where he was. He didn't need her to draw any pictures for him. She walked to the powder room to repair the ravages of the fates that were tearing her apart.

She sat staring into the mirror looking at her haggard reflection. There were dark circles under her eyes. Her face was taut with the residue of fatigue from her expenditure of emotion at the meeting.

"You don't look like any whiz kid now," she said aloud. "In fact, you look like hell." She shook her head as she reached into her bag for some blusher and mascara. She applied the makeup listlessly.

They don't give any courses in the way the real world works at Harvard, she thought. I've been with this firm less than a year, and I look ten years older. I've lived on airplanes and spent more time in hotels than I have in my own apartment. I've been going straight up like a rocket. Now that rocket seems to have run out of fuel, and I'm headed straight down. She shook her head as she put on some lipstick.

Is this the career, the life I really want? Would I have been better off in some less competitive environment? Would I have been better off with Peter? She looked at herself carefully in the mirror. The face that stared back at her reflected a mixture of self-pity and confusion. Her eyes were raw with fatigue, but they still had that unflagging determination. Deep within her she knew where she belonged. She may have blown it at Baldwin Cooper, but she had tasted challenge and opportunity, and she knew that she could not let that go. She stood up, her expression more determined. It's like a Greek play, she thought. The fates conspire and take their course and smash you on the rocks. She looked at her reflection one last time. She brushed her hair quickly. She turned quickly and left the small room.

Chapter 33

WHENEVER A MAN was in her apartment it seemed smaller to her. Somehow her apartment had come to fit her like a well-worn pair of gloves. It had assumed a shape that was hers. George, sitting on the love seat, seemed to shrink the place.

"It was thoughtful of Howard to buy you a drink," George said.

She was sitting on the ladder-back Shaker chair facing him. She sat very erect, looking at him but not really seeing him.

"Howard is sweet," she said remotely, as if she were alone, talking to herself.

George put his drink down on the end table. He looked exhausted. They hadn't eaten dinner, and it was almost ten o'clock. The apartment was dimly lit, the street quiet. Even the continual subliminal hum of the traffic on Eighth Avenue seemed lost to the hushed September night. He looked at her, his voice edged with exasperation.

"For chrissake, Liz, will you snap out of it? Don't you see what you did this afternoon? I'm not saying you didn't have provocation, of course you did. But you broke one of the golden rules of business. You lost control."

"Lost control!" She stood up and pointed vaguely uptown. "That egotistical son of a bitch accuses me of lousing up his deal—makes me his sacrificial lamb—and you say I lost control!" She was shaking, she was so furious. "How dare you say that to me, George! You of all people. You and your god-damn Barkley—"

"You're doing it again, Liz," he said quietly. He waited as she tried to get hold of her temper. "Sit down beside me quietly, Liz, and just listen long enough to learn something." He was annoyed, and it showed.

She sat down beside him hesitantly, looking at him with a mixture of guilt, anger, and frustration. She was appealing to him with her eyes to support her, to tell her she was justified in her behavior.

"Liz," he said quietly, taking her hand, "you've got to learn that you have to take a lot of pressure in business. It's part of the game. If you can't handle that you shouldn't play." He paused. "Larry was wrong. He was unfair, unjust, but he happens to be the guy who runs the firm." George looked at her; her eyes revealed just how young she really was, how inexperienced. "You've had it your own way for so long, Liz. You've been a winner all through school, and you've been burning up this firm. Suddenly you have to take a couple of steps backward and you feel as if your whole world is coming apart. It isn't. But you don't get up in the middle of a meeting and resign from the firm. That's not the way the game is played."

"Then maybe I'm sick of the game. Maybe Peter was right. What am I doing with my life? I've worked like someone demented ever since I got here. I've lived like a nomad on planes and in hotels. For what? So I can buy alligator bags and have a house in Southampton? Are those my goals? Do I want to be associated with people who are cold and avaricious and just plain damn unfair?"

He thought she was going to cry again. "Liz, if anyone was ever cut out for this business, it's you. You've got the drive, the guts, the smarts, the looks. You've got it all. But you're just twenty-six years old. You're not dry behind the ears yet. Bob and I spent the better part of the afternoon pointing out just how unfair Larry had been."

"And what was his reaction?"

George sighed. "Liz, Larry is a very opinionated guy. He doesn't back off easily."

"Meaning he still thinks I'm to blame."

George got up and poured himself another drink. He turned

to her. "If you had just sat there quietly instead of letting him
have it like that. No one talks to Larry Baldwin that way. No
one."

He was standing hear the love seat looking down at her.
She was looking up at him with a growing understanding of
what he had been trying to tell her. The yellow light of the
small silk-shaded lamp beside her softened the taut lines of her
face." I couldn't go back to that firm, George, even if I wanted
to."

"That's nonsense. Larry knows your value. He knows talent
when he sees it. The fact that he hasn't fired you ought to
prove that."

"So that's it! I'm supposed to be grateful to an egotistical
jerk—"

"Larry's no jerk, Liz," George said evenly.

"He may not be a jerk, but he hasn't got the guts or the
character to accept the responsibility for something that none
of us could control. He's supposed to be our courageous leader.
Then let him lead. Don't let him try to squeeze out of something
as ludicrous as this Barkley thing by laying the blame on an
associate. That's not what a person of character does. That's
not how the head of a firm behaves."

George swallowed his drink and shook his head. He put his
glass down. He looked at her, sighed silently, appraisingly,
heavily. He knew this wasn't going to be easy.

"Do you think you are mature enough to handle what I'm
going to tell you?" he asked.

She didn't answer him. She kept watching him with that
same expression of anxious quiet tinged with anger and frustration. She longed for his support and was terribly hurt by
what she perceived as his condoning Larry's position.

"Liz, you're going to have to apologize to Larry."

If he had hit her, she couldn't have been more surprised.
She was so shocked that for a moment she was speechless.
She stood up and faced him, her hands clenched into fists at
her side. Her voice hissed at him. "That's what you want me
to do? Are you mad! Don't you know anything about me?"
Her eyes blazed at him. "Well, I may be wet behind the ears,
and I may be immature, but in the wildest creations of your
warped imagination, do you really think that I would go crawling back to him to apologize?" She was standing close to him

now; she was tall enough so that her face was nearly on a level with his. Her eyes were locked into his; her voice ground out at him through clenched teeth. For a minute he thought she was going to hit him.

"George, I know that life isn't always fair. I also know that people sometimes behave foolishly. Perhaps I did this afternoon. Perhaps I should have let him berate me for things I didn't do and accuse me of actions I neither precipitated nor could possibly have foreseen or controlled."

He was about to speak, but the look in her eyes warned him he had better keep quiet.

"I'm willing to admit that I might have explored my feelings about Tim more thoroughly," she continued. "But that's all I'll concede. I could have searched from hell to breakfast for what was going on in that man's mind and never had a clue. He was the psychiatrist, not me." She looked at George in disgust and poured herself another drink. She turned and stared at George, her expression one of disbelief. "You don't understand a thing about me, do you?"

"Now wait a minute, Liz—"

"You don't. You've known me under intimate circumstances, yet you don't know a damn thing about me."

"I know you're about to louse up a hell of a career. I thought that was what you wanted. Miss President, or is it Ms.?" He could feel his own anger rising, and he was trying hard not to let it erupt. He had a hell of a temper when he blew. She had never seen that, but she was coming close to seeing it now.

"You're being a damn fool, Liz. You've got a hell of a shot in this firm. This will blow over with Larry, but you can't expect him to accept the harangue you dished out today without an apology."

"Why should *I* apologize?" she hissed at him. "He should apologize to me."

"Liz, for chrissake, this is your first real job, your first shot. Are you going to blow it because of your pride?" He put his arms around her and drew her close to him. He could feel the rigidity of her body. "Liz, I admit that Larry is being unfair . . ."

She pushed him away and walked into the kitchen to boil water for tea. It was mechanical; something to do. Her mind was leaden from the events of the afternoon, and she still had a bad case of jet lag. She stood over the stove in the small kitchen, lost in thought. George came in and put his arm around her. She wanted his comfort, but a part of her felt that he had let her down.

Maybe I'm being unfair, she thought. Maybe he's just trying to tell it to me like it is, but there is no way in God's earth that I am going to apologize to Larry.

They sat down at the drop-leaf cherry table in the kitchen and drank their tea quietly. A gulf separated them, even though they wanted to be together.

"Why don't you take some time off, Liz? Go away someplace. Let things simmer down. Howard, Curt, and Arthur will hold down the fort. I'll pitch in, too. Look, Liz. Don't be a damn fool. Give yourself time to cool off and let Larry get rid of a little steam."

They sipped their tea quietly, looking at each other, aware of the empathy between them.

"I'd like to stay with you tonight," he said quietly.

"I'd like you to."

They lay in the small Empire bed confused and frustrated by the circumstances that had snatched them off their mountain in Switzerland.

"Were we ever really there, George?" she asked softly.

He held her tightly to him. He could feel the silk of her hair against his face, the smooth, lithe body pressed against his own.

"It seems impossible, doesn't it?" He paused. "We were there, Liz. It exists, but I admit that it's hard to believe that forty-eight hours ago none of these problems existed for us. We had the mountain and the sky and those incredible clouds . . ."

"They kept moving all the time," she said. "They reminded me of great white galleons sailing across the sky." She tried to move closer to him, but that was impossible. "That will be an experience I'll always remember," she said. He kissed her long and tenderly. He stroked her hair gently. "Will you take some time off to think about all this, Liz?"

"What will Larry say about that?"

"Nothing. You're my responsibility."

"It seems I'm becoming more of a liability to you."

"Cut it out."

"No, I'm serious."

"Well, don't be. Larry has been unfair. Bob and I will work on him. We'll make him see that."

"Oh, George, I'm sick of talking about Larry and Barkley. I want to talk about us."

"What about us?" he asked.

"There's a better-than-even chance that I won't be able to work for Larry with the same career path expectations I had before this Barkley fiasco, even if I do apologize, which I can't see myself doing." She paused. "Suppose that's true? Where does that leave us?"

"Where do you want it to leave us?" He hesitated. "You know what I want, Liz?" he said quietly. "I want to marry you." He felt her body stiffen.

"What is it, Liz? Don't you love me?"

"You know I do," she said softly.

"Then why can't we get married?"

She waited a long while before answering him. "Because I'm not sure I'm ready for marriage. I haven't done what I set out to do, George. I haven't really done anything. I don't want to be tied down with children—"

"So we won't have children."

"But you want them; I know you do. You didn't have them with Claudia, and I know how you feel about that. I want them, too, but not now."

He touched her lips with his fingers. "Don't you think we have enough to worry about without creating more problems?"

They listened to their own silence. They began to respond to the tactile movements of their bodies. They made love knowledgeably, with a passionate sensitivity and understanding of each other's needs.

"You're so marvelous at this, George," she said hungrily, as her excitement was rekindled by his desire to please her.

"Don't forget that when you're away," he said jokingly, but with more seriousness than she understood.

They lay together like spoons inside a drawer, satiated.

"Where will you go?" he asked her quietly.

She thought for a while.

"I've haven't seen Mother for a long time. I haven't spoken to her in weeks."

"That sounds like a good idea." He waited. He didn't want to ask her, but he had to. He had kept it bottled up for a long time. "What about Peter?"

She had thought about Peter. She felt that she owed him some explanation of what she was doing with her life. She hadn't heard from him since he went to England for the summer. She didn't even know if he was back at Harvard.

"I should see him, George."

"For what?"

"To tell him about us." She paused. "I owe Peter an explanation."

She could feel his annoyance.

"Peter warned me about the problems I would find in this kind of life. He pointed out the value judgments I would have to make, the ethical choices I'd face between the excitement of earning money and achieving power and a more conventional life with less obvious, but perhaps more meaningful, rewards."

"And you don't think you can do both?"

She waited a long time before replying. "I don't think so," she said quietly.

He was afraid that he had fallen in love with a woman whose indirection in her personal life would either prevent them from coming together or be responsible for tearing them apart. She sensed his understanding; she was frightened by it herself. She had once told him that she wanted it all, and he had advised her that no one could have it all. Was this the immaturity he had referred to earlier? Was it part of the emotional malnutrition she had suffered as a young girl, in the small silent house in Maine, with its waxed fruit and polished furniture that held so many memories, so many sad and tired ghosts?

Chapter 34

SHE HAD HAD enough of airplanes. She was absolutely determined not to fly to Boston and Portland. She had rented a car and was driving on the Wilbur Cross Parkway between New Haven and Hartford. She had planned to skirt Hartford and pick up Route 86 to connect with the Mass. Turnpike and the Expressway to Boston. She had telephoned Peter and her mother, saying that she would arrive in Boston about four in the afternoon and had reservations for the night at the Ritz.

As she drove, the October reds and yellows of the maples flamed the ribbon of highway, interrupted by the deep emerald of spruce and fir. The blue sky was scattered with white clouds. The midmorning light was sharp and clear with dark stripes of tree shadows across the road. The day was a Sisley painting.

She had chosen to drive because she wanted to think about the irresolvable conflict between her career and her life as a woman. Maybe other women didn't have the problem with this that she had, but then, other women hadn't led her life. She knew what it was to have a working mother, to be a latchkey child. She was damned if she was going to be that kind of mother or be responsible for inflicting that kind of a life on her child. As I see it, she thought, I have to decide what's right for me. If it's a career, then children are out. She paused in her own mind as the force of that conclusion hit her. It was a Delphic choice. She was certain that if she tried to do both, she would screw it up. She knew herself well enough for that. She was too driven, too motivated, not to adhere to her own high standards. Maybe that was why she was on her way to see Peter and her mother. Perhaps they could point her in a direction she could live with.

She watched the Porsche approach rapidly in her rearview mirror and then pass her as she edged toward the far side of the right lane. She hadn't driven in so long that she felt timid in the aggressive turnpike traffic. The reds and golds flashed by her in kaleidoscopic sweeps of color.

"The only thing I do know," she said aloud as she clutched the wheel with both hands, "is that if I don't make up my mind about this I'm going to have to see a shrink."

The image of Tim Haley flashed through her mind. I wonder where he is, she thought. I hope they catch him. She paused, remembering how shrewd and manipulative he was and how skillfully he could use his specialized training. She thought of Tim and of Larry and George, and her hands whitened as she gripped the wheel savagely. She wondered what the road ahead had in store for her.

Boston was always the dangling tendril of her roots, the first reality of New England. Anything farther south than Boston simply was not New England and in the final analysis, she was a Down East Yankee. The materialism of New York, the exotic sophistication of San Francisco, the sprawling cultural desert of Los Angeles were only way stations for her. Boston was where she could first catch hold of her roots and as she followed them, they would lead to Maine.

She felt awkward meeting Peter at the Ritz. On the drive up she had thought about it carefully, and yet Cambridge was too personal. It would hurt too much to see St. Vincent's Avenue and Soldiers Field Road. The sight of the Charles River and Memorial Drive would bring back too many memories. No, the Ritz was the right place. Peter didn't like it because for him it symbolized a materialism he found distasteful, but it would help her keep some distance between them—a space, a separateness, that she would need. Too much of him still lay very close to that hidden core deep inside her where she permitted entry to no one, not even herself, not fully. Too much of what was there was strange, complicated, unfathomable, and, at times, frightening. It was a place for secrets; darkness was its friend, light its enemy. She didn't want to get anywhere near that place, and the cool, brittle sophistication of the Ritz would help protect her from it.

She showered and put on her makeup carefully. She was nervous about meeting him. She hadn't spoken to him since he returned from England. She had meant to call, but the frenetic pace of her work had always left her too busy. And then there was George. As her relationship had developed with him, she began to feel guilty about Peter, and maybe that was the real reason for their lack of communication. So why was she here now? Why was she sitting at her dressing table making up her face as skillfully as she knew how, brushing her hair until the copper highlights held a soft radiance? She was honest enough with herself to acknowledge that a part of her still loved Peter. She had even told George. But she knew, too, that the relationship wouldn't work over the long term. After George's forceful yet sympathetic lecture to her yesterday, she wondered whether a relationship with George would work. Maybe she was one of those women who could not get along with a man on a continuing basis unless she could dominate him completely. "God forbid," she said aloud as she moved the soft complexion brush across her cheeks. She checked her nails on which the clear lacquer had dried. She had brought an emerald green cashmere dress that molded and flattered her figure. She put on her mother's pearls, and looked at herself in the large mirror that hung between two framed floral prints in her room. Her room overlooked Arlington Street and the Boston Gardens. The day was moving toward that indefinite time between late afternoon and dusk, when the sunlight faded to an amorphous gray and the sharp outlines of shadows blended into a montage of colorless half-light that was neither day nor night.

She sat down in a small silk-upholstered chair by the windows that overlooked the gardens and tried to read a magazine. She felt herself becoming increasingly nervous. She kept looking at her watch. It was nearly six o'clock, the hour at which they were supposed to meet. Peter was normally very punctual. She thought about the last time she had met him here at the Ritz, when she came to Boston to see Family Care. Tim had reserved a suite for her. As her mind turned to Tim, her face became taut and bitter. That son of a bitch has probably cost me my job, she reminded herself, and maybe cost Barkley his business. She hesitated. I don't really believe that. After all, the system worked. It caught both Tim and Barkley. Poor Nick Barkley. She winced at the thought that she had introduced Tim to Barkley. Maybe there was some merit to George's argument, she thought. Maybe she had behaved badly toward Larry Baldwin. The thought of having to crawl to him and apologize made her blood boil. But her certainty of her position was being slowly eroded by the gnawings of self-doubt.

She slammed the magazine down on the table and got up to pace the floor. The door buzzer rasped. She stopped in the middle of the room, feeling the spears of anxiety, anticipation, hope, longing—a melange of powerful memories. She checked her appearance quickly in the mirror. It would have to do. She gave a few quick last-minute touches to her hair and then opened the door. "Come in, Peter." A deep rush of emotions flooded through her at the sight of him. They stood in the middle of the room looking at each other. They didn't touch. There was something intangible, an unspoken acknowledgment, an understanding that life had separated them.

"Liz, you look wonderful."

"So do you."

He was looking at the fatigue and anxiety in her eyes, which no amount of makeup could hide. She was studying him carefully. She knew him so well, remembered so much. She sensed that he was perusing her.

"How long has it been, Liz?" It was an ice-breaker, something to say.

"Let's see . . ." She thought, hesitated. "It was midsummer when I came up to see Dr. Haley."

"How is Dr. Haley?"

Her face clouded. "Don't mention that bastard's name," she said icily.

He had read about Haley in the papers. "What's going on?"

"Look. We've got the whole evening to talk. I want to talk about that bastard, but not now."

He was used to her temper, but not her language. She had changed. He could see that; he could feel it.

She had aged, if that's possible, in less than three months. There was a new maturity to her, or was it a world-weariness. How could someone twenty-six years old be world-weary? But there was definitely a brittleness, perhaps a new cynicism that hadn't been a part of her before. He didn't like it.

"You haven't changed," she said, as if reading his mind.

"You know us academic types. Not much excitement in our lives. Nothing much changes." He looked around the room. "So it's still the Ritz, is it?" He walked across the room, looking out at the gathering darkness and the lights of Boston, the dark areas of the garden and the Common. He turned to look at her. "I don't think I'll ever get used to meeting you in this hotel." He never took his eyes off her. "It's too far from St. Vincent's Avenue." He paused. "I can't get used to the elegant, sophisticated Elizabeth Clark from New York."

"Don't say that. I'm still a Yankee girl, Peter."

He shook his head. He smiled ruefully. "No, Liz," he said quietly, still studying her. "Something's changed. I'm not saying that Maine is gone; I'm just saying that you've absorbed something from New York by osmosis." He saw her frown. They were still standing, quite far apart now. It was awkward; not what either expected. She had become more practiced than he in the art of obfuscation.

"How was England?"

"Nothing much changes there, especially in the country. I was glad to see my parents. They are getting on, you know."

They were still standing apart nearly the full length of the room.

"How's your mother?" he asked, continuing the innocuous small talk.

"I'm going to see her tomorrow." She was embarrassed to have to say it. "I haven't spoken to her in weeks. I've been so busy, traveling so much."

"Yes, I know. I've called a few times..."

She was surprised. "I didn't know. I haven't had any messages."

"I didn't leave any. You were always away someplace. I just didn't bother."

It annoyed her. She realized instantly that she was being unreasonable, but she was still annoyed.

"I'm glad to see you, Liz," he said softly.

She felt a lump in her throat as she looked at him. One thing was absolutely certain. She felt it in the bedrock of her being, a part of her would always love him; that would never change.

He has the damnedest way of looking at you, she thought—
sensitive, perceptive, incisive, yet sad—as if he's always saying good-bye.

"Will you let a girl buy you a drink?"

He shook his head. "I'm afraid not, Liz."

That tired, shy, stubborn smile again.

"I can't afford the drinks at this place. There's a little place
on Newbury Street. We can walk there."

He helped her on with her coat. It was strange for them
both, this reticence, this physical separateness. Neither of them
felt comfortable. It was enervating.

The restaurant was small. The room was narrow with a shelf
recessed into the painted stone wall beside them, which held
pots of pink and white impatiens bathed in the eerie violet glow
of the hidden plant lights. A candle set in a large cylindrical
glass holder on their table trailed a cotton wick that floated in
white kerosene. The small flame cast a yellow glow on their
faces. Concealed spotlights in the ceiling kept the light muted
and intimate.

Though the wine helped to ease their strain, the meal pro-
gressed slowly. She tried to get Peter to talk about himself, but
she had to admit inwardly that there wasn't much to talk about.
He wasn't doing anything new, and she wondered why he
wasn't bored by his life. God knows she would have been.
The conversation was impersonal. He had read the Twenty/
Twenty story in the Boston papers, but of course he had no
knowledge of her involvement. She found herself explaining
her role in the bizarre affair.

"And your boss, this Larry Baldwin, blames you for introducing Dr. Haley to Barkley?"

She nodded.

He tapped the edge of his wine glass. "You did introduce
them . . ."

She looked at him coolly. "I did introduce them, but only
after discussing it with George, Bob, and Larry. It was an
offhand suggestion. I had warned them that Nicholas Barkley
was unpredictable, that we ran the risk of having this whole
deal blow up in our faces. I never dreamed, of course, that it
would take the turn it did. We were all sitting around a table

looking for an idea. I said that Barkley needed a shrink, and I happened to think of Haley."

"But San Francisco is full of shrinks. Why import one from Boston three thousand miles away?" He said it quietly with a certain detachment that annoyed her. She was more annoyed because she had no logical answer to his question.

"I suggested Haley because he was the only shrink I knew."

"But you really didn't know him." He was watching her carefully as he said it. He could see her flush of anger even in the muted light.

"You sound like Larry Baldwin."

"I don't mean to."

Her face was grim. The chill of fear spread through her. This is what George had told her, and now Peter was telling her the same thing. The two most important men in her life were implying that she was responsible for the Haley affair. Her growing understanding of what Peter had just said frightened her. It cast her off the moorings of her own certainty, but she still clung to the stubborn though battered belief that their criticism of her was unfair. Only now, she was not so sure. She toyed with a spoon, her eyes averted. She felt removed from Peter, almost as if he were a stranger. She felt angry as well. She had expected more from this meeting after so long a time. Her lips tightened as her mind replayed her thoughts like an old movie. She could feel him watching her, studying her. Why did she feel so disappointed in this evening? Why had she expected support from him? Perhaps because he had always given it to her. Whenever she had needed him he had been there for her, emotionally. What right had she to expect his support now, after George; after all the weeks and all the miles that had separated her from Peter; after the long absence of contact.

They sat in silence. It was obvious to even the most casual observer that they were not enjoying themselves. She began to feel a sense of isolation. First Larry, then George, now Peter. Were they right?

Maybe what she wanted and expected from Peter was succor, support, someone to hold her hand, and he wasn't doing that. Why? Perhaps it was unreasonable for her to expect anything from him after the decisions she had made affecting both their lives. Perhaps she had hurt him, and how he was hurting her. Was he doing it purposely? A part of her mind didn't think so, but she ignored that. She needed someone. Damn, she thought, at the moment there was no one. She was alone in a man's world.

They walked back to the hotel not saying much, no longer attempting small talk. They had known each other too long, too intimately, and they had too much respect for each other to pretend what they didn't feel. He was her first real love. She had given him so much of herself, and he had given of himself in return. They had touched each other deeply, but she had sacrificed their relationship on the altar of . . . what? What had she given up with Peter? What had she gained with George? They were both so different. She loved them both so differently, but this was the end of the line for her and Peter. If she had learned anything this night, she had learned the pain of her past decisions, the results of the destruction of those things that build relationships—the danger of taking someone for granted, the eroding effect of giving too little. She had done it all, and yet she still expected more than this silent walk along Newbury Street, past the lighted shop windows that depressed her like an Edward Hopper painting. She didn't want him to come up to her room. She felt too confused, too removed, too puzzled by her ambiguous feelings toward him. She did not wish to prolong this evening. She could no longer bear to witness the erosion of what they once had.

They stood in front of the elevators, not knowing what to say. She could not remember ever feeling that way.

"I think we had better say good night, Peter." She said it softly.

He was looking at her with a resigned sadness that made her want to cry. He didn't say anything. What could he say? She had come to him for support, and he had not been able to give it.

Can you love someone and withhold succor from them? Peter wondered. Is love so irrational that it demands support even when it isn't warranted? Was he expected to stand by her even though she had struck out on a path he couldn't follow? Even though she had destroyed their relationship by taking too much for granted? He didn't know the answers to those questions. He looked at her. She was a part of his life that was about to be lost to him, in the Ritz, on an autumn night in Boston. He wondered why the fates had chosen him for such silent, persistent torment.

"Good night, Peter." She offered her hand, and he took it. They looked at each other, and for some reason she remembered that day last spring when they lay on the grass near Memorial Drive. On that day, she had loved him more than her life. Now she had come back to Boston to find something of that love. Perhaps she was foolish to expect it. In any case, whatever she had expected had gone, and she was responsible for the loss. She seemed to have a way of losing things—men, her career. She walked into the elevator; the doors closed, and she found herself going up. Or was it down?

Chapter 35

SHE HAD CALLED her mother from New York and had been surprised when Betty Clark asked her to meet her at Nate Halsey's house. She knew something was going on between her mother and the widower, but she had no idea how far the relationship had developed, if indeed one had. She felt guilty for not having called her mother in so long. It was no use rationalizing that she had been busy. She had simply been thoughtless and selfish. She knew that. But, on the other hand, phones worked two ways. Her mother, as far as she knew, had made no attempt to call her; neither had she written. But as Elizabeth Clark pulled up to the weathered gray-shingled house with its white trim and flowerless white windowboxes, she knew why she had come. She was annoyed that she had to share this time with her mother with Dr. Halsey. She turned off the ignition, but didn't get out of the car immediately. She looked down the slope of trimmed grass to the sun-speckled gray-blue of Casco Bay, with its darker patches of cloud shadows. The American flag whipped smartly from the white wooden flagpole. The skiff was tied by its painter to the float off the end of Dr. Halsey's wharf. The small sloop rode at its mooring, bobbing up and down in the brisk, choppy sea. She looked out at Fox Island and remembered that day last summer when she, Peter, and her mother had come here from the refuse-strewn commercialism of Harper's Cove. She and Peter had rowed the skiff out to the island. They had made love on a patch of sand in a grotto of rock.

She had loved him so deeply then. All that had deteriorated so quickly in so short a time. Last night had been the end.

The front door opened, and her mother came out followed by Dr. Halsey. He was as she remembered him: tall, with full hair cut short, streaked with gray; face tanned, sun wrinkles at the corners of the light blue eyes that were surprisingly like her mother's. Her mother, however, had changed. There was a new spring to her walk. She looked younger, more relaxed. For the first time Liz could remember, she seemed happy.

"Why are you sitting out here all alone?" Betty Clark asked.

Liz got out of the car. Greeting her mother had always been awkward with reticence always restraining their emotions. But not now. Her mother came toward her swiftly, like a young girl, embracing her and kissing her. Liz was unprepared for such an overt demonstration of affection. But though she was embarrassed by it, she was pleased by it, too.

Nate Halsey held out a tan, weathered, age-spotted hand. "Good to see you again, Liz. It's been a long time."

"Good to see you again, Dr. Halsey."

He wagged a finger at her formality. "I think you're old enough to call me Nate." They all laughed. For some reason Liz felt uncomfortable calling him Nate, but Nate it was.

They sat in the parlor in the comfortable, lived-in chairs, seeing through the picture window the view that Nate Halsey had looked at for thirty years. They talked about this and that, skirting subjects that were important. They ate succulent crab-meat salad for lunch. Liz had forgotten how good Maine lump crabmeat could taste. They drank tea and continued their pleas-ant, innocuous conversation, but everyone understood that there were important things to be said on both sides, and they were using up their staple of pleasant conversation. Nate pushed back his chair and got up.

"I've got to make rounds at the hospital, Bet." He turned to Liz. "It shouldn't take too long. I'll see you two in a couple of hours."

Liz felt his experienced appraisal. She and her mother watched him walk to the garage in the crisp light of early afternoon. Liz turned to her mother. Betty's expression was teasing, smiling.

"There wouldn't be something you want to tell me about all this, Mother?"

Betty Clark blushed. Being happy was so new to her that she couldn't believe her joy was real. She felt that it would vanish and she would find herself back in the small, silent house in Falmouth. That was why she had waited so long to tell her daughter. Suppose it slipped away? But it wasn't going to slip away, not with a man like Nate Halsey. This is what she kept telling herself, what she now allowed herself to believe in her most precious and private musings.

They stood looking at each other, one older with a new joy, one younger with new sorrows.

"Mother, for heaven's sake, it's as plain as the nose on your face. You're radiant. You look like a young girl."

Betty Clark beamed at her daughter. She didn't move to embrace her again. She stood there quietly, almost serenely joyous.

"Nate and I are going to be married, Liz. I was going to write; then I was going to call, but I just couldn't. I was so afraid something would happen." She paused. "He's such a good man, Liz, and a fine doctor."

"Oh, Mother, I'm so happy for you."

"Thank you, dear."

"When is the big day?"

Her mother paused. "We were waiting to find out when you could make it."

Liz's laughter had a brittle, almost metallic sound. "I don't think my schedule is going to be a problem, Mother. As a matter of fact, I'll be lucky to have any schedule at all."

Her mother's serenity flicked away like a passing shadow and was replaced by concern. She had guessed that something was wrong when Liz called from New York. She was intuitive where her daughter was concerned; a psychic umbilical cord kept them in subliminal contact.

"What is it, Liz?"

Liz sat on the sofa and looked at her mother. Her concern, fatigue, exasperation, anger, and self-pity all welled up from the depths of her private misery and despair, but she retained control. She had been bred to do that, to have pride and strength of character, not to whimper. That pride seemed to be getting in her way with the men in her life, with her career. She sat facing the woman who had passed that pride and independence and self-reliance on to her through her genes. It was a gift of blood, or a curse, depending on how you looked at it. Her lips trembled as she began to speak.

"Mother, it's such a long story. I'm exhausted from thinking about it, living through it." She paused. She sat erect, facing her mother. Her face looked drawn with her effort to control the emotions that roiled within her. She took a deep breath and told her mother about Tim Haley, Nick Barkley, and Larry Baldwin.

"Do you think Lárry has been fair, Mother?" Liz asked after telling her what had happened.

Her mother thought about the question. "I don't think it's a question of fairness, Liz. Larry Baldwin's point of view probably seems reasonable to him, but I agree that a man of character would not place the blame for such a piece of business on an associate." She thought for a moment, her face reflecting her sympathy and her genuine desire to come close to the truth. But then what was truth? She had spent the better part of a lifetime suffering from what she considered the injustice of truth that her own stubborn pride had locked her into. Where had that gotten her? She had been unhappy for twenty years. Was it *truth* her daughter had come to her to discover or was it help, support?

"It seems to me," Betty Clark said quietly, looking at her daughter intently, "that who was right or wrong in this has very little to do with it. Mr. Baldwin probably needs someone to blame this on for reasons that are known only to him." She paused. "Maybe he doesn't fully understand those reasons himself. If he didn't need to lay the blame on you or someone else he would have accepted the situation as a collective problem for which the whole organization was responsible. But something probably makes him want to focus that blame on someone in particular, and unfortunately that person seems to be you. That's unfair," Betty Clark said. She stopped and looked at her daughter. "But, unjust as it is, you're going to have to apologize and forget about who's right and who's wrong. You don't want to sacrifice a career like yours . . ." She let her voice trail off. She watched her daughter's face reflect changing emotions: annoyance, frustration, and finally resignation. Liz looked at her mother and sighed.

"You're right. I'll do it. George has been telling me I'd have to apologize." Liz laughed sardonically. "But it will have to be one beaut of an apology, Mother. I practically resigned from the firm when I walked out of that meeting."

"You'll straighten it out, Liz. Give yourself a chance, and give Larry Baldwin time to regain his objectivity."

Their conversation turned mercifully to the wedding.

"We'll be married here, Liz, in this house. It will be just you, Nate, and me, and the minister, of course. Nate's two sons are in California. We're going to stop and see them on our way to Hawaii. We'd like to be married this month. The sooner the better."

The wind had come up; they could hear it howling around the house. They talked mainly of her mother's new life. Liz felt a growing envy. The man who would make that life possible had just returned from the hospital. They heard his car pull into the garage, followed by the rumbling of the garage doors. Nate Halsey walked into the room and looked at Liz. His eyes smiled at her. "I guess your mother has told you."

"Yes. I'm so happy for you both, Nate." Liz got up and extended her hand. He took it warmly and held it while he looked at her with those steady, wise, honest eyes.

"I'll take good care of her, Liz, I can promise you that. Bet's going to quit her job at the hospital," Nate said. "I'll remain on the staff, but take a lot more time off. We want to travel."

"She's in good hands, Nate. I'm thrilled for both of you."

The daylight waned, and Nate went out to take down the flag. They spent a quiet evening in the peaceful house discussing her mother and Nate's plans.

Dinner was clam chowder and boiled lobster. Their happiness was contagious, and Liz forgot about her own problems as she listened to their plans. She was overjoyed for her mother.

The storm that the late afternoon wind had foretold began to blow angrily at the house. The night was dark, and clouds covered the moon.

"Well, I guess it's time to head home," Betty Clark said. Liz looked at her mother in astonishment.

"Aren't we staying here?"

Betty looked at her daughter and smiled. "A lot has changed in Maine, Liz, but not so much with people like Nate and me.

Nate's lived on this street for thirty years. We'll wait until after we're married." Betty watched Liz's expression of incredulity change to one of distaste. Liz disliked the small house on Beach Street. This was a peaceful house, a loving house. The one in which she grew up on Beach Street was hateful to her. It was lifeless and cold and silently vindictive. There were too many tears connected with that house, and Liz didn't want to spend the night there, not in this storm.

They said good night to Nate, and Liz promised to be back for the wedding. She watched him standing, framed in the lighted doorway waving at them as Liz started the rented car. She pulled out of Nate's driveway and faced a steep hill. The fierce wind buffeted the car. They started up the hill toward the hated house. Her whole mood had changed. Gone was the brief period of peace that had infused her in Nate's house. She was about to go back into her past, which was disturbing enough. When she thought about her future, it disturbed her more.

Chapter 36

WHEN SHE RETURNED to her apartment in New York, she called George at the office.

"I didn't expect you back so soon," he said.

She hesitated. "I'd like to come back, George. I'd like to talk to Larry."

"Today?"

"If he'll see me."

Long pause. "I'll see what I can do. Why don't you come into my office first, say around two."

"I missed you, George," she said quietly.

"I missed you, too. Very much."

"I'll see you at two," she said.

Larry Baldwin, Bob Cooper, and George sat in the firm's dining room, having finished a desultory lunch. The atmosphere was repressed, explosive, needing only a spark to ignite it. Their faces were tense. Bob Cooper's was flushed, giving his skin almost a sunburned look. Larry was pale and tense, his face drawn, the muscles expanding and contracting along his narrow jawline. His impatient energy had given way to a silent, determined stubbornness; an inflexible attitude that was implacable, unyielding.

"We've gone around this subject twenty times, Larry," George said. Larry remained silent, avoiding George's eyes.

"Look," George said. "If anyone should be taking the rap for this, it's me. If Liz didn't check Haley thoroughly enough, that's my responsibility. That's what you pay me for. If you want someone to resign, that person should be me."

Bob Cooper's husky, chain-smoker's voice was filled with exasperation. "For chrissake, George, no one wants you to resign. You're too valuable to this firm."

"Then someone is going to have to explain to me why we have to get rid of one of the most promising associates this firm has ever recruited."

Larry turned to George, his face white with the effort to control his temper. "This is the last time," he said quietly, menacingly, "that I will tolerate the senior members of this firm wasting their time discussing Elizabeth Clark." He looked squarely at George. "Do you have any idea how much pressure has been exerted on me because of her? Do you know how many phone calls I have had from brokers, from the members of the selling group, from the directors of Twenty/Twenty" —his voice rose in pitch along with his temper—"from the chairman of the First Manhattan Bank, from the insurance companies, from every son of a bitch who has a telephone? I can't even escape at home. The bastards call me in town, out on the island. There's no getting away from them." He looked at George with those fierce, penetrating, intelligent eyes. "Liz got us Haley, and that son of a bitch brought us hell on earth."

"Larry, you've blown this thing out of proportion," Bob said. "So you've taken some flak, so what? It won't be the first time or the last." He paused. "Come on, Larry. I've never seen you like this. You've got a bug up your ass about this thing. It isn't like you."

Larry's voice was so low they had to strain to hear him. He was hissing at them with the menace of a pit viper. "I want her out of here today. Not tomorrow, not two weeks from now, today."

"For chrissake, Larry," Bob said, "that's not even legal. She could sue us. She's a woman and smart as hell. She knows her rights. There isn't a court in the land that wouldn't find in her favor if we just toss her out. It could cost us a bundle."

"The hell with what it costs."

"Larry, what is this thing with you and Liz," George said. "You've got some pathological antagonism toward her. Bob is absolutely right. A good lawyer could make her look like the victim of unfair management, and I'm not sure that's not what she is."

Larry shot George a deadly look. "Is that what you believe we are—unfair management?"

George faced him squarely. "That's how I believe we are behaving."

"There couldn't possibly be any personal prejudice on your part, George, in favor of Liz?"

"You know damn well there's a serious relationship between us, Larry. I've never denied that."

"Do you think it shows good judgment to become involved with an employee?"

"That's none of your business, Larry. And if you're uncertain about the quality of my judgment, I shouldn't be here."

Larry looked at George for a long time. "I want you to tell her today," he said, his voice low and menacing, like an insistent, quiet drill intent only on accomplishing its purpose.

"You're the one who wants her to leave, Larry. Why don't you tell her?"

"Because that's what I pay you for."

George looked at Larry for a long time; their eyes locked. "I'm afraid you don't pay me enough, Larry." He pushed back his chair and stood up. His face was white with fury, but he had played the game long enough to know losing control was a cardinal sin. "I'll have my resignation on your desk tomorrow, Larry. I'd like my capital and all monies owed me by the firm to be paid as soon as the lawyers and accountants can work out the agreements." There were a thousand other things he wanted to say, but he said none of them. He wanted to punch that egomaniacal bastard into oblivion, but he didn't raise a hand. These things got around fast enough, and he didn't want to leave more to embellish than necessary. The grapevine would do that on its own. "I'm sorry it's had to come to this, Larry."

It took an extraordinary effort of will to restrain his tongue, but control was vital. Liz had yet to learn that. An idea occurred to George as he stood there: Liz's defiance of Larry may have touched off a psychological fuse which, once lit, refused to go out. He didn't know, and he no longer cared. He walked out of the room.

• • •

She entered his office promptly at two, and the moment she saw him she knew something was terribly wrong. He was as pale as death, and his silent, constricted mien told her that he was very upset. Some instinct warned her that this was no time to talk to him. He gathered up the file folders on his desk and then buzzed Martha Wainright. She left her desk and stood in the doorway. "Martha, please pack my personal things and send them to my apartment. And call a meeting with Howard, Curt, and Arthur for ten o'clock tomorrow."

Martha looked at him with the understanding that comes from years of experience as a top-notch private secretary. She nodded an anxious acknowledgment of his instructions and left.

Liz felt like an intruder. He was not looking at her.

"George, what is it? What's going on?" She felt frightened, anxious.

He looked up at her for the first time since she had come into the room. "I've resigned."

She was stunned. Totally shocked. She stood there open-mouthed. "You can't be serious."

He looked at her a long time before answering. His voice was strained. "Would you mind if we put off our talk until this evening, Liz? I've got a lot to think about."

She wanted to go to him, comfort him, but she realized that this was not the time. Her mind simply refused to comprehend what he had told her. She thought that *she* might be leaving the firm. But him? Never. He was far too valuable for Bob and Larry to let go. The knowledge that he had resigned struck her like a bullet. She was numbed by it. Oh, my God, she thought, could it have been because of her? Her face reflected the horror of her thought. He could see her consternation; it was wounding.

"Liz, I'll see you at your place. We'll have dinner. We'll talk." His voice sounded so tired, so strained, that she wanted to weep for him. "I'll be there about seven." He tried to smile, but only his lips moved; his eyes reflected the stunning blows that had been hammered at his life.

She turned and left without saying another word.

• • •

It was the longest afternoon and early evening of her life. She spent the rest of the day walking the streets of the Village, poking through small, dusty antique shops, looking, touching, turning things over in her hand, not seeing them. She walked past the grime-darkened, flat-roofed buildings, past the fruit stands and grocery stores. She didn't see the faces that tried not to see her. In the city people didn't look directly at one another; that could prove dangerous. She was like a somnambulist, lost in her own private world.

When she was physically exhausted, she returned to her apartment on Weymouth Place, hung up her coat, and sat on the love seat in the small living room. She was preoccupied with the series of thoughts that revolved around George's astounding announcement: "I've resigned." Each time she examined that statement, she came back to the same conclusion: George had resigned because of her. He said he had resigned, not that he had been forced to resign. It had to be because of her. But if it was, why didn't he tell her? Even if he wanted to spare her feelings, he would have given some sign, some indication that it was she who had caused his resignation. There wasn't any other reason that made sense.

She sat there as the apartment darkened. Only when she realized that dusk had passed and night had come to the city did she become aware that she had not changed her clothes or checked her appearance since this morning. She had forgotten everything except her one overwhelming concern. She couldn't go back over the year since she had first met George at Harvard. She was too mentally weary for that. Her mind had turned off. She got up and turned on the lights. Then she sat and waited for George. Her nerves were like live electric wires sparking dangerously.

At first she didn't hear the knock on her door. It took considerably louder knocking to pull her out of her trance.

She opened the door and saw George standing there. She had expected him to look dejected, distraught, but he seemed composed, serious, not at all melancholy.

George looked at her and realized the agony that waiting for him had put her through. He could never remember seeing her so unnerved.

He closed the door behind him, took off his coat, and dropped it over a chair. He took her in his arms and held her. They hadn't said one word. He felt her arms tighten around him, her head press against his chest. They stood there holding each other, silently giving each other comfort and strength. She lifted her head and looked at him, her eyes filled with tears. She hadn't spoken to anyone since she left him this morning. Her voice was husky.

"For God's sake, George, tell me what happened. I'm going out of my mind." She paused, looking at him. "Did you resign because of me?"

"Let's sit down," he said quietly.

They sat on the love seat facing the window, through which they could see the steps that led up to the street.

"I didn't resign because of you, Liz." He said it quietly, with an earnestness that she found believable but not reasonable.

"But why, then?"

He thought about that for a long time before he answered her. "You know, we really have to stretch our ethical principles in this business. I'm not implying that people in our business are dishonest. Sure, some of them are, but so are people in any walk of life. But we become so involved in getting the job done that we sometimes forget about the human cost of accomplishing that." He paused. "I resigned today because I had reached my limit as to how far I was willing to go in dehumanizing myself. Do you understand that?"

She nodded. She still believed she had caused him to resign.

He looked at her searchingly. "Liz, I'm going to start my own firm. It's something I've wanted to do for a long time. The Twenty/Twenty deal has earned me a grub stake, but I'll need partners. I think I can get them. I have a reputation that should give me the support I'll need." He paused, looking at her intently. "Will you come with me? We'll do it together. What do you say?"

She was speechless.

"Liz, this is the compromise you've been looking for. It will give you the chance to be a woman, a mother, and a wife, and still have a career. It will give you the flexibility you've always wanted."

He watched the tears course down her cheeks. He wiped them away gently, tenderly with his fingertips. "I have only one small request. I'd like you to marry me," he added.

She sat there looking at him, unable to see him through her tears. Her lips trembled. She still couldn't talk. All she could do was look at him. The phone rang, and he answered it. It was Bob Cooper.

"George, I don't want to interrupt, but I've got to talk to you. Larry and I have had a hell of a row. I've told him that if he accepted your resignation, I was going to take my money out of the firm. George, Larry's willing to forget the whole thing. He admits he got a little carried away. He has been under enormous pressure. George, don't be a damn fool. You've got a hell of a deal with us. Don't throw that away. We'll take Liz back, too. We're lucky to have both of you." Bob Cooper paused. "Will you think it over? Oh, I damn near forgot. Larry got a call from his friend at the State Department. The Dutch have picked up Haley in Amsterdam. The son of a bitch was arranging a buy of—get this—fifteen million in diamonds. But the reward that the First Manhattan put up did the trick. The dealer Haley was working with turned him in. He'll get a half a million American bucks, which is better than taking a chance of winding up in a Dutch prison." Bob paused. "George, think it over and get back to me in the morning."

"Bob, I appreciate this call more than I can tell you, but I've decided to open my own firm. If you really decide to leave Larry, I'd very much like to talk to you about joining me."

There was a long silence on the other end of the line. When Bob finally spoke, he sounded weary and dejected. "I was afraid of this."

"I'll be in to talk to you and Larry in the morning about winding up my affairs." He paused. "There is something you can do for me, Bob . . . not really for me." He paused. "Claudia is dying, Bob."

"My God. I didn't know."

"She's set up a foundation for the study of oncology. I'd like to give her a check for fifty thousand. She doesn't have much time."

"I'll have the firm draw a check from your account in the morning."

"I appreciate that. You've been a real friend, Bob, and I am proud to have had your support. I'll see you in the morning." He hung up.

Liz had been watching him. Her mind was still trying to

absorb the shock of George's resignation, his decision to open his own firm, and his offer to have her come with him. It was too much to absorb so quickly.

George put down the phone and looked at her. He didn't come toward her.

"Will you marry me?" he asked softly.

As she looked at him, her eyes started to mist. She realized as she stood there, separated from him in the small room, not touching, that she had been from the top to the bottom with this man, from the beginning. She had slowly fallen in love with him as their careers threw them closer and closer together. She had come to know the humanity that was hidden under the pinstriped suit.

"I might make a lousy wife."

They still hadn't moved toward each other.

"I might make a lousy husband."

"George, I'm not being coy. It's just that so much has happened."

"Do you need more time to think about it?"

She hesitated. "I'd like a little more time."

"Will you come with me in my new firm?"

"I'd like that, George."

Something so fragile stood between them that they both sensed that it would break if they came toward each other. He picked up his coat. "I'll call you in the morning." He seemed taut, almost annoyed. She didn't blame him. Most women would jump at the chance to marry a man like George. He closed the door softly. She watched him climb the outside steps.

Chapter 37

SHE COULDN'T SLEEP. She kept going over the last few weeks of her short career, of her short life. She had gone so far, so fast, and she had crash-landed. But she had been able to get up, to walk, to breathe. She was young, and she had much to learn. She thought about George in the dim light of her small bedroom. He could teach me so much, she thought. We'd make a great team. What about as husband and wife? She thought about this long into the night, until the illuminated numbers on the digital clock read 3:30. The street outside was quiet. She reached for the phone. His voice was thick with sleep.

"Liz?"

"Yes."

"Is everything all right?"

She could hear his sudden anxiety. "Everything's fine." She paused. "Is your offer still open?"

He sounded irritated. "I told you I wanted you in my firm. Is that why you called me at three-thirty in the morning?"

"Not exactly."

"Well, what, then?"

She began to laugh. "I believe you asked me to marry me earlier this evening. Have you forgotten so soon?"

He was now wide awake, his voice alert. "Will you marry me, Elizabeth Reed Clark, you stubborn, unpredictable, bad-tempered Yankee?"

"I will," she said softly. She paused. "Do you think we could have a double wedding?"

"A double wedding?"

"Yes. My mother is marrying Dr. Halsey in two weeks. If she doesn't want a wedding all her own, it might be fun."

Long pause. "Why couldn't you have said yes earlier this evening? Liz, you're exasperating."

She put the phone next to her ear, resting it on the pillow. Suddenly her frustrations, her anxieties, her fears left her. "I wish you were here, George," she said softly.

"I could have been."

"Yes, I know. I'll have to make that up to you tomorrow night."

"And the next, and the next, and the next," he said.

"Whoa—wait. When do we work?"

He laughed. "Tomorrow. We can start looking for office space."

They both began to laugh. She looked at the clock. It was nearly four in the morning. Their new life had already begun. They had hit the ground running. Together.

Bestselling Books
from Berkley